Seur Ranegonde's eyes had a febrile shine; her short dark hair was matted on her face. She had drawn her chemise as far down as her lifted knees out of modesty, but there was little she could do to cover herself until the infant was out of her. "It hurts," she said breathlessly as Père Guibert made the sign of the cross over her.

"Give me your confession, ma Fille, so that you may be spared the pains of Hell if it is the wish of God that you leave this life. Tell me how it is that you carry this babe, and who fathered it."

She convulsed suddenly. "He came, saying that he would give me a child . . ."

Père Guibert leaned forward. "They say that demons are black and hideous, that they are endowed like stallions and are cold as ice."

But Seur Ranegonde was shaking her head. "No. He is tall and slender, with hair like an angel and eyes lighter than Mère Leonie's."

Père Guibert tugged his stole from her fragile grasp. "You cannot save yourself with lies about a youth like an angel. No demon is as fair as the morning, with such eyes." He looked wildly about the cell. "You cannot say such things, ma Fille, and go unpunished. . . ."

A MORTAL GLAMOUR

A
MORTAL
GLAMOUR

Chelsea Quinn Yarbro

BANTAM BOOKS
TORONTO • NEW YORK • LONDON • SYDNEY • AUCKLAND

A MORTAL GLAMOUR

A Bantam Book / January 1985

ISBN 0-553-24587-2

Published simultaneously in the United States and Canada

Bantam Books are published by Bantam Books, Inc. Its trademark, consisting of the words "Bantam Books" and the por-
trayal of a rooster, is Registered in U.S. Patent and Trademark
Office and in other countries. Marca Registrada. Bantam
Books, Inc., 666 Fifth Avenue, New York, New York 10103.

for
MALCOLM
because

In 1305, the Roman Catholic Church elected Bertrand de Got Pope. This Gascon from Villaudraut was a subject of the king of England, much of the western part of France then being ruled by the English. De Got, reigning as Clement V, established his papal court at Avignon, beginning the period in the history of the church known as the Babylonian captivity. The papacy remained at Avignon until Gregory XI decided to return the papal court to Rome; he left Avignon in September 1376 in order to end the antipapal league forming in Italy. He reached Rome the following January and died there on March 27, at forty-nine years of age. The cardinals in Rome elected Bartolomeo Prignano Pope on Thursday, April 8, 1378; he took the name of Urban VI and reigned in Rome for eleven years.

The French cardinals, however, did not believe that the election of Urban VI was proper; they elected Robert of Geneva Pope, and he took the name of Clement VII, beginning the great schism of Rome and Avignon, which was exacerbated by Urban VI's abrasive personality. His successor, Pietro Tomacelli, who reigned as Boniface IX, was a much more diplomatic man, but by then the damage had been done, and it was not until the Council of Constance elected Oddone Colonna Pope in 1417 that the church was once again united under Roman rule. There had been constant intrigue during the reign of the Avignon antipopes (Clement VII and Benedict XIII), which ended in a subtle shift of power from the papacy to the various royal courts of Europe and eventually led to the Renaissance and a return to humanism.

During this time, the Black Death (bubonic plague) ravaged Europe. The first epidemic lasted from 1347 to 1349; the second, from 1361 to 1362. The third and less virulent onslaught lasted from 1383 to 1384. The overall mortality rate for these three epidemics approached thirty-five percent of European urban populations.

This novel is fiction, though much of the background is taken from factual material. The characters, situations, institutions, relationships, locations, occurrences, and/or experiences portrayed are the product of the writer's imagination and do not, nor are intended to, represent any actualities of this or any other time.

French usage in the book is archaic, taken from medieval Provençal sources and based on maps, ballads, poems, and letters of the period.

They are dazzled.

Like those whose eyes hurt: they are pained and blinded by the light; but the dark, which disguises everything, they yearn for, it is so pleasant and desirable. Thus are they party to their own deception.

Dio Chrysostom

The time is 1387–1388
Charles VI is king of France under the regency of four
uncles
Richard II is king of England
Geoffrey Chaucer is writing The Canterbury Tales
Flanders has been subdued by Burgundy
Sigismund of Brandenburg is king of Hungary
Pope Clement VII reigns in Avignon
Pope Urban VI reigns in Rome
Milan Cathedral is being built
Byzantium is losing ground to the advancing Turks
The first English-language translation of the Bible is
almost complete
Universities are being founded at Heidelberg and
Cologne
Bologna has established a medical school to study
diseases of the lungs
The war between England and France has started up
again
Jean d'Arras is finishing L'Histoire de Lusignan

Chapter 1

In Saunt-Vitre-lo-Sur, most of the houses were deserted; rye and oats stood unharvested in the frost-shriveled fields. Lean pigs and half-starved children scavenged the vineyards for grapes long since turned to raisins. At the door of the squat stone church, four women waited, three with listless infants in their arms, for the priest to bring them the thin, meatless stew charity required he provide them. A dank, neglected odor hung over the place, lending an inward chill to the February afternoon, where shadows lay like bruises across the land.

There was one brighter spot in the desolation. Some little distance beyond the village rose the cracking whitewashed walls of la Tres Saunte Annunciacion, where the Assumptionist Sisters had attempted to keep the soil tilled and the orchards bearing. A century before, there had been more than eighty nuns at the convent—now there were less than thirty, and those women who remained worked as strenuously as the hardiest farmers.

From her place under the barren trees, Seur Marguerite, who tended the hives, was the first to see the wagon approaching, its sides heavily curtained so that even the portly monk who drove the pair of steaming horses could not see his passenger. The nun stood absolutely still, as if she were a doe attempting to hide from a hunter. Torpid bees settled on the frayed linen of her coif, but she made no move to brush them away. As the wagon turned up the lane to the convent, Seur Marguerite sighed and crossed herself, murmuring a prayer to la Virge.

"Holà!" shouted the monk as he got down from the

1

driver's box at the convent gate. "Open up here, good Sisters!"

There was no response; the thick-hewn doors remained shut.

The monk began to pace, rubbing his thick hands together to warm them. His back was sore from the hours of jolting over hard, rutted roads, and he was in no mood to be denied his well-earned food and rest. "Open! In le Bon Nom!" His voice was hoarse with fatigue and too much wine.

From a grilled window to the side of the doors came a discreet cough. "God be with you, Frère."

"And with your soul," he answered automatically.

"What do you seek here?"

"It is not I who seek anything. I come to bring you what *you* have sought. The cardinal himself has sent me to you, in answers to your prayers." His husky laughter was taunting, more flirtatious than was proper for a monk addressing a nun.

"What prayers are those?" asked the voice, suddenly haughty.

"Why, for a new Mère, of course. Is there anything else you wanted that I do not know about?" He winked but was wise enough not to face the grilled window when he did.

"A Mère?" the unseen nun repeated, as if she dared not believe what she had heard.

"That's what I said. Cardinal Seulfleuve himself has entrusted me to bring her to you."

"With what escort?" the nun demanded.

"I am he," the monk replied, offended at her reasonable surprise.

"No men-at-arms?"

Frère Odo hawked and spat. "There were none to spare. You insisted that you needed your superior as soon as possible, and so . . ."

"But to travel without armed escort . . ." the nun began, shock quieting her words.

"It was that or wait until spring. Your priest said the need was urgent," the monk insisted, turning sullen.

"But to come now, without escort—"

"All the more reason to think that your new mère is in the favor of heaven. Our passage was safe enough."

"For which you should humbly thank God and His saints for their care," the nun on the far side of the grille snapped. Another voice whispered behind her, and there was a brief, barely audible exchange.

"Well? What is it to be, then?" the monk called out. "Do you open the doors to your mère or do we wait here for Père Guibert or Père Foutin to insist that we be permitted to enter." He was annoyed at having been ignored longer than he liked.

"In a moment," the nun called with less certainty than before.

"Your Mère is weary with travel. As am I," he added.

"Oh. Yes. Of course. At once." This was another nun, more flustered than the first.

"And do something for the horses, will you? The beasts have got to carry me to Avignon again the day after tomorrow." He had learned to seize any opportunity offered him, and he recognized that this was one such. "They're hungry and thirsty."

"We will tend to them, Frère," the second nun promised him.

"When? Soon?"

"Yes. Yes. At once. We will."

There were more voices now, some shrill, some scolding, and the sound of hurrying footsteps. The heavy bolt on the inside of the doors was tugged noisily back; then the enormous iron hinges moaned as the doors were slowly pulled open to allow the wagon to enter the convent.

It was an old building, built around a square courtyard. On the east was the hospice, the tallest part of the convent, rising almost three stories from the old flagging. On the north were the nuns' quarters, the refectory at one end, the rest of the two levels given over to the chapel and to the individual cells. Next to that was a more recent addition, with storerooms, stillrooms, and at the far end, a stable. The wall on the south completed the square and closed out the world.

There were about twenty women gathered now, all in gray habits. Two of them had removed their coifs and rolled up their sleeves—clearly these Sisters worked in the convent's kitchen. Gradually, all of them clustered around the wagon, most of them afraid to speak louder than a whisper.

Frère Odo, full of self-importance, tugged at the corner of one of the draperies that enclosed the wagon. "Mère Léonie," he said in his most imposing way, "we have reached your destination."

"May God bless you as I thank you, Frère Odo," came from behind the hanging. "La Virge will reward your service with her prayers and intercessions."

"Praise be to God," the monk declared, crossing himself deliberately while he glanced over the nuns, hoping that one would catch his eye.

None of the women paid him the slightest attention. All of them were staring at the wagon as the draperies were drawn aside.

The hush that fell was eerie, at least to Frère Odo's ears. It boded ill, he thought, to have nuns so quiet.

"May God send His peace, which is not of this world, to guide and comfort you," said the tall young woman who climbed, unassisted, out of the wagon. Her voice was low, almost masculine, and in another might have been thought seductive. Though she moved slowly, she gave the promise of energy, perhaps even zeal. She looked around her. "Oh, very good," she said warmly. "Most surely good."

The Sisters gaped at her, some with relief, some with dismay, for none of them had expected such a replacement for the old and saintly Mère Jacinthe. Most superiors were of a respectable age and demeanor, grave in countenance and somber of disposition, not glowing and gracious like the newcomer. Even the gorget and wimple could not hide her attractive features or disguise the vitality that coursed through her. Two of the older nuns exchanged sharp looks.

"It has been so long," Mère Léonie said softly, speaking to herself or some inner part of her soul. "How I have yearned for this."

Only Seur Elvire heard her clearly; she knew that she would enjoy unusual attention for a day or two as she related this remark to the other nuns.

The wind whipped around the courtyard, tweaking the hems and cuffs of habits, disarranging coifs and causing the horses to snort.

"Your convent, Mère Léonie," Frère Odo said unnecessarily.

"Yes. Pray to our Lord we will do well." She gazed up at the slated roof of the hospice.

It was an awkward moment, for none of the women wanted to put herself forward, yet all knew that one of their number must greet the new superior.

One young woman, standing a little apart from the other nuns, spoke up first. "And my Savior send His blessing to guide you, ma Mère," she said in a carrying voice whose accents, as much as her carriage, revealed a noble background.

Mère Léonie crossed herself. "As I most humbly beseech Him every day." She advanced a few steps, meeting the eyes of her nuns forthrightly.

Frère Odo came swaggering along behind her, his coarse features spread over with a smug look that just missed being a grin. The soft drone of whispered conversations stilled as he passed, and he knew that the nuns were speaking of Mère Léonie—he could hardly blame them for that—and perhaps of him as well. He whistled a hymn tune very quietly through his teeth.

"Ma Mère," said one of the nuns dressed for the kitchen. "It is Seur Lucille who should greet you; she is the oldest of us and the one with the longest vocation. But she is supervising work in the orchard. At Vespers, she'll . . ." She looked around for aid.

The well-born young nun came to her rescue. "Seur Fleurette is right, ma Mère. Seur Lucille is supervising work, as she said. The almond trees did badly for our last harvest."

"It is not important," Mère Léonie said gently. "There is no need to disrupt yourselves for me. A good mother does not set an example by disorder." She looked around her, sensing the doubts of the women she had been sent to lead. "Return to your appointed tasks, my Sisters, and I will wait until the end of the evening meal to speak to you." Her eyes fell on a tertiary Sister. "Will you guide me, Seur?"

The Sister looked up sharply. "I thank God for the honor," she said, but her tone was slightly distracted, as if her mind had been on other matters.

Frère Odo looked up at Mère Léonie's summons. "I need your aid, Frère," she said, nodding toward the two leather cases she had brought with her. "If you will follow us?"

The monk grumbled but did as she ordered him. He had decided that he would try to get a few moments alone with one of the younger nuns, a great strapping girl who looked as if she had been raised on a farm doing hard work. Such women, he knew from experience, were often eager to forget their vows for an hour or two. With his mind still on the possibility of conquest, he climbed up into the wagon and brought down the larger of the cases, then trudged after Mère Léonie.

"The old refectory is in the far wing," the tertiary Sister was saying to Mère Léonie as Frère Odo caught up with them. "The community being reduced in size, we use it only as a hospice for travelers."

"And when there is illness?" Mère Léonie inquired. "Is aid provided here?"

"It was, for a time. This valley was much taken by Plague the last time it swept the land. From what we have been told, we fared less well than many other villages." She looked away, crossing herself in a vague manner. "There were many deaths, you see."

Mère Léonie also blessed herself, her face grave as she listened. "Is that the extent of it, or has there been worse?"

"There is always worse. Mercenaries sacked Mou Courbet last year—"

"Mou Courbet?" Mère Léonie repeated.

"The village at the end of the valley, just where the road turns toward the pass. It was more than twice the size ten years ago, or so I'm told." She frowned once more. "We have prayed to God and the Virgin for aid, but it has not been granted us. Mère Jacinthe, toward the end, warned us that our sins would cost us all dearly if we did not forsake them and repent."

"Is the convent so full of wickedness?" Mère Léonie marveled, permitting herself a gentle smile.

"We must be," the tertiary Sister answered. "I dare not think . . . that God, being just, would . . . require that—" She was unable to finish.

"Well, in Rome, they would say it is because we are faithful to the true pope at Avignon, though Rome has seen the Plague of late." Her head turned away. "Is that the chapel, Seur?"

"One of them. There is a larger one. This chapel is for our own devotions." She stood aside so that Mère Léonie could inspect the little stone-floored room. "When there were more of us, and there were three priests at the church in Saunt-Vitre, we had masses every day."

Mère Léonie left the chapel. "May I know your name, Seur?"

The nun blushed. "Seur Philomine, ma Mère. I've taken only tertiary vows, so that if my family should—" She almost said "relent" but stopped herself in time.

Mère Léonie nodded. "Your family has suffered much?"

"As have all families in these days," Seur Philomine said at once, not wishing to appear self-pitying.

"And for which we must pray all the more for our Lord's grace," Mère Léonie added in a careless way. "Have your relatives' fortunes suffered reverses?"

Seur Philomine blushed. "There have been some reverses," she admitted with difficulty.

"It must be similar for many of the nuns," Mère Léonie said sympathetically. "I should learn these things, that I may better fulfill my duties toward you all," she added as explanation. "Since the church has been weakened by the . . . rift between Rome and Avignon, many tasks have been neglected that—"

Seur Philomine shook her head in confusion. "Ma Mère, it is not my place to hear these things."

"Forgive me," Mère Léonie said at once, then

turned back to motion to Frère Odo. "Where shall he put this trunk?"

Once again, Seur Philomine was surprised to have the new superior confide in her. "Your cell and study are at the end of this hall, to the side of the chapel."

"Excellent," Mère Léonie exclaimed. "Take those cases—the one you carry and the one remaining in the wagon—to the study."

Groaning a feeble protest, Frère Odo moved to do as he had been told.

"But don't you wish to see your quarters?" Seur Philomine asked, unable to conceal her puzzlement.

"There are more important things for me to see, aren't there?" She smiled at Seur Philomine. "I will need to see the grounds and the storerooms. Will you guide me, or should I ask for other escort?"

"I suppose I may guide you," Seur Philomine told her, wondering why she had been chosen to do this.

"God send you His blessing for your service," Mère Léonie said at once. "Do you read and write?"

"Sufficiently for the demands of our service," Seur Philomine said, averting her eyes from the new superior. "I was not the first daughter, and so . . ."

"And your older sisters?" Mère Léonie inquired as they came to another turn in the hallway.

"They married, as was arranged, but . . . then they died." She crossed herself and coughed once.

Mère Léonie said with a touch of sternness, "As superior, I am required to acquaint myself with the lives of those in my charge."

Seur Philomine accepted her rebuke with all the humility she could find within her. "It was wrong of me, ma Mère."

"Of course. It is not astonishing that all of you here would be cautious of a newcomer, even one sent to lead you." Her faint, equivocal smile, framed as it was by gorget, wimple, and coif, was strangely sinister, a thing out of place in that handsome face. "I pray that you and your Sisters will guide me in the days that are to come."

"Amen to that, ma Mère," Seur Philomine said as she opened a door and stood aside. "Here is the antechamber to our kitchens. We offer charity to those in greatest need, especially to travelers and women with children."

"But the priests in Saunt-Vitre-lo-Sur, don't they provide for—" Mère Léonie made a gesture that implied that it was not the responsibility of the nuns to do such work.

"For the village itself, yes, they do, but there are others who are without homes and shelter who pass this way. Mère Jacinthe enforced all the devotional offices required of us. Before the Plague came the last time, it was not as urgent a need. Now, you—well, you saw how it was, didn't you?"

"Yes," Mère Léonie answered thoughtfully. "Yes."

"She troubles me," Seur Catant whispered to the woman on her right. "If she were not tranquil, she would be—" She stopped, breaking her small, flat loaf and placing it on the wooden trencher before her as the blessing was invoked for their evening meal.

Beside Seur Catant, Seur Elvire listened with slight attention; Seur Catant was known to be discontented with her lot.

The voice of Mère Léonie rose above the others, bringing the whispers of conversation to an end. "I am saddened to see you so lax in the rule of our order," she said, turning this observation into subtle and damning condemnation. "In these times, with war and the might of the Plague around us, we must be the more rigorous in our devotions. God will not forgive our lapses now or at any time. 'Who among us is safe?' you ask when you pray, and do not trust God to care for you, though He promised His care and gave the life of His Son in bond."

The nuns looked around uneasily, and one of them made a sound that could have been jeering laughter or a choked sob.

She rose. "I have been with you for seven days, and I have wanted to speak each of those seven days, for all that I saw distressed me more than I have the capacity to express." Her hands pressed at her thighs through the shapeless drapery of her habit. "It is not that you have fallen into sin and worse, for if that were the case, it would be easily dealt with; the convent would be closed and rites of purification carried out so that once again worship could be given cleanly. But that is not what concerns us." She paused, her eyes measuring the women before her. "What has happened here is more insidious. You have fallen into the error of liberality, which leads to corruption and such vileness that I cannot speak of it. This is a fault, and you have all succumbed to it. I cannot inform the Pope in Avignon that you have served your vocations well; you have not."

One of the nuns, the thin and nervous Seur Odile, had begun to weep, but the others did not dare make so obvious a display of their emotions.

"Let me advise you: I will ask you to renew the fervor and full dedication of your vows, and I will petition the church for a strict review of the practices here. It does not become me to speak ill of one who has led you, but in good faith I must protest that Mère Jacinthe did not do all that she might to instill the gravity of your position. My Sisters, outward ills cannot pardon inward loathsomeness. You must search inwardly for your failings and imperfections and do all that you can to eradicate them from your character so that la Virge in heaven may look upon you as handmaids deserving of honor, handmaids who have preserved themselves in perfect trust through the years of suffering and trial. For that reason, I wish each of you to pray for one hour each day, fully prostrate, in the chapel, so that it can be determined that the simplicity and purity of our order is restored and each of you is once again secure in her vows."

Two of the younger nuns stared at the new superior, one of them not able to conceal the panic that had entered her eyes.

"Let each of you accuse herself of her transgressions, and where you have most offended, let you scourge that fault from your body and soul. If gluttony or lust or melancholy has taken hold of you, it must be the body that pays the price, for these are sins of the body. We are only permitted to chastise with willow branches,

but see that you use them with a will so that you may be
the more preserved against greater offense."

There was a soft, terrible cry from one of the nuns.
"Oh, ma Mère," Seur Marguerite wailed, unable to contain herself, "I have seen too much—Plague, yes, I have
seen it. You must not condemn me to remember those
things. You cannot, in charity, demand that of me. I came
here to find refuge!" She lifted up her clasped hands to
Mère Léonie.

The superior studied the old nun and recalled all
that she had heard about her. "Come, bring your heart to
me, Seur Marguerite. You have endured much, and it
may be that there are other devotions that will aid you.
The prostrate prayers are required of all sisters here, and
you must not seek to avoid them. But if you fear damnation for what has been in your life, then meditation on
damnation may answer to grace as well."

The other nuns, hearing this, exchanged uneasy
glances. All of them were aware that Seur Marguerite
was not entirely sane and could not be held to the same
code of behavior as the rest of them; nevertheless, they
could not suppress a twinge of guilt at the thought that
Mère Léonie might grant her an exemption. Seur Elvire
almost drummed her fingers on the table but could not
summon the courage for so outrageous an act.

"Ma Mère," said one of the nuns in a tone that suggested dissatisfaction, "why do you require this of us
now, when—"

Mère Léonie turned toward the upstart. "Were you
moved to speak by the fullness of your heart, or is this
petulance?"

The young nun set her jaw. "I am not used to—"

"Seur Aungelique"—Mère Léonie cut her short—
"when you have finished your meal, you are to go to the
chapel where you will find a willow scourge waiting for
you. Use it when your prayers are done."

Seur Aungelique flushed with indignation. "I am
the daughter of le Baron Michau d'Ybert who is—"

"Titles of the world have no meaning here," Mère
Léonie reminded her. "Recall that you are not free of

vanity while you try to purge yourself of gluttony and
lust."

For once, Seur Aungelique was too shocked to
speak. She was shamed by the rebuke she had received
and wished she could become invisible.

"For the rest of you," Mère Léonie went on, "I will
expect to speak to each of you alone in my cell, where
you may unburden your souls of the doubts that have
festered there so that together we may find remedy for
your afflictions." She looked around the room in that
keen, searching way that impressed and worried the
nuns. The long tables were no longer full of Sisters; the
walls that were once whitewashed and pristine were now
dingy from neglect. "There is much to be done if we are
to overcome our enemies and the destruction of our
faith. The conflicts between Rome and Avignon are the
very essence of the Church, and from the outcome will
all of Christianity take shape. Those who believe that it is
of small consequence if Rome or Avignon makes the
pope forget that it is the Pope who speaks for God on
earth, and if we hearken to false counsel, then we damn
ourselves as surely as if we have made a pact with Satan
and signed it with our life's blood. You must pray for the
wisdom to decide in these matters, for although we are
only women, our mission takes us above our sex. We are
required to show the acumen of men in the conduct of
our vocation and thus seek ways to glorify God that honor
Him as He demands."

Seur Elvire dropped her wooden cup and looked
about guiltily at the noise it made.

"You have not had Scripture read to you at meal for
over a year, or so I have been told. That will be remedied
at once. You." She pointed across the room to Seur
Aungelique.

"Mère?" the young nun asked.

"In preparation for your evening penance, you will
read from the Book of the Prophet Jeremiah," Mère
Léonie ordered, motioning to one of the nuns to bring
the large, unused Bible.

"Deo gratias," Seur Aungelique muttered as she

came forward, glaring at the superior. "I am poor at my letters."

Mère Léonie smiled. "Where you falter, I will help you." She dropped gracefully to her knees and gestured to Seur Aungelique to do the same. "You may begin where you like, Seur Aungelique."

Seur Aungelique lay on her bed, feeling the hempen slats through the two blankets that served as a mattress. She could not sleep. Her thighs and belly ached where the willow had lashed them, bringing pain at first but now something else. Seur Aungelique rolled onto her side, but the disturbing warmth did not subside. Impetuously, Seur Aungelique threw back the heavy wool blanket she was permitted in the cold of winter and drew up her shift as far as her waist in the vain hope that the chill February air would give her a measure of peace.

There were a number of sensitive tracks across her abdomen and on her thighs, and when she touched them, no matter how gingerly, pain spurted through her. She gave a little gasp, but it was not entirely for hurt— the touch of her hand had awakened other aches, deep, abiding aches that she feared now would not be banished with prostrate prayers and willow switches.

It was a sin to touch herself; Seur Aungelique knew that from the many harangues she had endured since before her breasts had been bee-sting bumps on her skinny chest. Her fingers slipped—of their own accord, it seemed—between her legs, to the strange little nubbin that jumped for ecstasy at her ministrations.

"Virge Mère Marie," she whispered as her fingers rubbed and plucked, "you were a woman. You bore a Son. Surely you knew what it was to have . . . oh! Jesu, Jesu! . . . to be filled with . . . ah! . . . It is not lust, Mère Marie. It is too . . . Dieu, Dieu! . . . not lust." Her brow was slick with sweat, her prayers jumbled in her mind as she writhed and tried to keep from moaning aloud. Under her wimple, her short-cropped hair was damp, and though she trembled, it was not from the icy embrace of the night but from the rapture that her fingers wrung from her.

She would have to confess, when Père Guibert came, that she had failed again, that she had succumbed to her body. She began again to search out the unimaginable release that she knew was terribly wrong but so very, very sweet. Her hand teased and pressed; it was easy to imagine that it was not her hand at all but someone else's, something else, that pleasured her. Did not the saints themselves often wrestle with demons, combating lust as well as terror? She was secretly horrified that she should compare herself to saints, for that could be heresy or worse. Bad enough that her carnal desires should be known, but—Her thoughts dissolved in a burst of pleasure that drove her far beyond caviling argument to thrashing release.

In the floating, sated tranquillity that followed, she at last found some little sleep, and for that short time between her satisfaction and the call to morning devotions, Seur Aungelique was not troubled—in sleep, she found a kind of peace that eluded her in all her waking hours.

Père Guibert gazed warily across the courtyard of la Couvent de la Tres Saunte Annunciacion. His eyes ached, and his feet had long since stopped hurting and become numb. His mule sighed with almost human exasperation and refused to move again until Père Guibert climbed out of the saddle and drew the animal forward with the curve of the reins. With thumb and forefinger, the priest rubbed at his gritty-feeling eyes. For more than twenty years, he had striven to do honor to his order and to his God, but of late he had found it increasingly difficult to accommodate all the demands of his calling. A noise distracted him; he saw Seur Ranegonde come toward him from the hospice door, her habit in some little disorder. "God keep you, good Sister, and send you His peace," the priest said, blessing her in a mildly distracted way.

"I thank you most humbly," the nun answered, crossing herself before she came nearer.

It was a chore for him to summon up the necessary phrases, and he did not bother to do so. "Is the stable ready for this beast?" Père Guibert asked testily.

"Of course, mon Père," Seur Ranegonde said, as if there were nothing churlish in his behavior. "Let me take him for you." She was thinner than the last time the priest had come to hear confessions.

"How do you go on, Seur Ranegonde?" Père Guibert inquired; he realized belatedly that his manners were hardly worthy of his calling.

"I do as God wishes me to," she responded; waiting for the mule, her hands trembling.

By now, Père Guibert began to feel shame for his brusque words. "You have taken the decoction that Père Sannule—"

"Of course, and I thank God for it," she said, then looked over her shoulder.

The hospice door had opened again, and this time Seur Aungelique came out, approaching the priest in an unusually subdued way.

"God be with you, ma Seur," Père Guibert murmured, and automatically gave her his blessing. He was startled to see how pale the young woman looked, how deeply her eyes were sunk into livid shadows.

"And with your soul," she responded. "We did not think to see you for a day or so. There is so much going on that—"

"Excellent," Père Guibert said, recalling the apathy that had seized the convent after the death of Mère Jacinthe.

"We have much to do now that Mère Léonie is here," Seur Ranegonde said quickly.

"Yes. Your new superior." He patted the neck of his mule. "I don't wish to trouble Seur Ranegonde, who plainly has yet to return to blooming health. If you would be kind enough . . ."

Seur Aungelique nodded at once. "Yes, mon Père. Deo gratias." She took the proffered reins and tugged the mule toward the little thatch-roofed stable.

Père Guibert gazed after her, thinking that he had never seen Seur Aungelique so tractable.

"I would have been willing to take the mule, mon Père," Seur Ranegonde murmured. "I do not want to shirk my duties and put greater burdens on my sisters."

"Naturally," Père Guibert said, falling back into his usual demeanor of stern benevolence. "You are a nun of rare vocation, Seur Ranegonde, and it is an example of your vocation that you do not wish to give burdens to others. But you must also accept the mandates of God, and to attempt tasks that are for a time beyond you only shows pride, not vocation."

Seur Ranegonde lowered her eyes at this reprimand. "I will pray to be worthy of my order and my faith."

"It is not God's way to burden you—" He stopped, trying to forget the last time he had so admonished a nun, for it had been during a visitation of the Plague that had ravaged the kingdom of France and the lands around it not so many years before. His helplessness weighed on his soul intolerably then, and there was no remedy for it. What had that burden shown him, and why had God put it upon him? The question was like a mouse in his thoughts, gnawing, gnawing with sharp little teeth.

"Mon Père?" Seur Ranegonde ventured, her face not quite averted and her eyes downcast.

"I am tired," he offered as an explanation. "The sun is dropping in the sky, and my soul turns inward. Forgive me."

Seur Ranegonde nodded. "Thus does God touch our lives." Then she looked away toward the hospice again. "Would you allow me to bring you to our new superior so that she may greet you?"

"I would be most grateful." He permitted Seur Ranegonde to lead the way, observing, "It will be Vespers soon," so that Seur Ranegonde would feel free to speak to him.

"It will. My Sisters will come together for devotions then." She stood aside so that he might enter the building ahead of her. "Mère Léonie spends this time in the chapel at her devotions."

"I will wait for her; I do not wish to distract her." This information surprised him, since he could re-

member the many times Mère Jacinthe excused her
nuns from strict exercises of faith. He was more curious
than before about the new superior.

At the door to the chapel, Seur Ranegonde once
again stood aside. "Mère Léonie is at prayer," she said,
and bowed her head before turning away.

"You need not wait, Seur Ranegonde," Père Guibert
said, his attention already on the prostrate form of Mère
Léonie.

"Deo gratias," Seur Ranegonde whispered. She
waited a moment in case there should be any other service required of her, then hastened away.

Père Guibert stepped inside the chapel, crossing
himself and sinking to his knees some little distance behind Mère Léonie. He quietly began to recite his beads
while studying the figure in gray who lay facedown with
arms outstretched in front of the altar. He was struck, as
he had been with increasing frequency, with the ano-
nymity of religious life. Even the habit conspired to remove all trace of the person who wore it. There might be
anything inside the garments. He stifled a sound in his
throat and was not entirely displeased to see Mère
Léonie look up.

"God be with you," she said as she got swiftly to her
feet.

"And with your soul," he answered, caught off
guard.

"You are our priest? Père . . . Guibert?"

He liked her confusion; it made her less of a puzzle
to him. "I am a day or two early. I could not reach Fôrlebene, and so I came directly here."

"Has the winter been so severe?" Mère Léonie inquired.

"Apparently so." He felt that he had to explain his
lack of tenacity a bit more completely. "If I still had my
escort, then it would have been another matter."

"Of course," Mère Léonie agreed. She knelt for his
blessing. "You are thrice welcome here, Père Guibert.
My Sisters have great need of you, I fear. With so much
despair and suffering around us, there is . . ." She made
a gesture of resignation. "There is much to . . . to pray

for," she finished, though Père Guibert had the oddest feeling that she had intended to say something else. "I am grateful you have come."

Such a forthright declaration was disconcerting to Père Guibert. "Mère Léonie—"

"Mon Père," she interrupted him, "my concern prompts me to tell you of my worry." She looked up, as if appealing to heaven itself. "These nuns, this convent . . . all are . . . neglected."

This touched so closely to Père Guibert's doubts that he almost spoke of his own anguish, but frowned deeply and made a compromise admission. "We have reason to worry."

"Yes. I have seen that. Yet though I pray for the salvation of all mankind, it is this convent that has been entrusted to me, and before I turn my eyes and my prayers to the world, I must first tend to the well-being of my sisters, for if I cannot bring peace to them here, what chance has the world?" Her eyes flashed, and Père Guibert had the sensation of being challenged. "My Lord sets each of us tasks."

"Mère Léonie, you—" He stood back and blessed her a second time. "If we must speak of this, rise and—"

"We may come to my study. Doubtless that is where Mère Jacinthe spoke to you, and it is fitting that we should converse there." Her manner was entirely accommodating, but Mère Léonie bothered the Cistercian. She stood aside for him, but nothing suggested that she was prepared to render him unending and humble service. "When our evening devotions begin, I will have to return here. It is not fitting that I should shirk the duties I require of my nuns."

"Certainly." Her attitude was entirely correct, Père Guibert thought as he went down the hall ahead of her. Still, he longed for a more deferential attitude from Mère Léonie. "It is wise to observe all the rites." His tone was measured, even ponderous, but he felt as if he had lost all direction with the young superior. "A true Mère imposes upon herself all the exercises she requires of her charges, but to take on more or less is improper, for this distinguishes you and causes rancor to rise in the hearts of your Sisters. Our Lord—"

"Be pleased to enter," Mère Léonie cut in, opening the door to her study. "I will take the stool so you may have the chair."

Père Guibert tried to convince himself that he was not, in fact, obeying an order but taking his rightful place in the room. "You have begun well, Mère Léonie."

"If it appears so, it is to the credit of my Sisters, who are sincerely devoted to their calling and the glory of God."

"Of course. It is true that those who are unworthy are . . ." He fumbled with his beads as he strove to bring order to his thoughts. "Mère Léonie, you have accepted a great task here, for it is the will of God who . . ."

When Père Guibert fell silent, Mère Léonie folded her hands and waited. There was an unrealized smile in the curve of her mouth, an air of expectation. "I have taken the liberty of imposing stricter penance than my predecessor did," she volunteered once the stillness had become intolerable.

"But . . ." He broke off again. "Do the sisters acknowledge their sins through their penance?"

"There are a stubborn few. Seur Aungelique was one but has bowed to the necessity." She saw Père Guibert nod. "Seur Elvire is not of a patient disposition, and so I have assigned her to keep the night watches in the hospice chapel. Seur Fleurette is given to folly; I have told her that she must care for the ailing children that the women bring us from the village. Seur Marguerite . . . well, God has deprived her of half her wits; she continues to tend the hives, but I have required that she sing psalms, as she works, to the praise of God. Seur Philomine is only a tertiary, and I have not the authority to impose upon her. Seur Odile is of uneven disposition, and for this she is set to mend cloths and prepare bandages so that she may see that steadiness in small things gives merit in heaven. Seur Lucille, who is advanced in years, has come to believe that she has greater—"

"Mère Léonie," Père Guibert protested, holding up

his hands to stop her. "May God grant you strength for your tasks in years to come equal to what you show now." He caught himself wanting to reprove her for giving penance; Mère Jacinthe had left such matters to him, though she might well have done so on her own authority. He felt usurped and would have to do penance himself for the resentment Mère Léonie awoke in him. "Let me first hear confession, to discover what improvement your rule has wrought here. If the penances have corrected error, then God will reward you for your diligence, but if there have been lapses, we will decide upon another course."

"As you wish, mon Père," she said without expression.

In order to mitigate his warning, he went on. "You do not come from France, do you, Mère Léonie?"

She shook her head. "No, mon Père. I am from Dalmatia, which thrives under the banner of the Venetians. My family is distinguished." She looked away from him. "It is of no consequence here, and it was not for pride that I told you." She crossed herself. "We have long been devoted to the service of Our Lord."

"Most commendable," Père Guibert said, delighted to have found that hint of pride in her.

"It pleased heaven to bring me here to tend to these women in the time of our faith's greatest travail. I do not know what I will do if Rome is victorious over Avignon in the end." She wrung her hands, distress in her handsome features.

This was more the attitude that Père Guibert expected, and his initial impression was mollified. "In your zeal, ma Fille, you bring too great importance on yourself, which is an error. All we may do is pray and live as we were enjoined to live by Our Lord. God sees our lives, and His power guides the world. Do not think that He will permit evil to rule forever."

"No. Not forever." Mère Léonie crossed herself again. "I thank you, mon Père, for all you have said to me. I will keep your thoughts foremost in my mind. And may le Bon Dieu and la Virge bless us."

"Amen to that, with all my heart," Père Guibert

agreed. He took on a more indulgent manner. "You must not be too anxious, ma Fille."

"I will pray for tranquillity, mon Père," she vowed. "I wish to impart something of myself to my Sisters. If I am distracted, I will fail as surely as if I were venal and corrupt."

"Oh, that is too harsh, surely," Père Guibert chided her. "Who among us has been free of the taint of sin? To believe any but Our Lord is so is as great a fault as venality."

"Where there is the greatest sanctity, there is the greatest danger," she murmured. Then she looked directly at the priest. "Forgive me, mon Père."

At last Père Guibert permitted himself to relax his guard. "Your devotion is most admirable, especially in so young a woman, but those of us who have been about the world a little longer know that error cannot be uprooted in a day."

Mère Léonie looked toward the crucifix hanging over her prie-dieu. "You are right. Evil cannot be uprooted in a day."

Chapter 2

On this first market day of spring, the muddy road from Saunt-Vitre-lo-Sur to Mou Courbet was busy; carts and wagons lumbered along through the deepening ruts, the drivers cursing the various beasts harnessed or yoked to their vehicles. In Saunt-Vitre-lo-Sur, a space had been cleared, and there the people gathered, as eager for the visit of their neighbors as for the produce and goods that would be offered for sale or trade.

A pasty-faced man on a donkey turned aside at the lane to la Tres Saunte Annunciacion. He dismounted and led the animal toward the hospice entrance where he rang the travelers' bell.

Seur Aungelique answered his summons. "God give you good day, stranger."

"If you and your Sisters will give me a meal and a place to sleep, He certainly will" was the answer he offered in a sarcastic tone. "I haven't eaten since day before yesterday, and my donkey hasn't had anything but what grows by the roadside."

"Then come, stranger. There is food ready and a place to sleep. I will take your donkey to the stable and see that he is fed." She made the offer almost jubilantly, her eyes shining.

"Thanks," the man said shortly, and went into the hospice without another look at her.

For a moment, Seur Aungelique was consumed with worry. But, she thought, the d'Ybert blood had always been wild, and those who had it, were reckless. A chance like this would not come again, and she was a fool if she let it go by. Resolutely, she dragged the donkey off toward the stables, determination in every line of her body.

By nightfall, the village of Saunt-Vitre-lo-Sur was as lively as it had ever been in the previous dozen years. Roistering marketeers reeled between the squat houses, singing loudly and taunting those who remained indoors. No one paid much attention to the hooded monk on the donkey who passed down the narrow main road toward Avignon.

By the time the Sisters rose for worship, those who had caroused for market day had fallen into heavy sleep.

"Mère Léonie," Seur Philomine said timidly as she knocked on the door of her superior's cell. "Forgive my interruption of your prayers, but I fear it is urgent."

Mère Léonie answered sternly, "What is it you require of me more important than my devotions?"

"There is trouble, Mère Léonie." Seur Philomine hated to say it so baldly but could think of no other way to inform her.

"Is it one of the Sisters?" Mère Léonie demanded. "Is someone ill, or worse?"

"Not that, ma Mère," Seur Philomine said, her

courage all but failing her. "It is . . . Seur Aungelique."

This time there was a sharper sound in Mère Léonie's response. "What of Seur Aungelique?"

"She is . . . She is not . . . here." There. She had said it, and the worst that could happen now would be facing the brunt of Mère Léonie's displeasure.

The door to Mère Léonie's cell opened abruptly, and the superior, already fully habited and prepared for morning prayers, appeared. "Tell me the whole."

Seur Philomine ducked her head. "It fell to me, Mère Léonie, to wake the others. I had the last vigil in the chapel, and . . ."

"And?" The question was asked politely, but behind it there was an ominous disapproval.

"When I rapped at the door of Seur Aungelique's cell, there was no response. I waited, as our faith requires, then tried again, more firmly so that it might be heard through slumber."

"And Seur Aungelique ignored you." This time the superior seemed almost satisfied, as if a prophesied disaster had at last occurred.

"No." Seur Philomine faltered. "Not . . . that way."

"Then what way?" Mère Léonie rapped out.

"She . . . I entered the cell, with a prayer for forgiveness if I trespassed. I was prepared to explain why I had done so, and . . ." She knew she was babbling, but dreaded coming to the final revelation. "I . . . I looked at Seur Aungelique's bed, Mère Léonie. She was not in it. I felt the blankets, and they were cold."

"A-a-a-h," Mère Léonie sighed. "We must search her out."

"I have . . . already looked in the chapel." Seur Philomine felt she had to justify in some way her failure to locate the missing nun. "I thought that she might have gone there to pray again."

"Not she," Mère Léonie murmured. "Well, we must gather now, for the rule requires that we worship, and it would be a greater failure on our part to put the folly of one Sister ahead of the good of the souls of all the rest." She straightened up. "Wake the rest, if you have not done so. We will speak more of this after prayers."

By midafternoon, Seur Aungelique wanted to stop and would have done so, but fear of pursuit drove her on, and the donkey began to falter when the way grew steep. She had thrown back her hood in order to watch more carefully, but once she caught sight of the distant palaces of Avignon, she no longer dared to reveal her face; even in a monk's habit, her features were feminine beyond any doubt.

When at last she caught sight of the villa hidden in a tangle of fruit trees left to riot on their own, Seur Aungelique dismounted and led the donkey along the meandering lane that ended in front of the squat arch at the entrance to Une Noveautie, where la Comtesse Orienne de Hautlimois lived.

"A pleasant evening, Frère," said a servant who had appeared just as Seur Aungelique reached the doors. "Have you lost your way?"

Seur Aungelique decided then that a bold answer would be best. "No," she said, making no attempt to disguise her voice. "I hope I have found the way."

If the servant was surprised by the revelation of this monk as a woman, he showed no indication of it. He bent his head as courtesy required. "You are welcome here, Demoiselle, but I fear my mistress will demand some explanation of you."

"Fine," Seur Aungelique said at once. "Only let me present myself to her, and I will answer whatever questions she desires to put to me."

The servant made a gesture of compliance. "Your animal will be tended. You must follow me."

A second servant, much younger than the first and boyishly pretty, appeared in the door. He took the donkey's reins without comment and left Seur Aungelique with the elder.

"What . . ." Seur Aungelique asked as the first servant bowed her into the house.

"The donkey will be properly tended. Do not fear." He was walking through a long entryway skirting the main part of the little palace. There were signs of the luxury for which la comtesse was famous: carpets on the floor, thick and beautiful, so that all steps were muffled; braziers fueled by sweet-smelling herbs and spices stood along the walls, giving off fragrant smoke along with a moderate amount of light. The scent of the place was heady, like new wine, and Seur Aungelique was hard-pressed not to succumb to it.

"If you will come through these doors," the servant said, changing directions again and leading Seur Aungelique toward the rear wing of the palace.

They found la comtesse in a garden, within a striped pavilion that had been erected to protect her from the chill of the afternoon. Inside the pavilion, there was an enormous stone basin so carved as to resemble a sea-shell. Hot perfumed water frothed in the basin as la comtesse lounged in her bath. Her antics were accompanied by the plaintive sounds of the rebec and shawm.

The servant leading Seur Aungelique said, raising his voice to be heard over the sound of music and splashing, "Fairest mistress."

Comtesse Orienne stopped playing and turned her head. She was a beautiful woman and would be for a few more years. Her hair, caught up in braided loops and covered by a golden crespine net knotted with jewels, was the color of dark honey. Her long, languid eyes were the reddish brown of chestnuts. Her figure was ample, with high, round breasts and a deeply curved waist. Her brows, plucked almost to nonexistence, raised at the sight of Seur Aungelique. "What manner of monk is this, pray?"

"She came to the door, ma maîtresse," the servant said.

"But how odd," la comtesse said, then laughed, mockery making the sound harsh.

"I came here," Seur Aungelique said unexpectedly, "for sanctuary."

Comtesse Orienne was shaking her head. "No one comes here for sanctuary, ma Frèrée," she stated. "There are other things offered here, but not what you are seeking."

"But you *are* what I seek," Seur Aungelique insisted. "I swear to you, Comtesse. If I had not been told that you—"

"Told?" la comtesse echoed. "Who told you of me?"

For the first time, Seur Aungelique did not speak promptly. "I have a kinsman, a distant kinsman, but . . . He told me of you many times, and how you live here. He said you are the most beautiful woman in the world and that there is no pleasure of the senses that you do not know as art." There had been other things her third cousin had told her, but Seur Aungelique did not dare to repeat them.

"And who is this distant kinsman who told you of me?" Comtesse Orienne asked as she resumed rubbing her skin with pungent oils.

"He is le Duc de Parcignonne, Pierre Fornault." She raised her chin as she answered, and her expression was faintly defiant.

"Oh-ho," Comtesse Orienne exclaimed. "So Pierre has been telling tales, has he?" Her smile, contented and feline, gave the lie to her supposed rebuke.

"I wanted to know all about you," Seur Aungelique admitted.

"But why, ma Frèrée?"

"Because I want to be like you," Seur Aungelique burst out.

Comtesse Orienne gave a signal to the musicians, and they set their instruments aside. "And that is why you have come here?"

"Yes." Without warning, Seur Aungelique burst into tears. "They want to make a nun of me, but I won't. I *won't*."

"Not if you live as I do," Comtesse Orienne agreed as she came to the edge of the shell-shaped basin and climbed out of it. Immediately, a page approached, holding a drying sheet out to her.

"And so I . . . I ran away and came here."

Comtesse Orienne stopped in the act of wrapping herself in the sheet. "We will talk, ma Frèrée. You will dine with me. Then we shall see."

Père Guibert bowed his head as he listened, shame filling his heart. "I will follow after her, of course, ma Fille," he said to Mère Léonie.

She paced the short length of her study. "You have heard her confession. There may be things she spoke of—no, I have no desire to know what she has said under seal—that may tell you where she has gone. Her father, perhaps?"

"It is not likely," Père Guibert said with a heavy sigh. "One of the reasons she had been sent here was that she and her father could not agree about an acceptable husband, and she refused to take the man he had chosen for her, preferring another." He looked at Mère Léonie with an expression at once miserable and ludicrous.

"So I surmise," Mère Léonie told him over her shoulder. "It is a misfortune that many convents have had to contend with, however, especially in these times, with plague and war making havoc of the most careful plans." She laughed once, and Père Guibert was startled to hear it.

"It is true enough, but it is not an easy thing to tell a discontented parent this." He hated the way this excuse sounded, as if he, too, were caught up in worldly exercises.

"You will inform le baron of Seur Aungelique's actions, however?" Her hands were on her hips, and for all the demure lines of her gray habit, she looked martial and ready for conflict.

"I am required to do so. And I will send a messenger from Avignon. I must go there, you understand. I have to report this."

"Of course," Mère Léonie agreed. "And what of the sisters here? What do I tell them?"

"Of Seur Aungelique? They must know that she left."

"They know that she stole a donkey, fashioned some sort of disguise, and fled into the night. I wish to offer them good counsel, but how am I to do it if I have nothing more to offer them than that you have gone to search for her?" Her proud head ducked a moment, and Père Guibert thought he understood the sense of shame and failure that troubled the new superior.

"Pray for guidance, ma Fille, and God will read your

heart aright." He blessed her without looking at her, and
then went reluctantly to the door. "I will see that you
have news from me as soon as it is possible."

"Deo gratias," Mère Léonie answered without any
other sign of courtesy.

Distressed, Père Guibert left the study and went
into the courtyard where his mule was saddled and waiting for him.

Though the sky was cloudless, it was empty, as if a
fine blue bowl had been inverted and clapped over the
world. Comtesse Orienne stood in her solar at the tall
windows and stared out into the afternoon. "My gar-
deners say it will rain," she remarked to Aungelique,
who reclined on one of the larger silken cushions. "I will
have to have the oilcloths put up, I suppose."

Aungelique shrugged. "There are other rooms,
Orienne, and your banquets do not need a cloudless sky
to be enjoyed." She had been with her hostess for little
more than a week; she no longer dressed in shapeless
gray wool but in a samite cote the color of oranges and a
surcote of heavy rust-colored linen that was ornamented
with a center row of large amber buttons. Because her
hair was short, crespine nets were not suitable to her,
and so she wore instead a capuchon with elaborate pleat-
ing around her face. On Orienne's suggestion, she had
opened the lower part of the close-fitting hood so that
from her throat to her bosom her skin was bared. The
pale saffron color showed her olive flesh to advantage.

Orienne sighed. "Well, you're probably right—I
could serve the meal in a byre and half of them would not
notice. They are not fools, but they do not think of . . ."

"Of?" Aungelique asked when Orienne failed to go
on.

"Oh, of a thousand things." She turned away from
the window. "I suppose you're right. I will tell the steward to move all this down to the lesser hall and have the
fires built up so that we will not feel the drafts." She
smiled unexpectedly. "Are you looking forward to this
evening, ma petite? Do you want to taste debauchery at

last, or do you only want to watch and be shocked by what we do?"

"Inspired," Aungelique corrected her with an arch look. "I believe I have a talent for debauchery, if what Mère Léonie told me is right."

"Ah, yes, the penance and the willow wands." Then Orienne turned more serious. "It is not something to feign, Aungelique. It must be a riot in your blood that is as undeniable as the phase of the moon. This is not an acquired skill like the making of cloth or hunting of stags; it is more a talent, like what my musicians have."

Aungelique was taken aback at the strange turn of their conversation. "The church speaks of the Devil, who leads us into . . . into vice."

"Pafth!" Orienne exclaimed as she spat. "There are those who cannot hear the difference between the lowing of cattle and true voices, either, and say that there is no such distinction. Those of us who are held by fleshly chains know otherwise, as young Jaques knows his notes."

Aungelique shivered as she recalled the nights she had lain, sleepless, with the taunting needs of her body gripping her as tightly as a lover. "I have known those chains."

She came to another of the larger cushions and sank down on it. "I did not know at first what it was that ruled me, for I was sent young to a husband who was a stranger to me. The marriage had been arranged when I was still a child, and when they knew I was a woman, the wedding took place as my father wished. My husband was . . . well, he was not a young man, and his tastes were gone in dissipation by the time he took me to wife. There were other women for him, and boys. Of me he required nothing but heirs. I gave him two before the . . . Plague came." She toyed with one of the fringes on the cushion. "I did not mourn him long; the children, too, were lost before . . . it was over." She leaned back. "And so now I live as I wish, and the flesh is my master and I his thrall."

Aungelique said nothing, though there were questions burning in her mind.

"My husband was like a ram tupping ewes when the desire was on him. He had as much imagination as a ram, as well." This last was said with a weary sarcasm that puzzled Aungelique.

"But if you love the flesh . . ."

"There is no flesh in what he did. It was all over as quickly as it is in the barn." She forced a laugh and glanced at Aungelique slyly. "Do you think you would want that, my little Frèrée? Just one or two plunges? No?" She let her head fall back. "Well, tonight you will learn for yourself, and you can decide then."

"I hope I will do more than decide," Aungelique said as brazenly as she could. "I want to know what it is that I am supposed to rid myself of."

Once again, Orienne laughed, and this time she did not sound as if she were compelled to do so. "I want to see you when you make your discovery."

Aungelique smoothed her skirt and then pressed her hand over the lowest of the amber buttons. "Tell me; is my kinsman likely to be one of the company?"

Orienne gave a knowing look to her young guest. "It is possible. Why?"

"There is no reason." She got up suddenly. "I will assist in setting up the lesser hall. Otherwise, the steward might not finish the work in time."

"How considerate." She knew that Aungelique did not want to discuss Pierre Fornault with her, so she added with a touch of spite, "They trained you well at that convent, didn't they?"

Père Guibert had been gone little more than three days when he sent word back to Mère Léonie of his progress, stating that it was his belief that Seur Aungelique had taken refuge—if it could be called such when in association with so vile a woman—in the little summer palace of la Comtesse Orienne de Hautlimois. Although he was not able to bring himself to be more specific, Père Guibert did tell Mère Léonie that he was afraid that lasting damage might already have been done to Seur Aungelique. The guilt that possessed him as he wrote that was almost unbearable to the priest, and he knew it would be a very long time before he would be able to expiate his error in caring of Seur Aungelique.

There were musicians in the gallery above the great hall; two sackbuts, a cythara angelica, two gitterns, three buisines, and a tabor made up the consort. A few couples danced to the melodies, but most paid little attention to them, preferring instead to eat, drink, and converse. Only an adventurous few were openly salacious, for the evening was young.

Aungelique was uncertain of what was expected of her. She was not anxious merely to sport with Orienne's company but wanted to find a proper companion, one who would not bore her or use her ill.

"Alone, sweeting?" asked a light, equivocal voice near her left shoulder.

"Rather keeping my own . . ." Aungelique turned and faced the beautiful young man who had spoken to her. "Yes. I am alone," she whispered, caught up by his presence.

"A pity. You need not be." He was slender and graceful, dressed splendidly in pale blue and silver, which brought out the icy color of his pale eyes. It was odd, Aungelique thought as she stared at him, that such light eyes could be so hot.

The musicians made a flurry of sound and launched into a throbbing, plaintive tune.

"Do you know the words?" the young man asked.

"I don't . . . no." Speaking to him was an effort but terribly pleasant.

"It says:

"Alas, that I should be without dreams
For my soul is parched for lack
Of their gentle consolation
Of the glamour of their touch.

"Doesn't that stir you, little sweeting? Does not your heart know that wish?"

Aungelique was not sure if the youth was taunting her with his questions, but she did her best to answer him in the approved, arch way. "Good bachelor, this is enchantment enough."

He chuckled. "Is it? What is this but a dream?"

Again, Aungelique wondered if he were making mock of her. "I cannot grasp the substance of my dreams."

"Can you not, little sweeting? Is there no torment in your soul that cannot be quieted outside of your dreams?" He reached out languidly and brushed her cheek with the back of his hand.

"If you seek to affront me—" Aungelique began, but the young man interrupted her.

"No. Never that, little fledgling. I would only ask to bring an end to your suffering, not to burden you more." He smiled once and moistened his lower lip with his tongue. "Perhaps another time, sweeting?" He inclined his head and passed on.

"You've caught his eye?" Comtesse Orienne demanded as she came up to Aungelique as soon as the newcomer had sauntered off.

"I don't think so. He said a few things, but nothing to make me think that he had . . ." To her disgust, she felt her cheeks grow rosy. "Who is he?"

"His name, so he tells me, is Thibault Col, Chevalier de Bruges." She brushed impatiently at the open neck of her houppelande to be rid of imaginary crumbs. "If manner and wealth are any gauge, he must have some nobility. He came with Ferrand. You met him? Le Baron de Montpaiet?"

"I think so." Aungelique did not want to trouble her thoughts with the pale-eyed young man any longer.

"He comes from the north. Col, that is. Well, his name says as much." She flashed a wide, meaningless smile to three women who sallied toward them. "We will talk later, ma Frèrée. In the morning." With that, she was gone into the crowd.

In the end, Aungelique spent the night alone, and sometime before dawn she rose and wandered the halls, looking at the aftermath of the festivities with a critical eye. The musicians slept in the corner of the great hall, crowded together like a litter of puppies. Three sleepy understewards were strewing clean rushes over the floor, covering the refuse from the banquet of the previous evening. In curtained alcoves, lovers kept their trysts, some of them still awake from the sounds that issued from behind the painted hangings. Aungelique paused to observe two of these meetings; her hands grew moist as she watched, and an echo of the pulse in her loins trembled along her body.

By sunrise, Aungelique was exhausted, but she could not bring herself to lie down. Restlessly, she roamed through the back of the little palace and then out into the gardens where the wild orchard was just starting to put forth leaves and buds. She could not bring herself to contemplate the lovers she had watched; it was too painful to know that she had become attached to no one.

"Sweeting?" said Thibault Col from the door behind her.

Aungelique spun around. "Do you always come up behind . . ." She dropped her eyes at his lazy laughter. "You do not deal with me honorably."

"And do you? A runaway nun who watches lovers at their pleasure? Who are you to chide me, sweeting?" He strolled toward her, one hand on his belt. "You desire to taste, but you dare not. Do you lack courage or only sense?" As he reached her, he held her eyes with his own.

"Who told you I was a runaway nun?" she demanded, taking the most obvious of his accusations.

"Does it matter? Last night, the only woman who covered her hair was you. Is it because it has been cut off?" He reached out and touched her capuchon. "I doubt I'm the only one who guessed its purpose." He moved suddenly, brushing her mouth with his own. "There. Now you have made a beginning."

Aungelique took a step back and folded her arms. "I did not ask for a kiss."

"Didn't you?" Thibault asked her. He, too, folded his arms, regarding her with amusement.

"Did you follow me?" Aungelique inquired, trying to find a way to disrupt him as he had her.

"Naturally. You seemed in need of company, and since you intruded on la comtesse and me, I decided that it would be permissible to intrude on you; you have not nearly so much a reason to be private as Orienne and I had." His mouth curved like a scimitar. "Did you?"

"I didn't realize . . ." she began lamely. "I thought that . . . I thought you . . ."

"You thought we took pleasure together," he stated flatly. "Did you learn anything, sweeting? Do you wish I would hold you the same way, touch and taste you the same way?"

"Don't," she said, wishing she could turn away from him.

"Perhaps tonight? We could come here, or if that is not to your liking, there are rooms apart from the others where no one would find us unless you desired more than what I—"

"Stop," she whispered, horrified that she did not want him to obey her.

"Is there not a gulf in you, sweeting? Does it not seek to be filled?" He grinned at her. "Do you deny it? Do you deny *me*?"

Aungelique gathered her hands into twin fists. "You must not seek me in this way. It isn't fitting."

"What have I said that you have not thought already?" He did not move, but there was an intimacy in his teasing that had not been there at first.

She had no answer for him; she searched for escape. "Why do you torment me?"

"Why?" he repeated. "Is it not what you want, sweeting?"

"No!" she protested wildly.

"But it is." He came toward her again, stopping less than a handbreadth from her without touching her. "How strong is your desire, sweeting?"

Desperately, Aungelique broke away from him, shoving him aside as she ran as if she fled from rapine or damnation or the plague. "*No!*" she shouted, not certain what she sought to avoid—Thibault's embraces or her own passion.

Père Guibert regarded Comtesse Orienne with cowed disapproval. "I have authorization to return Seur

Aungelique to her convent." He brandished the document as if it were a weapon.

Comtesse Orienne sighed and helped herself to a date. "Do you want one, Père?"

"You have the girl here, haven't you?"

"If you are here, you know that I do," she countered. Her head rang from wine and lack of sleep; charm did not come easily to her that day.

"I have not seen her for myself, but it is what I have been told," he said, being scrupulously honest. "I have been directed to restore her to her convent at once."

"Yes, I understand that part." She yawned. "Tomorrow morning, mon Père. She will be ready to travel."

Père Guibert stammered out his astonishment. "But . . . you do not object?"

"I am not a foolish woman. If I defy the Cardinal now, I will lose his protection. If I cooperate, however, I will be left alone. At least that is how it has always been in the past, or didn't they tell you about it?" Her smile bordered on malice. "Bon Père, you are naive if you think that Avignon is unaware of what I do and those I do it with." She clapped, and a page appeared. "Take Père Guibert to the kitchen and see that he is properly fed." She beamed at the priest. "I won't offer you the insult of my company."

"Deo gratias," Père Guibert muttered, confused by the conflicts Comtesse Orienne engendered in him. "Bread and cheese will be sufficient."

"Nevertheless, you will take what is provided and thank God humbly for it, or you will not be worthy of your calling."

Père Guibert glared at her as he followed the page from the room.

"You may come out now," Orienne said to the air. "Ma Frèrée."

"I'm not going back" were the first words Aungelique spoke as she emerged from behind a hanging that blocked one of the private alcoves.

"That may be, but you cannot stay here," Orienne said, attempting to speak as gently as her raging head would allow. "I cannot risk my whole way of living for your stubbornness, Aungelique."

Aungelique set her jaw. "Why not?" It was an unreasonable question, but la comtesse deigned to answer it.

"For the time being, the Church ignores me officially, and that suites me very well. But if your father should insist that the letter of the law be served against me, then I will find myself in prison or worse, and you, ma Frèrée, would still have to go back to your convent."

"Or worse," Aungelique said darkly. "It was bad enough being sent to the convent." She folded her arms. "And if I go back, what then?"

Orienne shrugged. "Who knows? In time, your father will die. Upon his death, you will be free to do as you wish unless your brothers hold you to your father's will." She reached out for another date and chewed it thoughtfully. "I would not mind having you here if that were the only consideration, but with your father's reputation, well, I have nothing to oppose him that would mean anything to those good men of the Church."

"I hate the convent," Aungelique whispered, turning miserable instead of defiant. "We pray and prostrate ourselves and whip ourselves with willow rods."

"You told me," Orienne reminded her kindly. "But I can't change the rule of the Order, can I?"

"And Mère Léonie . . . Everyone says that she is doing such good for us, but I think that she . . . that she is . . . is . . ." Her voice dropped to nothing as she searched her mind for an adequate description of Mère Léonie.

"She is new, ma Frèrée, and from everything you've said, she is trying to reform the whole convent at once." She recalled herself enough to offer Aungelique a date. "They're very good, and you won't have many of them at the convent."

Aungelique's eyes filled with tears. "No." She reached out and took five of the precious dates. "I'll have to eat them all before . . . before I arrive back, or I'll be made to do penance for them." She stuffed two of them into her mouth at once and began to chew vigorously. It was almost impossible for her to swallow against the tightening in her throat. She panted, like one of the little ferrets that Orienne kept indoors to eat the leavings of the banquet table and kill the rats and mice that lived in the rushes.

"You think it's cruel of me to deny you all the things you want so badly. It may be that God made me cruel; He has made many thus. I know that you suffer, but the whole world suffers, ma Frèrée, and God permits it. I will take my salvation now in flesh rather than in the spirit for eternity." She put her hands to her temples. "You are not in a position to do as you wish, but few of us are, Aungelique. If the Cardinal had not befriended me, I would have had my head shaved years ago and been given to one of my distant kinsmen for chastisement. It would be harder for me than for you."

"But . . ." Aungelique protested around the dates.

"No. I won't discuss it more. There will be another time when you will be able to come here without the threat of your father's wrath looming over you, and then, if you still want to share my life here, you would be most welcome."

"I won't whip myself." Her resolve, which had been weakening, was once again firm.

"That is for you to decide. I will not forget you, and should I hear word from Pierre, I will let you know of it, one way or another. You will not be wholly cut off, or—" She held out the last of the dates.

Aungelique hesitated only an instant, then took them. "I thank you, Comtesse, for your courtesy."

"And at the moment you want to scratch my eyes out. I would, too, if I had to go from here to a convent, whips or no whips." She rose languidly so that the throbbing in her temples would not make her ill. "I have ways to get word to you, ma Frèrée, and in time you will find the means to send messages to me, as well. It is often done, no matter what you hear."

"I don't *want* to find the means!" Aungelique shouted, unable to control her temper any longer. "I want to run away."

"And then what? They dare not take you at a brothel, and you are not one to sell yourself at the waterfront, are you? That is no more free than life in your convent, believe me. But that isn't what you mean, is it? You want to find yourself your own Noveautie where you may live for your pleasure and the delight of others." She sighed and held out her hand as if to make amends. "When next you come here, it will be different."

"Will it? Because I will then be so old and haggard that I will have forgotten everything I desired?" She trembled. "I want what you have, Orienne; lovers and food and pleasures and . . . the rest of it. I was never made to be a nun, and God will not be fooled by my father's determination." In one last attempt, she went on as emphatically as she could. "In fact, it may be that in returning to the convent, I am aiding him in the worst sin—pride, for he believes he can instill a vocation where God has not bestowed it."

"You are clever," Orienne interrupted her. "And perhaps you are right. But God's Will is not in question; your father's is. He has said that you will accept the bridegroom he has chosen or you will wear the veil, and until he is dead, you must abide by what he declares. I have already said that it is not in my nature to take up gauntlets on others' behalf. It is too dangerous, and there is no merit in it." She gave Aungelique an arch smile. "It is not forever, little one. That young man—Thibault Col? Is that his name?—will not forget you."

"That . . . has nothing to . . . do with it," Aungelique insisted.

"And if not he, then another will want you. There are always men, ma Frèrée, and they have their desires. Your Pierre cannot forget you, either, can he? And not only because you are cousins."

"Thibault Col will not remember," Aungelique murmured, thinking of the many things she had seen in her brief stay with Comtesse Orienne.

"There you are wrong," Orienne said, raising her head a trifle to take the sting out of the words she repeated. "He told me he wanted you."

Aungelique was too young and too pleased to keep from asking, "But when?"

"Last night," Orienne admitted. "When he lay with

me." Suddenly, she could not bring herself to remain in the same room with Aungelique; with nothing more than a quick, cutting glance for farewell, she left her young guest alone.

Three more hours and the first night of her penance would be over. Seur Aungelique felt the cold stones under her, pressing her naked body, the welts from her scourging like fire in the cold. If only she were not alone in the hospice chapel, far from her Sisters. The isolation Mère Léonie had imposed on her had been welcome at first but was turning out to be a greater trial than lying stripped and prostrate before the altar throughout the night. The hospice was empty; no travelers were abroad yet, with the spring so new and the officers of the Roman Church taxing every merchant seeking to enter France. Seur Aungelique moaned and dutifully resumed the prayers she had been told to recite.

> "Votis vocemus et patrem
> patrem perennis gloriae,
> Pater potentis gratiae
> culpam releget lubricam.
> Informet actus strenuos,
> dentem retundat invidi:
> casus secundet asperos,
> donet gerendi gratiam."

She said the words distinctly but without thought or understanding. How much more to her liking would be silken cushions under her instead of the stone floor. How much more welcome would be the sound of sweet instruments playing soft tunes than the muttered prayers she must say through the night. She almost interjected that into her prayers but feared that someone might overhear. Servants to bring her all that she desired, Seur Aungelique thought, and that would mean not simply cooks and musicians but lovers, men who desired her to madness. She squirmed against the flagging.

It would begin slowly. Slowly, so that the desire would build in them both.

"Laetus dies hic transeat:
pudor sit ut diluculum,
fides velut meridies . . ."

They would recline in the solar, on the silken
cushions, and her lover—let it be Thibault Col, she decided—would bring her a goblet of hot wine mixed with
honey and nutmeg and pepper, and they would drink
from the same goblet, letting their fingers touch as they
held it between them. There would be the same desire
in his eyes that Seur Aungelique had seen when she had
inadvertently watched the chevalier make love to Comtesse Orienne. La comtesse had cried out that she was
caught in the talons of love, and Thibault Col had tightened his hold upon her, his hand on her breast sinking
into the soft flesh in a way that Seur Aungelique had
thought should be painful, but if Orienne's gasp had
meant anything, was not. If she tried hard enough, she
could almost feel a warm hand laid across her aching but-
tocks, a lean, sensitive hand that stroked and then
probed, so that the pain of her thrashing was submerged
in pleasure. That hand—if she would wish it into pal-
pability!—would know precisely where and how to touch
her, and she would writhe with rapture at its ministrations.

There was a sound in the chapel like a low chuckle;
then the rear door groaned open, and Mère Léonie approached.

"You are sweating," she said to Seur Aungelique.
"Are you ill?"

Seur Aungelique felt the color deepen in her face
and neck as she strove to rise. "It is . . . nothing, ma
Mère." Had Mère Léonie overheard her? Had she forgotten her prayers in those ecstatic moments when her
dream was almost real?

"Are you troubled, Seur Aungelique?" Mère Léonie
asked. "Père Guibert will hear your confession tomorrow
morning."

"It's . . . not that, ma Mère." She feared her trai-
torous flesh would somehow give her away, that her de-

sires could be seen as blatantly upon it as the marks of the willow wand.

"Return to your cell and put on your habit. And think of your shame as you go."

Arms crossed on her breasts, her face averted, Seur Aungelique hurried away from the imposing, gray-habited figure of her superior. She had started to weep, and try as she would, she could not convince herself that she was going to the embraces of her lover instead of fleeing the scene of her abasement.

Chapter 3

Père Guibert strode restlessly through the cloisters of Fôrlebene, his face set in a forbidding scowl. It was bad enough that five of the Brothers had died there during the winter, but with an ancient abbot with a wandering mind, the brothers lacked direction. This was not the report that Cardinal Seulfleuve would welcome when Père Guibert returned to Avignon. He tried to compose his thoughts, but that only intensified his burden of guilt and failure.

"Père Guibert . . . ?" said a pleasant voice in the adjoining ambulatory.

"Yes?" He looked around sharply. "Who calls me?"

It was not a proper response for one Brother to give another, but the man who replied did not point that out. "If I intrude, I will beg your pardon and leave."

Inwardly appalled at his own behavior, Père Guibert attempted to make amends. "I must beg your pardon; my thoughts were elsewhere."

The stranger, in the tan and white habit of an Augustinian, bowed his head. "I fear your concerns are of a worldly nature, mon Père."

"Uh . . ." Père Guibert blinked in surprise.

"So are my thoughts turning," the Augustinian went on. "Those of us who revere our vows and our Church must be consumed with worldly thoughts, whether we will or no." He stepped into the cloister garden where several clumps of dried twigs gave promise of summer herbs.

Where had this man come from? Père Guibert wondered. He should have been informed if there were a new brother in the community, let alone an Augustinian with a peculiar accent. "I fear, mon Frère, that you have the advantage of me."

The Augustinian turned to look at Père Guibert. "I must. I am Père Bartolimieu Reiter. Although in the cantons, we are called Padre, not Père."

"Padre Bartolimieu," Père Guibert acknowledged, more confused than ever.

"I came here seeking . . . sanctuary?" He was tall, this Swiss priest, lantern jawed and spade handed. He was between forty and fifty years of age, his fringe of hair almost completely white, as was the tangle of his eyebrows. "Père Guibert, may I speak with you?"

Père Guibert folded his hands. "Of course. But Padre, why did you, a priest, seek sanctuary?" It was a tactless question, but Père Guibert was in no mood for endless, polite, evasive conversation. "If your fears are worldly, there are other places where sanctuary is more . . . appropriate, though la Virge knows you are isolated here." He paused.

"L'Etivaz, where I had my church . . ." He reached up and shaded his eyes against the glare of the sun as the scattered clouds opened. "When Rome and Avignon became . . . enemies, there was much distress. The cantons are wary of both Italy and France, and no one knew where our loyalty lay. In seeking to find the way, we abused the faith of our people, and for this we . . ." He coughed. "God strengthen my resolve."

Père Guibert frowned. "I don't . . . Padre, you are difficult to follow."

"Yes. May God forgive me for this cowardice." He crossed himself and for a little time was lost in prayer.

"There was Plague three years ago. This district suffered then, as well, didn't it?"

"Praise to the mercy of God for sparing so many," Père Guibert said quickly, hoping to placate the ire he recalled all too vividly. "It has been worse before."

"They have also said that so many have died already that there are not enough left to die now." He pulled absently at the ends of his belt. "We were mad with folly then, thinking that the plague would pass over more quickly if we determined where we must ally ourselves. For this neglect, we were sorely tried and punished, for the Flagellants came . . . You have encountered Flagellants?"

"Thanks be to God, not directly," Père Guibert said with deep sincerity. "There were some not too far from here, at Romans-sur-Isère and at Valence." He stopped, not knowing what more to say.

"They brought catastrophe," Padre Bartolimieu whispered. "They razed my church, and those whom the Plague had not claimed they buried in the rubble, smashing their limbs with the candlesticks from the altar before pressing them with stones."

Père Guibert crossed himself slowly. "And you?"

"To my everlasting shame, I ran," Padre Bartolimieu admitted. "When the Flagellants broke down the church doors and began first to defecate on the rushes, I fought them. Then they lit fires, and after they started to break up the central pillars, I ran. I have petitioned both the Pope at Rome and the pope at Avignon to assign me penance for my crime, but there has yet to be a response from either See."

"Do you know if your petitions were delivered?" Père Guibert asked, not wanting to pursue the priest's transgressions unless he had to.

"Not surely, no." He leaned against the empty fountain at the center of the garden. "Now I have come here and will stay here unless I have other instruction."

"I see."

"I doubt if the Flagellants will come here; it's too remote. And the Plague has already been here for the decade." He rubbed his face with trembling hands. "I have confessed already and done what was required, but my soul is foul with my act, and it is not enough."

"Abbé Christolfe has . . . much need of aid here" was Père Guibert's first tentative suggestion.

"I will do what is needed," Padre Bartolimieu said at once. "But this is not my order, and the Brothers follow another Rule." His helplessness went far beyond the immediate situation, and Père Guibert had nothing to offer him as solace.

"We must await a . . ." His voice softened. "God requires the faith of all of us, and when the world is most benighted, when we are most severely tested, then our faith is the brighter and our salvation the more glorious." Looking at the other priest, he knew his consolation was inadequate.

"I have prayed and meditated," Padre Bartolimieu protested, plainly untouched by what Père Guibert had said. "I suppose it was God's will that I flee, but He has not revealed to me how I am to live with this failure."

Père Guibert could find no heartening sentiments to lay before the troubled Swiss priest. "Flagellants and the rest of your suffering, there is no one who could come through such an ordeal unscathed."

"At night, in my dreams, I see my parish and the Flagellants with their whips, and I watch my church fall, and the guilt comes back." He folded his hands. "While I am here, I want to strive for tranquillity, but there is so much guilt on my soul that I despair, and that is a greater sin . . . I fear that I am lost, Père Guibert."

"Then you must beg God to show you His plan. Prayer is never unanswered." It was another lesson he had repeated so many times that it no longer had meaning.

"I know. I have trusted in that. But of late I have started to wonder if it may be that the answer God has for me is no." The Augustinian crossed himself as if to protect himself from these heretical doubts. "One day, it will be plain to me. But, in that day, if it should be that I no longer . . . God does not desert man; man deserts

God," Padre Bartolimieu said with harsh emphasis. "Only my failure will . . ."

A portative organ wheezed in the chapel, and the sound of the first monks gathering for holy service rustled through the cloisters.

"I should attend," Padre Bartolimieu said halfheartedly.

"As should I," Père Guibert seconded. "It will do my soul good to hear Mass with these Brothers." He hoped that this simple, ordinary observation would lessen the other man's despair.

Padre Bartolimieu looked away, out of the cloisters toward the distant peaks in the east. "Will it?"

"But mon Padre, that was the promise given in the Body of Christ." He crossed himself and waited for Padre Bartolimieu to do the same.

"Yes." He let his breath out slowly; his hands remained still. "But that was so long ago."

Six men-at-arms accompanied le Duc de Parcignonne to the doors of la Tres Saunte Annunciacion, remaining in the saddle when le duc dismounted and strode to the grilled window to announce his arrival. He was of a good height and burly, carrying his armor and weapons with habitual ease. His square face was seamed on the left cheek by a jagged scar, giving him a severe aspect that many found disquieting. "Good Sister!" he shouted through the grille.

After a brief silence, he was answered by an unseen woman who was still breathless. "Traveler, pray enter at the doors of the hospice. We do not give admittance here."

"I seek no shelter or lodging either for myself or my men. I am here at the request of my cousin, le Baron Michau d'Ybert, newly made Vidame de Figeac, who has charged me to speak to his daughter on his behalf. She is known here as Seur Aungelique." He slung his weight onto the hip where his sword rested.

"Sieur le Duc," Seur Odile began, her nervousness causing her words to tumble out in choked whispers, "I must . . . get the permission of our superior to . . . permit you to—"

"Then do that," Pierre said testily. "The sooner I have completed my commission, the better." He made no apology for what he had said and chose to ignore the scandalized silence that his opinion inspired.

"I'll seek Mère Léonie at once," Seur Odile said at her most prim.

"God reward you." He heard movement on the other side of the grille and nodded to himself in satisfaction. "You might as well dismount," he told his men-at-arms as he went back to them. "We'll be lucky if we get to Mou Courbet by nightfall."

"Trouble?" one of the men asked.

"Difficulties. Nothing more. Get down."

His men did as they were told and passed the time walking their lathered mounts back and forth in front of the convent in order to cool them.

"Too bad there isn't a stream," one of the soldiers said. "I could use a drink."

"As could your horse," Pierre added. "There is one the other side of the orchard; wait for me there. These poor women probably think they're under siege with so many knights at the door." He laughed at his own rough humor. "You. Antois. You're in charge."

As soon as the men-at-arms and their horses were away from the gate, it opened, and Pierre Fornault found himself facing a tall young woman in the stark and shapeless gray habit of the Assumptionist Order. "God give you good day, Sieur le Duc."

"And to you . . . um . . ." He waited for the nun to introduce herself.

"I am Mère Léonie, superior of this convent. I bid you enter and will permit you to speak to Seur Aungelique on behalf of her father. However," Mère Léonie added sharply as she took a step closer to Pierre, "since Seur Aungelique has transgressed most seriously, you are not to inquire anything of her but what her father requires. All other intercourse is forbidden. Do you accept this?"

Pierre was not used to such forthright speech from a woman, but he gave it his consideration. "I will try to respect your instructions," he answered with more caution than usual. "Will we be observed?"

"Perhaps." Mère Léonie stared hard at him. "Perhaps."

Fasting and long vigils at night in the chapel had reduced Seur Aungelique's body to gauntness and made her strangely lightheaded, so that when she first heard Pierre's voice in the hall, she thought it was another one of the pleasant dreams she had been enjoying more and more often of late. She had already begun to weave a tale about him in her thoughts when Seur Philomine tapped on the door of her cell. "What?" she called out, forgetting the proper forms for address.

"God be with you, Seur Aungelique," Seur Philomine said in gentle correction.

"And with your soul," Seur Aungelique answered, recalling herself. "What is it now, good Sister?"

"There is a person to see you. He waits in the sisters' chapel." She waited to give Seur Aungelique escort, for Mère Léonie had given orders that Seur Aungelique was to go nowhere unaccompanied unless stripped first.

"Very well. I am coming." Her head swam as she got from her knees to her feet, and she steadied herself against the wall before going the few steps toward the door.

Seur Philomine said pleasantly as she fell into step beside Seur Aungelique, "Mère Léonie would not ordinarily allow you this opportunity."

"Wouldn't she?" Seur Aungelique asked vaguely. "Is she afraid that I will run away again? She'd make me go naked, wouldn't she?" Her eyes moved uncertainly from Seur Philomine to the corridor walls, now freshly whitewashed.

"Surely . . ." Seur Philomine began, then faltered, recalling the severity of the superior's attitude toward Seur Aungelique's transgression. "In time, when you have repented your sins, you will have the same ease of

commerce we all have under Mère Léonie." Since she
had heard Mère Léonie make just such a promise, she
was confident in repeating it.

"For that, God will forgive you, ma Seur, because
you do not deceive with malice," Seur Aungelique said
in singsong tones. "This is to be my oubliette; my father
and the superior have determined upon it."

This accusation shocked Seur Philomine deeply. "I
will not listen to what you say. Your vigils and fasting
have brought about this fancy, and in time you will see
that you . . ."—She reached the door of the chapel and
stood aside respectfully—"Do not fear, Seur Aungelique."

She could not remember the proper response to
give Seur Philomine, but it hardly mattered. She caught
sight of Pierre Fornault standing near the altar, his head
lowered in thought. It was the stance that she felt was
most characteristic of him, and seeing it, she held back,
dizziness fingering her.

In the door, Seur Philomine saw Seur Aungelique's
confusion. "Here is your kinswoman, Sieur le Duc," she
announced before leaving the two alone.

Pierre had turned at the words and stood, arms
folded belligerently, brow creased. "God futter the
saints!" he ejaculated at the sight of Seur Aungelique.
"What has happened to you?"

"Good cousin?" Seur Aungelique said with sudden
joy. "Have you really come for me?"

"By Marie's tits." He came toward her with urgent,
angry steps. "What has happened to you, little bee? You
look ready for your winding sheet." He grabbed her by
the shoulders, pressing his fingers hard against her, making her wince as he scrutinized her face.

The dream was muddled in her mind, and Seur
Aungelique shook her head to protest his roughness.
"You must be gentle . . . good cousin," she said, sud-
denly unable to catch her breath.

"Are you ill?" Pierre shouted. He did not want to
have to tell her father that she was near death. "Aungelique, are you . . . what is wrong?" She was dressed in
her engulfing habit, and so there was no way he could

determine if the dreaded tokens were on her. "You're . . . dazed."

"Am I?" She brought up one unsteady hand. "Release me, good cousin. I pray you."

His large, calloused hands dropped to his side. "Forgive me, good Sister. Long acquaintance caused me to forget your vows from my . . . concern." He took two deliberate steps back from her. "Your superior did not tell me . . . you were not quite . . . yourself." Already he was seething, forming his interview with Mère Léonie in his mind.

"There is no reason she should. Is there?" Now that he no longer touched her, Seur Aungelique longed to provoke him, to find the secret words that would bring her into his arms. "I have had penance to do."

"Nom du Nom!" Pierre growled. "I've had prisoners in my dungeons who have been less . . ." He saw too late that there were tears in her eyes. "Forget my clumsiness, Seur Aungelique. If your soul has been in peril and this has saved it, no doubt it was little enough to—"

"I haven't repented," Seur Aungelique said in a small voice. "I try, but . . . I would run away to Une Noveautie and live there if I could." Pierre smacked one fist into his other hand. "Aungelique, what now? You were the one who told your father to send you here, and now you are here, you disobey and bring shame on your House. Why? What purpose?"

Seur Aungelique looked around her in confusion. "I didn't want to come here," she reminded him, looking at a spot on the empty wall. "My father made me choose."

"By God, Aungelique!" Pierre rounded on her, fearing that her wits had turned.

"I was told I would have to marry Jeoffroi or wear the veil. You have seen Jeoffroi. Anyone would refuse him, wouldn't she? He is old and drunken and stinking and keeps that hunchback woman for his pleasure. I . . . couldn't. I don't want him." She crossed herself in case anything she said might be thought blasphemous.

"Aungelique, your father did not arrange that match from caprice." He explained it patiently. "Jeoffroi is not the most delightful bridegroom, but he is very noble and powerful, and his estates are enormous and prosperous. If the Plague had not claimed so many, there could have been another for you, but your father had few choices that did not disgrace our name."

"It need not be Jeoffroi. I would have accepted another." She folded her arms, some of her old stubbornness returning to her. This was not what she had longed for, and she would not have her dream perverted.

"There was no one else!" Pierre bellowed.

"There was you!" she shouted back at him.

Pierre sagged as if from a blow. "Aungelique . . . Don't."

"There was!" she insisted, color coming at last to her waxen face.

"The Church forbade such a match." His voice was very quiet now.

"That was before the Plague. There are others, many others, who have had dispensations since. Why should you not wed me instead of Jeoffroi?" At last, she looked at him squarely.

He shook his head. "Aungelique, you aren't well . . ." He fell silent.

"I know that you have said that you do not want me," she reminded him with defiance, but her heart was leaden as she said it.

This was one of the possibilities that Pierre had dreaded when he agreed to bring Michau's message to Aungelique. "It isn't possible, Aungelique. Dispensations are granted to those where only one or two sons have survived the Plague. I have three brothers. You have two brothers. Your father . . . it is not in his hands." He rubbed the stubble on his face. "If there is war and more deaths, then in time your father might wish to try again, but it would mean that there were more losses. Why not forget this and accept your father's will?"

Seur Aungelique could stand this no longer. "Jeoffroi has bastards and mistresses in every village for ten leagues in every direction. They said that Jeoffroi has Venus' lice, and I would expect it."

"Half the nobility in France have Venus' lice!"

Pierre yelled at her, grateful that he was not one of them. "How many nuns have no lice on their bodies?"

"But not Venus' lice," Seur Aungelique insisted, starting to pout. She would rather dream of Pierre than talk with him at the moment. Her dreams were pleasant, and this was not.

"And that has nothing to do with it," Pierre grumbled. "Jeoffroi is not why I am here." He paced down the chapel. "Your father has . . . he has received proposal of another match."

"Another match?" Seur Aungelique repeated stupidly. Nothing made sense to her as she spoke to Pierre.

"It was brought to him a month ago, and he has given it his consideration. I have been deputized to bring you word of it."

"And my sisters? Were they not offered for? They are not in convents. Or has that changed in the last year?" She wished she were stronger so that she could give her remarks the force she felt inside herself.

"Your father has been informed of your . . . time with Comtesse Orienne, and rather than compel you to live here without true vocation, he has . . ." It had sounded simpler when Michau had explained it to him, and Pierre knew he was discharging his obligation badly. "Your sister Jeuell is not . . . marriageable, and Tereson is already promised."

"Not marriageable?" Seur Aungelique demanded. "How is that?"

This was not a thing Pierre wanted to discuss. "She suffered an injury. It doesn't matter, because . . ." As soon as he spoke, he knew he had bungled it.

"What accident. What happened to her to make her unmarriageable?"

"Ask your father!" he shouted. "There is an offer of marriage for you. It comes from a man of good family and fair reputation who has honor enough to satisfy the Church and your father. Le roi has tendered permission if you will accept."

Seur Aungelique was beginning to sweat, and the room felt too close. "Good cousin I do not know . . . My mind is not . . . Why did my father send *you*? Why not anyone else in the world but you? Pierre?" She started toward him, then fell to her knees.

For the first time, he felt real distress at the sight of her. He came to her, dropping onto one knee to steady her, holding her against his chest so that the linen of her coif was against his face. He could feel how slight she was through her shapeless habit, and it cut at him. "You must give me your word that you will consider the marriage. At least that."

"Or I will have to stay here, is that correct?" She let her head rest on his shoulder. This was more like the dream she had of him, more what she had hoped for as comfort; it was not enough. "You desire me, don't you?"

"Yes, I desire you," he answered quite calmly. "I desire women with fire in them, and you, Aungelique, little cousin, are a torch. I desire you. And I desire others. God made me lusty." There was little tenderness in his nature, but he had a kind of rough sympathy for Aungelique that moved him now. "Be a good, sensible woman for once in your life, sweet cousin. Listen to your father and accept his wishes."

"Why isn't Jeuell marriageable? Why does my father want me to accept the offer? Who is this bridegroom that you have told me nothing of? Why *now*?" They were questions that burned in her, yet she did not truly wish to ask them.

He wanted to shake her, and then he almost laughed, knowing that what he most desired was to ravish her, make a proper woman of her at last as she had wanted him to do since her first blood came. "That is for your father to tell you."

"Then it is someone dreadful, isn't it?" The dreams she so loved receded in her mind. "And this bridegroom is far away? In the mountains? A swamp? Is that what my father hopes for, an opportunity to have grandchildren and still immure me as much as I am now?"

"Aungelique. *Seur* Aungelique—" He dropped his hands from her shoulders. "Are you willing to entertain the suit, or do you wish to stay here?"

Seur Aungelique looked up at him and laughed miserably. "Stay here? What do you think? Would *you* stay here, given the choice? I would rather . . . No, I will not say that for fear my father will have word of it and wish it upon me." She crossed herself out of habit. "I wish to know who the bridegroom is and what it is that my father thinks to gain. But Pierre, for the love of anything you love, don't you bring the message next time, or in despair I might . . ." She looked away from him as he got to his feet. "My mind is not quite . . . clear. I do not sleep much, these nights, for penance, and . . ."

"And what?" Pierre demanded, knowing that he could not trust himself to stay too near her. "You have been chastised for good reason, little cousin. What possessed you to run away and bring shame on your father and on your Order?" He clapped his hands on his hips. "When I learned of it—"

"From Orienne?" Aungelique asked when he did not go on.

"Yes, from Orienne. I wanted to ride there myself and bring you back to your father across my saddle. This world does not forget such mischances, Cousin, and you . . . That your father has decided to find you a husband once again tells you how restrained he is. Thank God for the Plague that makes daughters valuable, Aungelique, or you would have more to regret than you already do." He was surprised at how much anger he could feel toward the pitiful girl and could not deny the desire that rode with it.

"Have you said all that you must, or is there more?" Seur Aungelique asked coldly. Her body ached, her eyes burned in her head as if infected, her hands felt as if each joint had been broken. She wanted to throw herself on Pierre and gouge a second scar in his face, anything to give back in part some of the pain he had forced upon her.

"I have . . . only your father's wish that you consider the offer and think of your life, Aungelique. He will abide by your decision. He gives his word on that, but he warns you"—this was the part that Pierre despised, that was against every honorable impulse he had—"that if you do not accept this proposed marriage, he will presume it is your preference to live cloistered and chaste."

"I have no inclination to marry a man I know nothing of and have never met. I also do not want to be a nun. I beg my father," she said through teeth gone tight with fury, "to permit me to go to a worthy court and serve there as a waiting woman. I will not burden him with my support, for that would fall to my mistress. I will not require that he leave me dowered or provisioned beyond what the Church demands of him. Tell him for me, Pierre, that I am not disposed to surrender my—" She pressed her hands to her mouth for fear that she would be sick.

Pierre came nearer to her, aggravated and worried. It was like Aungelique to put him in such a coil. "I will advise him to release you so that you may go to a suitable court. I will do that, Aungelique. I will tell him the depth of your conviction if I can. He may not listen to me; I don't know if it's possible for him."

"I must thank you for that, I suppose," she said as she got to her feet. Once again, she strove to keep the dizziness from overwhelming her. "I should return to my cell, good cousin." She bowed to him, not quite formally, and went toward the door, doing her best to ignore the darkness that hovered around the edges of her vision.

Pierre watched her go, wishing that he could follow her and explain how it had come about that he was charged with so unpleasant a task. Underneath this excellent impulse there was something darker, a need to convince her that he had made no error, no matter how much force it took. If she had been one of his squires, he would have taken her by the arm and so twisted it that she bent in half to submit to his will. Then he recalled that he had said he would speak to Mère Léonie when he had seen Seur Aungelique. Slowly, he went out of the stark chapel.

Mère Léonie listened to everything Pierre told her; her eyes remained fixed on Pierre, pale and cool as the gray habit she wore.

Pierre shrugged as he finished his report. "I do not know what more I may do, Mère Léonie." He shrugged and shifted on the bench she had provided for him.

"Seur Aungelique said that she had no vocation?" Mère Léonie asked.

"Yes. And I believe her." This addition was spoken more firmly, more like the capable leader he was.

"Do you suppose her father would agree to send her to court? It is not my wish to have nuns here who are not devoted to their calling." She tapped her long, thin hands together with worldly impatience.

Le duc feared overstepping the proper bounds more than he had done already. "I have no say in the matter, unfortunately, or I would see Aungelique wherever she wished to go."

Mère Léonie gave him a look that hinted at a smile. "Would that include taking her to Comtesse Orienne de Hautlimois at Une Noveautie?"

This challenge startled Pierre. "It is not in my hands, ma Mère, no matter what my cousin wants."

"Ah. I see." She nodded once. "And *you* know la comtesse?"

"I have met her," Pierre answered, continuing to evade her.

"And what do you think of her? Does she live as you wish to see your cousin live? Well?" Her fingers tapped together again, and Pierre had the uncomfortable feeling that Mère Léonie was taunting him. "What would you want, Sieur le Duc? Are you so wholly disinterested as you claim, or is there another reason for your compliance in Seur Aungelique's desires?"

"I . . ." This line of inquiry was vexing to him. "My confessor will know of it if my thoughts are corrupt."

"It may be that your presence recalls old doubts that you play upon, and thus you turn Seur Aungelique from her life here to that sink of perdition that Comtesse Orienne wallows in." Her fixed stare grew more intense. "I must ask, mustn't I?"

"If you perceive your duty that way," Pierre responded shortly.

Mère Léonie smoothed the front of her habit, pressing the rough fabric so that some of the lines of her tall body were revealed. "Seur Aungelique's confessor will know of your visit."

"That is fitting." Pierre wanted to look away from her, but that would mean a surrender he had no intention of awarding her. "Is there any word you wish me to carry to le baron d'Ybert?"

"Only my promise that I will continue to watch over his daughter to the best of my capacity." She stood up and turned, letting the shapeless garment swing around her. "No doubt le Bon Dieu will guide my thoughts and bring me wisdom to deal with your cousin."

Pierre was not entirely satisfied with this remark, and his pride was smarting from Mère Léonie's high-handed attitude. "You will find Seur Aungelique is not truly suited to be a nun. I will see that she is spared further . . . discomfort."

"Do you think she is not comfortable here?" Mère Léonie did not sound angry so much as teasing.

"Look at her!" Pierre demanded. "She's half starved and dazed for need of sleep."

With a sidelong glance, Mère Léonie at last released him from the magnet of her pale eyes. "But then, there are so many kinds of comfort, aren't there? And not all of them come with soft beds and full bellies. Do they?"

The messenger who came in the last dapplings of a spring shower wore the tabard of Avignon and carried a staff topped with the device of the Pope. He drew up his horse before the gates of la Tres Saunte Annunciacion and called out as custom required, but his voice was husky from other such announcements, and it took him several attempts to be heard at all, even by the warder Sister who waited at the grilled window.

"Those true and faithful to the teachings of Christ and His Church, give your attention to the will of your one true Pope, descendant of Saunt Pierre and reigning in glory at Avignon as Clement VII. This is the word of the Pope, repeated faithfully on pain of hell."

Seur Catant was watching the doors that day, and she heard the messenger with a shock. She shook herself and came to the grille. "Good traveler, may God be with you."

"And with your soul," said the messenger as he rode

closer to the grille. "Will you give me entrance so that I may speak to your superior and your Sisters?"

Seur Catant was entranced by the sight of the messenger's tabard and staff. Any objection she might have voiced was lost in her awe of him. "Naturally. It pains me to say that most of the Sisters are working in the fields just now, and there are few present to receive you."

"Just as well. I should find your superior first." He came out of the saddle with a sigh. "You must forgive me, but my horse suffers from saddle sores, and I do not wish to injure him more. The papal court does not look with favor on those who misuse their animals." It was a facile lie, one that came easily to his lips, so minor that he doubted he would bother to confess it when he returned to Avignon.

"Oh," Seur Catant said, chastened. "I will open the doors for you, but you must remain in the courtyard until I can find the superior."

"Yes," the messenger agreed promptly. "I will be pleased to do that." He welcomed the rest but knew better than to admit it.

"Very well." Seur Catant wished that there had been more nuns about to see such a triumph but consoled herself with the thought that she would be able to tell of the messenger's arrival for several days.

"You were going to fetch your superior, good Sister?" the messenger prompted her gently.

"Yes. At once." She gathered up the skirts of her habit and scurried away toward the nuns' quarters, breaking almost into a run once she was indoors.

The messenger would have been pleased to have more time than allowed, but very soon he saw one of the inner doors open and the tall figure of Mère Léonie approaching with six other nuns in her wake.

"God be with you, ma Mère," he growled, trying to raise his voice to a more acceptable level.

"And with your soul. Seur Catant tells me you have word from the Holy Father." She looked imposing, though her garments were as plain as those of the other nuns. "Be pleased to inform me of the Pope's wishes."

"This is more properly done in chapel." He was not

sure how to proceed with this young woman. "If you prefer . . . I'll read." He reached inside his tabard for the folded parchment he carried.

"I think of your voice, good herald," Mère Léonie said quickly. "I pray you will read to us all." She folded her hands in front of her, setting an example for the nuns.

"As you wish." The messenger capitulated as he opened the parchment and began to read. "'We, Pope Clement VII, reigning in the name of Christ for the glory of God, charge those who keep to the true Church and true succession to give their aid to their beleaguered faith. It has come to our attention that agents of the perfidious Roman impostor have been found among us, seeking to subvert the devotion of those who adhere to the rites of Avignon. Often have we been warned of the evil that goes through the world seeking to devour the souls of those who are among those blessed by the One Catholic Church and given to salvation by the Blood of the Lamb. Already we are sorely pressed, tested in ways that try our courage and our souls.

"'Be not suborned by these agents of Satan, for they are no less than that in their desire to supplant salvation with damnation and lure our flock to follow the teachings of their Antichrist whom they exalt as Pope in Rome. If you fall, you fall twice, and surely your damnation is the more appalling, for you deny all that God has given you in His Mercy. Those who are tormented by doubts are tormented by the Devil, and those doubts, engendered by others or by your errant body, are the very essence of Satan and his demons. Let none of you question this, for to do so is the gravest sin. Rather than become allies of these pernicious forces, immure yourselves in sacred walls and end your lives in prayer.

"'The Devil is everywhere, and his minions are going through the land in every disguise, from humble priest to ravening brigand, from simple child to godless soldier. Be vigilant so that this evil'"—the messenger, who had been growing steadily hoarser, paused to cough and clear his throat— "'may be defeated and your souls, each so precious to our Savior, may grace His Throne at the Last Judgment that will surely come, where each will answer for his life to the Holy Spirit.' It is signed and fixed with the seal and cipher of the Pope." He folded the parchment, taking care to crease it along already established lines. "I am charged to ask if there have been strangers here attempting to win your support and aid for Rome."

"Seur Ranegonde," Mère Léonie said sharply, "take the messenger and see that he is given food and medication. Seur Adalin, take his horse to the stables. The rest of you, come with me to chapel."

Her orders brought about a flurry of activity, and the messenger was hurried off to the relief he sought as Mère Léonie hastened to the chapel.

Seur Philomine bowed her head to the messenger and spoke in a quiet voice. "I have listened to what you have said," she began, "both in repeating the words of the Pope and in your admonition this morning after Matins. But I am only a tertiary Sister, and it is not appropriate for me to turn myself from doubts."

The messenger glared at her. "You leave but a crack in your faith and the Devil will enter." He did not want to listen to this young nun, or concern himself with what he feared were the trivial questions of an inexperienced woman.

"But might not the cessation of all questions be a sign that the Devil has triumphed and not God?" She turned away from him. "I do not have a true vocation, so I do not know what it is to have the love of God pervade my soul; my love is bound to this world and to the love of one . . . man. I cannot, in good faith, turn my heart elsewhere, not and do so in truth."

The messenger shook his head. "That is for your confessor and superior to consider." He wanted to be away from la Tres Saunte Annunciacion before the day was much older, and he resented being held up in the stable that way. "For your goodness, Sister—"

Seur Philomine stepped back. "I did not mean to intrude. I wished only to know what the Holy Father has said in cases such as mine. If he has said nothing, well, then I must resign myself to doubts and . . . all the guidance of the saints." She crossed herself. "May God speed you, good herald."

"And guide you, good Sister," he answered automatically as he mounted. He let the horse walk into the sunlight, frowning at the brightness. His eyes would be sore long before he reached Saunt-Elizair.

Seur Philomine watched the messenger ride away, her eyes shielded by her hand. She was not content, and nothing that had been said to her had resolved the trouble that made her restless and worried. She looked toward the orchard and saw the distant figure of Seur Marguerite bustling among the hives, for all the world like a cook tending her ovens. Sighing, she went back into the stable and took down the rake so that she could muck out the stall the messenger's horse had occupied the night before.

Chapter 4

Comtesse Orienne held out her gauntleted hand and offered the hooded and jessed jerfalcon to Pierre. "See? Isn't he a pretty darling?"

"Very nice." Pierre was tiring of the banter that Comtesse Orienne had indulged in since his arrival the night before. "Are you hawking today?"

"No, I don't think so. It's windy, and that makes the birds so wild." She let her eyes rove over him, not quite caressing him. "Another time, Sieur le Duc?"

"Another time," he said, shifting in the saddle. "I am charged to speak with you."

She laughed. "Oh? By whom? Have I offended one of your fellow ducs, or have the powers that be in Avignon decided to put me out of sight again for a while?"

"It is not so simple as that." He stared at the jerfalcon.

"Not your tiresome little cousin, surely?" She pretended to be weary of the matter and kept her tone bantering, but under her words were the first stirrings of apprehension.

"No. She is once again at the convent, and her father is determined she should stay there . . . Unless she cooperates." He knew that he should not discuss Aungelique with Orienne, but prudence gave way to his inner sense of failure. "I have tried to convince, well, both of them to bend a little—"

"You? Suing for moderation? Pierre!" She laughed again, deep in her throat like a purr. "A new experience for you." She nudged her horse to move forward, shifting in the saddle so that her skirts would continue to cover her legs, though she wore leggings to keep the leather from chafing.

Pierre followed her, since they were on her land. "I am charged by Cardinal Belroche to ask you certain questions."

"Par Dieu! You sound so dire, Pierre." She held her mount to a walk so that the jerfalcon would not be disturbed on his perch. "He is in a temper today, my pretty Cupid here. He sulks."

"Will you listen to me!" Pierre shouted at her. "Stop dallying with that infernal bird!" If he had not been on horseback, he would have strode to her and shaken her well for her obstinate refusal to be somber.

"You seem to be sulky, too, Pierre," she called over her shoulder. "Wait until we are back at my château, and then you may rail at me all you wish." She tossed her head and began to sing, sounding like a carefree girl, while her thoughts turned toward the trouble she might be embroiled in.

Behind her, Pierre accepted her demands for the moment, letting her horse set the pace for them both, while he tried to marshal his arguments for their confrontation.

Two grooms hurried out of the stable at their approach and waited to help Orienne and Pierre to dismount, then led the horses away.

Walking toward the garden where her bath was located, Orienne at last gave some of her attention to

Pierre. "Tell me what we are to argue about, Pierre." She had considered many possibilities, and none of them pleased her.

"First be rid of that bird," he responded brusquely. "Then cast your mind back to your more recent . . . entertainments."

"Very well." Her heart steadied. "To any particular event or person or simply the entertainments themselves?"

They entered the garden and were met by a page who held out his gauntleted hand for the jerfalcon to bear him away to the mews.

"He is not very sweet today," Orienne cautioned the boy. "One of my pages got careless and treated another of my falcons roughly." She laughed. "It was amusing to watch him flailing about with his arms and screaming as loud as the bird while the talons were at his face."

"Don't think you will distract me with anecdotes," Pierre said, his attitude bordering on surly now.

The garden shimmered with sunlight, and the wild orchards beyond were spangled with blossoms. The fresh breeze was filled with their fragrance and the rich smells of newly turned earth. Bees and butterflies drowsed among the flowers, and in the far corner of the garden near the wall, one of Orienne's ferrets was killing a fieldmouse.

Orienne indicated a bench near her shell-shaped bath. "Come. Let us at least be comfortable while you tell me whatever it is you are required to tell me." She spread out her long skirts so that the damask blue-and-lavender brocade outshone the flowers. "What dreadful thing has Cardinal Belroche decided I have done?"

Pierre put one foot on the bench beside her and braced his forearms on his raised knee. "It is not a time to be light with Avignon. His Holiness is a man at war."

"Then the more reason to turn his mind to strategies and leave me and those like me alone." She pulled off her gauntlet in an absentminded way and set it on the bench beside her. "I am not at war with anyone."

"That is precisely why I must speak to you." Pierre could smell the sandalwood with which Orienne perfumed her hair and the saffron in which her fragile underclothes were rinsed.

She tilted her head up at him. "Well? Are you going to ask me your questions, then? And tell me what this is all about at last? Or must I guess?"

"You *know* that there have been men from Rome coming into Avignon to spread doubt and dissension and not all of them are priests."

"I've heard that," she said, deliberately negligent in her attitude. "I've also heard that the Devil himself has sent his lieutenants to disrupt the entire court of Avignon."

"Don't mock, Orienne," Pierre said harshly. "You endanger yourself if you do."

She concealed her new burst of terror with a lighthearted shrug. "What do you want of me, Pierre?" She was petulantly flirtatious as a means of disguising her increasing fear. "Isn't it enough that the Devil sends the Plague? Must he also send Romans?"

Pierre saw the fleeting shadow of her apprehension pass over her face before she smiled, and it told him more than he wished to know about her thoughts.

Orienne got up from the bench and wandered over to her bath, where she ran her hands over the scalloped marble rim. "I am faithful to the true Pope Clement, but I am French. I don't know what will become of me; they say that's in the hands of God. I want to live here, in this pleasant place, and enjoy my life while I may. I am only a woman, and a widow, and I do not seek to rule through a husband or gain wealth through sons I have never had. I am . . . harmless. Why do this to me, Pierre?"

"It is not I who wants . . ." He stopped abruptly, hating himself for being evasive. "I am sorry, Orienne, that you are placed in this predicament. You are in a position to learn and hear and see much. Those who come to Une Noveautie are seeking respite from their lives, from their duty and their anguish, and when they are here, they do not guard themselves as they might in another place. In passion, a man says many things, and some of those things might bear on the hazards that—"

"And did it never occur to you that I might be one

who does not wish to remember too much? It does not please me to think that my pleasures might be taken from me." She shook her head in anger. "What a man says when he is in my arms has little to do with his duty, Sieur le Duc, unless it is his duty to please me. No one speaks of matters of state, not here. The Pope and his court are the targets of these Romans. Let them be on guard, then, and leave me in peace."

Pierre glowered. "I am not permitted to do that. I regret—" He stopped, studying her, waiting for her to say something. "You are angry with me."

"Of *course* I am. I would like to see you run through. But I will bide my . . . Give me a moment to collect myself, Pierre, and then you might as well say the rest. What does it avail me to refuse?"

He knew better than to assume she had truly capitulated, and he wisely held his tongue while he watched her pace down the weed-tangled path, then come back toward him with a fixed and artificial smile on her mouth. "Are you ready?"

"No. But that means nothing to His Holiness." She crossed her arms under her breasts. "I am not sensible to do this, but I am going to warn you that I will do you an ill turn when I may."

Pierre nodded. "I understand. In return, I will caution you: I am well guarded, and it would be foolish of you to make me openly your enemy." He cocked his head toward the door. "Do you wish to go in now?"

"Yes," she said with due consideration. "I believe I am cold." Her eyes glared at his, but she did not flinch as he took her elbow to guide her out of the sun.

Seur Aungelique blinked and shook herself as she stood up to face the figure that approached her from the bank of the stream. Her mind was in turmoil as she squinted at the figure in pale blue who came toward her out of the brightness of the afternoon sunlight. "You," she breathed, wondering if he were more than a vision conjured up by her loneliness and misery.

Thibault Col smiled as he approached her, one corner of his mouth lifting before the other. "So this is where you fled, my fledgling."

"I . . ." She looked around in panic, terrified that someone might overhear them.

"There is only the sister who tends the hives," Thibault said, smiling more insistently. His icy eyes were flatteringly insolent as they traveled over her habit.

"How did you . . ." Again, she could not finish her thoughts.

"Didn't you want to be found, sweeting?" He was very near, his voice light and persuasive, tantalizing. "Would you prefer I go away?"

Seur Aungelique shook her head vigorously. "No!" Impulsively, she seized his velvet sleeve, her fingers crushing the fabric. "It's just . . . Where did you come from?"

"Does it matter, so long as I am here?" He looked pointedly at her hand. "Well?"

Her fingers were shaking when she opened them. "You . . . have surprised me."

"I have? But I had thought you dreamed of me, sweeting."

Seur Aungelique flushed deeply, but she could not turn away from him. "I have . . . thought of you."

"And remembered me in your prayers?" There was no mistaking the mockery in his tone, or the force he exerted over her through it. "What did you pray for?"

"Stop," she whispered.

He took a step back. "If that is what you wish." He looked around the orchards. "What is behind the brambles?"

"Nothing. An open field," she said, confused by his question and still distracted by his presence.

"Very convenient," he said, chuckling.

She frowned toward him, wanting time to sort out her feelings. "You are . . ."

"Impertinent?" he suggested. "I am more than that, sweeting, if you desire. Would you not prefer me to be insolent?"

"Insolent?" she repeated, as if she did not know the

word at all. "Why would . . . You puzzle me, Chevalier."

"Do I? A strange thing." He made no attempt to explain his remarks. "You did want to see me?"

"Yes," she admitted. "I wanted to see you."

"Shamed, my fledgling?" He came to stand beside her, still not touching her, but close enough that he seemed to press against her.

"I . . . I . . ." She sounded like a chastened child who was resentful of her correction. "I fast, and I . . . keep vigils, and I pray, and . . . then I confess."

"And do you repent?" He lifted his long, narrow hand to touch her but did not.

"I . . . no." She stared down at the grass.

"Does that trouble you?"

This time there was more force in her reply. "No."

"A-a-ah." His fingers trailed down her cheek. "Do you miss Une Noveautie?"

"Yes."

"And me?"

She swallowed. "Yes."

"Most of all?"

"Yes."

Thibault touched the linen of her wimple. "More than your Pierre?"

Seur Aungelique's eyes grew round with shock. "How did you . . . Did Orienne tell you about . . ."

He ran his forefinger over her chin. "Do not blame Orienne, sweeting. She said nothing to me."

"Then . . ." She stopped her next question before the words burst from her.

"I learned it from Pierre, if that is what you want to know. It *is* what you were going to ask me, isn't it?"

She tried to avert her eyes, but they were locked on his. How could Pierre have betrayed her so, and to this stranger? She let out a little cry and clutched her hands together as if in prayer. "Oh, Bon Dieu."

"Do not curse him, sweeting," Thibault chided her softly. "He did not know what he did. And I . . . what would it benefit me to speak of it to anyone but you?" He bent and kissed her lightly on the mouth, then stepped back. "Could you not come to desire me instead, sweet-ing?"

Seur Aungelique crossed herself and spun away from him, not heeding her steps or the hem of her gray habit. "Don't."

He caught her as she stumbled and held her tightly against him, imprisoning her hands in his own. "Take care, little fledgling; you may fall."

"No." She squirmed in his grasp, and her breath came more quickly. She looked away, refusing to see his mocking face so near her. "You mustn't."

"Why not? When it is what you desire? Have you not longed for me to embrace you and caress you?" He kissed her again, as lightly and briefly as before. "Why do you deny me?"

She took one shuddering gasp and then started to weep, her overwrought feelings finding no other release. "You . . . you are not . . ."

Thibault held her but offered her no comfort beyond the strength of his arms. His light eyes turned even colder. "There is someone coming," he said at last, and released her, stepping back as he did.

"But . . ." Seur Aungelique protested, reaching out for him.

"Later, sweeting. It is what you wish, then? You de-sire me?" His scimitar smile flashed once, and he made her a mocking reverence.

"Yes!" she cried. "Yes, yes." With a quick, wild glance over her shoulder, she thought she saw a nun ap-proaching. "Can you wait!"

"I can always wait." He ambled away from her to-ward the bramble patch. "But can you?"

She wanted to say no, to demand that he let her come to him at once, now here, but though she had high-running passion, she was without courage, and this lack halted her as wholly and efficiently as if a poisoned moat lay between them.

"Seur Aungelique!" came a voice through the trees. "Where are you! Seur Aungelique!"

She wrenched her eyes away from the place she had

seen Thibault stand last, turning now toward the caller.
"A moment! A moment, ma Seur," she called, trying to
gain a better hold of herself and regulate her thoughts.
Perhaps she could say she had been praying or was filled
with sorrow for all she had done that offended heaven.
Such a lie, she knew, would stick in her throat and would
eventually be found out. Then there would be more vigils and fasts and prayers, and she might never be allowed
into the orchard again and would not see Thibault, who
would grow bored with waiting and leave, so that she
would be even more alone than before, abandoned by all
the world and trapped inside the walls of la Tres Saunte
Annunciacion until . . .

"Seur Aungelique, is anything wrong?" asked Seur
Odile as she touched the other nun on the shoulder. "You
seem so . . . distant."

"Why, no, nothing's wrong," Seur Aungelique answered in a distracted way. "I have been . . . thinking of
my father's offer. You must have heard that he has proposed another marriage."

"Yes," Seur Odile said quietly, "so I have been
told."

Seur Aungelique sighed, not wanting to be angry
with the inoffensive little woman beside her. "Yes. And I
have been trying to come to a decision. But I do not
know who the bridegroom is to be, nor where he lives,
and . . . I do not want to be undutiful, but . . ." It was a
clumsy fabrication, but apparently Seur Odile accepted
it, because she shook her head in commiseration and
tried to provide a little sympathy.

"Well, at least your father gives you the chance to
accept or refuse. My mother knew nothing of my father
until they went to church to marry. You . . . can be
spared that." She made the sign of the cross. "Come.
Père Guibert has arrived, and it is time for confession."

"Confession?" Seur Aungelique repeated. "I . . .
thought it was tomorrow."

"He is early; aren't we fortunate?"

Try as she would, Seur Aungelique could detect no
sarcasm in Seur Odile's demeanor. She mumbled a few
words and fell into step beside the other woman while

she turned her thoughts to finding a way to see Thibault
again.

Seur Philomine rose from the floor and crossed herself; she would not be permitted to dawdle in the chapel
with travelers in the hospice. There was food to serve,
and later in the day she would have to clean out the
stable. It was wrong of her to be resentful of that task,
she knew, and yet she could not free herself from that sin
entirely. She looked up at the sound of a cough and saw
Seur Catant staring at her from the door.

"God give you good day, Sister," Seur Philomine
said in a perfunctory way.

"And be with your spirit," Seur Catant responded.
"Is Seur Elvire about?"

"Not since prayers," Seur Philomine answered. "Is
there some trouble?"

"One of the travelers is ill. We have need of her
herbs." She made a nervous gesture.

"Ill? How?" Seur Philomine asked, trying not to be
too alarmed at this news.

"He awakened with bloody flux. It might be . . .
anything." She crossed herself. "And, I pray, oh, I pray la
Virge that it is not the Plague . . . I have seen it before. I
would rather face starving wolves than that." She pressed
her hands to her mouth.

"God forgives you, Seur Catant," Seur Philomine
assured her, going toward her at once. "He brings
nothing that we cannot bear, and all He asks is that we
give our sins to Him, for His forgiveness and our redemption." She had heard this said so often that she
could repeat it without thought.

"But Plague . . . It must not be the Plague. Why
does God permit the Devil thus to walk among us, un-
challenged, and garner souls for the fires of hell?" She
crossed herself again and stared at the altar. "Mère
Léonie has already warned us that we must . . . take
care." She looked about, distraught. "She has said that
we must observe charity but that we cannot expose others to so great a danger as Plague is. She told us that the
travelers must be protected as well and not permitted to

enter a place where there may be sickness." She clenched her hands and took a few hasty steps toward the altar, then dropped to her knees. "O God, Who has the sun and the moon in His hands and set the world in place in the void, spare us, your sin-ridden children, though we are unworthy of Your care. Do not bring the Plague among us, not again."

"Seur Catant!" Seur Philomine protested, shocked at the other nun's accusations. "You're distraught. You're not considering what you say, and for this you bring sorrow to la Virge, who will intercede for us in our need."

The look that Seur Catant shot over her shoulder was as venomous as it was vulnerable. "If you want to die for a stranger, you go tend him, and remember that you will bring Plague to half the world through your folly. Do not forget that if you minister to one who carries the Plague, you will have the Tokens, and you may sweat and thirst and fill your flesh with pustules before you die and see the same happen to your Sisters. But I won't!" She turned back to the altar and continued her prayers in silence over her white knuckles.

Seur Philomine looked about helplessly and wished she were back home, away from this enclosed place, with her family around her and her heart free from fear. Better yet, she would want to be in Brittany with Tristan, with no more objections to their marriage. As always, when she thought of Tristan, she felt the warm flutter of her love, a sensation that began in her chest and spread through her veins in a subtle tide. "I must . . . ask you to excuse me, Seur Catant," she said, and left without waiting to hear if the other woman had anything more she wished to say.

"I have . . . not freed myself of the lascivious thoughts that have possessed me all my life, and though I beg God for His aid and guidance, I am what He made me, and the thoughts persist." The sound of Seur Aungelique's voice in the screened confessional was unearthly to Père Guibert, though he sat with only a stone pillar between them.

"Have you kept the vigils Mère Léonie gave you?"

He had seen other cases where no vocation existed and the lure of the world was far stronger than the promise of heaven.

"I have tried, mon Père, but when I lie on the stones, they press me like a lover, and the lusts of the body are binding." She felt her forehead become moist, and she licked her upper lip. "Mon Père . . . uh . . . I cannot say this easily. I have . . . been met by a man, who . . . desires me."

This time Père Guibert could not turn away from her. "A man? How is this, ma Fille?"

"He . . . had met me before." Her breathing was fast and shallow, as if she suffered from a sudden fever.

Père Guibert felt himself grow cold. "You knew him from your family?" He doubted that was the case but needed to ask, to delay as long as possible the moment of actual revelation.

"I . . ." Seur Aungelique could not bring herself to admit that Pierre knew Thibault; the betrayal she felt would cut too deeply if she did.

"Then you met him . . ." He cleared his throat. "You met him where I found you?"

"Yes, mon Père." She lowered her head, unable to summon up any more demanding emotion than a general hunger for the life she had tasted so fleetingly at Une Noveautie.

"I see." Père Guibert had hoped that her wildness would be better contained. "This man; what did you do with him while you were . . . there?"

"I talked with him. He was a guest." She sensed Père Guibert's discomfort, and it gave her surprising satisfaction. "He told Comtesse Orienne that he wanted me."

"Seur . . . ma Fille, do not say so, or you place yourself in gravest peril."

"But he was pleasant to me and did not insult me." She wanted to flaunt all she had done, to retain some of the satisfaction she had felt while away from the convent. "I have prayed for the aid of my good angel, mon Père, and this man comes to me. What am I to think of that?"

"Some of us are more tested in our lives than are

others, and it may be that you are one such, ma Fille. In any case, you must not lose faith that your soul is as precious to God as any soul and that He will rejoice that you come purely to Him." He doubted that his words had much meaning for Seur Aungelique.

"But what am I to do? He stirs me, mon Père, as no one has before." She wanted Thibault to pursue her, as much for the chagrin it would bring Pierre if he ever learned of it—as undoubtedly he would—as for the smoldering desire within her that she sought to slake in Thibault's passion.

"Ma Fille, did you hear me?" Père Guibert inquired brusquely, and repeated, "Where did this man come upon you, and why did you permit him to speak with you?"

"I was . . . grafting the trees. I was *in* the tree," she lied. "He came to the tree, and I could not . . . Well, it was not possible to descend modestly."

"You did not call for help?" He was suspicious of Seur Aungelique. "God reads your heart and will judge lies told before him with severity and grieving for your sin."

"No!" Seur Aungelique shrieked, striking out at the screen with her hand. "No! If God wishes me to be chaste, then He should not torment me with my flesh. He should give me the courage to resist. He should show His will to me so that I need not be . . . what I am." Her anger satisfied her in a way that contrition could not. "I don't care if this means more penance and more vigils. It is not right for man to contravene the will of God, and that is what you are doing in forcing me to be a nun!"

Père Guibert had risen to his feet, and now, against all canon, he wanted to confront Seur Aungelique as a woman, not a nun, to castigate her properly for all the trouble she had caused at a whim, an inability to turn her mind from the gross demands of the body to the more enduring merits of the soul. "Who are you, a woman and not yet seventeen, to question the way of God? What pride in your heart shows you more wisdom than the judgment of heaven?"

"I am a creature of God, and I know how He made

me," she insisted, her wrath-pale face showing around
the pillar. "I belong to the world, and it is there I will
be."

"The world is the province of the Devil," Père
Guibert reminded her very soberly. "And you are likely
to fall victim to him if you persist in these dangerous
caprices. You put eternity at risk for an afternoon of idle
luxury."

"Then I welcome hell. I am eager for it so that I may
sooner end this travesty that you and my father have
brought upon me. I have said that I cannot be a nun, and
everything that I have endured here reveals the truth of
it."

"You are a woman, and you have a woman's weakness and a woman's place," Père Guibert said. "God has
given you the burden of Eve, but Saunte Marie has saved
you from it, if you will remain chaste." He despaired as
he watched her.

Seur Aungelique set her hands on her hips. "I want to
live as Comtesse Orienne lives, not as someone's brood-
wife, to bear children and keep accounts. I want to live as
the women the troubadours sing of and poets celebrate."

"Those women lived long ago," Père Guibert
pointed out.

"Then in me they will live again. Did Heloise turn
nun, shut herself up from the world while Abelard was
yet a man? Who is so foolish to think she was beset by
the Devil?"

"She died in holiness, an abbesse, repentant of her
lust."

Seur Aungelique laughed. "They do not remember
her as a nun but a lover. Who has said that Iseult was
anything damned? And do not remind me of her love
potion or the death of her knight, for that is what makes
her so splendid. The world hears her tale and says, 'Oh,
that there may be another like her, that we may love her,'
and for that they are called wise."

Père Guibert moved back from Seur Aungelique.
"You are not yourself, ma Fille. You have been . . . too
much indulged. Your father has permitted you great liberty, and you abuse it."

"My father is nothing like that. He is punishing me!" Seur Aungelique stamped her feet and very nearly tore off her coif.

"You must stop this at once. I will speak to Mère Léonie and ask her to give you a new penance and more contemplative exercise." He knew it was inadequate, but there was nothing he could think of that would deal well with so rebellious a nun. "Your father must be consulted." He would find a way to convince le baron that Seur Aungelique should be chastised.

"Go ahead! Do anything, it doesn't matter. I will never be a nun. Nothing you or Mère Léonie can do will make me a nun!"

Père Guibert tried to find a way to calm her. "But ma Fille, we wish that God will come to you, Mère Léonie and I, and all your Sisters. You must not turn away from God."

"Has He not turned away from me? Many of the Sisters here are truly devout, and see what has happened to them—they are set upon by disaster. Why does He not send a lion to raven here and be done with it?" She tossed her head. "For all that God has given to us for our faith, we might as well have fallen to the Devil and worshiped him instead!"

"No, no," Père Guibert protested. "You are in error, ma Fille."

"I am? Then what do you see around you? Disaster has been invited here!" She looked away from him, ignoring his determined attempts to speak more to her. "I will leave here and"—and "—she wiped the back of her hand across her mouth.—"What I do then is no concern of yours."

"What you do must always concern me," Père Guibert said sadly as he blessed her. "I am your confessor, and your soul is in my keeping."

"Then I reclaim it," she said, and rushed out of the chapel, leaving him to sit in worried silence.

Not long before sunset, Seur Marguerite paid a last visit before Vespers to her hives. She pottered between them, crooning to the bees, showing no alarm when they lit on her hands and face. "They are your kisses, aren't they?" she asked, and was content with the answer she heard in her mind. "All the babies are in the house, and the elfin king will guard you all." She bent down to put a bit of honeycomb on a broken plank of wood. "I have paid the price, and he will guard you."

"Leaving treats for the Devil?" inquired a light, pleasantly insulting voice.

Seur Marguerite turned. She saw a figure approaching out of the setting sun, a man of middle height, slender and graceful, whose clothes and features she could not distinguish without squinting. "God give you good day, stranger," she said mildly. "Have a care that my little ones do not hurt you."

Thibault paid no attention to the bees. "You treat them like children."

"And so I might; they are mine." She crossed herself and said a brief prayer. "God must remember the bees while I sleep."

"If He treats them as He treats His human children, you might desire other aid," he suggested.

"One must find aid where they may," Seur Marguerite answered after a moment.

The unmelodic clang of the convent bell caught the attention of both Seur Marguerite and Thibault Col. "There, ma Seur," Thibault said. "Like the bells on cows, it leads you home."

Seur Marguerite laughed vaguely. "Home? No, not to my home. I can never come home, for that would be worst of all. I would be prey to worse than you, far worse." She was wholly unaware of insulting the beautiful young man, for she smiled at him. "It isn't you I seek. There are others. You would not know them, no matter what you know. You would not find out from the bees if they knew. No one will discover it." There were sudden tears in her eyes. "There are men in the mists, filled with Plague, and they are worst of all."

"I have heard you have Plague here," Thibault said, casually insolent.

"No, no," Seur Marguerite responded at once. "It is pox. Bad enough for the likes of you, but there has been no mist, and the others have not come." She touched the side of one of the hives. "You have come here before."

"Perhaps."

"You are like the ones in the mists and have many guises. I have seen those in the trees, too, making the bark move when they are hungry. They strangle the birds in their branches and eat them when they fall."

"I will take care, ma Seur," Thibault said. "I will be here tomorrow. I would prefer you are not."

"My bees wait for me. You do not." She lifted up her skirts and started away from him toward the convent. "It is Vespers. La Virge opens to the Holy Spirit and labors all the night. I have seen her, sometimes, when she is about to birth. Once she birthed monsters." Her voice was slightly raised so that it would carry back to Thibault, who watched her from his place beside the hives. "You have seen the monsters."

Thibault gave her no answer but an equivocal smile, which Seur Marguerite could not see.

Chapter 5

Shortly before noon the next day, a priest on a lathered mule was admitted to the courtyard of la Tres Saunte Annunciacion. Before he was out of the saddle, he was calling for Père Guibert in a high, terrified voice that sent nuns scurrying to find their confessor. The newcomer paced distractedly while he waited for Père Guibert, only speaking to grant one of the nuns permission to lead the mule away to the stables. He stared about as he roamed, moving like a beast in a cage, too unpredictable to approach.

By the time Père Guibert came into the courtyard, he was seriously alarmed by the various descriptions he had heard of this new arrival. "God be with you, friend," he said cautiously.

"And with your soul," Padre Bartolimieu responded, rushing toward the other priest.

"Bon Dieu!" Père Guibert cried, recognizing the Augustinian. "What has happened, good Padre, that you come here?"

"We have had word . . ." He looked about at the nuns gathering in the courtyard. "Not here. There must be a place more private."

"Of course," Père Guibert said, understanding at once his hesitation. "Of course. There is a cell we may use where we will not be disturbed. You may tell me there." He signaled to Seur Elvire. "I pray you, inform Mère Léonie where I have gone and that I will need to speak with her shortly."

Seur Elvire, pleased at being singled out for this errand, ducked her head to conceal her satisfaction as she hurried out of the courtyard. There would be opportunity later on to whisper to her Sisters of Mère Léonie's response.

Padre Bartolimieu had grabbed Père Guibert by the elbow and was attempting to shove him through the main door. "We must not delay. God on the cross! It is . . . it is . . ." Again, he forced himself to be silent, gulping air as he glanced over his shoulder. "Do you remember what I said about my church? What became of it? Do you remember that? Do you?"

The urgency of the questions distressed Père Guibert. "We spoke of many things," he said in an effort to soothe the other man. "This way, good Padre. There are steps, just there."

"Hurry!" Padre Bartolimieu, heedless of this warning, lurched up the stairs, all but dragging Père Guibert after him. "You do not know how they can move when they want. Who knows what might . . . You must warn your village here and the others in the valley, if you can. Word must be sent at once. They will have to find arms and . . ." He took a deep breath and reached out to steady himself against the wall. "I left as soon as the messenger arrived, and still I don't know if I am far enough ahead of them."

Père Guibert indicated a door on the left, then

reached to push it open before Padre Bartolimieu fell through it. "Who is this you speak of? Romans?" He pointed to the pallet under the crucifix. "Rest, Padre. You are exhausted."

"I can't rest. I *must* not rest," he protested as he dropped onto the blankets. "There is no time for rest. Dear God, if I fail now, I will know without doubt I am to burn in hell forever and ever, with all my sins still fresh on my soul and my repentance worthless as perfume on a nun!"

Père Guibert bit his lower lip. "What is the danger, Padre? Is it Plague?" He did not wait for Padre Bartolimieu to answer, "Because if it is, your fears are unfounded. We have had pox here but not plague."

"That is bad enough," Padre Bartolimieu said, crossing himself for protection. "No, this is not Plague or pox or anything of that sort. There are men coming to kill us and ruin our church, this chapel, the convent, all of it. The village churches are the most in danger, but these places are not spared, not when the Flagellants come. They seek to bring an end to the church, for they believe that the Church has . . . deserted them and that God has shown His wrath with Plague and therefore they must destroy all before God Himself brings about the end of the world." He lowered his head. "If I can save one church, one convent, any true believer from these terrible men, then it may be that I will not be forgotten in heaven or cast into hell or outer darkness at the Last Judgment."

The pathetic expression in Padre Bartolimieu's voice, the wholly downcast posture, touched Père Guibert deeply, and he had to control himself to keep from weeping. "How did you learn of these Flagellants? Are you sure they are coming this way?"

"They cannot go through the passes yet; therefore, they must come here. It is the only way the road will take them, toward Avignon. To Avignon, to kill the Pope and destroy the Church. Is it not enough that we have Romans to contend with?" This last outburst was directed at the ceiling, as if he hoped for God to answer him.

"When did you learn of this?" Père Guibert asked, hoping he would be able to find out enough to protect la Tres Saunte Annunciacion as well as Saunt-Vitre-lo-Sur from attack.

"I left . . . yesterday. I stopped after sunset to sleep and was in the saddle before dawn. The damnable mule is a strengthy beast, but he has no speed." He set his jaw. "I must face them, Padre . . . Père Guibert. I owe that much to le Bon Dieu, for my cowardice before."

"If you think it is necessary," Père Guibert said dubiously. "But for the moment, rest. I will speak with Mère Léonie, and we will determine how best to proceed."

Padre Bartolimieu looked up at Père Guibert in hopeless resignation. "It is the Devil; he is winning at last. He has been the foe of God since the beginning of the world. He is the one who brings plague upon us, and for the weakness of our faith and the depth of our sins, we are permitted to fall to it, and the Devil triumphs. And the Flagellants, they are also in the ranks of the Devil, filled with his evil spirits, as were the swine into which our Lord cast the demons."

Pere Guibert did not feel as resolute as he sounded, but that did not keep him from speaking with conviction. "Word will go out today, and Saunt-Vitre-lo-Sur will have time to prepare, as will we."

"And if they do not? What messengers have you? Who will you send?" He stared around the cell. "There are only nuns here."

"Some of whom know how to ride a horse," Père Guibert reminded him. "And if they are devoted to their calling, they will not balk at such a task. In times such as these, it is not fitting for nuns to keep to their cloisters, but instead to come to the defense of their Church and their faith." He wondered how difficult it would be to convince Mère Léonie of that. "I know that the Cardinal would not approve of such a plan if we were to ask him, but there is not time for such a message to be sent—and who would carry it?—and so I must do as my conscience prompts me and ask the Sisters to aid us in this time of need."

"I pray it will succeed," Padre Bartolimieu said with more fervor than Père Guibert had ever heard from him.

Mère Léonie heard the priest out in silence. "You may have two nuns to ride for you," she said when he had finished. "The rest are to keep here, where we may do what we may to prepare for the coming dangers, if they are coming at all."

"But Padre Bartolimieu . . ." Père Guibert began, then trailed off.

"Very true. And it is most certain that he believes the gravity of the situation and that his warning is genuine, but, mon Père, you know as well as I that when word is sent, it is often magnified, so that what was a group of old men from Hungary becomes an army of sages from the Khan before the Lord's Day comes twice."

Père Guibert nodded, knowing that Mère Léonie was well within her authority to speak to him in this way. "I have heard enough of the Flagellants to believe we must at least take measures to ensure the safety of the convent and the village."

"Of course. God would not be pleased if we waited like sacrificial goats for the Devil to descend on us." She rose and walked down her study. "I will see that the message is carried through the valley and on toward Avignon, but I will not send one of my Sisters to the papal city; that would be incorrect in every particular, and the Pope would surely rebuke us sternly for such actions. I will, however, see that a messenger is sent to the Pope, and one to that duc . . . Seur Aungelique's cousin, who came here on her father's behest. He is not far from here, and he has armed men to follow him."

It shamed Père Guibert to admit he had not thought of so practical an approach to the problem. "You are right, ma Fille. You are seeing this more clearly than I am."

"Well, coming from Dalmatia, we learn to anticipate such things," she said, turning his praise aside. "We have Turks and heathen alike to deal with there, and we know from youth how to protect ourselves."

"I had forgot you were from there," Père Guibert admitted, grateful to have that excuse for his lack of preparedness. "Who will you send?"

"I think that it must be women of some rank—a pity that it cannot be Seur Aungelique, but it would be folly to permit her outside the walls—who have names that bring respect. Seur Fleurette and Seur Lucille are the most likely choices, though only Seur Fleurette is of a noble house. She must be the one to ride to the duc, I think. She is not as strong as I would like, but her good angel will see that she arrives safely. We have a plow horse, and she may have that for her mount. Seur Lucille . . . she is known in the villages of the valley, and there are many who will heed what she says no matter what they may think of her message."

The last of Mère Léonie's words startled Père Guibert, who had not considered until then that there could be so great a risk to the women. "They should not ride without protection."

"Yes, of course they should have escort and ride in wagons with curtains so that men may not look upon them. In plump and happy times, we may wait for such formalities, but this is not the case, and our lives and souls are forfeit if we fail."

Simply hearing these words brought the full weight of their danger home to Père Guibert. He crossed himself. "As you say, ma Fille. We are in the hands of God."

"But in the realm of the Devil," she reminded him with a somber nod. "In the realm of the Devil."

Barrels were filled with water and kegs with sap. The nuns were set to clearing away all the loose branches that had fallen in the orchard, and anything that might serve for fuel for a fire was brought into the courtyard and stacked. Stones were gathered up, and three enormous planks were brought from Saunt-Vitre-lo-Sur to reinforce the courtyard door. Mothers with small children were sent from the village to occupy the upper floors of the convent in the vacant cells. Cattle and sheep were driven into the distant fields and left with their shepherds and cowherds to remain there until all danger was

past. Villagers and nuns alike took strength from Mère
Léonie's calm assurance that they would come through it
all with the help of God. Watching her, Père Guibert felt
his guilt grow with his own profound doubts.

The two nuns, Seur Lucille and Seur Fleurette, had
accepted their instructions with proper humility and had
left the convent within the hour of Mère Léonie's request that they ride to warn others of the approaching
Flagellants. Both nuns accepted letters to deliver as well
as memorizing Père Guibert's instructions and information.

Activity continued at la Tres Saunte Annunciacion
for the better part of a day. Even those nuns usually not
active took part, and though all felt harried, they also felt
they were doing important and essential work, and most
of the time camaraderie prevailed at the convent.

"You have done well, my Sisters," she told them
after the evening meal, which had been served late. "You
have been brave and industrious, which is much to your
credit and will stand in your favor when you answer to
Our Lord. You have also been of steady and tranquil
minds, showing the surety of your faith." She turned to
address the mothers with their children who sat on the
far side of the refectory, warily regarding the nuns. "You,
too, have shown your faith by seeking refuge here, and
God will demonstrate His love of you with His protection." She nodded toward the priests. Père Guibert and
Padre Bartolimieu will hear your confession if you feel
the need of shriving before tomorrow."

All those gathered to hear her felt grateful and
pleased that they had done so well.

Yet the Flagellants did not come then or the next
day or the next, and the goodwill that had been created
and nurtured began to give way under the strain of
crowding and waiting. Père Guibert could see the courage of the nuns erode, turning to spitefulness and anger.

He pleaded with them to have a care and think of
the danger that waited for them. At first, it was enough
to stop the mutters of discontent, but as the hours
turned into days, the nuns were not so easily silenced.

"Seur Elvire," he admonished when he found her

arguing with one of the women from Saunt-Vitre-lo-Sur, "you must have patience with her; she does not know the ways of your Order, and she meant no harm when she took that piece of bread for her child."

Seur Elvire glared at him. "As you insist, mon Père," she said.

"Deo gratias," he said, reluctantly blessing her.

Mère Léonie continued, cheerful, untouched by the discord that grew around her in dissonant voices. "You are all dedicated nuns," she reminded her Sisters. "You have taken vows, and those vows were never more important than they are now. You must be on guard against acrimony. Those who cannot curb their tongues must come to me or Père Guibert to confess their error."

This instruction was met with silence and averted eyes. Seur Odile coughed delicately and stared long and pointedly at Seur Aungelique, who had resumed her nightlong vigils in spite of the suggestion that she should not.

"I do not wish to criticize any of you," Mère Léonie went on, "but there are those of you who are caught up in considerations of the world and the body, and for that you lead your Sisters into error and grief. You will not be so ready to complain when you face the Throne of Mercy. And you may be everlastingly thankful that God is merciful, for He knows better than any man alive what agonies of fear each of you must suffer with in the dark of the soul, where melancholy and fancy lay their snares. When the horror of our coming battle is too great, the hosts of angels should occupy your thoughts."

Père Guibert listened to this with some apprehension. He himself had often painted such pictures of hell, but what they faced now was not the everlasting fires but the immediate threat of pain and death. He decided to speak with Mère Léonie later about her warnings.

"When you say your prayers tonight, let each of you solicit la Virge to extend her aid to us, helpless women that we are in this world of armed men. She is our way to salvation and to the joys of heaven in the life hereafter. She alone can protect us." She crossed herself and waited while the nuns did the same.

The meal was even more silent than usual; the women from the village did not speak, and their children had been threatened into silence. Père Guibert ate slowly, finding the simple food hard to chew, as if the flour had become as obdurate as the tempers of the nuns around him.

At midday the next day, a swineherd came from Mou Courbet with word that there had been troops of men on the road, men in robes who carried lashes, which they used on themselves and one another. "There aren't so many of them, not as many as we feared. They march along, but with the whips and all . . ."

Seur Odile, who was warder for the day, nodded. "God be kind to you for your service," she said in her most condescending tone.

"Thank you, ma Seur," he answered, tugging his forelock and bowing toward the grille. "It might be just as well to send the women home. We're driving the stock in from the fields in Mou Courbet."

Mère Léonie heard the news with relief. "Well, God is good to us, is He not? He has shown His care in keeping us from harm."

If she was satisfied, many of the others were not. Seur Adalin, who rarely said anything either to the bad or the good, for once let it be known that she was disappointed.

"We have been in readiness, we have shown ourselves willing, and God will not test us!" she declared.

Several of the Sisters agreed; Seur Ranegonde added, "We *have* been tested, ma Seur, by those insufferable women from the village. We will have to whitewash all the walls again, and we'll be cleaning privies for the rest of the week."

Père Guibert heard some of these mutterings and was worried at the vehemence the nuns showed now that they were convinced they were safe. "You must not assume all danger is past," he cautioned them, and was politely but deliberately ignored. When he taxed Mère Léonie with his concerns, she chided him for his lack of faith.

"Mon Père, I know that there was much to fear, but it is past now, and we must return to our Order, grateful for the guidance and protection God has shown us."

"Have the women stay for one more night. Take that much of a precaution, ma Fille."

"But they do not wish to stay, mon Père," she countered. "What am I to do? Lock them in the chapel and set my Sisters to guarding them? Think of what these women have suffered already, and ask yourself if I am wrong to let them take their children and go home."

Père Guibert had no answer for her, and so he offered no argument. "They are in danger, Mère Léonie. The Flagellants are like mad dogs, everywhere attacking the faithful and spreading their madness as they go." He looked away from her. "May God forgive us for deserting them in this terrible hour."

"If you believe it is terrible, why do you not try to convince them? Tell them what the Flagellants have done to other villages. Surely that would be enough for God and your conscience." She said this kindly, and Père Guibert was annoyed that he imagined malice in her concern. "Mon Père?"

"It is nothing," he said, giving her his attention once again. "I want so to aid these families, and it causes me much . . . travail."

"*You* have admonished *me* for the depth of my fervor before. It may be that you, too, should think of what you are saying and how you have said it." She bowed her head. "Forgive me for the impertinence, mon Père. I will confess my error and beg God's understanding. He knows what is in my heart."

"Ma Fille . . ." Père Guibert began, but she would not let him continue.

"Who here is unscathed by danger? These Flagellants are like the Plague, aren't they? A thing that is capable of laying the whole world to waste but wholly unseen and unknown. I do not know what else to do but permit the village women to depart."

This burst of confidence was welcome to Père Guibert, who listened with indulgence. He reminded himself that Mère Léonie, for all her abilities, was a young woman who often expected more of herself than God had given her to do, and he had been concerned that she might have the seeds of pride planted deep within her. In time, he would school her to humility so that her virtues would shine all the brighter. "I think we would both benefit from an hour of meditation, ma Fille. You have shown a stalwart attitude that must be helpful to your Sisters but ultimately difficult for you. Your mind will then be once more at rest, and we may discuss the predicament again when we both have given our fears into the keeping of heaven and la Virge."

"I will beseech our Lord," she said submissively. "It is not fitting that I should subject the convent to my concerns and frailties, for each must carry the burden that Our Lord sends to us in the manner that we are made to carry it. That is the way of the world, isn't it, mon Père?" She crossed herself. "I would appreciate it if you would take a little time to speak with Seur Aungelique. She has imposed more vigils on herself, and this, I am afraid, is evidence of defiance, not acquiescence."

"It may be," Père Guibert said, feeling his heart heavy within him at the need to talk to the difficult young nun again. "I will hear her out if she will confess."

"Yes. You told me that the last time she was not very willing to surrender to the will of God." Mère Léonie paused, then continued. "You know how revels draw her and contemplation does not."

"Yes." He blessed the superior with an odd sense of dissatisfaction that he decided was apprehension from all they had dreaded as they waited for the Flagellants to come. He nodded gravely. "You have done well, ma Fille. You are not to think you have erred or—or done anything displeasing to la Virge."

"Deo gratias," she said. "I hope with all my heart that it is true. Our Lord is precious to me." She rose from her knees and accompanied Père Guibert along the hall, leaving him at the chapel door with a low bow and a gentle smile.

That smile remained flickering at the back of Père Guibert's mind while he tried to convince the village women—without success—to remain at la Tres Saunte Annunciacion for another day. He thanked God that Mère Léonie was dedicated to the Church, for such a smile on a worldly woman would be as devastating as the wiles of Comtesse Orienne.

In times of difficulties, it seemed that instead of drawing closer together, as God had often admonished His children to do, they remained apart and angry with one another. This stay had been such a case, with the village women coming to dislike the Sisters more with every passing hour and the Sisters reacting not with the compassion they should give but with contempt. How unfortunate it was, Père Guibert thought, when all they had wanted to do was protect the village from danger.

During the night, the Flagellants came.

It was near the middle of the night when the first men appeared on the road from Mou Coubert. They walked with steady determination, silent and inexorable. All of them carried whips. Some had short-handled whips with braided lashes tipped with metal, the scourges used by monks to beat the Devil from their flesh. Most carried carter's whips, great long strands of leather knotted for strength and weight. A few had bullock's whips, the heaviest and most punishing of them all, tight-braided horsehide that cut to the bone in a single blow. Many of the men showed weals and scars where they had been struck by their own weapons, but others were untouched, their stony faces without any sign of human feeling.

There were about fifty men in the first group, nowhere near the numbers Père Guibert or Padre Bartolimieu had feared, and they showed none of the frenzy that was said to be the mark of their damned fellowship.

Père Foutin and his sour-faced sacristan were the first to see the men approaching.

"What do you think?" the sacristan muttered.

"I don't know," Père Foutin answered, much troubled. "The village . . . they should be roused. Who knows what manner of . . . The bell. Ring the bell,

Frère Loys. Do that." He stepped back into his old, drafty church and closed the door. He would open it again, once the bell had been rung.

Frère Loys bustled toward the stairs leading to the squat bell tower when he heard the first sound the strange men made—an eerie rumble, like a growl, deep in the chest, no louder than the purring of a large cat. He stopped in midstride and nearly fell for the utter terror that coursed through him. Then he bolted, reaching out for the rope to the bell as he might grasp for the hand of an angel.

Père Foutin was appalled at the sound and knew that he did not need more warning than that to rouse the village. His hand moved in a blessing, but he was not aware of it. "For all that I have done to offend Thee, I beg You will forgive me now," he murmured as he pressed his forehead against the thick wooden doors that now seemed woefully inadequate to keep them safe. "I repent my sins and despise myself that I committed them, knowing that they were . . ." His voice dropped to nothing as he heard the rough clamor of the bell. He prayed, "O Bon Dieu, let it be enough."

The purring sound grew louder, angrier, deeper. The men gathered in front of the church, spreading out to bar the way to any who might seek to enter or leave.

The bell sounded again, more emphatically, as Frère Loys tugged and cursed.

Suddenly, the men fell silent once again, which was more awful than the droning they had made mere pulsebeats before.

"Virge Saunt Marie," Père Foutin whispered, "you who care for us at the hour of our death, intercede for me; tell them that I did not mean all the venal things I've done, that I did not intend to desert my brother when the Plague came. You know that I have. If I am weak, God must know it. You will remind Him, Supreme Virge, that He gave me little bravery. I did all I could with what I have." He crossed himself. "You may stop, Frère Loys," he called out, feeling weary to the marrow of his bones.

The bell was stilled; Père Foutin and Frère Loys waited in the darkness for the men to act.

By the time the swineherd reached la Tres Saunte Aunnuciacion, he was panting so much that he could not speak at all. He gasped through the grille to the warder Sister in a few incoherent syllables and was admitted at once by Seur Philomine, who had heard the bell of Saunt-Vitre ring in the distance. She escorted him quickly through the halls, knowing that it was improper for a man to be in that part of the convent without the express permission of Père Guibert and Mère Léonie. She was prepared to deal with the reprimand she would undoubtedly receive later.

"Come," said the superior when Seur Philomine rapped on her cell door.

"It is Seur Philomine, ma Mère. There is a swineherd come from—"

"Where is he?" Mère Léonie interrupted her.

"He is with me, ma Mère." She knew better than to offer apology for this; later, more than apology would be required.

"I see." The door opened. Mère Léonie, fully habited, stepped into the hall. "And?"

Seur Philomine was about to answer, but the swineherd took a deep breath and said, "Men. In the village. Around the church."

"I see," Mère Léonie responded with difficult composure. "Those unfortunate women."

"Ma Mère!" Seur Philomine protested, turning pale.

"We must be prepared," she went on. "If this is like the others have been, we will have much to do to ensure . . ." She did not finish her thoughts. Turning to the swineherd, she stared hard at him. "How long did it take you to reach here?"

"Not long," he answered in an intimidated way. "I ran."

"I should imagine. Seur Philomine, go along with him and see that he has some broth before he leaves."

"Leaves?" Seur Philomine repeated. "But Mère Léonie, if those are Flagellants . . ."

"I do not mean to send him back to the village, ma Seur. But he cannot properly remain here, and we will have much to do to prepare for what . . . may come." With that, she swept away from them down the hall toward the chapel, her gray habit billowing with the speed of her pace.

Père Guibert saw smoke rising over the village of Saunt-Vitre-lo-Sur, and he bowed his head in prayer. His eyes stung, and he told himself it was from the smell of smoke drifting across the sky. He heard the nuns' voices from the chapel, where the chants for protection were being sung. "I could ask that I have their faith," he mused, afraid to address his doubts to heaven. "I have asked for aid before." He would have to go to Saunt-Vitre and see what remained of the place, a thing so intolerable to him that he very nearly wished that he might not survive the day.

"Père Guibert," said Mère Léonie as she came into the courtyard, "my Sisters will be ready to carry out your instructions as soon as possible. Seur Lucille returned yesterday, and she will inform you of what she learned. When you wish her to do so, of course." This last afterthought was said in so offhanded a fashion that Père Guibert knew Mère Léonie had her mind on other matters.

"Forgive me. I am not quite myself." She began to pace, her long, boyish stride setting the skirts of her habit swinging in a distracting way. "I wonder if it might be possible for us to ask His Holiness for one or two of his vidames to guard us?"

"There are many convents that would wish the same, and the vidames cannot send away all their men-at-arms." He gave this chiding as gently as he knew how. "I, too, would take comfort in the presence of men in armor."

"I want to strike back so that we are not just so many virgin sacrifices for the glory of God." She stopped, her hands coming to her face before Père Guibert could express his shock at her outburst. "I did not mean . . ."

"It is difficult," Père Guibert agreed, wishing that he might give vent to his feelings as she had done.

She was much more composed now. "I wish I had sent the older nuns to safety."

"Sadly, we do not know how many more of the Flagellants are on the road or where they are bound. It might have endangered them more to send them away."

"Nevertheless," Mère Léonie persisted, "I wish I had done it."

"It was a missed opportunity," Père Guibert said, annoyed at himself for letting so obvious a precaution escape him.

Mère Léonie sighed. "Well, we will do as we must. That and trust to Our Lord to bring us safely through."

"Amen."

"Deo gratias," Mère Léonie said softly. "I will say it again with greater fervor if at the end of the day these walls are still standing and the Sisters unharmed."

"Do not treat God as a merchant, to barter for the preservation of your life and the salvation of your soul," Père Guibert admonished her as he tried to match her stride about the courtyard. "Rather ask la Virge to remember you and beg that your sins be set aside."

"The lives of my sisters and their honor are in my hands, and they are a great charge upon me. I will lose more than my own soul if this goes badly."

Père Guibert sighed in sympathy. "Then it might be better if your Sisters did not see you in such distress and learn fear from you."

She stopped, her eyes filling with tears. "I . . . I will do . . . Yes, mon Père. You correct me most properly."

"It is natural that you would be worried," he said, glad for the excuse to talk and to deceive himself with his own authority, to take courage from the illusion that he could influence Mère Léonie. "You wish to see your Sisters preserved by the might of God, as we all hope to be saved. Yet you know that God does not defend those who are heedlessly reckless any more than He condones those who do nothing but await the ax and abandon His children. Where does the line fall between the two?"

"We will know that tonight, I think," Mère Léonie said, exerting herself more sternly to an outward tranquillity. "The Sisters will be out of chapel shortly. You will have to tell them what to do."

"And you, Mère Léonie, ma Fille? Do you need any reminder?" He wanted her to open her heart to him, to reveal her fears so that he could console her and, through that consolation, gain some echo of it for himself.

"I fear that . . , I fear that no matter what I may do, it will fail Our Lord, and we will be lost." She crossed herself. "If it were possible for me to be a man now, then I might face those irreligious creatures with their whips and their fires and believe myself able to fend them off with my sword and my wits. But as I am, well, what woman can endure what those men wish to do?" She had begun to pace again, this time not so rapidly or frenetically as before. "I want strength in my arm. But we are a community of women, dedicated to the service of travelers, recalling the parable of those who entertain angels unawares. What means have we to defend ourselves from such as those?" She turned toward the smoke over Saunt-Vitre-lo-Sur.

"Everywhere we see that God has come to the aid of the weak," Père Guibert reminded her unwisely.

"And we see where He has not, where the Plague has been, and war." She paused to stare at the smoke again. "What had those few women done that deserved that?"

"Do not blame God but the Devil, who has inspired those men to do his evil works." He felt more confident saying those words, as if the questions he might have posed could be erased by his affirmation of the work of the Devil.

"If we may not bargain with God, may we not bargain with the Devil?" She shook her head. "You need not remind me, mon Père. To bargain with the Devil is to insult God and is a greater sin than falling to the hosts of the fallen angels."

"Yes," Père Guibert said, and was about to go on when he saw the other nuns coming out into the court-yard. "We will speak later," he said to Mère Léonie, and faced the other women, trying to find the phrases that would lend them their faith to get through their coming ordeal.

It was late in the afternoon before they heard the low humming growl that had so terrified Père Foutin and Frère Loys. The nuns, gathered in the courtyard for hours, looked about with expressions ranging from dismay to panic. Seur Odile nearly fainted and was held up by the sturdy bulk of Seur Theodosie, who milked the nanny goats and ewes to make the convent's cheese. Seur Ranegonde almost had to be taken back to her cell when it was noticed how pale she had become.

"There is burning in the village," Seur Marguerite announced, as if it had just been discovered. "There was a shepherd by my hives today. He is a simple boy, that shepherd, and has visions."

"When were you at the hives?" Mère Léonie asked with more sharpness than usual.

"Why, during the morning," Seur Marguerite answered. "My children were calling to me, and sure as God watches His children, so He has entrusted me to watch mine. They have their saints and Virgin, too, my children, and they exalt them." Her face was dreamy now and distant. "They are singing loudly today, aren't they?" She took a step toward the door. "They will sing for all of us if we let them in. Do not worry for their stings, for they will do no harm if you sing with them."

Two of the nuns grabbed Seur Marguerite by the arms and held her back. She looked at her captors in bewilderment, more disappointed than alarmed. Seur Tiennette tightened her hold as she looked to her superior for guidance.

"Seur Marguerite," Mère Léonie said, making her voice loud enough so that the other nuns would hear her. "That your bees are devout no one questions, for they are examples of humility and industry to the world. But as the Devil sends evil in many disguises so that the most virtuous and fair may be a sink of vicious iniquity, so there are those who emulate your bees and serve not God but the Devil with their wiles. You must not let your love of your bees render your judgment faulty." She looked around her. "You must heat the kettles and set up the ladders. I want us to have hot water to throw upon those heretics. You need not fear to see them scalded, for the fires of hell will do worse than scald them." She folded her arms. "You have been told your duties. You know what we must do. Those who are not able to defend with their strength must go to the chapel to pray for God's aid. It may be that men-at-arms have been dispatched, but we must not assume this is so. If God has marked this convent for destruction, then nothing will save it, nor should it be saved. If God has determined that we will come through unharmed, then we are in the palm of His hand, and what petty actions we take mean little." She had to speak louder, for the noise beyond the walls was increasing. "My Sisters, each of you must go to her task. You have been shriven and need not think of death with horror."

There was a loud report as the Flagellants threw a large rock at the convent door. The wood reverberated with the impact, and for a moment those gathered on both sides of the wall were still.

"God will be with you. Be sure of that." Mère Léonie turned to Père Guibert. "If you will give us your blessing, mon Père." And she knelt to receive it.

The benediction was hastily given, and the nuns dispersed from it with unseemly haste. Another volley of stones rattled on the door, sending all the women scurrying to their tasks.

Outside, the humming stopped.

"God save me," Seur Odile murmured as she went toward the refectory, where it had been decided that injuries would be treated.

"God will do as He pleases," Seur Aungelique told her. "It does not matter what they say or what they do." She leaned on the wall, her emaciated face framed by gorget and wimple and coif. "Listen to them. They talk and talk and talk, and it means nothing. God does not care what we do or we say or we think. God does not listen. God does not see." She met the terrified eyes of the nuns around her. "We are fools to talk and reason and pray."

"Seur Aungelique . . ." Seur Philomine said as she pushed her way through the other nuns. "You are to join the others in prayer."

"In prayer?" Seur Aungelique demanded, laughing in an immoderate way. "It will not save us to pray. We should have run when we had the chance. We should have gathered stones and barrels and weapons to kill these men rather than think that God will find a way to save us. They tell us that the Devil is the father of lies, but even God lies—He told Adam that if he ate of the tree of knowledge, he would die. That was not true, was it? Then why should we believe that God will keep His promise to save us when we know He has lied from the first?" She let herself be taken in hand and led into the hall leading to the chapel. "If those men put this place to the torch, it will mean nothing. If they rape and gut us, it will mean nothing. Nothing."

Seur Philomine could see the others begin to waver, and she decided to take the matter into her own hands rather than wait for the superior to learn of this harangue. She approached Seur Aungelique with a determined set to her face. "It will matter to *me* if any of those things occur, Seur Aungelique. Whether it is for true martyrdom or for nothing, the suffering is real. And I care how I conduct myself. If it matters to no one but myself, it is enough." She could see that the others were listening to her. "There are duties we must perform, and yours, whether you like it or not, Seur Aungelique, is to pray." She shoved the other woman through the chapel door, then turned to the nun near her. "If she is unreasonable, ask Père Guibert to take her in hand."

The nun was mildly shocked, but she nodded, saying nothing to the tertiary Sister as much from respect as surprise at her behavior.

When Seur Philomine got back to the courtyard, she could see that the ladders were already in place and Seur Lucille and Seur Tiennette were supervising the heating of cauldrons of water in the middle of the flagging.

"It is most important," Seur Lucille was saying to the nun beside her, "that you continue to brush cinders back into the fire, else they could bring fire to the whole building, and the heretics' work would be done for them."

Mère Léonie was by the door, studying it as the rocks thudded and rang on it from the other side. "It will hold awhile." She turned toward the nearest ladder. "We will start with the scalding water first. Be careful that you use the quilted gauntlets so that you do not burn yourself."

"Yes, ma Mère," Seur Elvire answered, looking more determined than Seur Philomine had ever seen her. "I will do all that I may."

"Excellent." Now that she was actually setting the nuns to defending la Tres Saunte Annunciacion, Mère Léonie appeared for the first time to be truly in her element. "I will inform the heretics of what we are prepared to do," Mère Léonie declared loudly, and started toward the nearest ladder. At the top, she braced herself against the wall and leaned over. "You!" she shouted in a voice that, though light, might have satisfied a herald. "You came here without provocation to do us grevious ill. We have boiling water, and we have lengths of wood that we will hurl at you, burning, if you persist in this attack."

One of the men with the long bullock's whip uncoiled it from his shoulder and swaggered toward the wall. In silence, he prepared, and there was only the slice of the lash through the air to disturb the fading afternoon.

Mère Léonie almost fell from the ladder when the end of the whip touched her face. Blood appeared over her right eye from a puckered cut. She steadied herself. "You will pay for this, craven," she said in a manner that was almost amiable. Then, taking care not to lose her balance, she went back down the ladder.

The blows of the rocks on the door increased, and a few now were hurled over the wall, striking where they might in the courtyard.

"Ma Fille . . ." Père Guibert said as he approached the superior. He saw the blood welling, running down her face, obscuring the vision of her right eye.

"I need only a cloth," she said curtly. "My Sisters!" she shouted. "Commence!"

Chapter 6

Six of the nuns had been injured by the time the sun went down. One of the company of Flagellants had been able to start a fire in the stables, and so far it had not spread, though no one had been able to stop it, and the screams of the animals trapped there were pitiful to hear over the cries and rumble of the fighting.

Seur Adalin, at the top of one of the ladders, had been struck by rocks; she would not quit her post, but it was apparent that she could not continue much longer without falling as much from exhaustion as from bruises. Seur Elvire had come down to help prepare the boiling water, and for the time being, Seur Philomine took her place, working coolly to drench the Flagellants in scalding water. There were a number of minor burns on her hands, but she paid them little notice.

On the farthest ladder, Seur Catant struggled with the largest of the enormous pots. The hoist, usually employed to aid the harvest of fruit in the orchard, wobbled precariously as it raised the cauldron up a few more precious inches. "Seur Victoire," she called down hoarsely, "I need more!"

"They aren't ready yet," she answered. "Mère Léonie has . . ." She tried to explain, but she could not pull on the ropes and talk at the same time.

"I fear they may try to come in through the stables once the fire has caught hold," Mère Léonie said with formidable presence of mind while she strove to stoke the fires with the scraps of wood taken from the orchard.

"We will have to be prepared for that." There was an ugly bruise spreading beneath her injured brow, and the lid was swollen enough to droop badly.

"Oh, no!" Seur Lucille objected. "We haven't enough to keep us . . ." She clapped her hands. "I need more water. Seur Morgance, fetch it!"

"At once," she said cheerfully, and though her blighted joints were twisted and painful, she hobbled to the well and began to draw up more buckets. "It will take time!"

"Hurry!" was the answer from Mère Léonie.

Another volley of rocks landed in the courtyard, one of them striking Seur Lucille in the back so that she staggered forward. The hem of her habit brushed the flames and in the next instant had started to smolder.

"Someone!" Mère Léonie ordered, pointing to Seur Lucille, who gazed in stupefaction at the fire. "Overturn the cauldron!"

One of the younger nuns rushed to do as instructed, and the largest of the vats, near boiling, was upset on Seur Lucille, who shrieked once in all-consuming pain and then fell unconscious in the steaming water.

The fire hissed, sputtered, and started to go out.

"More wood!" Mère Léonie shouted, and this time she caught the attention of the nuns on the ladders. Seur Philomine, seeing the chaos below her, almost decided to climb down to aid the others, but she saw that the attackers were aware that something had gone amiss and were pressing their assault. Resolutely, she hung on, waiting for more hot water.

Seur Elvire, recovering herself, reached to keep the wood fueling the flames. She wanted to get away from the courtyard, from the burning smell and the distress and the constant reminder that hideous agony awaited her if the Flagellants should break through the door.

Mère Léonie signaled to Seur Elvire. "Leave her. Go to the chapel and tell the nuns there that we need more than their prayers now. Tell them to get knives from the kitchen and anything else that they can use. Ladles, forks, anything that might hurt them."

Seur Elvire gave a garbled answer and fled, unable

to bear the sight of Seur Lucille any longer. She had
tried to pull back her habit to see how badly the nun was
burned and had found patches of skin clinging to the fabric. "At once!" she sobbed, and slammed the inner door
as she got through it.

"Seur Catant! What do you see?" Mère Léonie
shouted up at her. "How many of them are there now?"

"More," Seur Catant replied in despair. "There is
another company just approaching from the road, about
the same number—between forty and fifty. I don't know
what we may . . ." She stopped to cross herself and to
signal for another pot of water. "As much as you have,
even if it's a little."

"How many of them are still fighting of the first lot?"
Mère Léonie asked, giving no sign that this new information distressed her.

"Most of them, though some of them are badly
burned. They don't . . . care," Seur Catant remarked,
taking a moment to master the dread that revelation gave
her.

"That is the Devil, who cares nothing for their lives
or ours. God cares for our lives," Père Guibert cried out
as he heard this. He had been tending to one of the nuns
who had had her arm broken by one of the rocks heaved
over the wall. "They are all that God is against. Dispatch
them to the last, and la Virge and le Bon Dieu will sing
your praises on high!"

The nuns nearest him turned toward him in surprise, as if they had forgotten he was with them at all.
One or two of them crossed themselves and returned to
their work, but Seur Tiennette, laboring to fill another
enormous pot, glared at him. "You are not in chapel now,
mon Père, and we need more than your assurances to
give us strength. Rather than tell us of God's love, bring
your arms over here and help fill this pot!"

At any other time, Père Guibert would have been
affronted, but now he did not say a word against her. "If
you will forgive me." He excused himself from the injured nun and went to do as Seur Tiennette bade him.

Night was coming on, and it was increasingly difficult to see clearly in the courtyard. The fire, rekindling,

cast wavering shadows along the walls but provided little steady light. Seur Lucille, dragged away from the fire to rest against the most protected wall, was scarcely more than a mound in darkness now that the long shadows fell over her.

"I will need someone to keep guard," Mère Léonie announced. "Seur Philomine! Come down from there. Go to the stables and stop the fires. Seur Catant! Come down. Another will take your place. Go into the hospice and help them there." Her light-blue eyes were hot as little sparks, and she went decisively from one ladder to another. "Quickly!"

The women moved to obey her, but she did not linger. "Mère Léonie," Seur Catant began, and was waved away. "I do not want to die."

"Nor shall you," Mère Léonie promised her. "Not here, not for these deluded men." She hurried into the hall and went to the chapel. "Come, my Sisters. Darkness is coming, and we are the ones with the torches and lamps. I want all of them to shine brightly in our courtyard so that we may fight on while the heretics wear themselves to tatters in the night."

Seur Aungelique was the first who moved. "What are we to do?"

"I want you on a ladder, ma Seur, pouring water on the men. I want you to burn all of them that come near. Seur Marguerite, I want you to help Père Guibert, who is too busy to tend those of us who have been hurt. You see, none of us can expect to come through this . . . unscathed." She touched the flesh near her eye. "Seur Lucille has fared worst of all. She is in the greatest . . . need." The superior paced toward the altar. "Those heretics thought that we would fall, as the church in Saunt-Vitre did, without opposition; they are not prepared to wait for their victory. Our Lord has sent us this respite so that we may have a sweeter triumph in His name when we are delivered from their hands."

"Ma Mère," Seur Marguerite spoke up. "How have our Sisters come to be hurt at all when we fight for the glory of God? The Devil sends lies to us to make us think that some are dead when they are not. If the wounds are suffered for God, how can such wounds give pain? If the death is in the bosom of the Lord, it is not death at all, or so Our Lord has said. No one is dead, but waiting. Isn't that so?"

"So we are taught, ma Seur. You may do all that you can to remember that when you keep the night watches with your Sisters." Mère Léonie stopped in front of the altar and swung around to address her nuns. "Each of you must set aside her fears and commend your souls and bodies to the will of God."

"But how?" Seur Ranegonde wailed. Her head was throbbing already, and she knew that the weakness that was slowly claiming her would not let up its grip in exchange for a prayer or two.

"Through faith, ma Seur," Mère Léonie reminded her. "You cannot falter now."

"Anything to get them to fight, ma Mère?" Seur Aungelique taunted her. "Where is this ladder you want me to climb?" She sauntered up to Mère Léonie and smiled at her. "Show me. I will climb it for you. Perhaps I will jump off it."

"If you wish to throw yourself to those monsters outside the walls, you may do it and know that you have given yourself to the Devil." Mère Léonie became more stern with each word.

"The Devil is welcome to me, then, if he frees me," Seur Aungelique mocked, but left the chapel more quickly than the others.

Père Guibert found Seur Catant huddled near Seur Lucille, her eyes staring hard at the flagging where the firelight was reflected in pools of standing water. "Ma Fille." He had found many of the nuns had been wounded without realizing the extent of their injuries, and it had impressed and repelled him to see them carry on their battle while flesh was swollen and blood ran.

"Stay back," she warned him. "There are Devils in the land. They seek us."

One of the planks of the heavy doors had broken near the top when an especially heavy rock had struck it a glancing blow, and now splintered wood lay all over the courtyard. Père Guibert brushed it away without thinking and knelt beside the terrified nun. "Come, Seur Catant. We will pray together, and then God will give you the strength to go on in His Name."

"And what if the Devil comes instead? What if God does not hear or does not answer in time? It is the Devil outside. He is nearer, and nothing can change that. We are not saved, no matter what we do."

"Then beg la Virge Saunte Marie to come to your rescue and pardon your sins so that you may come innocent to God." He heard another rock crash through the gaping hole in the door, taking more of the wood with it and causing several of the nuns to cry out in anger and despair. "You cannot remain here, ma Fille. It is too dangerous."

"But Seur Lucille is here. She is the oldest of us all, and she is a good sister. Her burns are . . . Someone must take care of her." She explained this with exaggerated precision, as if there had been an argument and she was eager to set her position out as clearly as possible. "I have to guard her. She is without any other protection. You see that."

Père Guibert did not attempt to contradict her. "Come into the chapel, ma Fille, and someone will attend to you there." He strove to get the nun to her feet but failed.

"I cannot leave her." Seur Catant was weeping now. "It is as if she is dead."

"No, no, ma Fille," Père Guibert said quickly. "She is alive. You have to get yourself to safety. Then others will tend Seur Lucille." He could think of nothing else to say. "Mère Léonie has ordered it."

Seur Catant sneered. "She is the one who has lured the Devil here, and if she were not here, we would be living in peace, as God intended."

"But Seur Catant . . ." Père Guibert protested, trying to distract her from this tirade and to get her attention once again.

"She is the Devil . . . or his servant. She came to us to lead us into sin and thus bring ruin to the whole convent."

"It is your superior you call vile," Père Guibert said shortly, and all but dragged Seur Catant away from Seur Lucille.

She made little resistance, but her very listlessness, coming so quickly on her ire, troubled Père Guibert. "Come, Seur Catant." He urged her on toward the corridor that would protect her until she could gather her wits.

"We are marked. That is what has happened. God has given us to the Devil, as He has given so many before. We will be in his power, and nothing will deliver us from that complete damnation but the Last Judgment." She uttered a strangled sob and permitted Père Guibert to leave her in the corridor where, once again, she sank down and huddled against the wall.

Since the upper part of the courtyard doors had started to splinter and break, few of the Flagellants had come around to the stables, and Seur Philomine worked as quickly as she could to release those animals that had not been too badly hurt. "There, there," she said to one of the ewes that crouched, petrifed with terror, in the far side of the sheepfold. "I will get you out." She sank her hands into the soft, curling wool and tugged, prodding the sheep with the toe of her wooden shoe as she did. The ewe bleated, then bolted for the gate, leading the last of the sheep out of the stable. All that remained now that she could reach were two donkeys, and they were in the farthest pen. They milled together, walking restlessly, their long ears laid flat back when they were not swiveling to catch the sounds of the battle or the crackle of fire. Seur Philomine knew that it was not safe to approach them directly, for they might lash out with their hoofs and teeth; a sharp blow from a donkey's hoof could dash out her brains.

The fire was spreading in a slow, sullen way, eating its way through the wood and straw Seur Philomine had soaked with water when she first came into the stables.

"Calmly, calmly," Seur Philomine said as she tried to think of a way to get the donkeys out of the stable.

One of the donkeys laid back his ears and let out a long, high squeal.

"No, no, little one. It is the fire you fear, and I do not burn." She realized that God had not endowed these creatures with understanding, and for that reason, she must not blame them for their stubbornness. At the same time, she wished she had one of the Flagellants' whips to drive the donkeys with.

There were shouts from the courtyard echoing along the high walls and becoming strange, like drowned bells.

Seur Philomine could not let herself be distracted, she insisted inwardly. If there was more danger, then she must work swiftly. She searched about the stables, her eyes watering now and her nose running. Vaguely, she could see the charred perches where the chickens roosted at night. Hoping that they were not still too hot, she reached up and grabbed the nearest, putting all her weight behind the action. Her hands grew hot, but she hung on and was rewarded when the perch broke into a long, serviceable club. Gripping it with desperation, Seur Philomine went to the donkeys and struck them on the rumps and flanks, forcing them toward the gate in their enclosure. When they were near enough, she pulled the gate open, then stood aside as the two animals bolted, tails up, eyes a maddened white, to the field beyond the smoke-filled door.

Flames came sneaking along the floorboards, running like small, bright mice past her feet. With a falling scream, she stumbled out of the stables, still clinging to the perch she had brought down.

It was twilight, soft and tender, like the petals of violets and lilacs. Seur Philomine stopped her headlong plunge to blink her sore eyes and look about her in wonder. The orchard was still; the trees were dark, blossom crowned, like enormous heads rising out of the earth.

She was still in rapt contemplation when she felt a hand seize her and in the next instant was spun around to see two Flagellants, one bringing back his whip to strike her, the other about to strengthen his grip so that she could not escape.

"No!" she shouted, revulsion filling her. That her

beautiful evening should be contaminated in this way! She brought her club up and swung it with the full force of her emotion against the man with the whip. The wood shuddered as it struck, and she was jarred by the impact.

"What . . . ?" the man who held her began, then yelled as she kicked backward, her sabot smashing against his shin with a loud report. The man screamed blasphemously, falling away from her. "My leg! Balls of the saints!" He lay on his side, his leg drawn up, his hands over the injury.

The other man was starting to get to his feet, but he moved in a dazed way, and he drew each breath in a long, rasping sob.

Seur Philomine flung her club away and fled into the orchard, following her animals.

Two of the hospice windows had been breached, and there were now Flagellants within that building. The nuns had retreated, leaving locked doors between themselves and the invading heretics.

"I want torches," Mère Léonie announced. "If these creatures come through the door, set their clothes afire."

"But ma Mère," Seur Odile asked faintly, "what of *our* clothes? Won't they be afire, too?"

Mère Léonie answered at once and with great conviction. "There is always risk. But you do not cease to do your labor; you must think of what is worse: to have a little burn, or to die at the hands of the heretics, knowing that more has fallen than this building." She saw dread in the Sisters' faces. "As this building fares, so do we."

Seur Adalin said in the most plaintive way, "My faith has always been strong, even at the worst time of the Plague. Why can't—"

"Ma Seur!" Mère Léonie snapped. "You will ask God to pardon that thought when we have ended the battle." She stared up at the ladders. "Seur Aungelique! What do you see?"

"They are still here," she answered with a hint of a giggle. "It's too dark to count them, and they will not speak to us."

"Then tell me if they are as near our walls as before, or has night driven them back?" Mère Léonie ordered.

"I don't think they are fewer or farther away." She was the only woman still on a ladder, and it pleased her. The hazard meant nothing to her; she had come to enjoy it. "I will need more water, ma Mère."

"You shall have it," Mère Léonie promised her. "At once. Seur"—she looked around quickly—"Seur Tiennette, can you still man the fires for me?"

"Yes, ma Mere," the steadfast nun said flatly. "With God's help."

At this, several of the Sisters crossed themselves, and one of them began to cry. A few of the others hushed her.

"Come," Mère Léonie said in her most bracing tone. "Let us get our torches."

"What if we have no help? What if no one comes? What if these men break through and we do not live because of them? What then?" Seur Odile demanded, her tone high and terribly strained.

"Then we will live in Our Lord," Mère Léonie answered at once. "Remember that if you fear you will falter."

There was a general but unenthusiastic agreement, and Seur Aungelique laughed. "Beg the Devil for aid; only he rules here."

"That's blasphemy!" Seur Tiennette shouted at her.

"What is that to me?" Seur Aungelique challenged.

"Stop, the both of you!" Mère Léonie ordered. "We have better things to do than wrangle amoung ourselves."

"I only—" Seur Aungelique started, but was not allowed to go on.

"Keep watch, as you have been told!" Mère Léonie cut her short. "And do not let yourself be lulled into thinking that because you can see little, there is nothing to see!" She rounded on the others. "To your tasks, and at once. I do not want those heretics breaching any more of our defenses."

"What if we cannot stop them?" Seur Adalin asked,

more from curiosity than from fear, for she had gone beyond that now.

"Then commend your souls to God and ask the saints to listen to your prayers," she said. "Our Lord will see to us."

One of the nuns sighed heavily just as a pounding became more apparent.

"They have broken one of the doors," Seur Odile cried out. "Oh, God!"

"Get torches!" Mère Léonie said at her most terse. "At once!"

Seur Tiennette was the first to respond; she went to the fading bonfire and pulled two of the half-burned brands from the stack and held them out. "Start with these."

For the most part, the women worked in silence, taking the torches as they were handed them and finding vantage points that would permit them to inflict the most damage on the Flagellants when they broke through into the courtyard.

On her ladder, Seur Aungelique began to sing, tossing her head the way she had seen Comtesse Orienne do while she flirted in her great hall with the men gathered there. The song was worldly, and more than one of the nuns looked at her with anger and consternation for her impiety. This served only to make her singing more emphatic as she prepared to pour more water on the Flagellants still waiting at the courtyard doors, their whips held ready for the flogging to come. She thought that her father should see her at her post; surely this would convince him that she was made for the brave life and not hours on her knees before an empty altar.

Seur Philomine's feet were bruised, and her palms were nearly raw, but she found herself a position of safety on the far side of the brambles, where she paused to catch her breath. What ought she to do, she wondered. She could think of nothing. When Seur Aungelique started singing, Seur Philomine heard it, faintly at first, then in a stirring countermelody to the rattle of blows on the walls and doors of the convent. She listened in fascination, thinking that it was like Seur Aungelique to be so defiant.

She saw the fire in the stable grow, first as a bit of brightness in the smoke, then as a wavering flag in the gloom. Shortly, the walls of the convent would begin to heat as the wooden support beams charred and smoldered; then smoke would seep from every crack and fissure in the walls. She had seen fires of that sort before, long ago, when the city elders had ordered the pesthouses burned at the height of the Plague. She sank down behind the brambles so that she would not have to look either at the convent or her memories.

She was half dozing, her chafed hands limp in her lap, when she heard a new sound, a clanking, jingling accompaniment to the drum of trotting horses. She looked up, thinking that the donkeys must have returned, yet aware that they never made such a noise.

Around the bend in the road from Mou Courbet came a company of men-at-arms, more than thirty of them, led by torchbearing outriders in heralds' tabards.

"There!" the leader shouted, pointing his weapon— a mace or a maul; at this distance it was hard for Seur Philomine to see it clearly—toward the walls of la Tres Saunte Annunciacion. "At the charge!"

Seur Philomine found herself on her feet, running once again toward the convent.

From her vantage point on the ladder, Seur Aungelique interrupted her song to shout down to the courtyard, "There are armed men coming, I think!"

"Bon Dieu!" Seur Tiennette cried out, her indomitable calm shattered in tears.

"Not yet, not yet, ma Seur," Mère Léonie commanded her. "They are not here, and the heretics are!"

Seur Odile had already put down her torch, but at this grim warning, she gave a scream and ran from the courtyard.

"Let none of you flee," Mère Léonie warned her sisters in a genial way. "To fly now with aid at hand is worse than blasphemy. You have prayed for this, and now you will not do that little more that God requires for you to accept it."

This stern correction brought some of the nuns back to themselves, and they renewed their dedication to their duty, returning to their tasks with hardly more than a breath to revive them.

Seur Adalin dragged her sooty palm over her grimy forehead and pointed toward the inner door to the hospice. "They're almost through, ma Mère. It will not take them long."

"The chevaliers are nearly here. They have men outside to attend to, and then we will open the gates and allow them to deal with the heretics within the walls."

"You don't doubt the outcome?" she asked, not prepared to be as optimistic.

"What are heretics with whips compared to armored men on horseback with swords and maces?" Suddenly, she was lighthearted and curiously frisky. "Come, my Sisters, persevere in the name of Our Lord and enter into His kingdom for your efforts."

On the ladder, Seur Aungelique crowed with delight as she watched the men-at-arms close with the Flagellants for the battle.

The first rush of the men-at-arms caused havoc in the Flagellants' ranks, who broke, scattering in every direction to escape the hoofs and steel of the riders bearing down on them. Then there were the first thuds and blows of combat.

Seur Philomine stopped running as she saw this and stood swaying with fatigue as she tried to make out what was happening not far ahead of her in the dark. It was difficult to breathe for fear that she would expose herself. She heard moans and curses and the soft song of steel cutting through the air before striking home. The sound that followed brought bile to the back of her throat; she knew and rejoiced that the Flagellants were being cut down, but that pulpy impact, the splatter of bone and blood, turned her vitals to cold, hard fists. The fire in the stables did not give enough smoke to wholly obscure the light of the flames, but she could not see clearly, and she dreaded what she could make out.

One man broke and started to run, his hands pressed hard against his belly. He whimpered as he went, not looking before or behind him, only running to get away. He came near Seur Philomine, stumbled and righted himself. "You godless scum!" he spat at her. "You poisonous well." He went a few uneven steps more; then he fell, twitched in the long grass, and lay still.

Charity required that Seur Philomine render aid to those in need, and the man was certainly that. She could not bring herself to move. The man lying so close to her was a Flagellant. He carried a whip in his left hand. He had cursed her and declared himself her enemy. But he was a man and a creature of God who was hurt and in peril for his soul. She managed to take two hesitant steps toward him; then she heard the heavy pounding of a horse behind her, and she turned to see one of the men-at-arms bearing down on her.

"Hold there!" the man shouted in short, choppy breaths, the words muffled by the helm he wore. "Stop!"

Seur Philomine remained quite still, grateful to have the excuse not to tend to the fallen heretic. She would have to confess the fault, she knew it, and would have to do penance for her moral failure, but that she would bear with patience. At the moment, she felt nothing but abiding thanks for her deliverance. "Good Chevalier . . . I am . . ." she said, addressing the rider.

The man-at-arms paid no attention. He went to the Flagellant and leaned down in the saddle to drive his broadsword through the man's back. That done, he looked toward Seur Philomine, who gazed in horror at the prone figure. "Did he harm you, Sister?"

"What?" Seur Philomine asked stupidly, her voice girlishly high. "You . . . I don't understand." She could not say anything more to the man, afraid that she would give herself away if she did.

"These . . . damned Flagellants"—he modified what he had intended to say with embarrassed haste—"have done unspeakable things to some they have chanced upon." He dismounted. "Are there any others outside the walls, Sister?"

Seur Philomine pressed her hands to her cheeks, forcing her mind to be calm so that she might provide reasonable answers to the man-at-arms. "I do not think there are any others," she responded. "I have not seen any."

"That's something," he said, beginning to sound tired. "I can't escort you back to the convent. A little while, and all will be clear, but for the time being . . ." His shrug was more audible than visible, his armor clanking as he lifted his shoulders. "Is there a place we might sit? And I'll need some water for my horse. He's dry."

"There is a stream just off there," she said, pointing away through the orchard. "Be careful. The ground is uneven." She wanted to laugh at the ordinariness of what they were saying. Neither of them looked at the convent.

"Thanks. I will return shortly. You remain there unless more of those . . . vermin come this way. Then you run and hide, Sister. No use giving them a chance to harm you." He chuckled, sounding very young. "They've ruined old ladies; a morsel like you would delight them."

As the man-at-arms rode off, Seur Philomine sank to her knees beside the dead Flagellant and folded her hands in prayer.

As the ponderous doors to the courtyard were pulled open at last, the remaining Flagellants were driven inside by the men-at-arms. A few could not avoid being forced into the dying bonfire, and their screams were louder than the trampling hoofs and the ringing of blows.

The nuns retreated to their corridors and huddled there, between the courtyard and the chapel, their whispers unheard by anyone but themselves as they alternately thanked God for their deliverance and begged la Virge Marie to intercede for them in heaven.

Mère Léonie remained nearest the courtyard, her striking features unreadable in the dark. Only the glint in her icy eyes was noticeable, like the shine on the edge of a sword. She moved her lips silently, and as the battle progressed, she smiled.

"Oh, Mère Léonie, what are we to do?" Seur Odile yelled at her when two of the Flagellants nearly succeeded in entering the corridor.

"Patience, ma Seur. Patience and faith," she said in a loud voice. "We are in the hands of Our Lord."

Seur Odile crossed herself as she moved farther back toward the chapel.

A bit later, while one of the men-at-arms dragged a Flagellant over the flagstones by his heels, ignoring the screams of the man, Seur Adalin shrieked out a protest.

"Be silent, good Sister," Mère Léonie admonished her. "You would have fared worse than that if those heretics had succeeded here."

The Sisters became restless when they heard this; it was one thing to have that prospect in their thoughts, another to be so curtly reminded of it. Seur Tiennette pressed her lips together, determined to show no emotion. Across from her, Seur Aungelique giggled.

There was a sudden increase in the rhythm of the fighting, a scurrying of men, quicker, more abrupt cries and orders. While it lasted, it was unendurable, but it ended with awesome speed. Then the men-at-arms herded the remaining Flagellants into the center of the courtyard and brought their panting horses around them. Shortly after, a gravelly, deep voice called out, "It's over, good Sisters!"

Before the nuns could emerge from their shock at this announcement, Mère Léonie turned to them. "Thank Our Lord for what He has done for you, my Sisters."

The nuns took only a moment to respond to this familiar requirement. There was solace in prayer, and for that most of them sought the chapel.

"You enjoyed this," Seur Aungelique accused Mère Léonie as she prepared to follow the rest of the women.

"I enjoy the triumph of faith, Seur Aungelique," Mère Léonie said mildly.

"It's more than that," Seur Aungelique insisted.

Mère Léonie pretended not to have heard her. "Père Guibert is still in the refectory, and he must be informed."

Seur Aungelique shook her head but accepted her dismissal with more fatigue than meekness.

Pierre de Parcignonne dismounted, his sword already wiped clean and returned to its sheath, when Mère Léonie came across the devastation of the courtyard toward him. He could not see her features clearly in the low, ruddy glow of the dying bonfire, but he thought for an instant that he saw the flicker of a smile in her handsome features. "We've done what we can, Mère Léonie," he said by way of beginning his report to her.

"Sieur le Duc, I am more than grateful for your deliverance." She let him come to her, those last few steps. "Do you know yet how much damage they did?"

"No, and I will not be able to assess it for you until the morning. I've assigned three of my men to put the fire in the stables out and to keep watch through the night to be sure that the fire does not start again or spread." His hand was sore where one of the Flagellant's whip had struck him, and he could feel the stiff welt forming. It troubled him to think that he would not be able to wield his sword with ease until the wound healed.

"Are any of your men hurt, mon Sieur?" Mère Léonie asked, cutting into his thoughts with her solicitous inquiry.

"A few. Nothing to speak of. We're in armor and carry swords. Those madmen had nothing but their whips to protect them." He paused, thinking of what they had found in the rubble of the church in Saunt-Vitre-lo-Sur. "Still, that was enough."

"You must bring them to us for help," Mère Léonie said with warmth. "It is little enough for all you have done." She looked around the courtyard. "This will be tended to later."

"There will be those to work for you," Pierre told her, wondering why it was that her assurance of aid for his men made him feel so uncomfortable. He sighed deeply. "Rome might pray for such agents as these, for all they have done."

"Do you believe that Rome sent them, then?" Mère Léonie inquired, looking toward the few pitiful men who were all that remained of the heretics.

"I think that they are possessed of the Devil, for the pope has said that they are. I think that they are the servants of Satan and dedicated to the destruction of the Church. And the Pope has said that the Romans are wedded to the Devil and are deep in his clutches. They serve the same master, the heretics and the Romans." He turned abruptly to shout at one of his men. "Get them outside the walls and tie them up. The trees in the orchard should serve!"

"At once," came the exhausted reply, and the mounted men-at-arms began to do as their duc had ordered them.

"What will become of them?" Mère Léonie asked, a trifle unsteadily.

"The Church demands that they be put to death. It is not for me to decide or change." He recalled again what he had seen before and knew that Avignon would not permit the heretics to live and would not let them leave their flesh quickly. "Whatever the Pope decrees, I will . . . execute."

"Where will you take them, Sieur le Duc?" Her voice was low.

"Wherever I am told." He forced himself to move his attention from her. "Where are your sisters, ma Mère?"

"They are safe. Be sure of that."

"But *where*?" His demand was sharper than he had intended, but he did not excuse it for fear of bringing attention to his reaction to her.

"They are in the chapel, most of them," she replied with a trace of hauteur. "A few are in the refectory, a few are in the hospice, and there may be one or two outside the walls. Seur Marguerite has said that she wants to give the heretics a little of the honey from her hives, because her bees are God's creatures and holy."

"I see."

She lowered her head. "Seur Marguerite has charity in her, Sieur le Duc."

"Madness is not charity," Pierre corrected her.

"Still, hers is a worthy example, is it not?" She shook her head. "I should learn of her. I am entrusted with the well-being of all these women, and I have failed the mandate of Our Lord in these hours."

"Nonsense! How failed?" Pierre demanded, coming a little closer to her. It was not wise to approach a nun in this way, but she fascinated him, and he did not want to keep off from her.

"You may ask that, mon Duc, for you must fight in the world. But I battle for souls with a great enemy, and there is no quarter offered or given and no ransom that can be made either way. God might promise redemption, but not for those who turn their back on Him." She raised her head, directing her pale blue eyes directly at him, fixing him with their light as with the little blue flame in the heart of an oil lamp. "You do not have the same issues I do to contend with. Or do you think that God is the same as the king or the Pope?"

"The Pope is the voice of God on earth," Pierre said stiffly, looking down at his hand and flexing the fingers experimentally. "For that, our war is the same war."

"But fought in different ways," she pressed.

"It . . . may be," he allowed. "Well." He broke free of the spell of her eyes. "I must see to these heretics and the setting up of camp. You must attend to your Sisters. I was wrong to keep you so long." He turned on his heel and strode toward his horse, all the while looking forward to the next time he would have occasion to be in her presence.

Mère Léonie watched Pierre mount and ride out the ruined gates of the convent. There was something in her face—not quite like greed but close to it—that was unlike her usual expression. Then it was gone, and she went back into the corridor that led toward the chapel, where the nuns were waiting.

Chapter 7

What was left of Père Foutin and Frère Loys was laid in the earth beside the broken altar stone of their church. Père Guibert wept with anger as he said the holy words that would still the grief that raged in the hearts of the few peasants who had survived the attack of the Flagellants. He longed to fill their souls with an abiding hatred of the Flagellants that would endure to the end of the world and shine before the throne of God. With shaking hand, he wiped the sweat from his face before raising his head. "You have seen what was done here, what indignities and cruelties were visited on these holy men before God released them into death. I do not need to tell you their suffering. Think of that when your resolve is shaken by doubts, when you begin to wish that the heretics might not have to undergo the punishment that has been decreed for them." He paused. "Word has come Cardinal Seulfleuve has sent a messenger"— this was common knowledge, but he wished to remind all the people gathered around the graves of the magnitude of the crimes that had been committed there—"with word that the remaining heretics are to be stripped, placed over stretched hempen ropes with stout men at their hands and feet to drag them over and back the length of the ropes until they are sawn in pieces."

Pierre exchanged a glance with his captain-at-arms; his face was grim.

"You will all watch and benefit by what you see."

Among the nuns, Seur Aungelique began to laugh.

"Be silent," Mère Léonie admonished her.

"It is not a swift death, and they will have a taste of the punishment that awaits them in hell," Père Guibert said with satisfaction.

Mère Léonie brought her folded hands up, concealing her mouth.

"We are told that the Devil roams the earth and that we, the children of God, are his victims. Every thought, every desire, every act that does not lead to virtue gives aid to the Devil and admits some portion of his vileness in your lives." Père Guibert cleared his throat, and when he spoke again, his voice cracked. "Be very sure that you do not taint yourselves with secret sins and think you are safe because they go unconfessed. Do not imagine that anything is hidden from God, Who is omnipotent and omniscient. You are weak and imperfect vessels, all of you. Each of you is consumed with iniquity, but so long as you live in faith and hope, there is a chance that your evil will be purged. With the heretics, the purging of their sins is too late, for they are given to the Devil. You must all beg God to give you His grace, that you may not succumb to your base desires and appetites."

Seur Odile let out a long, keening sob.

"Be rigorous. Do not excuse yourself any little lapse, but chastise yourself the more for making light of sin."

A few of Pierre's men were growing restive, and two of the infants were howling. The sun, which had been veiled by gauzy clouds, was now beating down on the gathering.

"Go each of you to your beds tonight, and pray that all your sins may be revealed to you. That is God's Mercy to you—the heretics have forfeited it, and with it, they have lost their souls." It was not nearly enough, Père Guibert thought. Later, he would find other words, other phrases, to fire his flock with the zeal that smoldered in his soul.

"All right," Pierre said in his loud, rough tones. "Those of you who live here go home. You Sisters, come with us back to the convent. Père Guibert, let me offer you my horse to ride." This last was not an entirely sincere suggestion, and he hoped that the priest would not accept.

"I will walk," Père Guibert muttered. "Our Lord walked."

"As you say," Pierre agreed, and went for his mount.

Mère Léonie came slowly up to Père Guibert and took her place beside him, though not quite even with him, so that he would lead the nuns back to la Tres Saunte Annunciacion. "You are much moved, mon Père?"

"Yes, ma Fille. You should be, too." He was stung by her apparent lack of concern.

"Yes," she said promptly. "But I cannot turn my mind to such matters quite yet. Our Lord will show the way. I must devote myself to the securing of our convent before I will think it right that I pursue the cleansing of the spirits of my Sisters."

There was nothing in her manner that hinted at disrespect, but Père Guibert, excited to a rare level of passion, could not contain himself. "It is not enough! No, Mère Léonie. You are confusing the temporal with the eternal. You are entrusted not with the bodies of your nuns but their souls."

Mère Léonie crossed herself. "May Our Lord grant that I carry this burden as He would wish."

"Amen to that." He was being churlish; he knew it.

"But if they cannot keep their lives ordered and within our Rule, then I have not acquitted myself as I have vowed to do. Those living decently in cloisters preserve themselves in the eyes of the Church as well as of God." She paused. "Think what would happen with Seur Aungelique if I do not repair the doors and the walls."

Père Guibert blanched. "Yes."

"Then perhaps you will pray for me and guide me with your wisdom?" In another woman, her tone might have been thought taunting, but not in so devout a superior as Mère Léonie. Père Guibert, listening to her, railed at himself for his harshness, which only brought confusion, whereas he most wanted to bring light and salvation.

"Hear me, ma Fille," he said when he had gathered his thoughts. "You are the key to the peace of your convent and the protection of your Sisters, and for that God must put you in His especial care. You must humble yourself before Him and petition la Virge to intercede on your behalf in order that you might have not only grace for your tasks and your life but true piety as well." He walked unsteadily, his fatigue catching up with him at last and rendering him lightheaded. There was a pebble in his sandal, but he refused to bend down and remove it, trusting instead that this minor discomfort would serve to vilify his flesh and exalt his soul.

"I will do all that I am able to comply," Mère Léonie said, turning subservient in her manner. "Forgive me for treating your instructions improperly."

"Of course." He was already trying to frame his next sermon in his mind so that when he addressed the nuns again, they would partake of his faith and share in his saintly lust for vengeance.

Seur Philomine, keeping her vigil in the chapel, was the first to hear the strange cries that came from Seur Aungelique's cell three nights after the heretics had been sawed to pieces. Her thoughts were confused, and she welcomed the intrusion that the sudden urgent sounds provided. Then she heard a few jumbled words and rushed out of the chapel.

"Oh, no, no. Not that!" Seur Aungelique yelled, but not with repugnance.

Outside the door to her cell, Seur Philomine paused to listen to Seur Aungelique's protests, hardly aware of her own breathing. "God protect me," she murmured before she rapped on the door.

"No, no. Oh, God, no more. Don't touch me there!" Seur Aungelique whimpered. "Oh, not there. Not . . . there. You don't . . . Ah! . . . Jesus and Marie! . . . Your hands are . . . sweet. No." There were two or three high, childlike yelps, and then she spoke again. "You mustn't . . . Thibault, you must . . . must . . . not . . . Yes, there . . . There, Thibault . . . Oh, for Pierre!"

Seur Philomine frowned deeply as she knocked once, hesitated, and knocked again. "Seur Aungelique? Is there anything the matter?"

"AH-H-h-h-h-h-h!" came the sudden, desperate

outcry, trailing off into what sounded like exhausted panting.

"Seur Aungelique!" Seur Philomine repeated, this time more loudly. "Is anything wrong?"

Seur Aungelique's cell was quiet all at once. Then a bleary voice called out, "Who's there?"

"It is Seur Philomine," she answered. "You . . . called out in your sleep."

"Oh." The nun's tone was dull, listless. "I . . . must have . . . had a bad dream. The Devil sends such dreams, doesn't he?"

"So we are told," Seur Philomine said, not sure of it as she spoke. "Should I get Mère Léonie or . . ."

"No!" This was more forceful, and almost at once, Seur Aungelique modified her objection. "It would make . . . too much of a . . .bad dream. Let me be, Seur Philomine."

By rights, Seur Philomine knew that she ought to insist that Seur Aungelique open the door to her cell and admit her so that they might pray together, but she could not bring herself to intrude so much on the other nun. "I . . . others may have heard you call out."

"I will beg their pardon when we break our fast," Seur Aungelique assured her. "The . . . bad dream has worn me out." This last was breathless, almost like inward laughter. "You're kind to . . . bear with me."

Nothing of what Seur Aungelique said was satisfactory, but Seur Philomine did not press the matter. "I will have to speak of this to Mère Léonie. And Père Guibert."

"Do that. Oh, yes, do that." Seur Aungelique's words ended with a catch in her breath, as if she had yawned.

"I will pray for you." Reluctantly, Seur Philomine turned back toward the chapel and was startled to see Seur Odile standing in the door of her cell. "What? . . ."

"She's at it again, is she? It's bad enough with Seur Marguerite screaming when the fits are on her and Seur Lucille moaning of her wounds, but . . ." She crossed herself. "God will know what will heal Seur Aungelique. We may only pray on her behalf."

Seur Philomine looked down at her hands and fancied she could still see the burns in the gloom. "We paid a great price, we nuns, to keep our convent."

"That's pride, Sister, and for that you will beg your bread. Mère Léonie would be the first to reprimand you for such sentiments." Seur Odile shook her head.

Seur Philomine nodded, remembering the fierce sermon the priest had delivered the morning before. "I don't know if I . . ."

"What we know and do not know is not important where heresy is concerned; it is faith that matters, not knowledge." She raised her head, showing more importance than she had ever felt in her entire time as a nun.

"But . . ." Seur Philomine began, then stopped. "They say that the Devil may come here in order to corrupt us."

Seur Odile answered with satisfaction, "My faith is staunch. Let the Devil come and try me."

"Isn't that pride, too?" Seur Philomine could not resist asking.

"It is the strength of my faith. My path is clear to me, and my steps are guided."

Seur Philomine said nothing; her vigil had been penance for just such doubts, and she did not want to spend any more hours than necessary in the chapel at night. "May your good angel guard you, then, ma Seur," she said, and started away from the other nun.

"You will tell Mère Léonie what transpired?" Seur Odile called after her.

"I must," Seur Philomine said.

"Very good. Report what I have said accurately." A tinge of accusation had come into Seur Odile's tone.

"I will ask that you be present." It was the best solution she could think of, and as Seur Philomine said it, she decided that in the future she would always use such devices to avoid unpleasantness.

"Pray well, Seur Philomine," Seur Odile told her, and shut the door to her cell.

How many others had heard? Seur Philomine asked herself as she took her place prostrate before the altar. How many had listened to Seur Aungelique and lain silent in their beds? The questions haunted her as she recited her prayers.

A light spring rain was falling as Seur Tiennette bustled through the still room, turning the cheeses that had just been brought in from the creamery. There were fewer than usual. Seur Tiennette pursed her lips as she examined the rounds, sniffing each critically and inspecting its color. The first six had gained her qualified approval, but the seventh was another matter. There was a mold on the rind that did not belong there, and the smell of it was offensive, like the stench of rotting eggs. With disgust, Seur Tiennette dropped the cheese into the sack she carried, annoyed at the waste. The next cheese on the rack exuded the same dreadful odor, and the one after that. In all, five cheeses had gone bad, far more than Seur Tiennette might have expected.

"But it might have been for many reasons." Mère Léonie soothed her when Seur Tiennette reported her find to her superior. "You yourself said that you were not confident that the Sisters aiding you knew what they were about."

"But five cheeses . . ." Seur Tiennette protested. "And so far gone, too."

"Yes; you showed them to me. It is most unfortunate, and it may be that we will have to speak to the women in Mou Courbet to arrange with them to have a few of their cheeses. You are right that we will be hungry without them. Though," she added in a thoughtful manner," an occasional fast would not be a bad notion for the Sisters here. It may be that Our Lord has sent us this test to show us that we must nurture the spirit as well as the body. Let me think on it for a little while." She made a gesture of dismissal.

Seur Tiennette did not leave. "I do not mean to overstep my bounds, Mère Léonie, but I fear that we will need more than a few cheeses if we are to come through the summer without hunger. The heretics lost us more than our walls. We have fewer animals and only half the number of chickens as before."

"When Père Guibert returns, doubtless I will speak

of this with him," Mère Léonie said at her mildest. "You cannot think that I would neglect the well-being of my Sisters, can you?"

Seur Tiennette accepted this oblique chiding with a single nod. "You are more dedicated than Mère Jacinthe, ma Mère," she muttered.

"I have more need of devotion, perhaps. Mère Jacinthe served this convent well."

"That she did," Seur Tiennette said with feeling. "Would you permit me to sit with Seur Lucille this evening? She is my friend. God is requiring much suffering from her, and I believe that I must do all that I can for her before she is gone away from us."

"I see." Mère Léonie lifted one hand in benediction, though properly such a gesture was reserved for priests. "It is to your credit, Seur Tiennette."

"I do not sleep much, in any case. I might as well pass time with Seur Lucille." It was a simple admission, yet few of the other nuns would have dared to say that the night was more disruptive than day in the convent.

"We must pray for our sisters," Mère Léonie said by way of acknowledgment. "I myself spend many hours alone in meditation."

"It might be as well if you were to speak to us when there is . . . trouble." She waited for a rebuke.

"It is best, I think, if I do not dignify the nightmares and restlessness of some of our Sisters with my presence and comments." She looked directly at the older nun. "Or do you wish to correct me, Seur Tiennette?"

Faced with so direct a question, Seur Tiennette turned and fled.

Seur Marguerite was weeping when Seur Catant found her in the orchard. She looked up and managed to say, "My poor little ones," before she burst out in frantic sobs.

Seur Catant's patience had been tried to the limit. "What is it now? Are your wits wholly gone, or are you merely wandering in your memories?"

"It's . . ." Seur Marguerite could not bring herself to speak, and it was some little time until she could bring herself to explain her distress. "I heard them calling me," she said thickly. "They were all of them . . . and they have never done harm. They knew it was too late, but they wanted me to aid them. It is like the rest of us, calling to God, though it is too late and the Devil has come to us."

By this time, Seur Catant had realized that one of the hives was silent, and she stared in astonishment at the dead bees that littered the ground around it. "When did this happen?"

"Only yesterday. It was the Devil. He came and breathed on them, and that was poison to them, as it is to all mortals." She mopped her face with the sleeve of her habit.

"It may be the weather," Seur Catant suggested. "The spring has been humid, and bees do not take well to that." She remembered hearing her uncle say that many years before. "You'd better watch the other hives."

"The Devil has come here, and nothing is the same. I have seen him, fair as an angel, and he comes with ease to us, and we . . . he is like the Plague. One moment all is thriving and well, and the next all has sickened, and in time it will fade and die. I have seen it before. Never so plainly, never so brazenly."

Seur Catant stopped listening. Like the other nuns, she knew that Seur Marguerite was not right in her wits and was given to strange pronouncements and outbursts. "I must see to the grafts on the trees," she explained as she started to move away.

"They will fail, too," Seur Marguerite warned her, then wept again.

"There could be trouble, with the weather," she said. She crossed herself. "It's a sin to be cast down. That is doubt of God's love and therefore a great error." She did not want to have to beg her bread for it and shut it from her mind.

A light wind blew through the orchard, scattering petals capriciously so that they landed on Seur Catant's coif like a forgotten wreath.

At first, Seur Catant was buoyed up, and the gloom

that had closed in on her was dispersed. Then she inspected the grafts, and her apprehension returned, for where there should have been new sprouting limbs, there were only dark, brittle sticks fuzzed over at the base with rot. "Bon Dieu!" she expostulated, wrinkling her nose. "Let us hope that the others are better." She said this loudly enough so that all the trees could hear her.

Behind her, Seur Marguerite was crooning to the hives, putting her arms around the smallest and singing bits of the only song she knew, which was the threnody that had been sung in Lyon for the greater part of a year when the Plague held sway there.

Seur Catant tried to convince herself that the little petals had all been blown away, but she knew that was not the case. The orchard had been blighted, and something had to be done at once if the illness was not to spread.

Seur Ranegonde frowned at the shuttle and the broken thread trailing behind it. She had been weaving for more than two hours, and it was the fifth time her thread had broken. She drew the shuttle out of the web and looked at it closely. She ran her fingers over it slowly, searching for edges or nicks that might weaken or snap the threads. She found nothing. The end was frayed, as if the thread had simply come apart. She moistened the break with her tongue and carefully knotted the thread together again.

"Is something the matter?" Seur Adalin asked from her chair where she sat embroidering a new altar cloth.

"Oh, nothing, really." She guided the shuttle through her loom slowly, watching for any further difficulties.

"Perhaps you'd better speak to Seur Elvire and Seur Morgance; they're doing most of the spinning now." She held up her work so that the light could shine through it. "I've had some trouble with threads. And when I've dyed them, they haven't taken the color as they should."

"Mère Léonie says that we should not worry about

it. She says it is because we are indulging our sins instead of . . ." Her voice trailed off as the thread broke again.

"Instead of cleansing ourselves, as Our Lord bade us," Seur Adalin finished for her. "But Our Lord never was a weaver or a needlewoman, was he?" She gave an apologetic laugh.

"This thread is impossible!" Seur Ranegonde burst out. "No matter what I do, it breaks!"

"Can you use another spindle in your shuttle?" Seur Adalin suggested. "It may be only the one that is wrong."

Seur Ranegonde leaned back on the weaving stool and nearly overset herself. Exasperation flared, and she pulled the shuttle out of the loom and threw it at the far wall. "I will have to confess *that*," she admitted without chagrin.

"But . . ." Seur Adalin began, then stopped as she saw the redness puckering the other nun's eyes. "Go to the refectory and ask Seur Tiennette for some of that lotion to soothe your eyes."

Seur Ranegonde was about to object but could not bring herself to do so. "Perhaps you are right. The headache . . ." She started to get off the stool and was nearly overwhelmed by dizziness. "Heaven protect me."

"Seur Rane—" Seur Adalin started from her low bench.

"No!" Seur Ranegonde cut her off. "It's nothing. Just . . . the headache. You see?" She moved away from the loom. "I am better already."

Though she doubted this, Seur Adalin held her peace as she watched Seur Ranegonde make her way unsteadily out of the room.

The small company of men-at-arms that accompanied Pierre Fornault to la Tres Saunte Annunciacion were not pleased with their mission, though they did not complain directly.

Pierre made a last attempt as they reached the convent to calm them. "Listen to me. It isn't right that you should feel slighted by this work. The Pope himself has said that we are to discharge his orders here. You may receive recognition for what you do, and—"

"Fine recognition!" one of the men scoffed. "Are we to receive a vidamie for building convent doors? Will we be advanced in glory?"

"The Pope has given us orders." Pierre had a dogged attitude about the work; he liked it no more than the men he led.

"Then let God show us a little favor, a little help. Why not send an angel or two to fix the doors? These nuns are his brides, not ours. Shouldn't He protect them?" This was Ivo, who had chafed most openly at their task since it was assigned them.

"Don't let a priest hear you blaspheme that way," Pierre told him, not bothering to scold. "We have work to do. The sooner it is done, the sooner we may be rid of it." He looked up at the scarred and battered walls. The convent, to his eyes, looked more like a defeated fort than a refuge for devout women.

"They did a job on the place. I'll say that," Ivo allowed, nudging the man next to him with his elbow. "For peasants with nothing more than rocks and whips, they did a lot of damage."

"This is mild," Pierre said quietly. "You haven't seen where the church in the village was. They brought the whole building down."

This caused a momentary hush to fall over the men. Then one of the older ones braced his hands on his hips and laughed. "Surely they didn't have to go to these lengths to get at nuns, did they?"

From her post at the grille, the warder Sister—today it was Seur Victoire—listened to the men and felt her face heat.

"Isn't there supposed to be someone on duty here?" one of the men-at-arms asked.

"A warder Sister," Pierre confirmed. "I wonder . . ." He strode over to the grilled window and peered in, shading his face so that he could more easily pierce the darkness of the warder post.

"God be with you," Seur Victoire gasped out, running the words together.

"And with you, ma Seur," Pierre responded. "Will you carry a message for me to Mère Léonie?"

"I . . . I will," Seur Victoire said, wanting to bolt from the place.

"Tell her that le Duc de Parcignonne is here with men to rebuild your doors. He would like to speak with her before the labor begins." He imagined Mère Léonie coming to him, her long, clean way of walking showing the length of her leg against her habit, her light eyes like points of flame. "Ma Seur?"

Seur Victoire shook herself and nodded to the intruder. "I will d-do it," she said, abandoning her post with haste.

Pierre strolled back to his men, content to wait for Mère Léonie to come to him.

Ivo was pointing out the corner of the burned stable, saying to the others, "And doubtless we'll have to repair those as well. Do you think that will increase our glory or merely make our bodies ache? Why couldn't they send monks to do this? Why did it have to be us?" His indignation was shared by the others, and one of them spat to show his contempt.

"They sent us," Pierre answered, speaking with exaggerated precision, "because there are other heretics in this part of the country."

The men-at-arms nodded, a few of them shifting their weight uneasily. All but one of them had dismounted, but the man still on his horse reached for the hilt of the long sword slung across his back. "Let them come," he said with relish. "Anything to liven this ordeal."

"What about the Devil?" Ivo suggested. "Would you want to match blades with him, or will heretics do for you, Godellbert?"

"Either will do," Godellbert replied laconically. "I've fought Turks, and the Devil has nothing on them."

Though most of the men laughed at this, Pierre remained quiet. It troubled him that his men were restive. He had warned the Cardinal that it might happen, but his worries had been dismissed as foolish. He would have to find something more for them to do; repairing the convent would not be enough if they were to be kept from mischief.

"Pierre!" The call interrupted his thoughts, and he glanced over his shoulder to see not Mère Léonie but Seur Aungelique coming toward him from the vegetable garden. Her face was gaunt, her eyes sunken, like enormous pools hidden from the light. "Pierre! You've come!"

He folded his arms and scowled. "What sort of manner is this for a nun?"

Seur Aungelique grinned roguishly. "I need not worry about that with you, cousin," she teased. "You know that I am here under duress." She reached out and took his arm. "Have you brought word from my father? Will he let me go be a waiting woman?"

"Hush, girl," he admonished her. "There are others here."

"Well, if you don't wish her to speak, *I* will listen to her," Ivo called out, coming a little nearer. "You cannot mean to keep such a treasure to yourself."

"Curb yourself," Pierre growled. "You don't know what . . ." With an impatient grunt, he pulled himself free of Seur Aungelique's hands. "You should mind your conduct, cousin. These men are not monks and lapdogs, and you would not want to . . . fire them."

"Yes, I would. I want to fire the whole world." Seur Aungelique laughed loudly, her attitude becoming more coquettish. "I would not mind if every one of your men fell at my feet and begged to kiss me. It's better than spending half the night lying in front of the altar begging forgiveness for all the sins I wish to commit. Isn't it?" This last was a challenge, and she faced him squarely.

"For the honor of your House, Aungelique!" Pierre hissed at her. "Keep a guard on what you say."

"Why?" she taunted him. "So that you can tell my father more lies? That's what you want, isn't it?" Her accusations were hurled at him like weapons, and she was pleased to see him flinch at them. "Am I wrong, sweet cousin?"

"Not here!" he shouted at her, wanting to beat her for what she was saying.

"Not here!" she mocked him. "Because you don't want me to speak the truth?"

"Aungelique, I warn you—" He could sense the interest of his men, and it shamed him that they should witness this encounter. "Whatever you wish to say, you will wait until Mère Léonie permits us to speak privately!"

"And if she will not? You'd find that convenient, wouldn't you? You could tell my father that you wanted to have words with me but that Mère Léonie would not permit it. I refuse to be ignored by you, my good, sweet Cousin," she said venomously. "You have caused me pain and suffering and this—this *imprisonment*, and you will answer for it!"

Godellbert leaned down in his saddle. "Do you need a champion, Demoiselle?"

"Stop!" Pierre ordered him in such a dangerous voice that Godellbert backed his horse away from the duc and his strange cousin.

"Why did you do that?" Seur Aungelique demanded, and now there was a hint of despair in her voice. "Do you refuse me everything? Pierre! I feel as if I am in my grave already. My cell is a tomb."

"For God's sake, Aungelique," he protested.

"You're cruel, Pierre. You are destroying me. There are demons in the air, and you have abandoned me to them, yes. You *want* me to succumb to them so that you will be free of me. Better demons than a man of flesh; that's what you—"

"Seur Aungelique!" Mère Léonie interrupted as she came through the ruined doors.

The place was suddenly silent. Only the soft sound of the superior's sandals, like the beat of a rapid pulse, could be heard.

"Mère Léonie," Pierre began when he had recovered himself. "We were sent to you at the order of Cardinal Belroche. He wants us to see to the repair of your doors and whatever else may require it. I . . . did not know that my cousin would . . . be near."

"But you hoped, didn't you?" Seur Aungelique demanded stridently. "You cannot abide my love, but you seek me out because of it."

"Be silent, ma Seur," Mère Léonie said softly.

The look Seur Aungelique gave her superior was acidic, but she did not disobey.

"Now," Mère Léonie said, giving her attention to Pierre as if there had been no confrontation, "you say that you have been sent to help us rebuild."

"At the instruction of Cardinal Belroche and the behest of Pope Clement," he concurred. "We are also to afford you any protection you may require. We are armed and prepared to fight if we must. The Cardinal said that we are not to provoke attacks, but if such should occur, then we are to defend you and your Sisters to the death."

This was more to the liking of the men-at-arms, and they stood a little straighter at this suggestion. Ivo went so far as to salute the superior.

"Surely your men do not wish to be humble carpenters?" Mère Léonie said.

"No, they do not," Pierre admitted. "But they have been ordered to do this, and they are bound to comply."

"For fealty," Mère Léonie said, and needed no confirmation. "I am grateful that you are here, little as you wish to be." She let her eyes travel from one man to the next. "Your duties here may appear trivial to you, perhaps even demeaning? To us, you are angels of mercy."

Ivo, his color heightened, coughed once. The others were still.

"Mère Léonie," Pierre ventured when the silence again became awkward, "we must make a camp. It is not fitting that we stay too near your walls. What would you suggest we . . . ?"

She looked around. "There is the orchard, if that is to your liking, but there, beyond our vegetable and herb garden, you will be nearer the stream and at a better position, I would think, to keep watch on the convent and the road." She looked directly at Pierre. "If that is to your satisfaction, I will instruct Seur Tiennette to be sure you are fed twice a day. At Midday and in the evening, you may rely on us to fill your bellies."

Seur Aungelique gave a sound like a snort, but no words escaped her.

"We thank you for that, Mère Léonie," Pierre said, including his men with a sweep of his arm. "This afternoon we will assess what is to be done; in the evening, you and I should confer." It would provide him an opportunity to be alone with her, and he was pleased at the prospect.

"That is satisfactory. For the time being, I will leave you to your tasks." She reached out and took Seur Aungelique by the wrist. "Until this evening, then. Come, ma Seur." She permitted no opposition to this order, and it seemed to Pierre, as he watched the two women, that though both nuns walked at a sober pace, Mère Léonie was dragging Seur Aungelique back inside the walls of la Tres Saunte Annunciacion.

Comtesse Orienne was picking over the remains of a roast swan when one of her pages came into the solar. "Yes?" she said, licking the spice-flavored fat from her fingers. "What is it?"

"There is a monk to . . . a monk." He was young enough not to know what more to say. He swallowed hard and looked up at the ceiling. "He says he knows you."

"Another one of the messengers from Avignon, no doubt," la comtesse said wearily. "Well, you had better show him in and see that he is offered food and wine. If he's like most of them, he'll spurn it, but still, we must offer. Hospitality requires it, though I don't want him here any more than he wants to be here." She sighed in a languishing way.

The page bowed and went to do as his mistress ordered. In the months he had served at Une Noveautie, he had come to think that none of the tales he had heard were true and that there were no intrigues beyond amorous ones enacted within the villa's walls. Now, perhaps, he would learn otherwise. And then his masters would reward him at last for all he had done for them.

"Will la comtesse receive me?" the monk asked anxiously.

"Yes, mon Frère, she will. If you will follow me." He turned and led the way through the halls, wishing he had an excuse to ask questions of the monk.

"So," Comtesse Orienne said as the monk was escorted into the solar, "have you come for more useless answers?" She was helping herself to sweetmeats and did not look directly at the newcomer.

"I trust not, Comtesse," said the monk.

Comtesse Orienne turned at the sound of the voice, her eyes narrowing and the start of a predatory smile on her vixen's face. "Do they know you're out, ma Frèrée?"

Aungelique giggled as Orienne spoke. "By now they must. The cry will be up." She came across the room. "Is there any of that bird left? I'm famished."

Orienne reached up and pushed back Aungelique's hood in order to kiss her in welcome. "You surely look to be starving," she said as she regarded Aungelique's sunken cheeks. "What have they been doing to you?"

The page, unheeded in the door, gasped in shock, then turned quickly and left the room, thinking that this might not be the sort of information he had been sent to obtain but still could interest the men from Rome, who were so curious about what went on at Une Noveautie.

"They have been giving me vigils and fasts to drive the Devil from my flesh," Aungelique answered, gulping back laughter. "I could not bear it any longer, and so I have come to you. You will not send me away, will you?"

"No, of course I will not send you away," she promised, perplexed at the way Aungelique behaved. "You are still the defiant one, ma Frèrée?"

"Yes!" The answer was more vehement than it had been when Aungelique first stayed with her, and that vexed Orienne.

"That could be difficult," she said, indicating one of the other chairs in the room. "I will have wine brought. If this is not enough"—she indicated the remains of her meal—"then I will have them turn a capon on a spit for you and bring you white bread."

"My thanks," Aungelique said, her mouth dry one instant and wet the next. "I'm hungry. I've been hungry for months."

"You need not hunger here. There may not be much I can do for you, ma Frèrée, but you will not lack for food here." She leaned back in her chair. "What was it this time? Did they threaten to put you in a stricter Order?"

"No," Aungelique said, resisting the urge to reach out for the wing of the swan. "It was . . . many things."

Orienne was used to evasiveness and for that reason made no mention of it. She reached for a little brass bell and rang it sharply. "I will want food and drink for my friend," she told the page who answered the summons. "Bring the wine at once, and bread. And . . . yes, you had better tell the cook to put two capons on a spit with onions and apples inside them." She saw Aungelique nod eagerly at this order, which pleased her. "Bring the wine at once," she said as she waved the page away.

"I'm . . . delighted. I'm overjoyed to be here. Orienne, I have missed this place and you so much. I would dream of it as I lay before the altar, when I should have been confessing my sins and begging forgiveness for all I have done." Her giggle was high and frantic.

"We do not wish to bring the wrath of your father down on us. Now that he has been made vidame, he has taken to making a show of himself. We will have to be a bit careful of him so that he will not be able to complain to the Pope that I have debauched you." It was a real concern of hers, but more than Aungelique's father, she feared what the Cardinal might demand of her in exchange for his silence and cooperation.

"Is my father in Avignon, then?" Aungelique asked with a quick, worried glance over her shoulder, as if she feared he might be lurking behind one of the tapestries.

"He was a little while ago but not now," Orienne said, seeking to calm her guest. "It may be necessary to . . . prevaricate." She heard her page approaching. "For now, get a meal into you." She indicated what was left on the table as the page put a large earthenware decanter on the table. "Wine and food and a little rest and all will be clear to us."

Aungelique accepted the goblet of wine, taking one long draft of it.

Comtesse Orienne watched her, smiling, hiding the

feelings that filled her with a practiced courtesy. In time, she told herself, she would know how best to use her little runaway nun.

Chapter 8

In the end, it was Thibault who arrived at Une Noveautie. "Have you tired of piety, sweeting?" he asked Aungelique when he came upon her in the garden.

"I have been many things in my life," she said with a toss of her head, "but never pious."

"Perhaps; there are many sorts of piety, are there not?" He was dressed in light blue, as before, but the clothes he wore now were brighter and of better cut than the first time she had seen him. He hoisted himself onto the lip of the fountain and looked down at Aungelique. "Well, little fledgling, are you still afraid to try your wings, or have you learned to soar? A delicious morsel like you would tempt more than me, sweeting."

"Only tempt?" she inquired audaciously. She was enjoying herself as much for the risk of her words as for the attention of Thibault Col, Chevalier de Bruges. She was glad to see that he could not entirely maintain his composure, for that gave her a sense of advantage she had lacked the first time they met.

"What more would you have me do? Fall at your feet and kiss the hem of your houppelande? Sing songs in your honor? Tell me. What do you want of me?" He favored her with his charming, equivocal smile. "Or shall I tell you?"

"You don't know what I want!" His confidence stung her.

"Do I not? But that isn't enough, is it? You burn, and your burning only feeds the fire—isn't that so?" He held out his hand, and Aungelique surprised herself by putting her own into his. "Your veins are alive with desires you cannot name. Aren't they? And your flesh reels and aches as if you had been beaten. Do you deny it?"

Aungelique's eyes had grown huge. "How do you know these things? Who told you?"

"No one needed to tell me; it's writ in your glance, in the way you walk. Haven't you wanted someone to see this in you? When you pray for God to aid you, do you not imagine a lover, not a father or brother?" He let go of her hand. "Or cousin?"

"You!" Aungelique flushed deeply and turned away.

"Will you leave me, sweeting?" His voice was still light and teasing, but under it there was something more, a power that caught and held Aungelique as surely as if the fragrant garden were the deepest pit.

"You've . . . said—"

"Have I been cruel? But lovers are cruel, aren't they? Isn't that what the troubadours sang all those years ago? What lover had not suffered for love?" In a supple, feline movement, he came down from the fountain and sauntered toward her. "Isn't that what you wish to do, to suffer for love and cause others to suffer?"

"Not . . . only that." She stared at him, caught by his insinuating force.

"What more, then?" He came up to her, mockery in his light-colored eyes. "Or shall I guess again?"

She put out her hand as if to fend him off. "No. Don't guess." She no longer wanted to match wits with him, for she knew he would toy with her mercilessly.

He cupped her chin in his long, slender hand. "Sweeting, I am willing to gratify your desires; you have only to ask." Quickly, he bent, brushing her lips with his own, then released her and stepped back. "Or do you prefer your convent, after all, and your cell, where you may have your dreams and not be bothered with awkward bodies that grunt and sweat at Venus' work?"

"That's not so," she said, not looking at him.

"Isn't it? When you sleep alone here? When you leap like a startled hare at my touch? Would it be otherwise if I were le Duc Pierre? Or is he only another dream you keep?"

"You are wrong! I will have lovers, and they will . . . they will adore me." Her jaw was set, and she wanted nothing more than to be left alone.

Her tormentor smiled again. "Adore you? Like a monk before the plaster statues of the saints, no doubt. Ah, little fledgling, if it is adoration you seek, then so be it." He bowed deeply and started away from her.

"Wait!" she cried, to her own amazement.

He slowed a little. "Why?"

"I must . . ."

"Yes?" He was still now, gazing at her with disconcerting intensity.

"I do not want to be a nun. I want to live my life as Comtesse Orienne lives hers."

Thibault's smile was almost a sneer. "Why?"

"Because . . . because she is free!" Aungelique declared.

"Free." Thibault laughed. "Do you think her life is less constrained than yours? Poor Aungelique! You think that because this cloister has silken cushions and scarlet robes it is less a prison than your convent? Comtesse Orienne has her Order and her offices just as you have. You are deceived by the trappings, little one."

"But I want . . . I want . . ." She floundered helplessly.

"What—other than rapturous dreams?" He waited, saying nothing more.

"Oh, you don't *know* what it's like!" She took a few steps toward him, then hung back. "I want . . ."

"To matter?" he suggested. "To be desired? To be possessed?"

"Yes; to be possessed. I want you . . . to desire me to madness." She liked the sound of that. "And I want you to be obsessed with me and to think only of me."

"And you? You have said what you want of me. But what of you, sweeting?" One long hand rested negligently on his hip.

"You already . . . let me . . ." Her cheeks grew bright at her thoughts.

"Very pretty. It's a shame to waste you on the convent. All those faceless, bodiless nuns. Do you feel faceless, little one? When you keep your vigil with your flesh against cold stone, do you feel bodiless?"

She stared at him. "Yes," she said when she had thought about it. "I feel that I am nothing, that I am fading away. But . . ."

"But there is your desire, isn't there? As long as the desire is there, you are not quite gone, are you?" This teasing manner of his made her more frightened than a more serious approach might. She stared down at her hands.

"There were heretics, Flagellants, who tried to break into the convent. We fought them." Her hands twisted around each other.

"Did you? And how did you feel? Were you frightened? Were you pleased?" With each question, he came nearer, stopping just two steps from her.

"Yes. Frightened, pleased, all of it. Excited. They didn't get in." She giggled abruptly. "It was . . . wonderful, pouring scalding water on them and seeing them run."

"And would you want to do it again?" Thibault's smile had changed, becoming not quite as attractive as it had been but more genuine, revealing a trace of the sort of creature he was.

"Yes. Perhaps no. I would want them to know who I am if ever they came again."

"Such ferocious thoughts, sweeting."

"Well, my father is Michau d'Ybert. We are a fierce breed." She was feeling better now and was starting to enjoy herself once more. "Think, if those heretics had been suitors, what fun it would have been to see them run and to watch for the one who would not mind the scalding water."

"And what would you do with him after he reached you?" Thibault asked, more seriously than before. "A scalded man might be angry with you. He might be a poor lover, as well."

"Does that matter? If he were angry, then I would know how strong his passion was. Let his burns press against me; let him howl with it as he takes me."

There were birds in the trees beyond the garden, and their calls drifted in, adding their magic to the scents of herbs and flowers. Sunlight, warm and potent as an alchemist's elixir, flowed over them, nearly palpable in its intensity.

"And then what?" he inquired, offering her his wrist to lead her indoors.

"Oh, doubtless I would wake up." Her eyes danced, and she achieved a charming smile as they went in out of the light.

Furiously, Pierre flung the half-full goblet across the room, where it broke, leaving a stain like the splash of blood against the stones. "By the brass balls of God, what has come over you, cousin!" he demanded as she came into the small reception room where Comtesse Orienne had made him wait.

Aungelique, dressed provocatively, her short hair dressed with wreaths of fresh flowers, opened her eyes wide in deceptive innocence. "Have I offended you, cousin?"

"Yes!" he thundered. "You know you have offended me. And your father. And your House and your Order." The scar on his face was livid with his emotion.

"All that?" she asked, finding the meeting far more interesting than she had feared it would be. "For such a little thing?"

"You ran away from the convent. You came here— *here*!—where there is nothing but license and dissipation. You flaunt yourself to those men who come to be entertained by Comtesse Orienne—"

"As she has entertained *you*, cousin," Aungelique reminded him pleasantly.

He shouted, "You're a disgrace! Your father would be justified in sending you to prison or to be an anchorite. He may still do one of those things if you do not return to la Tres Saunte Annunciacion immediately. Do you understand me?" His voice was growing even louder, and he glared at her impatiently.

"I am not minded to do so," she told him with a sly smile. "If I must live at the convent with my father's blessing or live here without it, then I will pray for him and remain here." She found Pierre's rage stimulating, the more so because she sensed that it masked a desire he could never admit.

Pierre would not touch her, or he might shake her like an ill-behaved puppy. There was, he knew, an awakening desire for her, to put an end to her taunting by bedding her. "Do you know what women do here?"

"Certainly," she said, running her finger over the little lace ruff of her houppelande. "I do them, don't I?"

"Do you!" He rounded on her, this time making her fear him. "If you are no longer a maiden, your father will disown you." He lowered his voice. "Have you truly done the act?"

She gave him a blithe smile. "Of course, cousin. You would not have me, and I have said all along I have not the vocation to be a nun. What am I to do, then? At least here there are men who find me pleasant." She gave an adept imitation of Comtesse Orienne's throaty laugh. "I have appetites, cousin. God made me a thing of passions—and not the passions of the spirit but the flesh."

"Your father could imprison you." It was said quietly. Both of them knew it was a fact.

"But he won't, not if I'm the only one he can use to barter to a husband." It was her only power against her father, and she was determined to use it to her best advantage. "Other women have had lovers before they were wives, and their husbands have married them with pride. Why shouldn't I have the same fortune? Am I so ugly or so ancient that no man could regard me with favor?"

"That's not in question," Pierre admitted, his anger reasserting itself.

"Then what is? If I am not a nun, if I were a lady-in-waiting instead, the woman I served would set the tone of my morals, and cousin, no matter what my nature, I would abide by what my mistress wished." This was a more dangerous ploy, for it might be all the impetus Pierre needed to recommend to Michau d'Ybert that his daughter be placed in confinement.

"You don't realize what you are saying," Pierre protested. "You play at games you do not understand."

Aungelique moved closer to him. "Then teach me, cousin. Do not fight with me; teach me what I must know, or let me be wanton as God made me." She put her hand on his shoulder and was not dissatisfied when he brushed it away.

"You must stop this . . . nonsense," Pierre ordered her, but without real conviction. "You must school yourself to be obedient and biddable."

"But why?" She waited, and when he did not speak, she went on. "I have said that I will be obedient at court. I have said that I would marry a suitable man. I wish for lovers, many lovers, but I will forego that if my father will get a dispensation—surely his vidamie has *some* merit—that would permit us to marry." She saw the confusion in his eyes and pressed on. "You do not burn for me. But there are those who do. I will be satisfied with them."

"Aungelique, you're not thinking clearly."

She brought up her chin. "Nor are you. Oh, for le Bon Dieu, do not try me too far, or I will run away to Rome and sate myself with those servants of the Devil who rule there."

He knew her well enough to realize that she was capable of such a monumental disgrace, and so he responded cautiously to her threat. "That would be unwise, Aungelique. No matter what Baron Michau wished in his heart to do, he would have to cast you out of his heart for the honor of his House. And once he had cast you out, you would have no recourse left but to be the playing toy of those Romans, and your end would not be kind." He felt compassion for Aungelique as he explained this, but he could not be open with her; his honor as much as his desire made it impossible.

"He has cast me out of his heart already," Aungelique countered. "He takes no pride in me. He is a stern man, and they tell me he is just, but I do not see justice in what he has done to me."

"You're his daughter, and a willful one at that. You

would not think he was just unless he married you to the emperor of the East or Prester John." He set his feet apart, his thick legs, like tree trunks, holding up the mass of his torso. "You think you know what it is to be filled with passion, but you do not recognize it in your father, who has more passion for the glory of his House than half the kings in Spain. It is not passion that consumes you, Aungelique; it is lust and pride, and for that alone you will suffer in hell unless you purge them from your soul."

"If I am those things," she said, not bothering to check her anger, "then heaven has given them to me."

"The Devil has given them to you!" he shouted.

She turned on her heel and was about to leave the room when she decided to make one more offer. "I have thought of something. Let me propose this: that my father disown me entirely and declare that I am without family, and then I will not be a shame for him. I could live as I wish, then, and my father would not have to bear with what I do or how I do it." She shrugged. "It's simple, isn't it?"

"You've run mad," Pierre said with conviction. "You are not some peasant's bitch that can be turned out in the fields to run wild." He pointed at her. "I'll make a bargain with you, girl. You will return to that convent, and you will remain there for the next three months. I will speak to your father, and I will do my utmost to persuade him to reconsider. If he will not, then I will speak to the Cardinal and ask that he find a suitable court for you to enter. My oath upon it."

"But you won't ask for a dispensation to marry me, will you?" She flung this at him like a gauntlet. "You'd rather see me lost to the Devil entirely than your wife."

"God's nails, will you let be? Even if I wished to, I could not obtain that dispensation." He fell silent, studying her. "Well? Will you accept my offer?"

She considered it. "What is to keep my father from ordering me into prison while I wait at the convent?"

"Oh, come, Aungelique," he said, almost losing his patience with her again. "Your father does not want bad blood with me. He will accept my oath as his own, or he will lose my men-at-arms, and he knows it." He hesitated. "It is not a very long time, Aungelique. Won't you accept that in exchange for the life you say you are made for?"

Aungelique wanted to give him a sharp reply, but that would not permit her to gain his favor again. She rubbed her chin in unthinking imitation of her father. "For three months. If there is any attempt to deny me at the end of that time, I will run away to Rome. I swear it on the blood of God."

Pierre nodded, shocked by the depth of her feeling. "Three months. That is all."

"Yes, all." She offered her hand for him to touch. "My word is as binding as yours. Remember that, Pierre." Then she added a last proviso. "Since I am doing this at your behest, I want proper escort back to la Tres Saunte Annunciacion. Three men-at-arms and a driver for the wagon." It was tempting to ask for something more. "I will want another two days here. I have told la comtesse that I will attend her entertainment tomorrow night. It is not fitting that I decline her invitation, as she has housed me."

"That's reasonable," he said, being careful to say nothing that might cause her to do something capricious. "I will inform Orienne that I will be here, as well."

That made Aungelique frown, but she said nothing more than "It will be her choice if you do attend."

"I understand that," he said, knowing full well that Orienne would not refuse him as long as he was obligated to ask her about men from Rome. "If she declines, I will find other hosts."

Aungelique shrugged, thinking that she must find Thibault and persuade him to dance attention on her while Pierre was about. It was time her cousin saw that other men did not find her as repugnant as he appeared to. "Then it is settled," she said to him and to herself.

"It is settled." He touched her hand properly, inclined his head but did not kneel, then almost swaggered from the room, more relieved than he had been in days.

* * *

Père Guibert looked at Seur Philomine in amazement. "How is it that Mère Léonie has given such instruction?"

"She was so cast down by Seur Aungelique's leaving," Seur Philomine explained carefully, "that she has spent her time in her cell in prayer and meditation. None of us has seen her since Seur Aungelique disappeared." She folded her hands and looked down at them, concentrating on the way her fingers interlaced. "She has said that she is to blame, and for that she must seek to make amends for her sin and for her failure to be the mother to us that she has promised to be. She has chastised herself for dereliction. She says that Our Lord does not wish to have his nest unguarded."

"Commendable," Père Guibert muttered, wanting to know more. He paced through the courtyard, paying no attention to the mule he had ridden to the convent. "It may be," he said when he had given the matter some thought, "that in caring so much for the one, she is neglecting the many, and for that she will have more sins upon her head."

Seur Philomine knew that she could neither agree nor disagree without offending the priest. "Mère Léonie mentioned the Prodigal Son before she closed her door."

"That's entirely different. If that difficult child were not the daughter of Michau d'Ybert, I should have recommended that she be released from her vows more than a year ago." It was wrong of him to say this, but his temper was growing short.

Seur Philomine went and took the reins of the mule. "I will put him in the stable and see that he is fed. Unless you require something more of me?"

"No, no. You're right, Seur Philomine." He started toward the inner door, then turned back to her. "How does Seur Lucille do?"

"Alas, her hurts were too grievous. God called her and ended her suffering." Inwardly, Seur Philomine could not bring herself to grieve, not after she had tended the nun, whose pain could not be eased even with syrup of poppies and whose flesh had mortified beyond all healing.

"God is good," Père Guibert said, crossing himself. "We will have special prayers for her tonight." He paused. "Did Mère Léonie . . ."

Seur Philomine guessed his meaning. "Seur Tiennette made the preparations, and Seur Elvire led the Mass for her soul."

It was not proper that any nun should do this, but after the Plague had taken so enormous a toll, the Church had become lax in these matters. "I will say another mass," Père Guibert informed her.

"Deo gratias," Seur Philomine murmured, and led the mule away.

Père Guibert shook his head as he entered the corridor leading to the chapel. He had thought there would be trouble with Seur Aungelique again and had been confident that Mère Léonie was resigned to problems, as well. Now he discovered that the superior was secluded from guilt and the convent had been left to tend to itself. He paused at the entrance to the chapel, looking down at the prostrate form of Seur Marguerite.

The nun was praying, but at the sound of approaching steps, she paused. Without turning, she said, "For the love of God, ma Seur, let me finish before you begin your devotions. My children are dying, and God does not save them."

"Dying?" Père Guibert asked, uncertain what Seur Marguerite meant.

"They come to their hives, and they fall around them. The orchards are empty, and my children . . . God must hear me. It is cruel and wrong to do this, for they are harmless, my children, and they do nothing that is evil or harmful." She made the sign of the cross and wept bitterly.

Père Guibert stood still, feeling slightly foolish and inadequate. His expression was harsh because of his confusion, which caused Seur Victoire to think that the priest was angry with Seur Marguerite when she came to the chapel a few moments later.

"Mon Père," she said when she decided that it was all right to speak.

He was grateful for the interruption. "Yes, ma Fille?"

"Seur Tiennette has been told of your arrival and begs a few words with you as soon as you are free to speak with her."

"I will come at once," he said, hoping that he would learn more of what had caused Mère Léonie to shut herself away from her sisters in this fashion.

"We have been . . . puzzled," Seur Victoire admitted to Père Guibert as they hurried toward the refectory. "Mère Léonie is new, of course, but there has been so much bustle here since she came to us that . . ." Seur Victoire withdrew her hands from the sleeves of her habit to give a gesture of helplessness.

"She is still unknown." It was not appropriate for him to speak in this way of the superior to one of her nuns, but his aggravation had been increasing steadily.

"Well, certainly to some of the Sisters. She isn't French, and that troubles a few of us." She paused, then said, "All of us are worried for Seur Aungelique. Mère Léonie is not the only one who prays for her."

They had reached the refectory door. "I am sure that each of you knows her duty," Père Guibert said, not eager to hear of this woman's piety.

"Seur Tiennette is waiting," Seur Victoire announced, standing away from the door so that Père Guibert could enter on his own.

"My thanks," Père Guibert said as he went into the large, whitewashed room, wishing he had never left Mou Courbet or Fôrlebene.

His kisses were quick and eager but light, and when she reached to hold him, he stepped out of range and laughed. "Oh, sweeting, are you always so impetuous?"

Two bladderpipes and a hurdy-gurdy thrummed and bleated in the room beyond their retreat, and there was an occasional outburst of laughter.

"Speak softly," Aungelique ordered with a swift

glance back toward the brightness of the great hall at Une Noveautie.

"They are listening to the music and watching the mummers. They would not notice if ten naked satyrs pranced down the halls." Thibault looked around the cozy withdrawing room.

Aungelique thought of Pierre, who had been glowering at her throughout the evening, and she shuddered at the thoughts his presence conjured. "Let us only be silent."

"And what else?" Thibault inquired, coming toward her again. "Are you still in search of possession, fledgling?"

She reached out and seized his hand. "Thibault, there will be three long months when all I will do is pray and fast and keep vigils. I would rather feast and love, but it will not happen in the convent. Cannot you help me to have something to remember that will comfort me while I lie on the cold stones and recite prayers?"

His long, slender hands slid over her breasts and cupped them through the beautiful damask of her surcote. "Something like this, perhaps?" His thumbs rubbed her nipples quickly, lightly. "Well?"

Aungelique breathed faster as she felt her nipples harden and grow taut. At the base of her spine, something quivered, something like an itch but warmer.

"There are things I could do to you, sweeting, if your cousin were not here. I could take off your clothing until you were bare as a nymph. Would it please you to give me kiss for kiss and touch for touch?" In the darkness, his ice-blue eyes shone, lit by the distant scented braziers.

"Ah . . . more," Seur Aungelique moaned, fascinated by his voice as much as the intent of his words. "Go on."

He kissed her again, still without passion. "What would you want then? You are not a ewe to be covered by a ram for three heartbeats and released, are you?" His teeth nipped the lobe of her ear.

"N-no." She leaned against him, hoping that the

pressure of her body would banish his light-handed control.

"Then what would you wish? Hours of caresses that the Turks have learned for their luxury?" He had moved his hands, and now they slid down her sides to the top of her thighs and back up, hardly touching her but inflaming her as they went.

"Turks," she whispered, not knowing what she said.

"Or is your desire greater than that? Sweeting? Can you tell me?" He kissed her deeply once, then stepped back, taking hold of her wrists. "Come. The mummers are nearly finished, and Pierre is going to start searching for you."

"No. Not yet!" she wailed softly. She could barely bring herself to move; her excitement was intolerable.

"Later, sweeting? In three months, perhaps?" He flicked her cheek with one finger. "Think about me while you are away, will you not, sweeting?" Without waiting for an answer, he led her back into the great hall just as the mummers presented their last tableau.

Pale, her icy eyes intense, her habit impeccably neat, Mère Léonie emerged from her self-imposed isolation the morning after Père Guibert arrived. She entered the refectory where the sisters had gathered to break their fasts after morning prayers, taking her place at the center of the central table as if nothing had happened.

The nuns stared, and one or two of them murmured to others, but for the most part they were silent as Père Guibert intoned the blessing.

"Seur Adalin will read from the Scriptures today," Mère Léonie announced when the prayers were finished. She looked around the room. "You may all rejoice with me; I know that Seur Aungelique will return to us soon."

This time there was a buzz of conversation that Père Guibert halted as he stared hard at Mère Léonie.

"Have you had a message? Why was I not informed of it?" His voice was too high, and he knew he ought not to be curt, but he had more than enough to cope with in the last day and was not minded to tolerate any more from these Sisters.

"The messenger was from Our Lord," Mère Léonie said serenely. "It has been given to me to see her return, and for that I am especially grateful, for her return gives strength to Our Lord."

"You do not know it was a true vision. If it is not, you stand in great danger of heresy and apostasy, ma Fille," Père Guibert informed her testily.

"It is the truth. The other time when Seur Aunge-lique was gone, I kept to my cell and prayed, and she came back." She had already picked up the portion of cheese that was part of the breakfast.

"And if she does not return, what then?" Père Guibert asked, unwilling to give up his objections.

"Then I will pray again until she is with us once more." She turned to Seur Adalin. "Read, ma Seur, from the Book of Judith, and do not stop until you are instructed to do so."

"It is beneficial to hear holy words," Père Guibert declared, and the nuns prepared to listen while they ate their bread and cheese in silence.

One of the fat-tailed ewes had stopped suckling her lambs, so Seur Philomine had taken it upon herself to try to save the baby sheep. Twice a day she would venture into the field where the sheep grazed and would present the lamb with a rag protruding from an old wine crock that had been filled with milk. So it was that she was the first to see the escorted wagon turn away from the main road and approach la Tres Saunte Annunciacion. She faltered in her task, almost dropping the wine crock, then, in response to the lamb's demanding bleat, once again held the crock at the proper angle.

The little cavalcade drew up at the main gates, and one of the knights dismounted so that he could approach the grille and speak to the warder Sister. Seur Philomine narrowed her eyes, trying to see more clearly. The figures were too distant for her to recognize the devices on the cotes that covered their armor, but it was plain that the wagon belonged to the church, for the arms of Avi-

gnon and the Pope were emblazoned on the hangings
that concealed the passenger from prying eyes. As Seur
Philomine watched, the doors, newly repaired and refit-
ted and glistening with wax, were opened, and the
mounted men passed inside, the wagon following
them.

At her side, the lamb butted her hip, eager for more
of the milk. Dutifully, Seur Philomine finished her feed-
ing of the lamb before she started back to the convent,
her thoughts caught up in speculation about the new arrival.

Many of the Sisters had left their chores and come
to the courtyard, all wondering what the occasion of the
visit might be.

"It is Seur Aungelique," Seur Catant said without
much enthusiasm. "Mère Léonie said she'd come back."

"But why?" Seur Elvire asked. "There are others
who might choose to come here. It is not only Seur
Aungelique who has reason to—"

"And under escort. It is her baron-and-vidame father, you may be sure of that," Seur Catant announced.

Seur Morgance shook her head slowly. "It is wrong
to make too much of this," she told the others, who paid
her no heed.

"They bring the Devil," Seur Marguerite warned
them all. "The Devil is here, but he is sleeping. Now he
will be roused and will walk among us. My children are
dying because the Devil has breathed upon them, as he
breathed upon others and they fell from the Plague."

"By la Virge Marie!" Seur Catant hissed, reaching
over and pinching Seur Marguerite's upper arm. "Let it
wait!"

Père Guibert was late, coming into the courtyard
after most of the Sisters had already got there, and he
had to elbow his way through the nuns to reach the men-
at-arms. "I give you welcome; may God give you His
blessings."

"And to you, mon Père," said the officer, who had
been the first to dismount. "We are men-at-arms to le
duc de Parcignonne, and he has mandated us on his authority and the authority of Cardinal Belroche to deliver

one of your sisters to you." He touched his visor, then knelt for a benediction.

In an abstracted way, Père Guibert pronounced the phrases expected of him, though his mind was more taken up by the wagon, which had still not been opened. "Mon Chevalier, will you tell me who it is you bring to us in this way?"

"The cousin of le duc, who is one of this order," he answered properly as he rose from his knee. "I have been given the honor of providing her escort."

"Excellent," Père Guibert said faintly.

The nuns were conversing quite openly now that it had been confirmed that their superior had been correct, after all. Seur Victoire shook her head and said pointedly that it might be better if Seur Aungelique were to go away again, and a few of the others agreed with her. Only Seur Adalin objected. "She kept her vigils and fasts, and she was determined in the defense of the convent. We should thank God that she has been delivered to us safely."

"*If* she has," Seur Catant sneered. "Père Guibert has not heard her confession."

"Would the Cardinal provide her this wagon if she had lost her chastity?" Seur Elvire asked, addressing no one in particular.

"What matter chastity when your father is a baron?" Seur Catant countered.

"You will beg your bread for that malice," Seur Adalin told her.

The curtain was drawn back, and Seur Aungelique, in an enveloping and demure houppelande of dark gray wool, stepped out, her eyes lowered and her manner restrained.

Père Guibert helped her down and lifted his brows in surprise when she knelt for his blessing. "You are welcome, ma Fille."

"Deo gratias, mon Père," she responded softly. She was enjoying her little charade but knew it would pall soon.

There was another flurry of disruption as Mère Léonie came from the convent. Her handsome features were unusually cheerful as she caught sight of Seur Aungelique. "Ah. You *are* back."

"Mère Léonie said she knew you would return," Seur Elvire offered. "We did not know it . . . would be so soon." This lame ending was not what she had had in mind to say, but prudence dictated modification.

"Did you?" Seur Aungelique asked, looking at Mère Léonie in some surprise.

"Yes. Our Lord revealed this to me."

At the back of the courtyard, near the passageway to the stables, Seur Philomine stared at the gathering. It was not her Sisters that held her attention or the wagon or Seur Aungelique but one of the men-at-arms. She took hold of the crucifix that hung from her belt as if it would lend her support.

He was standing on the lowered steps of the wagon, reaching for the small chest Seur Aungelique had brought with her. Then, as he held out the chest to one of the other men-at-arms, he stopped, as if he had heard his name called. He scanned the faces of the nuns, seeing little more than wimples, gorgets, and coifs. And then his eyes met Seur Philomine's and held with the strength of Damascus steel. Distractedly, he released the chest and climbed slowly down from the wagon.

Seur Philomine remained where she was, knowing that he would come to her now that he had found her. How absurd that they should meet again, he in his armor, she in her habit, each disguised from the other. She wanted to tear off the restrictive headgear and remove the habit, don scarlet and samite, and run with him through the fields, away from the convent and his battles, so they might live as they wished to live.

Mère Léonie was inviting Seur Aungelique to enter the convent again, and as the nuns gathered around her, Père Guibert indicated to the leader of the men-at-arms that their horses should be taken to the stables.

Seur Philomine swung around and all but ran to the stables, knowing that in a moment, Tristan Courtenay, Sieur de Giraut, would follow her and they would be together once more.

Chapter 9

Moonlight stretched its pale fingers through the orchard, touching the man and woman who walked there. One should have been keeping watch, and the other should have been keeping vigil, but neither of them cared. It had been too long, and there was not time enough for all the phrases and courteous words that another might have demanded; they could not let their opportunity be lost on emptiness.

"Then why did you accept the veil?" Tristan asked, his dark blue eyes black as the night as he looked down into her face.

Philomine had removed her gorget, wimple, and coif, letting her fawn-brown hair curl around her face. "What else was there to do? I did not want to be a charge upon my House when I had no intention of agreeing to any match but you. It was not honorable in me to stay with them. Here I would do something . . ." She let her words trail away.

"But what?" he prompted her.

"Give food to travelers, minister to their hurts, tend their animals." She shrugged. "I have taken only tertiary vows, my dearest dear." She put her hand on his arm, glad that now all he wore was a short Flemish houppelande instead of a surcote with armor beneath it.

"Oh, Philomine." He stood still, hearing the movement of the wind in the grasses and the faint scratching of the trees as branches and twigs were jostled by the breeze. "There has never been a day when you have not been in my thoughts." He paused. "I did not expect that. It may be that the fires are banked, but they only burn hotter." He made no apology for his language, as he might have with another, for he thought of himself as a man-at-arms, not a poet.

In words that were half melody, Philomine said, "I will never forget; how green the grass was outside the window where we met." She laughed once, gently and freely. "I have wanted to make a song of it, but try as I will, I can find no more words."

"The grass was green," he agreed, and opened his arms to her embrace.

They were silent for a time, content to stand that way, knowing only their nearness.

"You," Philomine whispered at last. "You are what is real. And all the rest is . . . so much smoke. To have you here—oh, my cherished love—is so sweet it is almost unendurable." Her arms held him more fiercely. "Everything else is shadows; you are the sun."

He kissed the corner of her mouth very briefly, but he did not let her go. "What of God, Philomine?"

"God, the Devil, they are just other shadows, less than the women I see every day. I touch them, I hear them, I see them, but it means only that they are there and they speak. Your memory is ten times more vivid than that, and to be with you . . . I am whole." Their mouths touched.

"Don't speak of it," he said when he could speak again. "It's frightening."

Her fingers pressed his lips. "No, never frightening. How could this frighten?" She never thought of herself as a bold woman—often she held back in the presence of others and had always been known for her good sense and modest demeanor. What drove her now was more than the intense hunger of her body to know him, the salt of him, the weight of him, but to reach his soul.

The way her breast curved was profound knowledge to his hands, a thing to be treasured more than the heft of a worthy sword.

The night was chill enough to make them gather their discarded clothes around them as they lay under the trees. In the clover and long grasses, they welcomed one another, discovering the limitless delight in caresses and kisses, in looks that pierced the soul; each one different and complete while leading to other joys more fulfilling.

No hesitation marred their union; no lingering fear of intrusion or betrayal or shame held them back. They were as graceful as creatures of the sea, carried together as the tide carried waves to the shore, an exaltation that neither had known. Philomine held Tristan on her, within her, caught in the rhythm of his love. Soft, joyous cries like the call of night birds came from her to blend with unexpected laughter.

They lay joined long after their first passion was spent, murmuring loving, senseless words, savoring the way their emotions and their senses met and blended with all the intensity of their flesh.

"And tomorrow?" he asked her as the resurgence of his need made her quiver.

"Hush."

"I'll take you with me." He wanted to say it before the words were gone again from his mind. "I should have . . ."

Her fingers trailed over his arm. "You would feud with my father for life, should you take me. Do you want that?"

"No," he said, so quietly that she had to move even closer to hear him. "But if it were necessary, then . . ."

"Don't. I want no death touching us. That's for tomorrow, my ever dearest. Tomorrow is a shadow. You are all the world right now, and nothing is . . ." She did not finish, kissing him instead, rousing herself through his desire.

"Philomine."

Her mouth stopped her name; fingers, lips, a length of leg, the bend of elbow and knee, the rise of hip, each in turn glistened with moonlight and ecstasy in the new-leaved orchard.

It was nearly dawn. They sat together, their clothes draped over shoulders so that they might touch a little longer. Both were pale and tired—both were so exhilarated that sleep would have been impossible.

"Let me take you with me when I leave," Tristan

said for the third time that night. "I will petition the king to permit the marriage, and even your father must bow to that."

"But would he?" She shook her head. "It is worse since the Plague took my brothers and uncles from him. He rages like a caged lion for the glory he has missed and the battles he will be denied."

"But you are no nun," he protested as he tweaked the soft curls by her ear.

"No," she agreed. "I have no vocation. I was and will remain a tertiary Sister." She reached to touch his face. "You are what I worship. You are my deity."

"That's blasphemous. Or heresy." He said it automatically, but the words meant nothing to him, not as he said them.

"If it is, then amen to it. Why should I give my life to shadows when you are here?"

He took her hands in his. "You say that and will not come with me?"

Their eyes met. "Can you ask that, knowing the trouble that would come?" She rested her head on his shoulder in order to continue touching him. "You would hate me for that in time. Not at the first, perhaps, but eventually they would insist, and you would have to decide what to do. I would follow you anywhere, Tristan, Tristan, but I will not go home with you."

"Then I will leave France. There are places a man-at-arms can find work and princes who will offer good money and advancement for a skilled sword arm."

It was true enough, and both of them knew it. "It is wrong to turn away from your House and blood," she reminded him, but with a lack of conviction. "Promise me, Tristan, for the sake of loving me, don't act quickly."

"We've waited too long already," he said, bending to nuzzle her neck.

"We may wait a bit longer if it means that we will not part," she told him, the plan that had been shapeless an instant before now taking form in her mind. "We might find a way so that no one need suffer and you need not carry the weight of your father's curse along with my love."

"How?" He said it more sharply than he had intended, and she gave him a startled glance at his abruptness.

"Your House must be secure. The opposition to my House is too strong to be overcome by a marriage contract. Therefore, there must be another to succeed you, one that your father approves. Let him find a man-at-arms, a worthy man, to adopt as his heir and settle you with—"

"As if I were his bastard?" This time he was not gentle. His dark blue eyes turned darker, and his face was heated.

"Is that too much?" she asked sadly. "If it is, then I will be content to remain here."

He laughed in a harsh outburst. "You mean that this would be enough for you?"

"If it is all that we will have, then it must be enough. I cannot poison it with wanting more than we could have. It would be too bitter a price, my dearest." She looked down in confusion, trying to find another way to explain herself.

"No, Philomine," he murmured, the anger gone out of him. He drew her close against him and felt her tears on his shoulder. "Do not weep, my only love. Do not weep."

They kissed slowly, tenderly, shutting out all the hurt that the world gave them. Their faces were alive with longing and anguish at the need to part. It was terrible to have to leave, more terrible to be separated.

"I will make myself a bastard," Tristan vowed to Philomine in a whisper. "I will find someone—a nephew, a cousin, anyone acceptable—and I will step aside, taking whatever portion my father will grant me."

"I will wait for you and never forget this." Her lips brushed his. "I will tell my father only that I must leave since I have not discovered a vocation." She pulled on her habit, reluctant to let it come between them. "There are birds singing in the trees already. The Sisters will gather for prayers shortly, and I must be with them or risk answering the superior's questions."

To relieve the gloom that descended on him as he

watched her dress, Tristan asked, "Is she very strict, this superior?"

Philomine shrugged as she tightened her hempen belt and attached her rosary to it. "She has caused much excitement with some of the sisters, but I don't know why. She is capable enough, I suppose, but to hear Seur Victoire or Seur Aungelique speak of her, you would think she came directly from la Virge or the Devil."

"And what does she make of this?" Tristan inquired as he tugged on his soft chemise.

"Who can say?" Philomine answered, grateful to have this to speak of instead of their good-byes. "She is a cipher, that one, shaping her mood and her ways to those who are in her company, or so it seems to me."

"And the others?" He was pulling on his belt and checking the heft of his small sword now, his mind more on the details of dressing in the predawn half-light than on what Philomine said. He wanted to hear the sound of her voice, though all she said was children's songs.

"I don't know. It is strange that she would be so . . . flexible and still be thought rigid by many of the Sisters." With one hand, she smoothed her hair back, and with the other, concealed it beneath the coif. She was Seur Philomine once again, little as she liked it.

"You haven't got it all," Tristan said gently, coming up to her and tucking one trailing bit of hair under the coif. "There."

She pressed herself to him. "Do not be too long, Tristan. I will wait as long as I must—all my life, should it come to that. Yet if it must take time, let it take as little as possible."

"It will be soon. I don't think I can endure much more waiting. Philomine, do not think the less of me."

"Never," she promised him, kissing the corner of his mouth while he held her tightly. "I must go," she reminded him a bit later. "The bells will sound shortly, and I must be where they can find me then, or . . ."

His arms released her, though it was an effort to do so. "Shall I walk back with you?"

Seur Philomine shook her head. "No. The warder Sister might see us, and then it would be difficult for you as well as for me." She was trying to think of a way to account for the grass stains that she knew were on her pale gray habit. "It would be too awkward."

"As you wish, treasured one." He touched her shoulder, trying not to hold her back, yet wanting to keep her with him. "One day you will not have to answer that summons anymore."

"I pray that it is soon," she said with a half-turn toward him.

"You pray, after what you confessed to me?" It was not outrage but mirth that made him ask.

"You are real; the rest is shadows. Who better for me to pray to?" With this outrageous admission, she broke away from him and hurried away toward the tall convent walls, regretting every step she took.

"It is the Devil who does this to you," Seur Catant said to Seur Aungelique as she waited outside the cell door.

Seur Aungelique moaned and tugged at her dampened shift. "I am . . . loved," she insisted. "I am being taken in love."

It was wrong for a nun to sneer. Seur Catant was well aware of it; she compromised with a severe scowl. "There is only your lustful thought to blame for this, Seur Aungelique. If it were up to me, I would order you to leave this convent and the order so that your disgrace would not bring dishonor on your Sisters."

"You are jealous," Seur Aungelique said shrewdly. "There is no one who seeks to take what lies between your thighs, and you are angry that there are those who burn for me."

"No nun would wish to have any burn for her. You bring peril to all of us by your confession."

"Then where is God, to bring me to His forgiveness?" Seur Aungelique taunted her. She was half-off the cot where she slept, her shift sticking to her where sweat had moistened it. "All of you pretend that you have forgotten or never wanted the love that God made me to seek."

"Be silent," Seur Catant rejoined, wanting to be rid

of the other woman entirely. "You must not speak to me."

"Why not?" Finally, Seur Aungelique was enjoying herself. "Don't you wonder what it is like to have a demon come to you, to enter your flesh with a member the size of a log of wood? Don't you long for that pain?"

"Be silent!" Seur Catant shrieked, stepping back from the cell door. "You have been overcome by the Devil! You are infected by him, as those with the Plague are infected!"

Seur Aungelique laughed, shaking her head so that her hair swung free of its confining wimple. "Listen to you, you demented old crone. You are nothing more than a husk, and not even the Devil can fill you." She leaned back against the wall and began methodically to tear the neck of her shift so that her breasts were visible. "You bring Mère Léonie. I want to hear what she says when you tell her that you do not want the Devil to violate your virginity. Do you think the Father and Son will take turns with you, the way the Flagellants did with the nuns they caught outside of Mou Courbet? Hum?" She tore the shift the rest of the way so that it hung open to the hem at her ankles. "You have dugs as flat as an empty wineskin. I have something to offer a man."

"And you give it to the Devil!" Seur Catant burst out, then spun around and fled down the hall, shouting for Mère Léonie to come at once.

Smiling, Seur Aungelique lay back and began to sing the bawdiest song she had heard while she was at Une Noveautie. She had gotten to the fourth chorus when she was interrupted by hurrying steps in the hall. "Who comes, then?" she called out, and then went back to the outrageous lyrics.

Mère Léonie stood in the door, straight as a soldier, her pale eyes burning down at Seur Aungelique. "You have fallen again."

"Call it what you like," Seur Aungelique responded insolently. "Last night there was a lover with me who filled me and made me abase myself for his pleasure."

"Did he?" Her voice was severe. "And you forgot all that you have promised to God and la Virge, and you gave yourself to vice and sin."

"He is beautiful, a man made of beauty, a splendid man," Seur Aungelique said in a singsong tone. "He is slight, and his face is soft. His eyes are light, almost as light as yours, and his hair is pale as the light of the moon. He is carved from ice, and he burns cold as the stars." She pulled open her torn shift to show the bruises that markered her. "He did this to me, my Thibault did, and he will do it again, and worse, before he is through with me."

"Beg Our Lord to take you in," Mère Léonie said with increasing sternness. "In the meantime, I do not care that you wish to remain here. You will keep your vigil as you have been told to do, and you will go and confess your sins, no matter how heinous, to Père Guibert. You will beg your bread and water from your Sisters, whom you have offended most deeply. Is that understood, or must I be more plain."

"You are plain. You have a boy's face, not one that a woman would wish for. And nuns are the only ones whom you will hear call you Mère. No children will come from your womb."

"That is so, but it is the wish of Our Lord that this be so," Mère Léonie said with odd satisfaction. "You have decided that you must be debauched instead of taking the salvation offered to you. But not until Père Guibert hears from your lips your desire to leave this Order and the protection of this house."

"I have said that from the beginning," Seur Aungelique insisted.

"And there is also your father to consider. At the first chance, I will personally send a message to him begging that he grant us the right to send you away from us, into the world, where the Devil cannot reach us."

Once again, Seur Aungelique had to laugh. "The Devil is here. He is everywhere, and you are mad to think otherwise. You should keep bees with Seur Marguerite, not sing the praises of God." She wriggled out of her shift and held out the torn cloth to Mère Léonie. "See? I cast off the habit the same way, as if it were my shroud."

"You are being foolish," Mère Léonie remarked with more heat than before.

Seur Aungelique was examining the bruises on her abdomen. "Do you think that he will make me with child? Do you think that a child of his get will bruise me as much, kicking in my womb? Do you?"

"If that is what you want, then doubtless it will be what the Devil gives you," Mère Léonie said harshly, starting away from the door. "You will be confined here until morning. You will come on your hands and knees, naked as you are, to beg a crust of bread and a cup of water from your Sisters, who will be told not to speak to you. That is how it will be until you confess."

"Until I confess?" Seur Aungelique demanded with another burst of derision. "I do not confess anything. I take pride in being as God made me, and I will not defile His handiwork with false repentance. If I am to be the plaything of the Devil, it is His plan to make me such. Have you no answer to that, Mère Léonie?"

The superior studied Seur Aungelique, her face like a mask of saintly acceptance. "If Our Lord intends you to be an example to the Sisters here, then we must learn from you, I suppose.

As the door closed on her, Seur Aungelique called out, "If there is a demon here, if the Devil comes to me, there are no doors strong enough to keep him out, and I will not resist him, you may be sure of that!"

Mère Léonie turned to the two nuns who had stood just out of sight. "Seur Adalin, Seur Morgance, guard her. If she harms herself, let me know of it at once. Otherwise, ignore everything you hear. Think on the travail of Our Lord if you find it difficult to shut out her ravings, but do not let yourselves be tempted by that . . . woman!"

The two nuns bowed their heads in submission to Mère Léonie's commands, though both of them already listened to the cries that came from behind the bolted door.

Pierre braced his feet apart and glared at Mère Léonie. "How could this happen? How could you let her . . . do such things?" He had been silent for the first part of Mère Léonie's explanation of the latest crisis Seur

Aungelique had brought to the convent, but he had become more and more aggravated as the superior spoke and finally could contain himself no longer.

"I have little say in the matter," Mère Léonie said, spreading her hands out to signify her helplessness. "You see that I am unable to stop these . . . events, do you not?"

"I see that Aungelique is writhing about like a gaffed fish and screaming like one demented, and you can do nothing but pray!" This outburst shamed him, but once started, he could not hold himself back. "What is wrong with you, woman, that you permitted this to get so far out of hand? Do you know what her father would do if he saw her? She would be sent to a dungeon and chained to the wall with the rest of the lunatics, and the Pope would withhold his permission for marriage dispensations for the whole family. You know that Aungelique has been his only hope, and now she is making love to the Devil!" He stared hard at her, then looked away quickly; he had suffered enough from his obsession with her.

"What should I do? Should I beat her? You have seen her body, and those dreadful bruises and cuts were left by the Devil, or so she claims."

"Not the Devil. She says it was Thibault Col who came to her and who will come again." This was grudgingly said, as if he wanted to dispute everything Mère Léonie revealed.

"The Devil can take many forms, and the demons he sends are as like to be women as men. Why would they be ugly, Sieur le Duc?"

Pierre stared hard at her again. "God would not allow such treason," he said, and was dissatisfied with his remark.

"Our Lord . . ." She stopped, smiling strangely. "Think of the treason that cast Our Lord down into hell. God did not spare Him. Why should He spare a vocationless nun?"

There was nothing that Pierre could give to refute Mère Léonie, and it was infuriating for him. He came a few impetuous steps nearer. "I will say this once to you,

Mère Léonie: Aungelique's father intends that she will marry, and marry she shall, if she must be tied and gagged like a felon awaiting execution. But if she goes that way to the altar, you will be sent from here to the most remote part of France to say your prayers to rocks and snow. D'Ybert is a vidame, and the Pope will listen to him, since his vidames are all that stand between him and the deviltry of Rome."

If this threat worried Mère Léonie, it was not apparent in her demeanor. "You must do as your oaths bind you to do, Sieur le Duc. As I must abide by mine. Our Lord will send me where I am wanted, and it matters not what vidame and Pope do, for they are in the hands of Our Lord, as is everyone in the earth."

Pierre crossed himself and growled an "Amen" before resuming his argument. "You have a little time, and you had best use it well. When I return for that girl, she had best not be clinging to me and reaching for my balls. Is that plain?"

"Of course," Mere Léonie said with the same calm tone she had used all through their conversation. "And if she is correct, and she was made wanton, do you want us to find a village youth to indulge her, to sate her with the lust of his flesh so that she may be sent peaceably to her bridal bed? Or shall we keep her confined and raving? You have only to tell me what you require and it will be done." She stood up, smoothing her habit. Pierre's eyes followed the paths of her hands over her small breasts and down her lithe body. "What is it you want me to do?"

"By Christ's nails, I want you to make a reasonable woman out of her!" He folded his arms as if to barricade himself against her. "You are a reasonable woman yourself, Mère Léonie, and that is what I wish you to . . . to make Aungelique be."

"Then perhaps you are saying that I should instill a vocation in her, although we are both aware that none exists. You do know how much trouble she brings to this convent, do you?" She waited a moment, then strode past him toward the door. "You must give me time to pray for guidance. I cannot ask that God protect her if . . ."

"If she turns away from Him?" Pierre asked, reaching out to take her elbow. "Hear me out, Mère Léonie," he said, reveling in their closeness and the way his hand pressed her arm through her habit. "There will be no more talk of this Thibault Col. There will be no more laughter and swearing and declarations of ruttings, as she has been doing. I do not care how you affect this change, but Michau d'Ybert and I require it."

"Do not touch me," Mère Léonie said softly, her pale blue eyes boring into his. "If you lay a hand on me again, I will complain of it to the Cardinal and to the Pope, and you will have to answer for it."

The anger he heard in her voice fired the passion that already filled him; his hand closed more tightly. "Do you understand me?"

Mère Léonie raised her other hand, fingers curved so that her short nails became claws. "*Release me.*"

"Very well." He was pleased to see how she glared. "I only wish to impress upon you the magnitude of my concern."

"Those who assault nuns are castrated," she reminded him icily, stepping back as he released her. "When you come again, there will be other Sisters with me."

Pierre favored her with a mocking bow. "The daughter of Michau d'Ybert is not to be made the object of gossiping nuns. You will receive me when and where I direct, or you will be sent for and brought to her father." He grinned at her as her chin came up. "Then where would you be, without the Sisters and Père Guibert to protect you?"

"Our Lord protects me," she responded, her calm deserting her.

"With help from the chirurgeon's knife. Of course." He wanted to touch her again, to see the flames leap in her eyes. A woman like that, he thought, belonged at some important castle as chatelaine, not here with these terrified women.

"Leave."

"At once," he complied, turning abruptly and going

to the door. "I will be back by midsummer. See that Aungelique is ready."

"If that is the will of Our Lord, she will be." Mère Léonie stood straighter than usual, her shoulders squared and her head high. There was no lessening of her rigidity when she heard the courtyard door close and the sound of horses on the flagging. "Seur Odile," she called out.

"Yes, ma Mère," came the answer from the adjoining room.

"You heard what le duc said to me?"

"All of it, ma Mère."

"Then pray for him," Mère Léonie advised her curtly. "Pray that he will not bring more sin upon himself."

"Yes, ma Mère," Seur Odile answered.

"And pray for Seur Aungelique. We must do that in any case, but now it is of the utmost importance that we bring her into the hands of Our Lord." She held her rosary tightly in her long, lean hands. "We have reason to fear the wrath of God."

This last pronouncement made Seur Odile quiver, and she made the sign of the cross quickly in case she might have inadvertently exposed herself to the dangers of the demons said to haunt the air where sin had been committed. "She . . . may repent. She has begged her bread for four days."

"Without humility," Mère Léonie reminded the other nun.

Although she could not be seen, Seur Odile blushed for shame at her error. "Yes. Naturally. I . . . had not considered that."

"You have only to listen to her speak and know that she is as defiant as the fallen angels." Mère Léonie put down her rosary. "Père Guibert has told me that it is a great risk to all of us, keeping her here."

"Then . . ." Seur Odile began, finding it difficult to think of the proper thing to say. "There is danger enough in this world, ma Mère. Who are we to venture into more?" She came to the door and made a gesture of respect.

"We are the servants of Our Lord," Mère Léonie answered at once. "If we are tested more, it is that we prove the triumph of faith and the depth of our devotion." She straightened up. "Tell the others that if they ask you what they should do."

Seur Odile remembered that Mère Léonie had said something of the same nature when the convent was surrounded by Flagellants, and they had managed to come through that ordeal without ruin. "I will, ma Mère," she assured the superior.

"Deo gratias," Mère Léonie answered. "I must keep my vigil before the altar. Especially now, when I have been tempted to sin."

This last impressed Seur Odile, and she said to Mère Léonie as she withdrew from her presence, "I will think of those temptations that have been sent to me so that I might know them better and turn from them with a glad heart."

Mère Léonie rewarded her with a trace of a smile. "That would please Our Lord."

"God! Oh, my God!" The scream went through the convent like a winter wind. "What are you doing to me! *No, I cannot bear it . . . No!* Oh . . . oh . . . oh, do not hurt me again. *Don't.*"

The convent was roused abruptly, and nuns, came hurrying out of their cells, some of them calling for aid, others silent with wonder at what they heard coming from the barred door of Seur Aungelique's cell.

"*Thibault! . . . Thibault! . . . No!*"

Seur Ranegonde crossed herself, and the others copied her action. "What do you think."

"A demon," Seur Victoire said, not quite certain she was right.

"It must be. A woman like Seur Aungelique, what might she expect?" The words were condemning, but there was more fear than ire in Seur Elvire's face. "Where is Mère Léonie?"

"I . . ." Seur Philomine looked about. "No, she is not with us."

"She cannot be asleep," Seur Adalin protested.
"She must have heard . . . she *must* have."

"She is . . . praying?" Seur Tiennette suggested,
her large arms held over her girth. "Was it her hour to
keep vigil?"

"*Thibault!*" The name was wrung from her.

"Should one of us wake . . . bring Mère Léonie?"
Seur Odile asked in the most tentative accents.
"Shouldn't she be here?"

"And Père Guibert. He would know how to end
this." Seur Catant huddled in her shift as far from Seur
Aungelique's cell as she could. "Someone must know
what to do."

The next scream was more terrible than the others,
a wordless litany of torment that transcended mere suffering and became total despair.

"Bon Dieu," Seur Morgance whispered.

"It is not God Who touches her," Seur Theodosie
warned them, her large, brawny frame cowering now.

"My children . . . she hears them. They call to her,
and this is all she can do," Seur Marguerite explained,
but no one listened to her. "She has tried to find them,
and her heart is broken."

"By la Virge, be quiet," Seur Catant hissed.

"Leave her alone; she isn't clear in her mind," Seur
Adalin said, putting herself between Seur Catant and
Seur Marguerite.

"I meant only . . ." Seur Catant began, then
stopped when panting sobs came from the closed cell.

The voice shuddered, too exhausted to whimper,
and then there was a crack of low, pitiless laughter before
the weeping began, slowly at first and then building to
wretched sobs.

"I will get Mère Léonie," Seur Philomine said to
the others, and went before anyone could stop her.

"Sacré Mère Marie," Seur Ranegonde prayed, saying the comforting words without thought. "Pardon us
and intercede for us so that we are not lost on the Day of
Judgment and our souls go not into the pit."

Seur Adalin crossed herself and began to recite
prayers of her own. She heard Seur Elvire join her, and

the others followed their example, each of them speaking of her fears and helplessness.

Seur Philomine did not bother to pray as she rushed to Mère Léonie's cell. To her dismay, the superior was not there. "Mère Léonie!" she called out, hoping that she could be heard. "I ask forgiveness for intruding, but we must have your aid now. There is . . . trouble!" She went next to the study and saw that the small door leading to the convent's herb garden was standing open. With an impatient shout, she went toward it, raising her voice again. "Mère Léonie! Mère Léonie!"

The superior was at the far end of the garden, standing with her head bowed and her hands clasped before her. At this interruption, she looked up sharply and stared through the darkness.

"Who is it?" Her tone was sharp. "I am—"

"I have no wish to disturb your prayers, ma Mère, but there has been more trouble. It is Seur Aungelique. She . . . is in great travail and distress of spirits." That much was correct and could not later be questioned. "The door is barred, and none of us wishes to open it without your authority."

"I see. Very well." She crossed herself. "For us to relieve the burdens of this world, even for the foolish and wayward, God has made each of us what we are, and for that we must honor every creature." She was walking swiftly, passing through her study and her cell without pausing for anything. "Come, Seur Philomine. There is work for us to do."

Seur Philomine followed, grateful that it was not for her to minister to Seur Aungelique. She caught herself wondering, as she did more and more often, if she should have gone with Tristan when he offered to take her and ignored the consequences that would be visited upon them for so impulsive an act. Then she heard the sobs again and put her mind to Seur Aungelique's tribulation.

Père Guibert listened to all Mère Léonie told him in silence. His brow clouded as she spoke, and by the time she was finished, his expression was desolate. "How could it have happened, and here, of all places?"

"Then you believe that it is a demon, mon Père?" Mère Léonie asked.

"I will have to consult with Padre Bartolimieu, but it would appear to me that there is reason to fear she is possessed." He crossed himself, fighting an appalling exhilaration that was building in him. "We must pray that this is not so, but we must also prepare for that eventuality."

Mère Léonie looked down at her hands. "Surely it is only her lusts, mon Père. We have agreed that she is not a woman of vocation, and it may be that she yearns for release that is not permitted, and for that reason—not reason, but motive, perhaps, since no reason seeks out afflictions—imagines that she has become the victim of the Devil?" She had avoided his eyes, but now she stared hard at him. "To have the Church begin a process here might bring more harm than it ends."

He could not deny it. Other priests had begun processes that proved fruitless. All of them had been chastised and sent to parishes in parts of the world that were unpleasant to be in. "You may be correct in your caution, ma Fille," he allowed, hoping that he had not given away the degree of concern she had awakened in him. "I believe it will be best for all of us if I pursue this matter myself for a time. I may decide to ask Padre Bartolimieu to aid me, but that is not the same thing as a formal Process." He added, feeling inspired, "In times like these, when the forces of Rome demand so much of the Church's time so that their error will not spread, it is prudent to bring such problems as this one to the attention of the Church only when it is a sure thing that their skills will be needed."

"That is true," Mère Léonie agreed. "And it must be wise to question these things, for there are those who are quick to label sin as diabolic when in truth it is only the fallibility of man at work."

"God has made us fallible," Père Guibert concurred, afraid that he might be one of those. "We must guard against our blindness."

"Our Lord will guide us," Mère Léonie said with

great confidence. "Our Lord is our master and our greatest champion."

Père Guibert crossed himself, thinking of nothing more to say. "I will want to hear Seur Aungelique's confession as soon as possible. If she is not reluctant to give it."

"She has said that she is in need of it," Mère Léonie told him primly. "She has said that there will be no rest for her until she has confessed."

"Then it may be that she will repent and come to God if He moves her to cast off her fleshly desires. We must pray that God will choose to bring her to Him after much suffering." He shook his head. "Ah, ma Fille, surely God has given you great trials since He caused you to come here."

"I thank Our Lord for this chance to do His will," she responded quite properly. "If Seur Aungelique is the most recalcitrant nun I meet in my life, then my path will be an easy one."

Père Guibert was not certain that this pride was correct, but he did not want to contradict Mère Léonie, so he contented himself with a mild rebuke. "Do not bring more upon yourself, ma Fille, through the mistaken belief that you are capable of bearing the ills of your Sisters. It is God Who provides the strength, and it is He Who endows us with the patience to bear our burdens for His glory."

"It may be, but if it is, we will do what we must. The valley is lying fallow where grain grew before the last Plague. There are not so many men to work the land and few women to winnow the harvest. The miller died, and there is no one to grind the grain to flour any longer, so that the peasants must take their wheat and rye and oats to the next valley, to Sangchoutte, where they are charged more than they wish to pay for the milling. This year it is not a hardship, but the next, who can say?" She turned the corner in the hallway. "The hives are another matter. Poor Seur Marguerite mourns night and day for the two hives that are lost. There is a third, and so far it has not been touched by the blight that struck down the other two. The cheeses . . . Seur Tiennette said that they have been tainted with mold, but she does not know which kind. There are more cheeses curing, and it may be that they will all take, so that we will not have much of a loss there. With travelers so few, we have not had to deplete our supplies as we have had to do in the past, or so the Sisters have told me. Mère Jacinthe's records show that in other years there have been more men upon the road seeking the protection of the hospice."

"It is the Plague and the wars," Père Guibert said. "And the men from Rome, of course," he added as an afterthought.

Seur Morgance passed them, lowering her head in dutiful submission to her superior and their priest.

"How are the Sisters responding to Seur Aungelique's"—he almost said "possession" but stopped himself in time—"affliction?"

"There are those who wish to be rid of her, who believe that she will bring even more misfortune to the convent. There are those who pity her. And it may be that one or two of them envy her." She said this last as if the thought were new to her, and the silence that followed bothered Père Guibert.

Seur Fleurette stood in front of Seur Aungelique's cell, her back to the door. A large white scar on the side of her face was a constant reminder of the attack of the Flagellants, as was the limp she revealed as she approached Père Guibert.

"God be with you, ma Fille," he said, blessing her as he looked at the door.

"And with your spirit, ma Père," she answered as she crossed herself.

Père Guibert disliked having to consult Mère Léonie, but in this instance he had to rely on the superior to advise him. "Is it better that she witness, or must this be under the seal?"

"For the good of the convent, a witness would be best," Mère Léonie answered. She gazed at Seur Fleurette. "Guard your tongue and your soul, ma Seur, for what you hear is holy confession and not for idle talk."

"I am honored to obey you, ma Mère." She gave her attention to Père Guibert.

Père Guibert pressed his lips tightly together. "Has she claimed that the Devil has been with her since sunrise?"

"She has been quiet," Seur Fleurette admitted. "Last night was another matter."

"That was last night," Père Guibert said. "Today we must praise God for protecting His wayward child." He went to the door. "Remain nearby. This may be more vanity than Devil, but that is not an easy distinction to make when a nun is as obstinate as Seur Aungelique."

The two women lowered their heads and waited for what was to come.

Alone with Seur Aungelique, Père Guibert attempted to compose his thoughts, but the sight of the young woman troubled him more than he had assumed it would. There were massive bruises on Seur Aungelique's exposed thighs and deep scratches on her hips and abdomen, one of which had already begun to fester. The skin had been scraped from her collarbone, and between her breasts there were the crescent marks of teeth. Some of the discolorations were fresh, others, older, turning from purple to yellow green. Little of Seur Aungelique's beauty remained, and as he stared down at her, Père Guibert decided that it was just as well. "I am troubled to see you, ma Fille." He made the sign of the cross over her and was pleased that she copied his action.

"Then why do you come? Why not leave me to the demon that robs me of my sleep and my peace of mind? Don't you sense the corruption that has invaded me?" The challenge was spoken softly, as if she were too exhausted to do more than make a token show of resistance to him.

"God has given me His mandate of the priesthood," Père Guibert said. Then, to modify this statement so that it would not put her off, he added, "God wishes all His children to honor His commandments for their salvation."

"But surely God knows that He has made his children diverse and that they cannot come to him but that He calls them?" Seur Aungelique threw back her head and rubbed her eyes. "God is far off, mon Père, and the Devil is near at hand."

"God has given you his priests to aid you," Père Guibert reminded her. His eyes were drawn to a large, livid bruise on her thigh, near the place where it joined the hip, a purple splotch with a ruddy center, the size of his palm. What could have left such a mark? he asked himself.

She moved slightly, exposing more of her body. "Then how is it wrong to live as God made me to live, not seeking any change for fear that the change comes not from God but the Devil?"

"It must seem so to you, my poor child, with so much trouble in your . . . flesh."

"They say that women are weak and erring creatures, and for that they are the prey of demons." She ran one hand over the crest of her hip. "We are taught that we must be guided if we are to escape perdition."

"That is so," he replied uneasily. "Yet you have refused confession before. Do you truly seek it now?"

"Oh, yes, mon Père. I must have some peace, or I will be madder than Seur Marguerite with her bees." She lolled toward him, making no effort to touch him but still impressing him with her nearness. "The Devil has sent his servant to plague me, and I cannot endure it much longer. The demon has come to me often and has done such things to me that I fear for my salvation." She started to raise up on her elbows but could not accomplish that simple action without wincing in pain. "You see, mon Père, what has been done to me?"

"I see that you are much aggrieved," he answered her; it was an effort to avert his eyes, but he accomplished it and thanked God in his heart.

"It is worse, so much worse. When I try to enter the chapel, the enormity of my transgressions drives me to fits. I have almost fainted at the sight of the cross."

Père Guibert watched her with troubled eyes. He could not believe that she would permit such blasphemy to possess her—if possession it was. The nun was from a noble House, her father both a baron and a vidame, high in the esteem of the Church. His daughter could not be so steeped in evil that she would bring this disgrace on her family. "The cross," he said, swallowing once before going on, "will sustain you."

"It is the demon that does this to me!" she protested.

"What has taken place I do not know and must rely on your true and complete confession to inform me," he reminded her. "Are you prepared to do that, ma Fille, or are you still in the thrall of the demon?"

With a heavy sigh, Seur Aungelique crossed herself. "Very well. May God forgive me for my sins." She picked at a small scab on her hand, then licked the blood that welled there.

Père Guibert listened, frowning. "You should recall that when you are tempted by the messenger of the Devil, if it is truly a demon who comes to you."

"What else could it be? How could a lover reach me here?" She gave him an arch smile. "This is not Une Noveautie, mon Père."

"Think what you say, ma Fille," he scolded her.

"Yes, mon Père," she answered, once again contrite. "It is simply that I see such horrible things around me that I cannot endure the sight. This is a place of damnation, and hell stands open at our backs."

"No, no, ma Fille," Père Guibert said, extending a solicitous hand to her. "You must not be deceived. God protects His own, those who live with grace." He paused. "You have strayed from the flock, Seur Aungelique, and you have lost the way. What have you done to fall from grace, ma Fille? Tell me."

She shook her head as he said this. "I have done nothing, mon Père. Nothing. It is not I who have done this. My suffering has been visited on me by the Devil, who delights in torturing me through the . . . ministrations of his servant." She stared up at the ceiling, as if watching something there. "You know what I am, Père Guibert? A woman of the flesh and of the senses, and for that I am not a good nun, for the world calls me, and I cannot turn away from it without denying what I am, which is a great sin. I am carnal: that is as God wills and as I wish to live. But I am here, and thus am I tormented by the desires of my body until God brings me to His love. For now, I cannot be what I am wished to be. I have done the penance given me." Her chin jutted at that.

"This is known to me, ma Fille. What of the demon you claim visits you? What is his nature, and how does he offend you?" It was a foolish question, and Seur Aungelique made it plain that she did not wish to be made light of.

"You have seen my body; you know what he does to me." She breathed deeply once. "The Devil has come to me in the form of Thibault Col, Chevalier de Bruges. He is most personable, this young man, very fair and gallant."

"Do you say this chevalier is the Devil?" Père Guibert demanded, knowing how serious an accusation Seur Aungelique had made.

"I say that the Devil can assume any shape he wishes, and those that please us gain him an advantage. His demons are beautiful to see, so we are warned." She crossed herself languidly. "Thus this Thibault comes to me, or the demon in his shape. At first he only courted me, paying me compliments and putting his hands on my breasts as he had done before. Then he came longer, and he demanded more."

"You did not rebuke him? You did not defend your maidenhead?" His voice cracked on the second question.

"I wanted him. I desired he touch me and fill me. When he was gone, I was in terror that he would not come again. Had I been able to conjure him from the moonbeams, I would have done so."

"That is wrong of you, ma Fille." He had to look at something other than her ravaged flesh.

"Does that matter? God did not intend me for chastity. When Thibault came to me, he roused me as no prayer has done. He gave me pleasure in any way I told him I wanted." She yawned. "Later, he made demands of me, and they grew more exacting each time he came to me. Of late, nothing I do is enough for him, and he is more impatient with me." Tears slid from her eyes, and she wiped them away at once.

"Ma Fille, you are in the gravest danger," Père Guibert said as he clasped his hands in prayer.

"He comes to me each night," she crooned. "He feels all my flesh, and then he demands that I pleasure him however he wishes to be pleasured. He is too masterful for me to refuse him. He penetrates all my body, and if I am unwilling to accommodate him, then he bends me to his will with his body and his soul. His eyes burn at me." She laughed again, this time with more spirit. "It is painful and hideous, and he cares nothing for me."

"Seur Aungelique!" Père Guibert expostulated, shocked in spite of himself.

"Oh, how I scream and how I fight and how he overwhelms me." She smiled at Père Guibert. "He is endowed like a bull, and there are times when I fear he will eviscerate me when he is within me. I have never given him the satisfaction he has required of me. Even when I have abased myself completely." Now her voice was soft, husky with feeling. "Have I confessed enough, mon Père? Or do you wish to hear more?"

"I . . ." He could feel his face burn for shame at what he had heard. "You are not repentant, it would seem."

"Oh, yes. In the morning. But by the time midday has come, I know that night is on its way, and with it Thibault. Then I am satisfied with my lot." This time her laughter howled at him, and he stepped back from her.

"You are damned, woman! You are *vile!*"

Seur Aungelique murmured, "Perhaps he is not a demon, after all, since you agree."

For this, Père Guibert had no answer; his head rang with her words, and they were repugnant to him. Crossing himself for protection, he fled.

Chapter 10

Padre Bartolimieu listened to Père Guibert with somber attention. "And does this demon continue to . . . sport with her?" he asked when his fellow priest was finished with his tale.

"So she claims. One of the other Sisters has also claimed that she has been visited by a creature in the night, a strange, dark thing that does things to her that she cannot describe for revulsion. She is a frail woman, and I fear that such predations will harm her more than she knows."

"It will harm them all more than they know," Padre Bartolimieu declared as he paced the garden. "It was wrong of me to run from the confrontation of evil. It is not enough that I retire from the world." He lowered his head. "Tell me about this second nun. What has become of her since the demon assaulted her?"

"She . . . she is very bright in her eye, and her cheeks flame for the wrongs she has permitted this creature to do her. Seur Ranegonde is not strong, and when she is made to suffer in this way, her constitution fails her, and nothing provides her succor, not even prayers." He was distressed to say this, and when he was finished, he stared away across the garden. "Mère Léonie prays for her Sisters and has said that she does not want a Process unless it is necessary."

"She is wise, this Mère Léonie? Or is she subtle?" Padre Bartolimieu put his head to one side. "I recall her with favor; it may be that God has given her more wisdom than He provides most of her sex. They are cunning, women are, and those who embrace virtue are few. They must guard themselves, even in chastity, for it is their nature to yield to the flesh, as Eve did."

Père Guibert shook his head. "I pray that it is only the perfidy of women that must be corrected and not the incursions of hell. The Pope has recently warned that the forces of Rome are growing stronger and seek to undermine the proper authority of Avignon and the French throne. To have demons present would weaken his assertion that it is Avignon that has the right. It might be thought that these nuns were acting on behalf of Roman lovers and for that seek to cast doubt upon the sanctity of Avignon." He could not admit it, but this consideration was not his own; Mère Léonie had spoken to him on this subject shortly before he left to seek out Padre Bartolimieu.

"It may be so," Padre Bartolimieu allowed after thinking over what he had heard. "Rome is capable of such deceit, and we know that woman is a source of lies. It might be best if we observe these . . . trances and learn more."

A flight of swallows raced over the walled garden, and both men looked up briefly. Finally, Père Guibert resumed their conversation. "Then you will come with me, back to la Tres Saunte Annunciacion? Someone must advise me before I report to the Cardinal and bring the attention of the Church to this."

"It may be the wisest course," Padre Bartolimieu said after considering it. "I . . . I do not wish this burden. I have asked God to take His cup from me many times, but to no avail." He crossed himself slowly.

"The women there are . . . worried, with good reason."

"If there is a demon—"

"No, that is not their main concern. They worry that they may starve next winter. At the moment, they manage well enough, and they are able to give charity to those travelers who come to them. But in the autumn it may no longer be so, and they may be driven to fast for long days." He shook his head. "Mère Léonie has borne up well thus far, but she has not yet faced hunger such as they could know in the dark of the year."

"They must plan." He folded his hands into his sleeves. "It is well that they fast. Perhaps even now they should accustom themselves to the practice, knowing that it will strengthen their souls."

Père Guibert frowned. "I will recommend it to Mère Léonie. She will decide as she must."

"You are her priest. It is fitting that she follow your instructions." He took his foot off the bench. "Think of her awesome responsibilities and you will see that she must turn to you if she is to accomplish her tasks as she ought. She is too forward a young woman, mannish in her ways and proud in her carriage. It is wrong for her to behave thus, and it sets a poor example to her Sisters, who should seek to model their behavior on that of la Virge Marie, who was meek and obedient to the will of God." He began to walk toward the monastery. "Come, Père Guibert. I will inform the abbot that I must depart with you."

"I may require your presence some little time," Père Guibert said, wanting to be certain the other priest understood that.

"No matter. Should it become necessary, I will petition the Cardinal for leave to minister with you. No doubt he would be pleased to have another priest with you after all that the . . . heretics did." He walked more quickly, as if reminding himself of his failure spurred him to new action.

Seur Catant sat carding wool, but her eyes were distant. Her fingers moved as if they were not part of her, efficiently selecting wool, placing it on the toothed paddles, drawing them together until the wool was tangleless and fairly smooth, then dropping that hank into the basket at her side and picking up another bit to repeat the process. "He put his hand on my breast. I felt him do that," she muttered for the hundredth or the thousandth time. "I felt it. His fingers were long and cold. He put his hand on my breast."

Sitting apart from her, Seur Morgance could not hear what Seur Catant was saying to herself; she was occupied with darning old habits, repairing ripped sleeves and worn skirts where kneeling in the garden had worn the fabric thin. Her hands were stiff that morning in

spite of the warm spring weather, and she wielded the
needle with difficulty. A little conversation might have
helped pass the time, but Mère Léonie had enjoined all
the Sisters to keep silent because of the gossip that had
been spreading about Seur Aungelique and the demon
that was said to seduce her each night. There were other
things to talk about; there had been travelers the day
before who had said that they had encountered men from
Rome on the road who had boasted that Pope Urban
would emerge the victor in the dispute with Avignon.

Without warning, the carding paddles fell from Seur
Catant's hands. She let out a long, wailing shriek and
clutched her elbows. *"He touched me! He put his hand
on my breast!"*

"God protect us!" Seur Morgance said, looking up
in baffled surprise.

"Oh, God; oh, God! *He touched me!"* Seur Catant
dropped to her knees, rocking and sobbing.

Seur Morgance put her darning aside and got up
from her stool, then hesitated. "Seur Catant, are you
ill?"

"He touched me, touched me, touched me touched
me thouched me touchedmetouchedme," she repeated,
running the words together until they were only a bab-
ble.

"Seur Catant?" Seur Morgance said tentatively, and
when there was no response, she said, "I am going
to . . . get help. You need . . . someone. Mère Léonie
or Seur Tiennette." As she bolted for the door, another
name came to her—Seur Marguerite.

"And who else has been afflicted?" Padre Bartolimieu demanded of Mère Léonie as he stared at her
where she knelt before him.

"I told you of Seur Aungelique, Seur Ranegonde,
Seur Fleurette, and Seur Catant."

"And the others? Have there been others?" His
voice grew louder with each word, his hands clenched
tightly at his sides, as if he were containing a need to do
battle with her.

"Perhaps Seur Victoire and Seur Adalin, but we

cannot be sure. They have had dreams that disturb them and have come to me to tell me of them. It may be that they, too, have been visited by a demon, or it may be that with the screams and great turmoil in the night, they have had bad dreams only." She lowered her head. "I have listened to them, and I ask Our Lord to give them His help."

Padre Bartolimieu stepped back, mollified by her attitude as much as her words. "You did well, ma Fille. It is not for women to decide these matters but for men to act. Père Guibert and I will hear the confessions of your Sisters and pray for divine guidance in our quest."

"May Our Lord assist you," she said humbly, not looking up at him. "You are a good priest, Padre."

"That remains to be seen," he said, but stood a little straighter at this praise. "I must show the strength of God to those who are in doubt."

Staring down at the worn stones, Mère Léonie smiled.

Pierre came out of the saddle impatiently and tramped over to the warder sister's grilled window. "Le Duc de Parcignonne!" he snapped without exchanging proper greetings with the nun waiting there.

"God be with you, Sieur le Duc," said Seur Elvire in her most imposing voice.

And with your spirit, Sister. Now give entrance to me and my men. This is urgent." He was in no mind to visit the convent again, but he had been enough disturbed by what he had heard at Une Noveautie that he had decided to find out for himself if the rumors were true. He had been regretting his impetuosity for more than an hour, and now he was determined to make his stay as brief as possible.

"Mère Léonie must first be informed of your arrival. "There is shade in the orchard, Sieur le Duc, and you and your men may wish to go there."

"We'll remain here at the gate, if you please." He twisted around. "Tristan! What's the name of your—"

Before Pierre's unruly tongue could compromise her,

Tristan answered, "My friend here is Seur Philomine. She's a tertiary Sister."

"Yes. Well," he said addressing Seur Elvire once more, "you might mention our arrival to that Seur Philomine as well. Anything to get us inside more quickly."

Seur Elvire was affronted by his manner but grateful that he had come. Now there would be something to talk about other than demons and possession, of the ways those creatures offended God's brides with their importunities. "I will return as quickly as possible," Seur Elvire said to Pierre before leaving her post at the grille.

"Those doors are well made," Pierre said as he came back to his men-at-arms. "Did any of you work on them?"

Two of the men spoke up. "I didn't," Tristan said.

"Well, you did well. Christ on the cross, why did I bother to come here?" He had thought this from the first, and now he let his men share his feelings. "The sooner we are through with this, the better it will be for all of us."

"You don't think there is any real trouble here?" Tristan asked, and heard Ivo snort his derision.

"I think that Aungelique is up to mischief again. She was far too tractable when she returned here, and now I think she is trying to find another way to leave the convent without waiting for her father's permission to do so." He clapped his hands to his belt, hooking his thumbs over the thick leather. "When I heard that they're saying the nuns are bedeviled here . . ." He broke off, knowing that he should not say so much to his men. "We will see what she has done, and if her behavior warrants it, we will remove her and return her to her father. I will not have the disruption of a convent laid at my door or the door of my House."

Ivo laughed and nudged Choce. "There are many ways to disrupt a convent, wouldn't you say?"

The other man-at-arms winked and was about to add his own comment when Tristan cut them short.

"These are dedicated women, most of them, and have good reason to retire from the world."

"Listen to Courtenay Le Durand," Ivo said. "He cannot have his woman out of here, so he must make saints of all of them."

"Stop it," Pierre ordered the men, and glared at them as they fell silent. "I don't want to give them any reason to complain of us."

A short while later, the doors were drawn open, and the men were bade enter the courtyard, not by Mère Léonie or one of the other Sisters but by Père Guibert, who regarded Pierre soberly.

"I am grateful that you are here, Sieur le Duc, though I confess you were not expected. Mère Léonie has retired to her cell for meditation while this . . . investigation is under way."

Pierre heard this out with growing consternation. "By the brass balls of . . . Pardon, mon Père." He cleared his throat. "I have heard certain disturbing rumors. I came to find out if they are true." He looked about for one of the nuns to take the reins of his horse and was startled to find that only Seur Elvire was present.

"I regret that you will have to stable your beasts," Père Guibert said with embarrassment. "Most of the sisters are in their cells, meditating."

"Ivo, see to it" was Pierre's brusque order.

"As you wish," Ivo said, dismounting quickly. "What of Choce and Courtenay?"

"They'll have work to do, never fear," Pierre told him. "What has been going on, mon Père," he went on to the priest, "that the nuns stay in their cells during the day? Is it true that there are demons here?"

"There is something, mon Fils," Père Guibert told him. "Padre Bartolimieu and I are attempting to determine what it is." He belatedly made a blessing for Pierre and the three men-at-arms. "It may be that these sisters will need your protection before we are finished."

Pierre wanted to protest but knew that he could not. "My men will not torture women, mon Père, not even for the Church. If that is what you need, send for one of your own to do it."

"You say this after the two women you raped in Huy demanded recompense from you?"

"They were not nuns, and well you know it, mon Père. Merchants' daughters, that's all they were." He shrugged. "There are many who do not balk at having a man of my rank in their beds."

Père Guibert did not want to make an issue of it. "We do not intend to use such methods unless it is absolutely necessary."

Pierre turned to Tristan and Choce. "We'd better make camp in the orchard. See to it at once."

Both men compiled without comment, leaving the courtyard through the passage to the stable. Tristan looked back once, but Choce only grumbled and followed le duc's orders.

Père Guibert watched the men depart, then faced Pierre squarely. "What have you heard, Sieur le Duc, and from whom?"

Pierre fixed his gaze on the top of the courtyard wall, squinting at the sun. "I was at . . . well, you know the place: Une Noveautie. That fair-haired courtier from Bruges was there, paying attention to Comtesse Orienne. He made a point of speaking to me, telling me that he had heard from travelers that this convent was not available to them because there were demons here who were ravishing the nuns. He laughed at that and said that as far as he was concerned, Aungelique had enough of the Devil in her to make every nun in France forget her vows." He coughed once. "I assumed he was making light of Aungelique's desire to leave the Order and told him that it was no service to her to speak in that way. He said something more, and it caused me a little worry; he said that if ever there was a convent that begged for a demon, it was this one." Finally, he looked at Père Guibert. "Pardon, mon Père, but that is what the man said to me."

"Yes, pardon; naturally," Père Guibert said in a distracted way; he was still trying to make sense of what he had been told. "I did not know they had turned any travelers away."

."Perhaps it was before you arrived," Pierre suggested. "Col learned of it somehow, and he is not the sort to make pilgrimages."

"No," Père Guibert said, his tone still vague. He gave himself a shake and put his mind on his unexpected visitor. "Doubtless you are right, and Mère Léonie did not mention it to me. When she emerges from her seclusion, I will ask her about it." He indicated the door into the convent. "Come. We must discuss what has been going on."

"Demons and all?" Pierre asked, falling into step beside the priest.

"I think it is more likely that we will find Romans behind this, not demons." He entered the corridor half a step ahead of Pierre. "This man you spoke of—do you think he might have been suborned by the Romans?"

"He's not a Roman, mon Père, just one of those parasites that thrive at court. They long for gossip and rumors as a peasant longs for butter." He chuckled at his own humor but did not fail to notice how distressed Père Guibert was.

It was nearing sunset, and he rode in from the west so that Seur Elvire saw him as a dark blot on the road that swelled as it came nearer.

"We are not permitted to have travelers here, stranger," she called out in a quavering voice.

"What?" came the light, taunting reply as Thibault Col dismounted and sauntered over to the grille. "When I have come all this way, ma Seur? How can you admit le duc de Parcignonne and deny me?"

"I . . . I do not know that, stranger." She leaned forward, peering at him.

"Come; I am not an adventurer to make demands of you." He leaned close to the grille, smiling with half of his mouth. "I am Thibault Col, Chevalier de Bruges."

"Le duc did not say that there would be others." For some reason she did not understand, she was breathing faster.

"There are not others, ma Seur," he told her with a flick of the reins he held in his hand.

Seur Elvire crossed herself. "I will have to speak to Père Guibert."

"By all means. I will await you here." He braced his shoulder against the wall and gave her his most affable smile. "Go at once, ma Seur."

"Yes," she said, not at all confidently. "I will return. Shortly."

"Fine," he said. "God be with you, ma Seur."

Chagrined that she had not greeted him with this phrase, Seur Elvire blurted out the response, "And with your spirit," and then hurried away into the convent to seek our Père Guibert.

The priest took longer to answer this summons. When he did arrive at the gate, it had grown noticeably darker. "Seur Elvire said that you wished to stay here."

"That's not exactly what I told her, mon Père, but let it pass," he said in answer. "I have come here because I saw that le duc was coming here, and I am, I admit it, curious about everything I was told." He smiled at Père Guibert. "I am somewhat connected with your Mère Léonie."

Père Guibert drew back, not entirely pleased with this revelation. "A relative, Chevalier?"

"In a manner of speaking," Thibault said, winking once. He held out his hand to Père Guibert in common greeting, his light blue eyes alight with some unreadable emotion. "Look at me, good priest. There is a resemblance between me and Mère Léonie, or so we have always been told."

Grudgingly, Père Guibert did as he asked. "Yes, you have something of the look of Mère Léonie," he said with a sigh. "The door to the hospice is there. Once you have stabled your horse, you may seek out Seur Tiennette for a meal. She is in the refectory."

"May Our Lord reward you, mon Père," Thibault said, and strolled away without waiting for a proper blessing.

It was a dream, Pierre thought as he saw the tent flap draw back. It had to be a dream, for it was inconceivable that Mère Léonie would come to him in the night in a shift of linen so fine it was nearly transparent. He gazed at her, fascinated, as she came nearer, her pale eyes fixed on his face, her body, glimpsed through the linen, as strong and lithe as a boy's.

"Sieur le Duc?" she said, now less than an arm's length from where he lay. "Am I welcome?"

"Christ!" he burst out, thinking he was shouting instead of whispering. He wanted to grab her, to plunder her body until his passion for her was gone, but he dared not. "You're a dream," he said.

"If that is what you want." She touched the scar on his face with her long, lean fingers. "Do you dream of battle, then? Do you dream of love? Tell me, Sieur le Duc."

He grabbed her hand, pressing it to his face. "You're convincing, I'll say that for you. When I wake, I'll—"

"You doubt your senses? You hold my hand; isn't it solid enough for you?" The linen of her shift brushed against his arm. "Well?"

Pierre pressed her hand to his face, biting her fingers lightly. "I like so much. Teton de Marie, this is sweet."

Mère Léonie made a sound between purring and laughter. "My breasts are sweeter than la Mère Marie's," she said. "Taste them. See for yourself."

"Oh, God," he groaned, seizing her shift in both hands and tugging at it with all the strength he could muster. The fabric held, then was rent from her neck to her ankles. His fingers brushed her leg. "Jesu, Marie!"

"Do you want me, Sieur le Duc? Though it is a sin and may cost you your soul." She tangled her hand in his hair. "Is there a nobleman in France who does not have lice on his head?"

"Bald ones," he growled, reaching for her, wrapping his arm around her hips and pulling her down to him. "Dream or no dream, I *will* have you."

"Though it cost you your soul," she repeated, holding him off.

"My soul, my title, for so sweet a dream, I will give anything." His blunt fingers sank into her hip, and he thought with satisfaction that if she were real, she would have marks to remember him by. "Be rid of that shift; it's ruined, anyway."

"In a moment, a little moment." She seemed to mock him now as she let him touch her. She bent and kissed his face, just to the side of the scar. "You want me?"

"Christ, yes!" He stared up into her hot, pale eyes. "Must I say it again? Come here, woman, and I will show you how I want you."

"Enough to serve me, Sieur le Duc? Enough to get on your knees to me as you have to your sovereign?" She braced her arm against his shoulder and to his amazement kept him from drawing her any nearer. "Answer me, Sieur le Duc. Would you get on your knees to me?"

"Certainly," he said, hardly paying any attention to what he said, so great was his desire for her. "Anything. Once I possess you."

"Ah, no," she taunted. "First you will get on your knees, and you will *crawl* to me."

He half-rose at that. "I crawl to no man!"

"But I am a woman. Crawl." She stepped back from him, avoiding his hands as they grasped at her. "I am waiting for you to crawl to me." She stood just beyond the end of his camp bed, holding her torn shift open so that he could see her body. "I have no lice. My flesh does not stink of sweat. I will open my legs to you if you will crawl."

Desire and rage coursed through him as he stared at her, and a fever like the passion of battle took hold of him. He flung his blankets away and yanked his chemise over his head, casting it aside. "Crawl, you say? To a duc of France?"

Her movements were like dancing. She escaped his first lunge and his second. "You will not have me that way, mon Duc. If you crawl, then you will have me." She stood out of reach, deliberately cupping one small, high breast with her long fingers. "Don't you long to do this? Wouldn't you like to put your lips here?"

"Don't goad me, woman!" he shouted at her, striving to get hold of her once more.

"Crawl, mon Duc. On your knees, if you want me."

He had no answer but the determination to catch her, and the more she eluded him, the more determined he was to have his vengeance on her. Finally, he stopped and stood, panting heavily, his body wet from his exertions. Each beat of his pulse felt like an explosion behind his eyes. His lust had not diminished; if anything, it had grown as he pursued her.

"You need only crawl, Pierre," she said softly. "I will be so pleased to see you crawl that I will let you have me."

"If I reach you, I'll throttle you!" he threatened.

"You will reach me when I want, mon Duc, and not an instant before. That will be after you crawl to me." This time when she smiled, her face was predatory. "Think, Pierre, what it will be like to lie atop me— you wish to be on top, don't you?—so that you can crush me. My thighs against your legs, my arms around your neck, my lips under yours—that is what you crave, isn't it?"

"Damn you! DAMN you!" he bellowed at her as she slipped out of reach once more.

"Why don't you crawl, Pierre?" She was close enough for him to put his hands on her, but he was not able to, for as soon as he moved, she danced away from him. "You could be inside me, Pierre, if you will crawl."

He threw himself at her, arms flailing out toward her, then fell, his breath tearing through him. "I will have you," he vowed between clenched teeth.

She came up behind him and lay down on his back, her body cool against his. "Tell me you will crawl and I will let you feel my thighs, Pierre."

"You're a devil!"

"Not a demon?" she teased him. "Poor Père Guibert; he must be looking for the wrong thing." She kissed the nape of his neck, then moved lightly away as he wrenched himself around.

"Stop!" he ordered her.

"I do as I wish." She stopped, and the hot light of her eyes licked over him like fire. "You are the one who has desired me. So be it, Pierre. I am the thing you seek. Now, *crawl!*"

He dropped to his knees. "Oh, no."

"Yes. Yes, Pierre. Crawl, Pierre." Her voice captivated him, so low and ripe it was, the very note he had imagined so many times before and never heard. "You will crawl."

"I will," he mumbled, and reveling in his disgrace, he did as she ordered, his head down so that he could not see her. He felt wonderfully despicable, loathsome and marvelous at once. When he reached her, he pressed his lips to her knee.

"Kiss my foot, Pierre." She raised her heel so that the arch was presented to him.

In a rapture of misery, he obeyed, taking her foot in his hands and holding it like a revered object, a holy treasure that the Church would defend with force of arms. He was so base, so foul that there was nothing he could not do, for he could not dishonor himself further. "Now I will have you."

She bent down, taking his head in her hands. She turned his face upward and kissed his mouth avidly. "You have groveled; you've earned the right."

Ordinarily, he would have been stung by what she said, but not now. He grasped her by the waist and forced her to come down onto the earth with him, under him. He went into her heedlessly, hammering at her until he was spent, his seed wrung from him so thoroughly that he could not believe he would be able to father children for a year.

Mère Léonie rolled him off her with contemptuous ease. "Next time you will crawl without such fuss," she whispered as she held the lobe of his ear between her teeth.

He had hardly breath enough to answer her. "I will never crawl again."

"Won't you?" She was on her feet now, watching him flounder in an attempt to rise.

"God's prick, woman, what did you *do* to me?" he groaned. He felt a quiver of fear run through him at his uncanny weakness.

"Only what you wanted, beau Pierre." She gathered up her shift.

"You're monstrous," he accused her as he sank back down on the earth.

She lifted the tent flap. "You are not the only one who has said so," she said very softly, then stepped back into the night.

Pierre stared at the place she had been. "It was . . . a dream? A dream." He rolled onto his side. It had been a dream. Mère Léonie would not come to him, more debauched than he had thought possible. He ought to confess his desires and cleanse his soul. And perhaps he would do that when he had tired of the dream.

As the Sisters chanted Vespers, Padre Bartolimieu hovered outside the door of Mère Léonie's cell. It had been six days since she secluded herself, subsisting only on bread and water left for her at midnight at her order. He wanted to open the door, to insist that she come forth and aid in the examination of her Sisters, but he dared not.

"Troubled, Padre?" Thibault asked as he came down the hall.

"You are not supposed to leave the hospice," he said by way of an answer.

"It is a dreary place, the hospice." He fingered the slashing of his blue silken sleeve. "Nuns have so little to entertain them, haven't they? Can you blame them for preferring a demon to boredom?"

"If Mère Léonie were not your kinswoman . . ." Padre Bartolimieu began, then caught himself.

"No doubt you would have le Duc and his men remove me under escort." He made a gesture of contempt. "Is it true that two more Sisters have been visited in the night?"

"Of course not," Padre Bartolimieu said much too quickly.

"That makes seven now, doesn't it?" He nodded as he saw the priest's face darken. "Pity the poor demon with so much to do." With mock humility, he crossed himself. "Our Lord protect us."

"Amen to that, little as you . . . or any of us deserve it," Padre Bartolimieu said.

Thibault snickered. "You priests, with your abasements and denials, you are the worst of all—thinking that you have access to God. You are usurpers, every one of you." He winked at Padre Bartolimieu, whose face had gone ruddy with wrath. "It takes so little to annoy you, doesn't it?"

"You are speaking heresy!" Padre Bartolimieu accused him.

"And blasphemy, too, I should think. I will confess it and make an act of contrition." With this flippant assurance, Thibault bowed slightly to the priest and strolled away down the hall. "If you wish to harangue me, I will be in the refectory," he called over his shoulder.

It took every bit of will he possessed for Padre Bartolimieu to let Thibault depart without railing at him. "He will be with the goats," he muttered, and was satisfied with the thought.

"Padre Bartolimieu!" Seur Adalin cried out to him as she rounded the corner.

He started at the sound of her voice. "What is it, ma Seur?"

"In the chapel! Come quickly, I beg you." She was breathless and on the verge of tears.

"Yes, yes," he said, responding at last. "What has happened now?"

Seur Adaline put her hands to her face. "Seur Fleurette—she has fallen into a fit. She says that there are demons in her flesh. O Saunt Marie!"

A high, delirious voice filled the hall, keening. "What it does!" she cried over and over again.

Padre Bartolimieu crossed himself and restrained Seur Adalin for a moment. "When did this begin?"

"We . . . noticed it just now. But we have been chanting. She might have started before—" She stopped abruptly. "May we be forgiven for that lapse."

Padre Bartolimieu moved once more, wondering where Père Guibert was. He entered the chapel and saw the nuns in the twilight, their gray habits making them look like old candles or pillars of smoke. He pushed his way through the disorder to where Seur Fleurette lay huddled on the floor, her knees drawn up to her chest, her face in a rictus of terror. "God fortify me," he whispered as he knelt beside the nun.

"What must we do, Padre?" the nearest Sister asked in faint accents.

"She needs your prayers." As he said this, he reached out to Seur Fleurette.

She screamed as if she had been touched by a hot iron. "NO!"

Padre Bartolimieu hesitated. "What . . . ?"

"She said that the Devil sent imps to her," Seur Morgance volunteered.

"She tried to scratch, but when she drew blood, then she started screaming," Seur Elvire told him. "What is to become of us, mon Padre?"

"Is it demons?" Seur Odile asked, afraid to hear the answer.

"It may be." He moved back, resting on his heels. "Is Père Guibert close at hand? Should he be called?"

"You are a priest," Seur Victoire reminded him, sounding shocked that he could speak in this way.

"But Père Guibert is her confessor." It was an excuse. Yet the nuns accepted it. "I am a stranger."

"I'll find him," Seur Adalin offered, hurrying out of the chapel once again.

Seur Fleurette continued to shriek in the steady, methodical way of an angry infant. Her eyes were screwed shut, and her lips had drawn back from her teeth.

"We need Mère Léonie," Seur Odile said, and the others agreed with conviction.

"She has secluded herself, good Sisters," Padre Bartolimieu reminded them, speaking loudly enough to be heard over Seur Fleurette's noise.

"Then we must ask her to come out of seclusion," Seur Tiennette declared. "She is a good and pious superior, but now she must attend to us."

"But she is helping my children," Seur Marguerite objected. "Without her, the last of them will die. Mère Léonie has saved them, and she must—"

"This is not the same as a few dead bees," Seur Catant snapped. She was huddled against the edge of the altar, staring at Seur Fleurette as if she were an adder.

"She kept the Flagellants away from us; she must help us again," Seur Odile demanded. "Make her help us, mon Padre."

"I . . ." He faltered. "Yes. I will speak to her. I will try to convince her to come to your assistance." It would get him out of the chapel, away from the hysterical Seur Fleurette. He stood up, feeling dizzy, then hurried out of the chapel, the screams pursuing him, driving him like a heretic's lash.

Off in the dusk the stream gurgled softly; frogs and crickets creaked and chirped, an owl hooted, and the grasses whisked against the wind.

Tristan said to Philomine as they walked through the fields, "I fear for you, off in this demented place."

She could not dispute with him, nor did she want to. "Will your duc allow you to take me with you when you leave?"

A week earlier, Tristan would have said yes without hesitation. "I don't know. I wish I did. Parcignonne has not been like himself of late. There are times you would think he had been cursed." He held her hand more tightly in his. "If he will not permit it, then I will leave his service."

"You have an oath to honor," she said, not looking at him. "You have bent the knee to him, and you wear his badge."

"But he has his obligation to me as well." He paused, looking at her with unwonted intensity. "If he will not defend me and mine, then he is not worthy, and I am not bound to him."

"You would bring shame on your House," Philomine said sadly.

"Just as well, if we are to be together," he said, chuckling. "I will speak to le duc as soon as I may."

"Tonight?" She held his hand more tightly.

He let go of her hand in order to put his arm around her shoulder. "It will be soon; it must be." They walked in companionable silence for a little while, enjoying the sounds of the night and their nearness. "Parcignonne troubles me. He goes through the days with his eyes haunted and his mind . . . distracted. He has said that he cannot leave yet. Then he says that he must leave at once for the good of his soul."

Philomine listened to this sympathetically. "He is as unfortunate as the sisters, then." She stood still, turning toward him. "If he stays here, so must you."

His smile was slow, deeply content. "That is so. And for that I am grateful to my lord."

She leaned her head on his shoulder, glad that she wore none of her required headgear. "I wish you might stay with me forever."

"For all my life, Philomine," he whispered. "There is nothing that will separate us but death."

"Hush, Tristan." She kissed his face.

When she did not go on, he said. "They cannot harm me. Not while you and I are together."

Philomine trembled. "Don't speak that way, Tristan. I . . ." She had no way to tell him how much she dreaded becoming like the other nuns. "Let me be with you, and the whole world is real. If you are lost to me, then even I am . . . nothing, and the rest is less than nothing."

He held her more closely. "Then be with me, Philomine, and we will both be real." Their kiss was long; their need was shared. "Is there time?"

She laughed. "Yes. Not much, but enough time." As she said it, a frisson passed through her, for she felt she was speaking not of making love but life itself.

"Do you mind that it must be . . . quick?" He tilted her face up to him.

"Of course I mind," she answered. "I want to lie in your arms all night long and wake to you." She put her arms around his waist so she could feel his body through their clothes. "I will not forgo this chance simply because it is not ideal."

He stepped back, but only far enough to be able to strip off his surcote. "Do you need help with your habit?"

"Oh, Bon Dieu!" For the first time, she felt merry.

"I have got in and out of it every day for three years."

His answering smile was strangely shy. "I am sorry it has been so long."

She stopped undressing and touched his arm, her face calmly serious. "It has been what it has been. Now we are here, and this is the time we have."

He looked steadily at her. "Yes. Oh, Philomine, yes."

Half dressed, shivering in the cool of the evening, they clung together, seeking one another with ardor. They finished undressing slowly, caressing each other as their garments fell into the long whispering grasses beside the stream.

Chapter 11

Guards flanked the door of Georges, Cardinal Belroche, their swords properly sheathed but braced before them. Père Guibert and Padre Bartolimieu glanced at them uneasily as the papal page opened the door and stood aside to admit them.

The Cardinal, a squat, sour-eyed man, sat at his writing table, a sheet of vellum spread before him. He looked up, squinting at the newcomers, and called out in his high, metallic voice, "Who's there?"

"It is Padre Bartolimieu, Swiss, and Père Guibert, French," the page said, knowing that the cardinal's eyesight was failing and that the prince of the church did not like to be reminded of it.

"Your Eminence," Père Guibert said, kneeling before the table, his head bowed. Beside him, Padre Bartolimieu did the same.

"Oh. You're the ones with the convent." He snapped out his words, looking in the direction of his page. "Have I time to speak to them now, or . . ."

He waved his hand to dismiss his page, then made

the sign of the cross over his visitors. "You have until he comes again to explain your report. What is this nonsense about demons?"

"I fear greatly that it is not nonsense," Père Guibert said, his head still bent as much with shame as with respect to the cardinal. "There is something that is wrong at the convent, and if it is not demons, we do not know what it is."

"I have seen nuns in the grip of those . . . forces," Padre Bartolimieu declared, his voice high with emotion.

The Cardinal said nothing. One of his large sandaled feet tapped in irritation.

"We are in need of aid," Père Guibert ventured in the uneasy quiet.

"You say in your message that le duc de Parcignonne has brought men-at-arms to your nuns. Surely he can aid you." His tone was becoming more terse and impatient. "You circuit priests!" the cardinal scoffed. "All you think about are those few religious and peasants you hear confess. You believe that they are the Church. Mon Fils, *we* are the church, we of the papal court. The rest are the flock we lead, as we must, but it is not they but *we* who *are* the Church." He slapped the flat of his palm on the table, a sharp explosion of sound. "And *we* are under assault as surely as if there were an army at the gates of Avignon."

Padre Bartolimieu coughed. "The Devil sends his minions in many forms, Eminence," he said awkwardly. "Roman spies to you and, it may be, demons to the good Sisters of la Tres Saunte Annunciacion."

"Hardly the same thing," the cardinal said. "You report that there are those who are abused with fleshly dreams and others who fall into fits. There was much of that when the Plague was visited on us before, and most of them died who were afflicted in such wise. Is there Plague in your valley, perhaps?" He drummed his fingers on the table. "If there is Plague, it is a sin not to inform me of it."

Père Guibert said, "There are demons, but there has been no Plague."

"There were heretics not long ago," Padre Bartolimieu interjected,

"Those were the ones the Sisters fought off, weren't they?" Cardinal Belroche asked. "There was mention of it in your report."

"Yes," Père Guibert answered, startled that the Cardinal should be familiar with what he had said. "They defended themselves and their convent until le duc de Parcignonne and his men arrived. They were valiant, the Sisters. One of them died from her wounds."

"Unfortunate," the Cardinal said in a crushing manner. "Tell me of these demons you fear. How long has the convent been infested with them—if it is infested at all?"

"For seven weeks, perhaps more," Père Guibert answered apprehensively. "There is one Sister, Seur Aungelique; she does not have a vocation and has been compelled to enter the convent. She has been a . . . disruption."

"Ah. And who is this nun?" He folded his arms and belatedly motioned for the two priests to rise.

"The daughter of Baron Michau d'Ybert," Père Guibert said with sudden trepidation.

"The new vidame?" the Cardinal asked with sharper attention than he had shown before. "Why did you not mention this?"

"It . . . it was part of the report. I informed Your Eminence that Seur Aungelique is the cousin of le duc de Parcignonne," Père Guibert answered, his discomfort increasing unpleasantly. "I did not intend to . . . to misrepresent her to you, Your Eminence. Mère Jacinthe, the old superior who died last winter . . . she made no disposal either way to me, and it was natural that I . . . that I . . ." He forced himself to stop babbling. "Of course I should have made it clear that Seur Aungelique is d'Ybert's daughter."

"Indeed you should," the Cardinal agreed, not as dauntingly as Père Guibert feared he might. "And you, Swiss?"

Padre Bartolimieu coughed once. "I have only recently attended the nuns, at the request of Père Guibert.

I do not know them well." He disliked his cringing answer but could not change it.

"The Swiss always equivocate," Cardinal Belroche declared, leaning back and pointing to two low benches not far from his writing table. "Sit down, priests. I will hear you out."

"May God bless you for this," Padre Bartolimieu said, and intercepted a critical glance from Père Guibert.

"Naturally," Cardinal Belroche said. "I would prefer He eliminate the Romans, but God does not always bless us in the way we choose."

Pére Guibert stopped the rebuke before he uttered it; instead, he said, "It is not for us to question God's Will."

"Sadly not," said the Cardinal. "And in the meantime, there are these demons or Romans or other agents of the Devil."

"And we must be rid of them," Padre Bartolimieu said, the depth of his loathing in his voice.

"The demons cause them to be wild and lascivious, your message indicates," Cardinal Belroche sighed.

"That is so," Père Guibert said, already convinced that their errand had been in vain. "We have seen the distress it causes the nuns, and we wish to do all that we may to rid them of this terrible affliction."

"Yes, that's clear enough," the Cardinal said. "But you must understand my predicament, good Père. You have a few souls to concern you, while we in Avignon have the fate of the world in our laps. If this were a case of Roman intervention, then it might be that we could spare you assistance, but as it is . . ." He shrugged.

Padre Bartolimieu at last spoke up. "But you've warned us that the Romans are the servants and tools of the Devil. So it may be that what has happened at la Tres Saunte Annunciacion is inspired by Rome." He was breathing more unevenly when he finished. "God will not permit us to do nothing and then seek the rewards of paradise."

Cardinal Belroche raised his shaggy eyebrows. "You've had some schooling, haven't you, Padre? And you believe that you may challenge Avignon in this way. You are not very wise for all your learning."

"I did not . . . mean to challenge you, Eminence." He looked toward the floor, smarting with acute embarrassment.

The Cardinal snorted, then went on. "Still, it may be that you have discovered some new incursion, and it would not be proper for us to ignore it entirely."

"Yes, that is what I feared," Père Guibert seconded him.

"Not as I have feared it, but in your way, you have some little concept of what threatens us, I suppose." He lifted up the vellum and peered at it. "I cannot spare you much." He crossed himself. "God guides our hand, and we are His servants."

The two priests made the sign of the cross, waiting to hear what the Cardinal had decided.

"There is a bishop, recently elevated to his office, whose town was most harshly treated by the heretics not so long ago. He is dedicated to the eradication of the evil Rome has visited on us. He cleared his throat. "The man is Évêque Amalrie Tordrer, and I will send my page to him this evening so that arrangements may be made to begin this . . . investigation."

Père Guibert was on his feet before Cardinal Belroche had finished. "Oh, a thousand thanks, Eminence. We are grateful to you, more than you will know, for it is what we had hoped for." He fell to his knees, crossed himself, and began to pray.

"My page will show you to the chapel where you may return thanks to God more properly," Cardinal Belroche said hastily.

As he looked up, Père Guibert had tears in his eyes. "You are His instrument, Eminence, and it is fitting that you should know how indebted we are to you."

"It is for the Church that this is being done," Cardinal Belroche said impatiently. He gestured for them to depart and endured the ritual of his ring being kissed with ill humor. "Be on guard for men from Rome, good priests. They trouble me far more than a few nuns who scream in the night."

"Yes. Of course," Padre Bartolimieu promised, adding to Père Guibert as they left the Cardinal's apartments, "It may be that he is correct in his assessment. We may have permitted ourselves to act precipitously."

Père Guibert frowned at the other man. "It hardly matters now, does it, since it will be for Évêque Amalrie to determine if there is a demon." He walked a little faster, annoyed at himself for being irritated by the Cardinal. "Whatever problems beset the Church," he said, hoping to convince himself, "they must be grave, otherwise, our message would have been given more attention."

Behind him, Padre Bartolimieu shuddered. "Be grateful for our insignificance, mon Père. It has saved us as surely as la Virge died chaste."

Évêque Amalrie was younger than Père Guibert had expected him to be—hardly more than thirty, with a smooth moon face that was marred by high, disdainful eyebrows and an arch of his small lips that hinted at unsatisfied appetites. He met Père Guibert and Padre Bartolimieu the day after they had spoken to Cardinal Belroche in the ambulatory of la Eglise de Saunt Antoine, not far from the papal palace.

"I will bring a page with me and also Frère Renaut to record what we learn. There will be a wagon ready to take my suite the day after tomorrow." The brows rose even higher.

"We will accommodate you as we may, mon Évêque," Padre Bartolimieu assured him without looking at Père Guibert. "It is an honor that a man of your high rank should condescend to aid us in our travail."

The bishop pouted. "I had hoped to aid Avignon here, where there is so much intrigue and turmoil. But Cardinal Belroche and Pope Clement have ruled otherwise, and I am obedient to their wishes." He paused for a moment. "I have read the message you sent to the Cardinal."

"We are sad to have caused you any distress," Padre Bartolimieu said; he did not like the young bishop, but he still deferred to him.

"Any fall from the grace of God must cause me distress," he said, and turned to Père Guibert. "You are silent, mon Père. Is there anything you wish to tell me, or have you fallen into reverie?"

Père Guibert shook his head. "Your forgiveness, mon Évêque. I was concerned for the nuns. We have been gone several days, and it troubles me that they should be left alone for so long when they have endured so much already."

"Very wise. Women are subject to visitations of the spirit more than men, and they are not strong in reason. You must not forget that when in sin, they are subtle and sly, clinging to their vices because they delight in repeating the errors of their Mother Eve." He folded his hands in front of him. "The wise man remembers this when dealing with women."

"These are sincere nuns, most of them," Père Guibert said, wanting to defend them without contradicting Évêque Amalrie.

"It is for the shame of their sex that they become religious." He walked on in silence, letting the two priests trail behind him. "You see, young as I am, I have learned something of the nature of woman, and I am prepared to counter any wrongs I find."

"They wish to live in accord with their Order," Père Guibert said, waiting to hear the Swiss priest attempt to curry favor with Évêque Amalrie.

"We will encourage them in this, and we will root out the Devil, if Devil there is." He was satisfied at that pronouncement, and he turned back to the priests. "I will want to consult with you every evening so that we may compare all we have heard and seen and know that we are not being caught in the wiles of the Devil through enchantment and glamour."

"It will be great instruction to hear you, mon Évêque," Padre Bartolimieu said with an emotion similar to fervor. "I know that your learning and piety will guide us in our investigations." He came a step closer. "There are those who think that we are too apprehensive and too severe on the women of la Tres Saunte Annunciacion, but you will see when we arrive how much has occurred and what it has done to the Sisters."

"Yes," Évêque Amalrie said, beaming at Padre Bar-

tolimieu. "Doubtless that is why Cardinal Belroche and
Pope Clement selected me for this work. Some of us are
gifted in these matters, and the burden of such inquiries
falls upon them." He lowered his head. "Be sure, good
Fathers, that I will be vigilant and stern, for all my
youth. There is no one at the convent who will escape my
notice and no vice that will go undiscovered. For that,
God be blessed and praised, for He gives the victory to
those who are His most humble servants and devoted
children."

"Amen," Padre Bartolimieu said, crossing himself
with the bishop.

Père Guibert made the sign of the cross in silence.

Seur Odile was warder Sister when the priests with
the young bishop and his two attendants returned from
Avignon. She watched them approach the convent with
curiosity and doubt: her mind was weary from lack of
sleep, and there had been another disturbance when the
nuns had gathered in the refectory to break their
fasts.

"God be with you, ma Fille," Père Guibert said as
he left the wagon and came to the grille.

"And with your spirit, mon Père," she said in a rush.
"I will tell Mère Léonie that you are here." She caught a
sob and attempted to turn it into a cough.

"What troubles you, ma Fille? Is there more difficulty?" He was certain she would not invent problems
where they did not exist.

"Yes, mon Père," she whispered. "Since you left, it
has been worse." She paused, aware that she had ex-
ceeded her authority in saying so much.

"Then inform Mère Léonie that we have brought
aid. Évêque Amalrie Tordrer, from Flanders, has been
sent by Cardinal Belroche and Pope Clement to help
us." He was able to say this without much feeling.

"God shows us grace at last," Seur Odile exclaimed.
"A bishop to help us. Mère Léonie will be filled with joy
to learn of this."

"Excellent," Padre Bartolimieu exclaimed. "It is
well when nuns accommodate the superior understand-

ing of men in orders." He turned toward Père Guibert. "Is that not so, mon Père?"

"It is the teaching of the Church," he said in an emotionless voice.

"And for that we must thank God," Padre Bartolimieu said, growing more enthusiastic, "for it was God and the Savior who founded the church and gave authority to the Popes to rule in Their holy names." He smiled at the round-faced young man. "God has shown wonders in His works, has he not?"

"And so has the Devil" was Évêque Amalrie's depressing answer. "That is why we are here, and we must be on guard against all the lies and subterfuge that the Devil has given to his servants to use against the servants of God." He stood in the wagon, the curtains pulled aside, and he glared at the doors of la Tres Saunte Annunciacion. "It is for us to determine what evil has been done here and to bring it to an end."

The two priests nodded but not with the same motive. Père Guibert wanted only to be left alone with the Sisters he had been given charge of and was now in danger of losing. "I will be pleased when this is resolved," he remarked.

"As will we all," Évêque Amalrie said, his mouth turning down, making him look like a baby about to have a tantrum. "And we will determine who is responsible for this outrage. For then the Holy Father in Avignon will know how it is that the Devil works against him and who has given the enemy of God aid and refuge." His eyes raked over the two priests. "And if nothing has occurred that warrants this attention, then those who have distracted the Church from its duties will feel the wrath of the Church. Be sure of that."

He had been making such grim pronouncements since they left Avignon. Padre Bartolimieu echoed them. "Yes, when Père Guibert came to me, I did not wish to have this known, for it would take men from the Church who would better be serving her in her battle against Rome."

"So you have said," Évêque Amalrie responded in quelling tones.

Padre Bartolimieu might have gone on, but there was the sound of the bolt being lifted, and the huge doors swung open.

Instead of the usual dozen or more Sisters that greeted new arrivals, this time there were a mere four, and one of them was the superior.

Mère Léonie appeared to be haggard and elated at once; her handsome features were sharpened, as if with fasting, but she moved with her accustomed vigor. "Be welcome in the name of Our Lord," she said as she came up to the wagon. "Things . . . have gone poorly here, good Fathers, and many of us are tired from our labors."

"Is it bad, ma Fille?" Père Guibert asked, for once grateful for her strength of character.

"There are times when Our Lord is mightily tried," she answered, and turned to kneel to the bishop. "We are honored that one of your station should be willing to come to the aid of such insignificant women as we are."

Évêque Amalrie leaned down from the wagon, extending his hand with his episcopal ring to her. "It is my responsibility, ma Mère, to serve where God and the Pope send me to magnify the glory of God." His bland features were set in a disapproving expression as he permitted her lips to brush the ring.

Padre Bartolimieu got down from the wagon and signaled to the recording monk and the page to prepare steps for Évêque Amalrie. "If the Devil has caused more depravity, then it must be ended at once," he announced, with a covert look at the bishop.

"We have striven to keep order here. Our Rule does not permit chastisement with rods, or the most obstinate would have felt them by now," Mère Léonie said, watching the bishop preparing to get down.

"And le duc?" Père Guibert asked. "Are he and his men still here?"

"They are." Her satisfaction was entirely disguised from the priests. "Le duc has said he will remain as long as there is need." She stepped back to give Évêque Amalrie plenty of room to step down. "With such guards as all these, what will become of the demons?"

"They will be sent to hell," Évêque Amalrie said,

halting on the second step that had been lowered for him.

"Where they belong," Padre Bartolimieu seconded him. "And if it is caprice, the sisters will suffer for it."

"My Sisters have been much put upon already, mon Padre," Mère Léonie said, with averted eyes. "I would not want them to suffer unnecessarily."

"As any superior would not, as it would cast a bad light on her leadership," Évêque Amalrie declared as he reached the ground. He was not quite as tall as Mère Léonie, and this distressed him. He glared at her. "Pride is the greatest sin of all, ma Fille, even when it is for the honor of one's Order."

Mère Léonie turned toward him. "Pride *is* a great sin. But protection is not, is it, mon Berger?" She used his pastoral title submissively but deliberately. "We who are given the souls of others into our care must guide them in the name of Our Lord so that they are not disgraced or maligned."

"There may be demons here," Évêque Amalrie said in his most disapproving tone.

"And if there are, I must do all that is demanded of me to see that they are routed," Padre Bartolimieu interrupted, coming alongside the bishop. "You have fired me with zeal, mon Évêque," he went on, deliberately ignoring the tug on his sleeve that Père Guibert gave as a warning.

Mère Léonie had signaled to Seur Philomine, who went to the heads of the mules that pulled the wagon. "See they are stabled, fed, and watered. Harness and tack should be put in the antechamber to the vestibule. If you need help, Seur Elvire or Seur Tiennette may be asked for it. They are still relatively able to work."

Seur Ranegonde, who had watched all this in awed silence, suddenly dropped to her knees, turning her face up toward Évêque Amalrie. Her thin cheeks were stained with fever, and her sunken eyes were glazed to brightness. "Praise God that you are here to give us your protection," she said as she seized the bishop's hand and kissed his ring.

"You overstep yourself, ma Fille," he said stiffly.

"In another instance, I know that, mon Sieur. I know that you are above me in all things, but for that I look to you to banish the evil that has come here." She waited, and when there was no further rebuke, went on. "I believe that you are the one who will show us how to escape from the clutches of the dreadful thing that has come here."

"Seur Ranegonde," Mère Léonie said when she could safely interrupt the frail nun in her outpouring, "You may retire to the chapel to pray until vespers summons you to join us in our devotions."

Seur Ranegonde lowered her head. "I . . .I hasten to obey you, ma Mère," she whispered, then got awkwardly to her feet and retreated rapidly.

"Are they all so . . . distraught?" Évêque Amalrie asked once Seur Ranegonde was gone.

"Some are affected in different ways," Mère Léonie answered with unusual caution. "A few do not appear to be under the influence of any demon or derangement of mind. Most, however, have fallen to the spell of . . . whatever has cast it." She looked at Père Guibert. "While you were here, many of the Sisters were able to fight the feelings that this . . . thing engenders, but now, well, I have done what I can."

"Ma Fille," Père Guibert said with genuine concern, "you must not hold yourself to blame. If there are demons here—"

"If there are demons here," Évêque Amalrie declared loudly, "then it is for us to cast them out, as the Savior cast out demons when He walked among us, for He has given to His Church the rights and powers to work His miracles. If you are simply in the toils of the deception natural to your sex, then you will be treated in other ways." Évêque Amalrie pointedly turned away from Mère Léonie to his recording monk, Frère Renaut, saying more easily, "I will begin to hear confessions after Vespers. If we discover any true demonic influence, you must aid me in exorcism."

Frère Renaut bowed his head. "As you wish, mon Évêque."

"You are bound by the rule of the confessional, unless it is revealed that the Devil is at work here, and then it will be required of you to reveal to Cardinal Belroche what you heard and recorded." He looked back once at Mère Léonie. "If I decide that it is prudent, you will hear confessions with me, ma Fille."

Everyone in the courtyard knew how irregular these orders were, but all of them acquiesced. "If you require that of me, mon Berger, I will accommodate you." She made another sign to Seur Philomine, who had finished unharnessing the mules from the wagon. "Remember what you heard, ma Seur, and testify to it if Cardinal Belroche or Cardinal Seulfleuve demands it."

Évêque Amalrie's mouth pursed more tightly. "Very wise, ma Fille. You are most circumspect."

"In these times, I must be if I am to serve Our Lord." She genuflected to the young bishop, then rose, indicating the corridor Seur Ranegonde had used. "Will you not enter, good prelates, and give us the benefit of your succor and wisdom?"

"You are insolent, ma Fille," Évêque Amalrie accused her.

"I? Toward you? What sort of a nun would I be if that were so?" She stood aside so that the two priests, the bishop, the monk, and the page could precede her out of the sunlight.

As he put down his earthenware cup, Évêque Amalrie said, "I am shamed, *shamed* by what I have heard. There is such debauchery and concupiscence among these nuns that it is a discredit to the Church and the Pope that this convent exists." He rubbed his hands together, then reached for the subtiltie that Seur Tiennette had made for him. "I have heard over twenty confessions, each more disgusting than the last."

Père Guibert watched the bishop carefully. "It is a dreadful thing that these Sisters should be made the victims of demons."

"Rather invited, if what I have heard is the truth. They revel in their degradation and beg for more." He licked his lips slowly, then had another draft of the acidic wine made in Saunt-Vitre-lo-Sur.

"That may be the case with Seur Aungelique," Père Guibert said slowly. "I cannot believe it of the others, who have resisted the demon with all their mights."

Évêque Amalrie nodded, licking his fingers as he did. "It is well that you defend them, mon Père. I heard Seur . . . Catant? Yes, that was her name, Catant, who is filled with strictures against her Sisters, reveal that when she has retired for the night, a great, shapeless being like an enormous black bird comes to her and gouges her flesh with his talons before ravishing her with utmost brutality." He finished his wine.

"Seur Catant is . . . a difficult woman, mon Évêque. She has faced many disappointments in her life, and I fear that the convent is one of them. Her father was a scholar of some repute who had taken her with him to Paris and to Genoa while she was a child, and she was used to the company of learned men. Then the Plague came, and she was sent to her aunt in Anjou. The only man who offered for her was a merchant, and her aunt decided that it would be best if she gave one of her own daughters to the merchant instead of her niece. She has been at a disadvantage ever since." He looked at Évêque Amalrie, hoping to see some touch of sympathy in the young man's demeanor.

"It is not for women with a true vocation to question what the Order requires of them. It is presumptuous and improper for a nun to behave as she has; I am not surprised that the Devil has found her a vessel for his purposes." He gave a satisfied smile. "I have not heard all the confessions yet, but when I do, I am certain it will be plain that you were right and that demons have come here. Cardinal Belroche will be informed, and Frère Renaut will send messages for us as we progress." He made the sign of the cross over the remains of his meal. "For the time being, we will order the hospice closed and send warning to the taverns and inns along the way to tell travelers that they must not come here, for there is a great danger."

Père Guibert hesitated before he responded to this new order. "If you believe that is best, then . . ."

Évêque Amalrie nodded again. "And I have told

Duc Pierre that it would be best if he and his men-at-arms leave. The men are constant lures to them, and we cannot permit the women to indulge themselves in such fancies, for it gives access to the Devil." He stood up, smiling complacently. "We have much to do here."

"Yes, mon Évêque," Père Guibert murmured, thinking he had better warn Mère Léonie of Évêque Amalrie's plans.

"I will need to speak to Padre Bartolimieu. He depends on the leadership of others, which is as it should be, but he is not willing to exercise his own judgment without supervision, which is regrettable. Still, he is preferable to a priest who cannot see the dangers here and who is more devoted to the nuns than to God."

Père Guibert bowed his head in acceptance of this undisguised criticism. "If I have erred, it is not for lack of faith but for care of my flock."

"Naturally. But it has made you shortsighted. You have heard the confessions of the nuns and have yet to see how debased they have become. Now that you have others to guide you, no doubt you will be more alert." He started toward the door, then paused. "I do not think it would be wise to explain too much to le duc. You know how the nobility can be. He will want reasons that a soldier may understand. He knows the hazards of desire, I would guess. That will suffice."

"As you think best, mon Évêque," Père Guibert said, feeling very tired.

"There are those who would try to abandon the nuns to their fate. But they are in need of correction, much in need of it, and the man who can lead them again to the grace of God will have much to recommend him in the Church." He blessed Père Guibert in a casual way. "Be certain, mon Fils, that I will be thorough in my examinations."

"I did not think otherwise, Évêque," Père Guibert said, not entirely able to hide his disgust of the man.

Évêque Amalrie chose to believe it was the plight of the nuns that caused him to show such an expression. "If it is too repugnant to you, you are excused from the proceedings, Père Guibert."

"I did not think God or the Church existed to spare us pain," Père Guibert countered, his annoyance mildly expressed so that Évêque Amalrie could not challenge him. "I will pray for guidance and for clear vision."

"God and His angels send you good counsel," Évêque Amalrie said brusquely. Without waiting for Père Guibert's "Amen," he left the refectory, walking more quickly than usual.

Père Guibert sat alone, his appetite gone and his heart constricted within him, as if held in a mailed fist.

With a faint whistle, the lash fell, striking the pale flesh; a slap that was loud in the chapel. Seur Odile gasped and steeled herself to endure the next nine blows.

"You must understand, ma Fille," Padre Bartolimieu told her softly, "that this is not to punish you but to drive the demons from your body so that you will not have to suffer greater pains in this world or the next."

"Deo gratias," Seur Odile whimpered as the next blow struck. She felt tears on her face and wished her hands were free so that she could wipe them away. But Évêque Amalrie's page held them firmly. She wanted to faint.

"You have permitted demons to enter your flesh, haven't you?" Padre Bartolimieu asked as the lash hit for the third time.

"I . . .I did not mean for it to happen." Her words came out in a rush so that she would not scream.

"No one means for such calamity to happen to them, ma Fille," Padre Bartolimieu said sternly. "That is why we must be vigilant and examine the state of our souls at all times. The Devil is subtle, and he changes you in ways that you cannot see or feel, except that you turn from grace and seek vice."

"I did not seek vice," Seur Odile insisted. She could feel the sweat on the page's hands as he held her.

"But you allowed it to use you," Padre Bartolimieu reminded her. "Think of the sins you have indulged in and what they have done to you. You confessed that you felt a monstrous man possess you."

"I took no pleasure," she objected.

"Do you hear yourself? You are defending your lapses; the Devil has turned you away from humility and made you stiff-necked."

She could not keep the wail from her voice now, nor did she try. "Père Guibert never required fasting and lashes of us."

"For which he was seriously lax." Padre Bartolimieu turned his head quickly at the sound of a step in the door. "Mon Évêque!"

"Padre Bartolimieu," the young bishop said, staring down at Seur Odile, naked and prone on the stone floor. "What progress?"

"This is the third one today. I have three more blows to deliver before the allotted ten have been administered. Still she maintains that the Devil came to her without her knowledge."

"Is that so, ma Fille?" Évêque Amalrie asked, coming closer to Seur Odile.

"I have prayed to God to show me how I fell, and there has been nothing to guide me, mon Berger." She stopped, letting the sobs come.

"Then you must be doubly grateful for your chastisement that will cleanse your soul and show you your error at last." He cleared his throat. "Another five lashes, beyond the ten, should assist her. I will watch to see what happens."

Padre Bartolimieu delivered the next two blows in silence, paying no attention to the muffled shrieks that Seur Odile gave. "You see that she has started to bleed. Shall it be one more, mon Évêque, or six?"

"Six, I think. If we falter now, God will see that we lack purpose." He folded his hands and watched her. "Strange that there are no postulants here."

"This is not like Avignon, where the daughters of noblemen come for the privilege of serving in any convent." He lifted the lash and brought it down with more force than before and was rewarded with a scream.

"That is better, mon Fils. You must not be lenient, or the Devil will have the victory." Évêque Amalrie bent over slightly. "Ma Fille, do you still persist in your error?"

It was almost impossible for Seur Odile to speak. "I am . . . thankful that this . . . is my reward and . . . not the fires of hell . . . mon Berger."

"Ah. You are learning wisdom. When the next five blows are over, you will be prepared to make a full confession. You must reveal all that the demon did and said, all the indignities he heaped on your flesh. It *was* a male, was it not?"

"Yes. *Yes!*" she cried out.

"Not a female, to wrest all your chastity from you in forbidden ways?" He sounded more disappointed than curious. "Have you been spared that, or do you seek to deny the whole of your debauchery?"

"No women," Seur Odile protested. "What could a woman do?"

"That is something," Évêque Amalrie said to Padre Bartolimieu. "We have reason to be grateful to la Virge, it would seem. The next five blows, mon Padre? Not too gently, I think."

"Yes, mon Évêque," he said, not quite smiling.

Pierre scowled at the sealed letter Père Guibert held out to him. "Why do you not present it yourself, mon Père?"

"I am afraid of what might happen here if I leave," the priest answered nervously. "Évêque Amalrie and Padre Bartolimieu are very . . . strict in their reprimands and their methods. I . . . I wish Cardinal Seulfleuve to know of it."

"Not Cardinal Belroche?" Pierre demanded, his hands braced on his hips. "It is not my wish to leave at all, mon Père, and still less my desire to be embroiled in the feuds of clerics."

"This is not a feud!" Père Guibert snapped, hoping that he was telling the truth. "You saw what they've done to Seur Aungelique, and you know that no matter what she has done, she does not deserve that." He held the letter more emphatically. "She is your kinswoman, she is without vocation, and she has been made to suffer."

"That's true enough," Pierre said with a sigh. "This

is a strange place, mon Père." He looked at the high white walls. "There are demons here, or so I have come to think. They should be got rid of. They should be driven . . . driven . . ." He did not finish his thought.

"But not at the cost of all the nuns, surely," Père Guibert said, striving to keep a reasonable tone. "They are helpless creatures, women, without the means to save themselves from the predations of hell. But we who have been given the task of caring for them may do things as harmful as neglect or punishment if we do not use them as they ought to be used."

"Use them. Well, if they are subject to demons, they *are* used, and in ways that are far from God's guidance." He shook his head, the scar becoming a ragged shadow across his face. "What do you ask of Cardinal Seulfleuve?"

"That he take time to discover what Évêque Amalrie has ordered and how he has proceeded here. If the Cardinal agrees, I will accept the whipping and the fastings, and I will listen to confession with a calm heart. I express only my doubts at the force of the methods employed to obtain the confessions. Where there are demons and the nuns desire them, then racking is most certainly proper, but there is yet no proof that the nuns called up the demons to love them. I know that this is a place of fears and dreams, and it may be that these nuns, more the slaves of their humors than men, have become confused. Even I, upon occasion, have had such dreams here as would make me tremble if such things were truly happening to me. Such an angelic youth has come to me and abused himself and me that the grace that shone from his features was turned to the lurid flames of hell. If I, a priest, may be so disordered, what may we think of the nuns, whose reason is not strong and who have come to look upon themselves as under the attack of hellish messengers." He paused, looking closely at Pierre. "Do you believe they have called up demons?"

"Not . . . not that, no." He coughed. "Any man does dream here . . ." He was able to speak more firmly as he reached out for the letter. "But demons will come if they find your weakness, won't they, mon Père?"

"But to confess their intervention where it is lacking is a grave sin," Père Guibert reminded him.

As Pierre took the letter, he flushed. "I will deliver this, mon Père, but I will say nothing; this is a matter for clerics, not fighting men."

Père Guibert frowned, sensing more than the usual reluctance in his warning. "Mon Fils, are you troubled? Is something the matter."

"Nothing that concerns you, mon Père." He straightened up, tugging at his belt as he did. "Dreams are only that, and what we see in them are naught but the fumes of the brain." He repeated his old lessons with confidence. "I will give your letter to Cardinal Seulfleuve, my word upon it. And when it is permitted, I will return again. As you say, they are not treating my kinswoman well, and that demands my attention."

"I am grateful and will remember your act in my prayers, Sieur le Duc." He tried to find a better way to express his appreciation, but there was nothing he could do or say that would be correct in such a situation as this one.

"I am grateful, as well. But I will not interfere, not without the authority of the Cardinal to guide me, for God did not make me to serve Him but His Church and le roi."

"That is acceptable to me, mon Fils," Père Guibert said, thinking that it was less than he had hoped but more than he had expected.

Pierre tucked the letter into his belt. "No one shall take this without my knowing of it."

"Good." He made the sign of the cross and went back toward la Tres Saunte Annunciacion.

"Must we leave?" Tristan asked as he came up behind Pierre.

Le Duc jumped, as though he had been awakened from a dream. "Ah! You. I fear we have been told to go. What is wrong here"—he shuddered as he searched for words—"does not need force of arms but something else. I will not let the priests keep us . . . waiting on their pleasure."

Tristan did not speak at once. "And the matter I mentioned to you?"

"The woman?" Pierre asked quickly.

"Yes. Philomine." Tristan did not press further, while Pierre glowered down at his boots.

"I know why you want to take her away from here, Courtenay. But if you took her now, while that Évêque Amalrie is still in charge, it would appear that she was carrying the demon with her and that you were its servant." He strode toward his horse, glad to have the illusion of action if not the reality. "You would bring suspicion on her."

Tristan nodded, though Pierre did not see him. "I will need a little time to tell her. She had hoped to be gone from here by this evening." He did not bother to argue further with le duc, for he had seen that expression in his eyes before and knew it brooked no dispute.

"You may have a little time. We will wait for you," Pierre called back to him as he prepared to mount.

Chapter 12

Cardinal Seulfleuve was an older man, harried in manner and of a scholarly disposition. He held out the message from Père Guibert to le duc de Parcignonne and shook his head. "I'm sorry, Sieur le Duc, but you must understand that Cardinal Belroche has already approved Évêque Amalrie's methods and any questioning of it now would only serve to make it worse for the sisters at la Tres Saunte Annunciacion. From what I have read here, there would be a process and burnings and all the rest of it."

Pierre shook his head. "Évêque Amalrie is enjoying himself from what I saw of him."

"That's possible. But there are others like him, and they are in great favor right now—their zeal gives them power that they might not otherwise be granted. You can't be certain that they will not report you to the pope or his personal assistants, and then there *would* be trouble." He put the message down. "It's those perfidious Romans, mon Duc; that is what makes them all so determined to protect the church at any cost." He went on hastily, "The Devil rules in Rome, and we are the last bastion against him. In March, a whole monastery was burned, with its monks, because they had become suspect. It could easily happen at la Tres Saunte Annunciacion."

Pierre shrugged. "Why plead with me, Eminence? You admit that I am not part of the Church."

"But you are part of the nobility, and as such, you must do what you can to maintain the Church, by your oath." He looked around the library, where they were speaking. "They have removed books from this room, believing them to be dangerous to the souls of men. When books are burned, mon Duc, it is little time before the people meet the same fate." He shook his head. "I have done the only thing I could think of: I have recommended that the decision be left to the civil authorities. It will keep the hounds at bay for a time." He paced down the room, his hands clasped nervously at his waist. "I have done everything that I could without bringing the attention of—"

"Yes, you've said so already," Pierre interrupted. "I would be pleased to be the administrator of your instructions. After all, I have a kinswoman there, and she is one that they claim to be afflicted."

Cardinal Seulfleuve shook his head slowly. "It may be so many things. The Devil is subtle, and so are his Romans. If you were to agree to watch this until we are more certain, then I would be most grateful. I have some authority in the issuance of vidamies, and it may be that you will receive one for this service."

"It would be welcome," Pierre said honestly, knowing how much his house would gain from the church title and the revenue from the lands. "Since the Plague, my House has been struggling with its holdings. We lack peasant tenants to work the land, and much of our acres are fallow."

"A vidamie will not change that," the cardinal remarked.

"It will provide fields in good heart with men to work them. That, in turn, will give us the revenues to acquire more tenants. There are peasants that would be glad for a fief with a living lord and an assured succession." He paused, giving the cardinal a little time to get to the end of the long room and turn back toward him.

"You will have word from me regularly. Courtenay, one of my men-at-arms, can write, and I will take him with me."

"You are astute, mon Duc," Cardinal Seulfleuve said with a faint trace of a smile. "It is wise to be careful."

"So I am learning." He rose when the Cardinal had given him his blessing. "I will tell you this, Eminence: I would rather face Turks in battle than remain here with the intrigue and deception and hypocrisy you find around you. With Turks, you know where you are, but here"—he lifted his hands to show how inadequate he felt—"a sword is about as useful as a plow in a river."

"Sadly, I must agree with you," the Cardinal said. "In time, the Pope will be grateful."

"I do not hope for that." Pierre knew that he must not expect Clement to act on his behalf, especially in a matter as delicate as this one. "His Holiness has other concerns than this."

"Lamentably," Cardinal Seulfleuve agreed. "Well, I will bid you Godspeed and pray that you have less to contend with than you fear."

"My thanks, Eminence." He was halfway to the door when he added, "I do not want Cardinal Belroche to alter my instructions."

"He will not," said Cardinal Seulfleuve with more sternness than Pierre had heard before.

Pierre nodded. Bargains of that nature he could understand and appreciate. "Let me learn of any change."

"You have my assurance on it," the Cardinal promised, and waved him toward the door again. "You must recall, however," he reminded le duc, "that we are speaking in camera and that nothing we have said is official in the Church."

"Of course," Pierre said, and backed out of the library.

Long after sunset, the halls of la Tres Saunte Annunciacion rang with voices, some raised in prayer, some screaming obscenities and profanities, and some reduced to terrible laugher. Mère Léonie called those nuns who could respond to the chapel and ordered them to devote themselves to prayers on behalf of the other Sisters, those would were not able to pray for themselves.

"I wish the night were over," Seur Victoire confided to Seur Philomine between responses to the devotions to Saunt Jude.

"Hush," Seur Philomine whispered to her.

"I wish I could petition the superior general of the Order to send me to another convent." She sounded both petulant and wistful.

"*You have been the refuge of those beyond hope, who have lost every battle*," Seur Philomine said with the others in the modified Latin of the Church.

"Don't you want release from this?" Seur Victoire asked, prodding Seur Philomine in the side with her elbow.

Seur Philomine was goaded into answering, "You must be silent, ma Seur, so the prayers will be recited properly."

"To the Devil with prayers," Seur Victoire said lightly, her eyes turning away. "Everything else goes to him—why not our prayers?"

"What is your discussion, my Sisters?" Mère Léonie demanded from the altar where she had stopped the liturgy.

"Nothing," Seur Philomine said quickly. "We are frightened, ma Mère."

"She wants to go away from the Order. She told me," Seur Victoire said, more loudly than Seur Philomine.

"And for that you have interrupted holy service when the convent is in such dire need of aid?" Mère Léonie asked, her voice sweet and her eyes more icy than usual. "Would you care to explain to your Sisters how this comes about?"

Seur Victoire tossed her head. "I have done nothing, ma Mère."

Seur Philomine started to protest, but Mère Léonie cut her short. "If you have done such a wrong, ma Seur, you should be chastised as Évêque Amalrie has chastised others. Do you long for the caress of the thongs, or are you pleased with the misfortune that has been visited upon us."

"You know I am not," Seur Philomine said, feeling indignation rise within her. "I have been devoted to this convent, and though I am a tertiary Sister, I have performed my duties with contentment and humility." It was not entirely true, but she did not feel she was lying.

"Which you boast of?" Mère Léonie challenged. "You are guilty of a great wrong, ma Seur, and it is for me as your superior to correct it; Our Lord commands us to obey him, and we who are in His service are pleased to do so. To be afraid, as you say you are, doubts the very strength and majesty of the God you say you worship and trust. Think again: do you require more than this minor admonition to be rid of your sins?"

Seur Philomine had gone pale, but she kept her composure. "You know that I love and serve God, but another has achieved the crown of my heart, and God has not seen fit to change that. Therefore, since I do not know the adoration of those with vocation, I falter and know fear."

Seur Marguerite, who had been caught in her own inner reflections, suddenly addressed the Sisters. "It is not wise to listen too much. I remember how it was before the Plague came—everyone talked, and it was worse because of it, I think." She crossed herself. "My children always talk among themselves."

"That is not important," Mère Léonie said with great control. "It is for Our Lord to enter your hearts, as

Seur Philomine has said. But ma Seur," she went on to the tertiary Sister, "you must fast and pray; for Our Lord comes where he is wanted."

"And where He has made a place for Himself by giving a true vocation," Seur Philomine said, knowing that her defiance would go against her.

Mère Léonie stepped back so that she was braced against the altar. "Let us give one day to fasting, all of us, so that the tempestuous fires that have raged here will have the chance to be stilled and the soul regain its tranquillity."

"Fasting?" Seur Victoire cried out. "Starving, rather. We have not enough food, and the village can spare none for us. So we fast, pretending that it is because our souls are in need of it." She abruptly left the chapel.

Most of the nuns were silent now, trying to avoid Mère Léonie's piercing gaze. At last, the superior addressed them once more. "Yes, we have not as much food as you or I would wish, but that does not mean that Our Lord will neglect us, for we are His servants, and we are doing all that we may to honor Him." She moved away from the altar, walking up and down the chapel between the nuns. "You each have doubted God. You have demanded that you be saved now, in the body."

"There are too many souls to save," Seur Marguerite announced to the nuns. "There are so many that they are beyond counting; I do not know how many of them have died. There is not space in the earth to hold them at Judgment Day. How can the earth give up so many?"

"Sacrilege!" Seur Morgance shouted, and threw herself at Seur Marguerite, reaching to claw at her face.

In an instant, the chapel was in disorder. Seur Marguerite whimpered in hurt and confusion as Seur Morgance bore her down, knocking aside the two Sisters who knelt beside her. One of them began to scream, while the other scrambled on hands and knees for the door.

"This is forbidden!" Mère Léonie shouted.

Seur Morgance rolled on her side and drew her knees up to her chest, reciting the first line of the Pater

Noster over and over quickly and softly. Seur Philomine
put an arm across her to shield her, but one of the Sisters, caught in the scuffle, reached out and struck her as
she attempted to escape.

Two other nuns were fighting now, one of them ac-
cusing the other of unnatural desires. One well-aimed
blow caused a nosebleed, and shortly there were small
stains on many of the gray habits.

"By God's Grace!" came an outraged voice from the
door as Évêque Amalrie rushed in. "What has—" His
face was rigid with fury as one of the distraught nuns
grabbed him around the waist and clung to him.

"Forgive them, mon Berger," Mère Léonie shouted
to him, hardly audible over the din. "It is the Devil's
doing."

"The Devil may have begun it, but God will stop it!"
he promised, his eyes sweeping over the Sisters in utter
contempt.

Mère Léonie lowered her head as the chapel became silent once more. "We are in the hands of Our
Lord."

"What are you telling me?" Pierre demanded as he
faced Seur Aungelique in the herb garden; the scents of
sage and thyme hung in the air.

She tossed her head. "I am with child." She made a
sound that was intended to be a laugh.

"But . . . how?" Since his return to the convent two
days before, Seur Aungelique had been attempting to
speak with him. He had avoided her and now wished he
had continued to hold her off.

"You know what it is that men do to women. You've
done it many times, haven't you?" She plucked a sprig of
tansy and sniffed at it.

Pierre's face grew harder. "You know what I meant.
Answer me. Was it someone at Comtesse Orienne's
gatherings?" He had heard many of the men speak of
Seur Aungelique when she had been at Une Noveautie,
admiring her.

"Yes. And no." She cocked her head to one side. "It
happened after you brought me back. I know. My

courses came after my return." She added angelica to the tansy. "But you know what it is to be a lover. Mine came to me, to possess me."

"That's"—he was about to say "ridiculous" or "absurd" but could not bring himself to speak—"impossible."

Her expression was taunting, but her voice was angry. "What? Do you doubt that I could inspire such devotion simply because *you* do not wish to love me?"

Pierre restrained himself, though he wanted to strike her or shake her. "You are not with child. It's a stupid game, cousin, and one that may reap you a bitter harvest."

"Other women have bastards," Seur Aungelique pointed out, making mock through reason. "They have lived well, those women, with pleased husbands and honored children."

"They may have bastards, but not while living in a convent," Pierre growled.

"They don't? How strange. I had heard that other women have forsaken God for the flesh while in His house." As she came up to him, she held out the herbs she had picked. "Will you wear these for me, mon cher cousin?"

He struck out, casting the sprigs aside. "Stop it! *Stop!*"

"It is too late to stop, Pierre. The babe will be here by Christmas, just like Our Lord." She held her wrist where his hand had hit her.

"Stop this jeering. It gains you nothing!" His voice had risen, and he strove to lower it.

"It gains me satisfaction," she said, bringing her chin up. "You will not have me, my father does not want me, the Church is a farce, so what does it matter that I will have a child? It will be mine."

He took a step back, his heel crushing the stalks of half-grown basil. "God and the Martyrs, girl, you're inviting disaster."

"Well enough. If that is what God intends for me, I will embrace it. I will bend my will to God's Will. And you can do nothing to change that. You are not God." She crossed her arms, her eyes narrowing. "Of course, you could marry me, and then there would be no problem, would there?"

"Why not marry your lover? Or is he married already? Or is he a priest?" He aimed the questions at her as if they had been quarrels to pierce armor.

She beamed at him. "But you have heard the priests, Pierre. My lover is a demon. They have decided that, those three eunuchs, between them. And Frère Renaut records it all, to tell the men at Avignon." She pointed to his feet. "Stop walking, mon Duc: you are ruining my garden."

"What do you mean, they are recalling you?" Évêque Amalrie asked Frère Renaut as they waited to hear the confession of Seur Catant.

"I cannot easily refuse such orders, mon Évêque," Frère Renaut said. "There are the priests. Both of them can read and write after a fashion; enough for your purposes."

"But . . ." He folded his hands. "They are subverting my work here. They are making it impossible for the Devil to be routed. Whatever they put their hands to will be contaminated by this."

Frère Renaut shook his head. "Your feelings are just, mon Évêque, but I beg you not to say such things to me, for I will have to report them when I return, to Pope Clement." He went toward the door to the hospice. "I must hasten, since the orders require that I leave here before sunset."

"Tell them to authorize a replacement for you," the bishop insisted.

"I will tell them that you are in need of another monk to record for you. But I am in no position to do more, mon Évêque." He forced a kind of smile to his lips. "We are servants of more than God when we are in the church."

"The Church! The Church!" Évêque Amalrie flung up his hands. "That is why we are here, Frère Renaut. They have lost sight of that fact, it appears. They are subverting the very work we are mandated to perform!" He paced the length of the room. "First they send that infu-

riating Parcignonne to interfere—and he is not a churchman but the most worldly noble—and then they remove
my aid. They are chasing Roman specters as a cat chases
mice. *This* should have their attention, not what the Roman Cardinal did with his nephew in bed."

"Mon Évêque, please—" Frère Renaut began, and
was cut off.

"Don't you see? They must be *made* to understand
what danger we're confronting here. They do not *appreciate* what is at stake, and so they are proposing to abandon
their daughters to the degradations and degeneration of
demonic possession. And you. You! You obedient hound,
fawning at their feet and wagging your tail because they
have called you in from the stables. But this is not a stable; it is a *cesspool*. They do not have the knowledge
to . . . to . . ." He made a complicated gesture to indi-
cate how vast the hazard was. "You have not recorded all
the confessions correctly, and that has deceived them!"

"Évêque Amalrie—" Frère Renaut protested, his
face alive with distress. "When you are cooler, we will—"

"When I am cooler? Who are you, *Frère*, to determine if I am fit and if I am able? Or is there more to this?
Have you been sent not to record these confessions at all
but to watch me on behalf of my enemies?" He approached Frère Renaut with an unpleasant grin on his
rosebud mouth. "Is that the game they are playing? They
remove one spy—you, mon Frère—and give me another—that confounded imbecile of a duc!— in order to
keep me from fulfilling my purpose here. I have been
blind!" He was a deep, plummy shade, and his small
eyes bulged with his emotion.

"Mon Évêque, this speen is—" His tone quivered.

"Out of my sight! Out! Go back to those lickspittles
at Avignon and slander me! *God* is my defender and the
force of my arm!" He turned away from Frère Renaut.
"Do not think that I will ignore your perfidy, Frère Renaut."

Frère Renaut watched the bishop storm away, and
his heart was tight in his chest. He knew of Évêque
Amalrie's unruly temper from other monks who had had

the misfortune to work with him, and now he understood their frustration in dealing with the man. He shook his head, this time slowly. He would have to include all this in his report to the Cardinal as well as the less official message he would send to Tuscany where it would be relayed to Rome. He was contemplating the possible rewards he would receive when he heard a footfall behind him.

"Frère Renaut?" said Mère Léonie.

"Yes, ma Mère?" he responded, facing her.

"You have had some disagreement with Berger Amalrie?" Her pale eyes rested on his face, and she could see his embarrassment at her stare.

"Évêque Amalrie is a man of . . . strong temperament." He was drawn into her gaze, transfixed by the clean lines of her features.

"What has displeased him, then? You are not bound by the confessional, mon Frère, and may speak as openly as your conscience will permit." She came a step nearer, so that she was not quite out of reach.

"First . . . ah . . . he suggested that it was unfortunate that I should be recalled to Avignon." There was something about Mère Léonie that captivated him, enthralled him, and he could not still his tongue while she was near him. "You understand that he is convinced there is a demon here."

"Only one? With all that has transpired, the creature must be worn to a rag." There was just enough humor in her retort that Frère Renaut was able to laugh a bit.

"There is a demon here, ma Mère," he told her, but as softly as if he were entreating her love.

"Why do you say that? Because we have not perfected ourselves and are still weak in the flesh?" She smiled at him. "I know what women are, mon Frère, and I wish to bring them to Our Lord."

Frère Renaut dragged himself out of her gaze, moving away from her and looking toward the crucifix hung over the door. "There is a demon here."

She came up beside him. "I agree."

This calm statement astonished him, and he turned recklessly toward her. "Don't you know what that may mean for you and your Sisters?"

"That there will be a Process?" she considered it. "I would be surprised if the Church bothered to begin a process here."

"Évêque Amalrie has said something of the same thing," Frère Renaut admitted. "He believes that there is subterfuge behind it."

"Of course he does," she said, speaking very evenly. "He is an ambitious man. He does not want to be here, and for that reason, he punishes the nuns." When she heard the protesting gasp, she amended her condemnation. "He is afraid of the Devil. But he would rather he be sent to investigate demons in some place that will add to his credit." This time when she smiled, her handsome face was more open. "I have no illusions about la Tres Saunte Annunciacion, but I go where I am called, mon Frère. I am the devoted servant of Our Lord, and if this is where he wishes me to do His work, then I am content to obey."

Frère Renaut was more relieved than he could express. He would not have to battle the superior as well as the bishop. "God send us more such Mères as you are, Mère Léonie," he said, no longer resisting his urge to stare at her.

"To say amen would be vanity and therefore a sin, mon Frère," she said, chiding him lightly. "But it was kindness for you to say so in this hour of trouble."

There were visions in his mind that he would have to confess, but he could not bring himself to leave her alone. He had never felt the flesh pull him as it did now, and not for a prostitute or other slattern but for a tall, lean nun with a face as handsome as a boy's and eyes of cold blue fire. "There is more I might say," he whispered.

She shrugged. "What is there to say until Avignon speaks or the Plague comes again?"

"That's not . . ." He coughed. "I will make my report in Avignon, ma Mère, and I will say that you have done all that you might to keep this place from being . . . infested."

"But that is not correct, is it? I hope you will tell the truth, for all falsehoods, even the most kind or flattering, are homage to the Devil and traps for the virtuous." She hesitated. "I wish only to accomplish the tasks Our Lord sets forth for me."

"I will do as you ask," Frère Renaut said, anxious now to be out of her disturbing presence.

"Deo gratias," she responded, her manner still humble but no longer quite as potent as it had been.

"I have seen how these things are dealt with in Avignon. I know how to tell them."

"Yes, and for that our Lord be praised," she said, then went away from him back to her sisters, who were waiting in the refectory for their midday meal.

By the time the second messenger came from Avignon, Évêque Amalrie had ordered eight of the nuns into a week of seclusion and had given floggings, with Padre Bartolimieu's help, to five more. He gave an elaborate greeting to the messenger, offering him a bench in Mère Léonie's study that he had taken for his own. "It has been more than three weeks since Frère Renaut departed for Avignon. Your arrival is most welcome, but I find it a little tardy."

The messenger was enveloped in a simple dark brown cloak, and the warmth of the day had made him sweat. He removed the cloak and revealed the splendid papal tabard beneath it. "We are told to travel covered so that Romans will not know where we go or why," he explained.

"I am aware of that!" Évêque Amalrie barked. "You are not dealing with a simple village priest who knows little more than the Mass and the Psalms."

"You have not been much outside of Avignon until now, mon Évêque," the messenger reminded him smoothly.

Évêque Amalrie pouted. "They have forgotten me out here." He assumed his most portentous manner.

"There are forces here that would cause even the most holy of men to blanch with fear."

"That is unfortunate," the messenger said, unmoved by the revelation. "You are being recalled to Avignon."

Évêque Amalrie sat in disbelieving silence. "To Avignon?"

"I have been sent to give you notice. The Pope has ordered you to return. He is concerned about the Romans, who have been busy again."

Évêque Amalrie looked with suspicion at the parchment that bore the huge papal seal. "Why am I being recalled at this time? Were there not Romans when I was sent here?"

"Of course," the messenger said smoothly. "And their numbers are increasing. There are political favors, as well, for those who are not too proud to take them." He looked at Évêque Amalrie. "You have said that you wish to serve the Church and defend her. God and the Pope have given you that opportunity."

Although Évêque Amalrie had some experience of courtiers, he did not often recognize them when they wore the livery of the Church, and so he took much of what he heard as vindication of his worth rather than the appeal to his vanity it was. "Avignon is the only hope of the world. But I fear for these unfortunate Sisters, who will have no one to watch over them."

"Their priests will be here," the messenger said, doing his best not to appear bored. "If there is any danger, le duc de . . . uh . . . Parcignonne is still mandated to defend them."

"Do you mean he is to remain *here*?" Évêque Amalrie demanded. "Here? His men near these women who have fallen to demons?" He half rose from his chair. "God will punish them all for . . ." He sat down again. "I will need escort back to Avignon. Since Frère Renaut has left—and doubtless told you many lies about what has transpired here—there is my page to lend me his protection, and that is not enough, especially in these times, when a papal messenger must travel wrapped in a cloak." He smiled in appreciation of his own wit.

"It is proper that a man of your dignity have escort,

yes," the messenger said in a bland, practiced manner. "Had the Pope created this area a vidamie, then it would be for the vidame to extend that honor, but His Holiness has not yet decided how this area is to be assigned."

This morsel was snapped up at once. "Yes, there are matters that we should discuss, the Pope and I." He leaned back, folding his hands in complacent satisfaction.

"I will inform the superior of your orders if that is your pleasure," the messenger said, rising. He had managed to discharge his obligation there without making more of an issue of the bishop's removal than the Cardinal wished, which would be to his credit later on.

"It would . . . be best that you do, I believe," Évêque Amalrie said. It would have been enjoyable to tell Mère Léonie himself, but it was more impressive and appropriate to have it done by the papal messenger himself.

"Then I thank you for your gracious courtesy, mon Évêque, and I pray that God will speed your return to Avignon." He knelt to kiss the ring Évêque Amalrie extended to him. "With some dispatch, you should be prepared to depart in two days. Is that reasonable?"

"If le duc is willing, then I will be at his disposal." Évêque Amalrie's small eyes glinted. "Avignon. I have longed to be there so many times."

"You will be there soon," said the messenger, and left the study. So intent were his thoughts that he did not hear a voice call out to him until the second time.

"You're the messenger, are you?" asked Pierre, striding along the narrow corridor, making the walls appear too close together. "How is it that they sent an old reprobate like you?" He clapped the messenger on his shoulder. "How many years, Jean? Five? Six?"

The messenger's expression changed at once. "Seven years, as well you know." He returned the hug Pierre gave him. "Now what in the name of all the angels of heaven are you doing on sentry duty here? When I was told you were keeping watch on this place, I almost went off in a faint. You, Pierre."

"I have a cousin here, and her father—d'Ybert;

you've met him—has just been made a vidame, so he is generous with his favors to the Church.

"Generosity is not how I should describe it," the messenger said. "You could be better employed." As he said this, he was not entirely certain it was true, for he saw deep lines of fatigue in le duc's face and noticed that the man was thinner than before, his eyes dark and feverish.

"Amen to that. Every time I have returned here, I have vowed it would be the last, but then something happens, and we are back here to fix the doors or keep watch for demons. It's a dreadful way for a good fighter to have to spend his days." Pierre made an exaggerated sigh. "My men. You knew Ivo, didn't you? He has said that if he comes back here, he'll rape a few of the women and say that the demon impelled him." He stopped and gave Jean a long look. "And you? What are you here for? And in that tabard?"

"My father is one of the new vidames, and he, too, is generous with the Church. You do not know what it is to have a family brought back from the brink in that way. Two of the old fiefs are gone to ruin since the Plague was there. Now there is a chance to save them, but it means that those of us who are able must give our service to the pope. I'd rather be fighting Romans, so—" He opened his hands in acceptance of his predicament.

"Do you think it will come to that? That we will fight the Romans instead of this eternal spying and bickering?" He spoke with animation, but Jean sensed that there was a more frantic need for battle than mere boredom.

"It might," he said. "My father heard one of the Cardinals say that he favored a war. But there are not enough men to mount a real campaign, not yet. If the English had not been so busy in the north, then we might have been able to do something before now. Oh, I think it may drag on another three or four years until both sides are more prepared. It cannot go on indefinitely."

"Three or four years is too long as it is," Pierre declared. "But that's a churchman for you—take more time and make it all much worse."

"True enough." Jean stopped, then said in another tone, "You do not approve of Évêque Amalrie, then?"

"He is one of those who likes to see men flogged, and so much the better if he can flog women. It is not such punishment as any sensible man must mete out from time to time but that other, reckless sort of beating that brings pain and dread." He hooked his thumbs in his belt. "That captain in Lyon—do you remember the man, with the yellow hair and dark eyes?—he used to have his men flogged so that they howled and gibbered. This Évêque Amalrie is the same sort."

"Strange that a man with such a bent should want to be a priest." He lowered his chin. "It's not as if his family sent him here. He is said to have a vocation." He began to walk again, motioning for Pierre to keep up with him. "Évêque Amalrie has been recalled to Avignon by order of the Pope, and you will be required to escort him."

"What? Why should I let my men be the lackeys to that miserable—"

"Be calm, Pierre," Jean said with a grin. "If you escort him, it may be that you will be able to appeal to the Pope to send others here next time, and you will then be free to return to your estates or to prepare for battle with Rome, whichever is more to your liking."

"That's possible," Pierre said slowly. "But so far, d'Ybert has insisted that I be the one to speak to his daughter Aungelique, who is a nun here."

Jean reached the door into the courtyard, but he did not go out at once. A reminiscent smile touched his hard, square mouth. "Aungelique. Is that the one that keeps running off to Une Noveautie? The one that Comtesse Orienne calls ma Frèrée?" He chuckled as he opened the door. Hot sunlight met them, making both men squint and shade their eyes.

"That is part of Michau d'Ybert's reason. He also desires to impress the Cardinal so that eventually he will regain the lands that are currently disputed by him and Courtenay."

"It is three generations already, and there is no sign of an end," Jean said, pleased to have something so remote to discuss. "But you. You are not bound to d'Ybert for that, are you?"

"By heaven, no. Courtenay's son is one of my men-at-arms, and I will not be asked to arm for d'Ybert should they ever come to battle over the land." He stared around the courtyard. "When are we to take this precious burden to Avignon?"

"You would do well to leave in two days. The Cardinal wishes to have the man back where he can reach him before the Cardinals meet to discuss the new vidamies that are being awarded." He gazed at the wall of the hospice. "Would there be room for me with your men? I don't relish passing the night in such a place as that one, not if the nuns are as Frère Renaut described them."

"In my tent, if you wish," Pierre said, then wished he might withdraw the offer. He had more visions of Mère Léonie, and if there should be another such while Jean slept near him, it might be a very bad thing.

Jean inclined his head, saying, "I thank you, and another time I would be most pleased to accept, but not, I fear, tonight. While I wear the tabard, I must keep to my own quarters. And in the morning, I will have to leave again. I have another message to deliver to Saunt-Elizair. It would seem that they caught a Roman and killed him after pulling out his nails and breaking all his teeth."

"What is the matter?" Pierre asked. "You would have done the same, wouldn't you?"

"True, and worse," he answered, shaking his head at the waste of it. "But we would have questioned him while we worked on him. That is what has me most concerned, Pierre. I confess it—many Romans, if Romans they are, are being caught and held and killed without any attempt at discovering what they have been sent to do. If the word goes out that Avignon is permitting the slaughter of innocent travelers, you know what that will do to trade and the treaties le roi has made with other rulers. There *would* be war then."

"Excellent!" Pierre exclaimed. "I would be ready in three days, with two dozen men to ride with me."

"And we are not prepared for war. We must have more intelligence if we are to prevail." He stared around the courtyard. "This is the most forlorn place."

"That it is. I'd rather a camp in the desert than this." They resumed their walk toward the doors. "I'll see if one of the Sisters will care for your horse. The one who usually does it has been ordered to keep to her cell and meditate on her sins and her lack of vocation."

"Nothing much growing, is there?" Jean observed.

"The whole valley is like that. There used to be more Sisters here, and the land produced what they needed with sufficient simple fare for the travelers who came to the hospice." He pointed to a row of spindly squashes. "They need water, but with all the nuns doing penance, the plants are withering for lack of care."

"A pity," Jean said, shrugging. "The Cardinal may order some relief, if he has time to do it."

"It would be sensible, I think," Pierre said, then abandoned the subject of the nuns for the more interesting matters of spurs and dirks.

As the men-at-arms grouped around the wagon that carried the petulant Évêque Amalrie, the Sisters came out of the convent to pray for his safe journey and to ask God's blessing for his great service to them.

"You are all in need of the grace of God," the bishop reminded them as he addressed them for what he devoutly hoped was the last time, "and you are all frail women without the aid of God's guidance to bring you to His glory. Prostrate yourselves, mortify the flesh for the glory of the soul, and it may be that God will show His Mercy to you and save you from the pit. You cannot do that by denying the evil that has come to you but by acknowledging the demon and welcoming the chastisements that must free you at last." He signaled to Pierre. "You may start, Sieur le Duc."

"'You may start, Sieur le Duc,'" he mimicked under his breath, then raised his right hand and called out his rough, ringing cry, "Onward for honor of the bees!"

which had been permitted to his family by le roi for service to him—the badge of the royal household was golden bees.

The men echoed his cry, and they moved out at a walk.

In her cell, Seur Philomine stood on tiptoe to see out the window so that she could watch the little cortege leave.

Chapter 13

Pierre broke their journey at sunset, motioning his men off the highroad onto a pleasant lane. "We will stay at this villa tonight," he informed his men and Évêque Amalrie. "It is not wise to be abroad after dark."

"Indeed not," Évêque Amalrie said, crossing himself. "Devils and brigands and all the dangers of . . ." He stopped, not wanting to frighten himself more than he already had.

"Mon Évêque," Pierre said smoothly as they made their way through the first, fragrant gloom of twilight, "this villa is the home of a noblewoman who is often in the company of Cardinals and other high churchmen."

Évêque Amalrie nodded, his smugness returning as he listened. "You are most proper, mon Duc. You, being a man-of-arms, may be at liberty to move in places that would bring odium to one such as myself." He drew the curtains of the wagon back even farther. "It *is* a pleasant building."

As they approached the front of the villa, two pages came running out, one of them holding a torch to light the entrance, which had fallen into deep shadow. "Good strangers, we—" began the nearer page.

"Jaques, tell your mistress that Pierre Fornault is here, will you? And say that I have brought Évêque Amalrie as well as a few of my men." He was already dismounting, rubbing his eyes, which ached from a day on the road."

Jaques bowed deeply, as was proper to honor Pierre's suzerainty as a grand seigneur of France. "You are welcome, mon Duc. My mistress," Jaques said as he took the reins from Pierre, "is in the pavilion in the garden and would be grateful to receive you there."

"The pavilion in the garden?" Pierre asked with a speculative smile. "Pray attend to the rest of this company, and be certain that mon Évêque is properly honored."

"It shall be as you wish," Jaques said, signaling to the other page. "Have grooms come, and then prepare the table in the smaller salon." He bowed again to Pierre as le Duc strolled away around the corner of the villa.

Évêque Amalrie, puzzled at the unusual reception, permitted the pages to help him dismount and instructed his own page to accompany the others to the servants' quarters while he sought the smaller salon with the men-at-arms. The heat had made him surly for a time; now he felt the renewal of appetite and interest. He addressed the page Pierre had called Jaques. "What place is this? I fear I do not know of it."

Jaques inclined his head and paused in his progress through the corridors. "This is Une Noveautie, and the mistress is Comtesse Orienne de Hautlimois."

Ordinarily, Évêque Amalrie would have been terribly offended by the familiar tone of the page, but he was too overwhelmed by what he had heard. Of Comtesse Orienne, he had heard such tales that he dreaded having to meet the woman. He was certain that she was not French at all but Roman, so appalling was her reputation. "I . . . thank you, mon serve," he managed to say through his suddenly tightened throat.

"The salon is there on your left," Jaques pointed out, and stood aside for the visitors to enter. "Refreshments will be presented shortly."

"I . . . ." Properly, Évêque Amalrie knew that he ought to refuse anything offered him in this iniquitous place. He was able to achieve a kind of compromise within himself. "I will wait until le duc has come to us."

Jaques shrugged and left the room, but the men-at-arms chuckled.

"That may be some little time," Ivo suggested as he found a padded bench and sank down on it.

"I am prepared to wait" was Évêque Amalrie's austere reply.

Oil lamps were hung in the pavilion, and their light gilded everything within it, including the shell-shaped bath where Comtesse Orienne lounged in scented water while her musicians played to her.

"Well met, Orienne," Pierre said as he strode through the door. "I see that you are—"

She gave a squeal of delight and flung water at him. "Pierre! Oh, thank goodness. I was ready to die of boredom and exhaustion, and then *you* come!" She half rose, the water running off her like golden tears. "I have missed you, Pierre. Where have you been?"

"No place you would enjoy, ma belle," he said, indulging her with his grin. "Bathing again? What does your confessor think of it?"

"He thinks that I am steeped in sin, of course," she replied, sinking back in the water. "But still, there are those who do not mind that I am steeped in sin. And some of them are churchmen." She trailed her fingers over the surface of the water. "Do you care to join me? You look as if you might be able to use a wash." She was teasing him, but carefully.

Pierre was about to refuse, then changed his mind. "I've never bathed in a tub like a seashell. That will be new."

She laughed and made a sign to her musicians. "Play outside the pavilion, my dears." When she had been obeyed, she gave an arch smile to Pierre. "Do you need a valet, or will I do?"

"I dress myself when traveling," he answered as he began to tug his surcote over his head. Shortly, all his clothes lay in a heap; the linen was dingy, and there were large stains on it.

"I will have that washed in saffron water if you wish,

mon Duc," Comtesse Orienne offered. The smell of the garment was even stronger than her perfume.

"As you wish. Just provide me one of those Turkish robes until morning and I will be well-content." He came toward her, completely naked now, and got into the tub as if mounting a fractious horse. "How am I supposed to sit in this engine of torture?"

"Just bring your knees up," she instructed, sliding between them. "There. You see how well it works?" She kissed him long and slowly. "It is good to have a man here again."

Pierre put his arms around her shoulder and was disappointed that he did not feel the rush of desire she usually inspired in him. He sighed, thinking that she was a beautiful woman with her lush body and her cat's face. But he could not free his mind from the tall, lithe form of the vision of Mère Léonie that tormented him so. "I have the honor to escort an ass of an Évêque back to Avignon."

She giggled. "Oh, dear. Is he that bad?"

"I fear so. He has spent several weeks whipping nuns, and he is disappointed that he will not be permitted to do so in future." Pierre moved a little, sinking deeper into the bath. "Ah, how good of you to do this." He let her wash him in silence; only the splash of the water competed with the airs of the three musicians outside the pavilion. "The bishop was sent to la Tres Saunte Annunciacion to investigate the claim that there were demons possessing the nuns there. He beat the Sisters and set them long and arduous penance until the demons should be revealed."

"Oh, my poor Aungelique," Orienne said with a sudden rush of sympathy. "She is not the sort of woman who benefits from a beating; she only becomes more headstrong and stubborn."

"She has not been much beaten," Pierre said with a trace of bitterness. "She is with child, and Évêque Amalrie will not touch her until it is known if the babe is demon's spawn."

"With child?" Orienne gasped. "But how could she?"

"She had plenty of opportunity here. She is a sly creature, that one, and she would lie if she thought it would benefit her." He propped himself more firmly by hooking his elbows over the side of the shell. "Do you believe that anyone here had her maidenhead?"

Orienne frowned, and for a moment she ceased her ministrations to Pierre while she thought. "There was Thibault Col, of course, but I did not think that they had gone beyond fondling and bussing. Perhaps I am wrong; she is a clever child, and she may have decided to do the act in secret." She recommenced her sponging of his chest and arms. "What of this churchman, then?"

Pierre gave one angry laugh. "He is one of those godly eunuchs who despises the flesh, or so he says." He grabbed her roughly and clutched her to him. "You can fire the loins of an angel, Orienne."

She slid her hands between his legs. "I do not seem to be doing that well with you, Pierre." She was not chiding him, but there was disappointment in her eyes. "I would rather fire you than an angel; these churchmen have no more notion of it than those pious camels." Gently, she kneaded his thigh. "Say you will take me, mon Duc. Say you will rut with me."

It was difficult for Pierre not to call out "Mère Léonie" as Orienne worked his flesh with her hands. He felt oddly dizzy, yet there was no answering thrust of his flesh. "I . . .I am tired, Orienne. It is the bath. Water enervates a man."

She went on with more determination. "It stimulates a woman."

He released her and pulled her hands away. "Leave off, woman! When I am rested, I will fuck you until your eyes bulge from their sockets." He fell silent, and she was wise enough to say nothing while he gave himself to his thoughts. "This churchman, though. I'll warrant he has never known any sheath for his dart other than his hand."

Her brows raised. "What pleasure then for me?"

"Perhaps not pleasure but satisfaction. Take this baby and make a man of him, and you may be sure that they will know of it in Avignon. He will crow his guilt like a cock in the sunrise."

She leaned back from him, considering his suggestion. "If I do this, what will you do for me in return?"

He sighed. "I have little to offer you, ma belle." He scowled down at the water. "What should I do that would benefit you?"

She lifted her shoulders, making that commonplace motion seem more sensual than anything else she had done. "Have I your word that you will serve me if I have need of a champion? I have your vow that you will defend my right?"

"You have," he said promptly. In the back of his mind, there was an element of caution, for he knew that once given, he could not be released from his vow except by the specific exoneration of the Pope himself. "I am your champion to death."

She smiled and began once again to wash him, this time concentrating on his thick-muscled thighs. "Very well, then; I will have my way with this Évêque and give you proof of it by first light."

"I will welcome it," he said, certain he would have the opportunity to revenge himself on Évêque Amalrie.

Seur Aungelique was on her knees tending the herbs when Seur Philomine came upon her. "The rosemary's not doing well," she said when she noticed that the other nun was nearby.

"That is unfortunate," Seur Philomine answered. "One of the lambs was killed last night; the village dogs got it."

"What a shame," Seur Aungelique said, straightening up to ease her back. "They say that I cannot feel it, but I know that it grows."

"Does that trouble you?" Seur Philomine could not help wondering.

"No. There are plenty of bastards in the world." She started to lean forward again, then stopped. "You are not permitted to marry that chevalier of yours, are you?"

"Tristan? If I had been, I would not be in this habit

now. Even in tertiary Orders, I find that this life is not
what best suits me." She got down beside Seur Aungelique. "Here. Let me help you."

"As you wish," Seur Aungelique said, and went on
with her weeding. "Do you think you will leave the
order?"

It took a while for Seur Philomine to answer. "If that
is what is needed, then yes." She pulled out four insidious creepers of morning glory.

"How can you be so serene when you know that you
are being kept from what you want most?" She sighed. "I
will not be able to tend this garden much longer, not if
the babe gets larger."

"Which it will, given time." She found a large pale
green spider hanging in the savory and pointed it out to
Seur Aungelique.

"Oh, kill it. I don't want it crawling over my hand
when I come to pick the herbs." She reached over and
squashed the spider under the flat of her hand. "There.
It's gone."

"Do you want the babe?" Seur Philomine asked a
little later. She had sat back on her heels and was wiping
her face with her wide cuff.

"Want it? Why not? If it is the Devil's get, then it will
mean that I am damned, and I will be free to live as I wish
to." She finished with a bed of parsley and moved on to the
borage. "You see that the leaves are rusty at the edges?"

"There is some of the same thing in the orchard,"
Seur Philomine said as she finished up with the penny-
royal.

Seur Aungelique saw what she was tending to. "I
might ask Seur Tiennette to make an elixir for me, using
that and the other plants that would rid me of the burden, and then we would never know whose it was—
man's or demon's. Seur Génève—you would not know
her, she was before you came here—was raped by one of
the monks that used to serve in Saunt-Vitre, and she had
such an elixir. She died of it, though. They found the
monk, too, and he was castrated for his sin. My father
had one of his enemies castrated, I remember. His family
has a standing challenge with ours now."

"It is not quite so drastic with our Houses, his and mine, but it is enough to keep us from marrying." Seur Philomine stared down at the plants, at the green light that filtered through them, staining the earth beneath with strange shades of olive and chartreuse.

"But you could go away with him, where neither family could reach you, and then if you decided to marry, it would be all right." Seur Aungelique said this as sensibly as she could. She went on with her weeding, paying no attention to the stains and grime on her habit. "I believe it would be best to have an island all to myself, where only my most worthy lovers could come, and only when I invited them." She looked over at Seur Philomine. "Would you enjoy such a life?"

Seur Philomine thought about it, concentrating on the question so intently that she almost pulled up two small thyme plants. "No," she said at last. "I was not made so adventuresome, ma Seur. I have one lover, and I pray that he will live for me, for I do not want to be in a world where he is not."

"There's always heaven," Seur Aungelique reminded her. "I am doomed to that whirlwind. I know I am. But are you not, as well?"

"I may be," Seur Philomine said. "If that is where he is, then I will be there, too."

"Such fidelity," Seur Aungelique marveled, trying not to laugh.

Seur Philomine gave her a serious answer. "No, not fidelity. It is something else entirely. It is as if together we are a coin; he one side and I the other. It would not matter through whose hands we passed or for what reason, because we are always the same coin, and wherever we were, we would each be part of the other. As long as we both lived, it would be thus." She shook her head, and sweat ran in her eyes.

"Then this is your ideal lover, this chevalier of yours you are a coin with?" Seur Aungelique was not so much mocking as doubting. "How can you want so much from only one man?"

"Not an ideal lover," Seur Philomine said seriously. "He is Tristan, and that is sufficient to my joy."

Seur Aungelique stifled a yawn. "What one man can encompass me? None of them are able. And so I will have the ones that please me while they please me, and then I will choose another until he bores me. Men have their wives and their mistresses and their whores, and I will do the same."

"You sound like a pagan, with one little god for each hour of the day and all the different aspects of life and death. You cannot love such things, Seur Aungelique," Seur Philomine said, no longer irritated by her.

"I can love them as I wish: easily. You, from what you say, would be cast out into eternal darkness if you lost that other side of your coin." She did not disguise her mockery and made no apology for it.

"Yes, I believe I would be." She said it quietly, with the certainty of faith.

"Then he would fail you," Seur Aungelique pointed out. "And he would be the flawed side of the coin for that, wouldn't he?"

Seur Philomine broke off a little basil and crushed it between her fingers; she looked across the herbs at Seur Aungelique. "You are right, Seur Aungelique. I was afraid I would go into darkness, but . . . I would not have his light, but my own would have to sustain me, or what he and I have is nothing."

"And with all this light, what of God and la Virge?" Seur Aungelique teased.

"They are names I recite prayers to; they are not a fire in my heart or the light of my soul. He is." She stopped, smiling suddenly.

"Évêque Amalrie told Père Guibert that a woman of my sort is worse than the Flagellants, for I wear the mask of piety. Imagine that! Piety! I *told* him I did not wish to be here, but it was for naught. He . . . he was . . ." She let her voice trail off. "There is something wrong with the tarragon. You see how the stems droop? This place! It has a plague of its own."

"Or it has caught it from us, as some take madness from the bite of a mad dog." Seur Philomine broke off one of the twigs Seur Aungelique had indicated. "It might be as well to pull up the whole bed and plant it again next spring."

Seur Aungelique laughed. "I will have my child at my breast and be wearing samite and damask instead of this endless gray." She got up with some difficulty. "The vegetables are next. Do you want to weed them with me, as well?"

"With Seur Victoire stricken by the heat—"

"And laziness, and the notion that a demon is trying to enter her body," Seur Aungelique interjected.

"It might be best that I do the weeding with you," Seur Philomine said as she trudged behind Seur Aungelique.

"Something has been at the carrots again," Seur Aungelique pointed out. "I suppose it's because the peasants are planting less and the animals are hungry."

Seur Philomine wiped her brow again, throwing her coif askew. "We will be hungry, too, if this continues."

Seur Aungelique said cheerily, getting onto her knees again, "Perhaps we should put up a shrine to . . . whichever saint looks after vegetable gardens."

"And perhaps we should get a puppy to chase away the hares," Seur Philomine suggested as she knelt near the three long lines of onions.

It was late afternoon, when the heat lay heavily on Avignon. Most of the men of the papal court had retired to their apartments for the day to meditate and rest. Cardinal Belroche longed for a nap, but he had granted an interview to Évêque Amalrie, which he now bitterly regretted doing. "You think that the demons have left la Tres Saunte Annunciacion? Is that what all this outburst means?"

"Yes," Évêque Amalrie panted, his skin the color of tallow, slick with sweat that stank of fear. "Yes, I have seen for myself how far the demons have come. We must take precautions now if the Devil himself is not to enter the city and besiege the Pope!"

Cardinal Belroche tapped his fingers on his writing table. "What convinces you of this danger, mon Évêque?

We are aware that there are Flagellants still abroad, but there are men-at-arms in pursuit of them."

"Not Flagellants, no. This is much worse! This is subtle and a snare for all virtuous men. I thought I had seen the worst of it at the convent, but beyond it is worse." He leaned forward, bracing his hands on the writing table. Mon Cardinal, you believe that because we are the servants of God, nothing can touch us, not the threat of hell!" He had to stop and gulp in air.

"Doubtless you believe that we have underestimated the hazard you encountered. Frère Renaut has reported as much to the college. Therefore, it might be best if you . . . had a retreat." He saw at once that this suggestion was a mistake. "Not at an inappropriate place," he amended. "There is a papal villa near the coast. A most pleasant place, with guards and a chapel and a good kitchen to make for—"

It was a terrible insult to interrupt a Cardinal, especially when he was speaking to the benefit of his listener, but Évêque Amalrie could not contain himself. "No! Are you unaware that the Devil is insidious, and he enters through all the sins that surround us, especially the pleasant ones, the ones that no one wants to give up entirely." He started to tremble but forced himself to go on in spite of it. "Your Eminence, you do not know what dangers we face here."

"Therefore we are the more desired victims of the predations of hell?" the Cardinal said, knowing this argument thoroughly.

"Yes, of hell, of Rome. We are the ones that must be defeated, not by force of arms or by dangers, which can make men stalwart instead of timorous." He was afraid that he was not convincing the cardinal.

"Now we are getting to the heart of the matter," the Cardinal sighed. "Very well, mon brave, what happened? Did one of those nuns in the throes of her possession cause you to feel lust? It is common enough." He pushed back, thinking that if he handled it adroitly, he would be away from this tiresome interview in very little time. "You are a conscientious man, mon Évêque, and

no one doubts it. Nothing comes to us but through Him
unless it brings us to damnation."

Évêque Amalrie slammed his hands on the table,
his face rigid with terror. "No! *No!* You have not listened
to me, Eminence. There is terrible deviltry close at
hand, and it is permitted to continue."

"Gracious," Cardinal Belroche said, his little eyes
brightening. "What have you unearthed, mon Évêque?"

"Concupiscence," Évêque Amalrie ventured, his
pasty features turning very bright. "The most terrible
sins are born of it."

It was an effort for Cardinal Belroche to keep from
bursting out in derision or anger. "Did you rape one of
the nuns, mon Évêque?" Once again, he saw that he had
erred and made haste to correct his mistake. "When the
Devil or his messengers are present, many terrible
things happen. Good, pious churchmen fall at such
times."

"No. I was on guard then. You do not know with
what care I examined my soul each night."

"Like a physician inspecting a wound?" the cardinal
suggested.

"Yes!" Évêque Amalrie seized on the idea. "Yes,
searching for laudable puss in the bandages." He
lowered his head. "I saw that the Sisters were chastised
and exhorted for their errors, yet the Devil is stubborn,
and when I was recalled, it was apparent to me that the
danger still existed there."

"You have done what the Church requires of you.
Do not be concerned, mon Évêque. God alone can perfect us, and until He chooses to do so, we must not aspire
to perfection but to as godly conduct as we have been
made to achieve." This, he hoped, would satisfy the
bishop.

Évêque Amalrie clapped his hands to his face and
dropped to his knees; now only his head was visible at
the edge of the table, eerily disembodied. "It was not
that. We are told that when the Devil enters our hearts,
then we are lost to the light of God, and we go into
darkness and fire." He crossed himself, and his hands

appeared at the edge of the table for a moment. "And the
Devil entered my heart, Eminence." His mouth shook,
and he had to compress his lips before continuing. "I was
under escort and returning here. We stopped for the
night at a villa near here. It was a wild place, with flowers
and fruit trees run riot."

"In fact, an Eden?" Cardinal Belroche said, smiling.

"If you mean the home of the Serpent, then it is
apt." He closed his eyes and began to weep. "Le duc de
Parcignonne was the one who brought me there, saying
that the mistress was a comtesse. Better I had slept in a
hovel than in those fine sheets." He wiped his tears. "My
sins stink to heaven."

Now Cardinal Belroche was curious. This self-
castigation perplexed him. "You have done nothing to
suggest you are beyond redemption, mon Évêque."

"I have fallen. The Devil sent his demon to me, his
golden siren, in a form so sweet and so bound in the
pleasures of the flesh that . . ." He stopped, swallowed
hard and went on. "I had not known what it was that the
Sisters felt when the demons came to them. I did not
know what it was to have a demon with . . . with me."
The last was a whisper.

"A demon came to you? At Une Noveautie?" Cardinal Belroche turned away so that Évêque Amalrie
could not see his expression. "What need of a demon
when there is Comtesse Orienne?"

Évêque Amalrie boggled at him. "But . . . you cannot know . . . what she did. What I did because of her. It
had to be a demon. You do not *know* what she is capable
of, what she can cause others to do. It cannot be . . . No
woman is so far gone in . . . corruption that she
will . . ." He turned a deeper shade of plum. "Women
are the seat of iniquity; this woman, this *demon*
was . . ."

Cardinal Belroche got to his feet. He looked at the
weeping man kneeling before his writing table. "There
are many who would think you were fortunate beyond
reckoning for what you have tasted, and I would be one
of them if I believed you knew what you have had." He
flicked a mosquito off the fresh vellum that was spread on

the table for his later use. "You have let yourself be seduced by the most accomplished courtesan in all France, and you fear that this is evil. God did not make you to be without these lapses." He blessed the young bishop. "Confess your sin, such as it is, and then accept the offer of a short time of retreat. You have magnified your transgression beyond all thought."

"It was a demon. It *was*. I tell you, I know that it was!" He had started to rise, his hands reaching out as if to grab the Cardinal.

"Stop this at once!" Cardinal Belroche ordered in so stern a voice that Évêque Amalrie quailed at the sound of it. "You are indulging yourself in your guilt. Take care that you do not sin for pride and vanity in this as in your piety." He stepped back. "If you intrude upon me again, I will have my guards remove you." He hesitated; there was no telling how far this difficult young man might advance within the Church. "Take heart in knowing that others have sinned as you have, and with less concern for their souls while they did it."

Évêque Amalrie gave a strange sob, then flung away from the cardinal, staggering toward the door. "Pernicious! Pernicious! There is sin everywhere. The Devil is here before me!"

"Mon Évêque—" Cardinal Belroche called out, but the bishop paid him no heed.

By the time Père Guibert reached the convent, he was too tired to want to do more than sleep. He rang for the warder Sister and had a considerable wait for a yawning Seur Odile to come to admit him.

"God be with you," he said to her as she swung the doors closed behind him.

"And with your soul, mon Père. We are grateful you have returned." She looked about, then said quietly, "You are alone?"

He held the reins out to Seur Odile and was startled when she did not take them. "Ma Fille? What is this?"

Seur Odile was in a quandary. "Your pardon, mon Père. I would take the mule, but the last time I ventured into the stables, the Devil found me there, and I was set upon by his fiends, who tormented me." She crossed herself. "I have prayed and fasted since then, and Mère Léonie has said that she believes the worst has passed, but I dare not go there again." Her breath was shaky. "Mère Léonie said to us that the Devil comes where he is welcome and only when he has been summoned, just as those who are saints are called of God."

Père Guibert heard this with misgivings. "Mère Léonie has the right of it, but not all of it. Those who are godly and in grace can nonetheless be tempted." He patted the mule absently. "Is there another Sister who will tend to him for me?"

"There is Seur Tiennette, who is still making cheeses in the stillroom, and Seur Marguerite is awake." It was all she could legitimately offer to him, and both were aware of it.

"Ask Seur Tiennette if she would mind stabling my mule for me." He stood still, waiting for Seur Odile to do something. "Seur?"

"Yes. I will tend to it," she promised, then crossed herself in fear. "Our Lord between me and evil," she whispered, then hurried away, calling back, "I will inform Mère Léonie that you have arrived."

"Deo gratias," Père Guibert said, watching her go. He did not like the time of day, when all but the last of the light had faded from the skies, when the stars began to show overhead, for at such times, he knew he was most vulnerable, thinking himself still safe.

"Mon Père!" Seur Tiennette called as she lumbered into the courtyard. Her girth had expanded of late, and there was a wheeze in her breathing that had not existed a year before. Her habit was covered with a patched apron, and it reeked of the curds she had been handling. "I am sorry to have to greet you this way, but I trust you will give me your forgiveness?"

Over the years, Père Guibert had come to regard Seur Tiennette as something of an older sister, a part of the family he could not remember, and he responded now with a warmth that was not often apparent in his manner. "I am pleased to have such industrious escort,

Seur Tiennette." He gave her the reins. "He will need water as well as feed."

"I am thankful for the task, mon Père," she said, then looked at him closely.

"Will they be back, those men from Avignon, or will we be left in peace, do you think?" She misinterpreted his silence. "I must do what I may to discover how much more of it I will have to endure."

"Endure?" he asked.

"Oh, I know that if there is reason for correction of sins, then we must be thankful for the rod that brings us once again to virtue. But I do not wish to be corrected for wrongs that are not my own." She stopped to put her hand to her brow. "It is nothing, mon Père. Do not listen to me. In the morning, I will have rid myself of these resentments."

This was so unlike what Père Guibert was used to from Seur Tiennette that he almost urged her to tell him more. But his back was sore, his eyes ached, and he could not give her the attention he felt she wanted, and so he made the sign of the cross over her. "God guide your thoughts and your steps, ma Fille. I will hear your confession tomorrow."

"Deo gratias," she murmured, then led his mule away.

Lightly the blows fell, lightly, persistently, to the count of the nun with the scourge in her hand. "Fifty-eight, fifty-nine, sixty," she said breathlessly. Here she paused, the sting and burn of her stripes making her dizzy when she struggled unsuccessfully to get to her feet. Her body was clammy to the touch as she pulled her habit back over her shoulders, trying to transcend the pain that blossomed in her like an enormous, vile flower.

"Seur Ranegonde," said the soft voice in the shadows.

"Apage, Satanas," she muttered, her eyes swimming as she searched for the speaker.

"I *am* behind you, ma Seur" was the pleasant response. "Or would you wish to face me?"

Seur Ranegonde closed her eyes, determined to shut out all awareness of the intruder. "Where hearts are pure and the devotion to God is genuine, then the Devil and his messengers cannot enter," she whispered determinedly to herself. "Where there is evil, goodness will drive it out. God does not bargain with the Devil."

"Doesn't He?" asked the gentle voice. "What of Job? Did not God and the Devil play for his soul?" He waited while Seur Ranegonde continued to pray.

"Virge Marie, hear me, for I am weak and in danger, and but for your mercy and the mercy of God, I am lost to the Pit. God made me pious, but I have no courage but what you will lend me."

"Poor Seur Ranegonde," Thibault said, coming up behind her. "Do you think the ceiling will open and Virge Marie will wrap you in her mantle?"

"Let me not hear the words that the Devil has spoken. Let me hear only the hymn of praise that the angels sing forever at the Throne of God," she said, her words coming faster and faster, as if their speed alone could carry her to safety.

"There are other hymns, Seur Ranegonde, and they are more pleasant to hear," Thibault said, deliberately placing his hands on her shoulders so that the hurt of her scourging rushed through her. "What good father permits his children to harm themselves in this way?"

"Bon Dieu!" she sobbed, stricken with terror. "Save me! O Thou Who brought Moses out of the desert, save me!"

"He brought Jesus to the cross, as well," Thibault reminded her in the most gentle tone. "What will He do for you if that is how He treated His Son?"

"I will not listen to you!" Seur Ranegonde cried. "You do not speak the truth."

"It is part of your faith, Seur Ranegonde. You cannot wait for God to serve you. But *I* will serve you, and not in heaven." His hands had moved down her arms so that he held them pinned to her sides. "You are weak with fever, little dove. What is so hideous that you must treat yourself in this way?"

"We are not worthy." Seur Ranegonde closed her

mouth firmly, determined not to be tricked into talking again.

"Of what? Of the death of a carpenter over a thousand years ago?" He gave her a little silence, then went on. "Do you think that whipping yourself to ribbons will make you more acceptable a sacrifice?" He sounded almost amused as he asked, and when she still remained silent, he made a third suggestion. "Tell me, little dove. Do you believe that you will be taken to the marriage bed by Father, Son, and Holy Ghost, to know at last what you have denied for so long?"

She wrenched in his arms, but her weakness was too great for her to fight free of him. "Let me go!"

"To what? To dream of a lover that is without body or passion?"

"There is passion! There *is*!" she insisted, then wished she could recall the words. "There is passion, but it is not—"

"Is not what?" Thibault cut in. "There is no surrender? You surrender in prayer hours every day. There is no embracing? You lie prostrate with your arms outstretched, and they hold nothing but stones. Little mouselet, you are afire, you kindle the flames in your heart, and then you strive to subdue the very embers you have fanned. That scourge will change nothing except the number of scars on your skin."

"No. No, no, no, you must not do this! Let me go. I swear I will pray for you and forgive you for what you have done if you will let me go." She knew that her pleading was more of a whine, and it shamed her that she should appear so craven to this diabolic creature that stood behind her and held her as easily as she might hold a day-old lamb.

"But I do not want your forgiveness and your prayers, mon ange. I want your passion as mine."

She felt one surge of hope. "I will lash myself for your sins as well as my own."

"What sins?" he asked in his most caressing voice. "After I have taken you, there will be time enough for that." Abruptly, he jerked her, and she found herself facing his hot, pale eyes.

"But not that—" She was afraid that she was about to weep, and there was nothing she could do to prevent him from seeing it.

He fixed his hands now, digging them deeply into cloth and flesh, and he began to press her down, ruthlessly, relentlessly, to her knees. "You desire to worship, little dove? You may worship me, and I will give you the reward you are seeking."

"I . . . you blaspheme," she objected, but so weakly that he guffawed. "No."

"Oh, yes. It is what you will offer your God, isn't it? You are prepared to lose your virginity, ma Seur, if it is sacrificed to the most puissant lord, and you will give him sacrifice and honor, won't you?" And then he was atop her.

She gritted her teeth through it all, her eyes closed. She could feel his movements, and the weight of him was enormous for a man so slight. For all the indignity and humiliation, the only hurt she had came from her shoulders, from the welts she had put there with her scourge.

When he had finished, he still lay atop her, giving her no option to move. "You will have a child of this, and I will come for it."

Seur Ranegonde finally wept, but without a sound. "I want nothing of yours," she said hollowly.

"Oh, it is not of mine. Demons have no progeny; we have only the seed we carry from others." She stiffened under him. "You are not the first tonight, my mouselet. I would not have been able to start a child in you but that another warmed me earlier." Thibault sniggered, then loosened his hold on her enough to let him be able to see her face clearly. "Why, ma Seur?"

Her eyes opened wide; she could not convince herself she had heard him correctly. "You gave me no choice," she said, loathing him and her admission with equal intensity.

"There is always a choice, my mouselet," he said, this time with sadness that distressed her; she did not wish to think what it meant.

"You were too strong for me," she said after a little silence.

"I?" He reached down and touched her face. "But I am weak." This was said with such forthrightness, wholly unlike the blandishments he had used earlier, that she blinked. "It is your desire that is powerful, not mine. You have the strength; I possess none of my own." He got up after that and dressed quickly.

She lay watching him, refusing to think. Many women, she knew, might be foolish enough to want him for his beauty, for his pale hair and pale skin.

It was as if he had heard her thoughts. "There are always those who desire what I am, who long for what I give them. Men, women, it makes no difference. I become what they want me to be." He made a fussy adjustment in the little ruff around his neck. "Where I am truly not wanted, mouselet, I am powerless to do anything."

He was almost at the door when she made herself ask the question that had been burning in her, that she dared not give voice to for fear it would confirm her inmost horror. "If you are not the father, who is?"

Thibault thought this over, then gave a mischievous, triangular smile. "I do not think I will tell you that just now. In time, you may discover it for yourself." Then he blessed her, and while she drew away from him in repugnance, he left her cell.

Chapter 14

Long shadows from the looming walls of the papal palace threw the chapter house of Saunt-Chrodegang into darkness at midafternoon. The small, octagonal building was dank, even now at the height of summer, and the two men who met there were chilled, as if they had come to a tomb.

"You have had no word, then?" Padre Bartolimieu asked of Évêque Amalrie.

Évêque Amalrie, very much thinner than he had been, plucked nervously at his lower lip. "No. I have heard nothing. Nothing at all."

"Then have they abandoned the matter?" Padre Bartolimieu asked, frowning at the other man. "You are a man of zeal, mon Évêque, and you have defended the church against her enemies. Surely it is known that you have been foremost in the battle against the forces of hell?" His voice echoed around the little stone room, the words more and more distorted.

"I asked the cardinal . . . Belroche, it was, to continue the investigation, to authorize a Process, but . . . he has not done so." He looked up into the gloom.

Padre Bartolimieu said, "What manner of man is this Cardinal that he refuses to act where God must be defended?"

It was a short while before Évêque Amalrie answered. "I do not know what manner of man he is." He walked away from Padre Bartolimieu. "There is great sin all around us, mon Padre, and none of us can escape it. We are doomed, and it is fitting that we bow our heads to the punishment meted out to us by a just God, for we have failed Him and are not worthy of salvation." He touched his hair as if to try to keep it on his head.

Padre Bartolimieu stood in dumfounded silence. He had been expecting many things from this meeting but not the quiet misery Évêque Amalrie offered him. "Then why did you call me here?"

Évêque Amalrie shrugged. "I had heard you had come to request that the investigation be continued, and I thought I might be able to stop you from taking so disastrous an action." He wandered across the cold floor. "I once thought that it was essential that we uphold the honor of God and the Church and that all measures were acceptable if they were used in that cause and that so long as the cause benefited God and the Church, it made a man proof against the errors and sins of the world. But that is not so."

"Has God touched your heart, mon Évêque?" Padre Bartolimieu asked, trying to follow what the bishop was telling him but with little success.

"It may be that He has. I cannot know what is in my heart." He sighed. "No. It is not fitting that I rebuke you when I am steeped in the transgressions of the world."

"What has happened?" Padre Bartolimieu demanded.

"Very little; I was proud, and for that I have been cast down, which God promised he would do to the proud. I believed that the Cardinals were determined on the preservation of the Church, but this may not be so." He made an aimless little gesture. "It is all for naught. We walk in darkness, as the Bible says, and that light we have been promised shines in the darkness more faintly than a candle. There may be those who have seen it, but if they have, it has made them blind."

"And for that we must persevere in our efforts," Padre Bartolimieu said forcefully, pleased to be on familiar ground once again. "Whatever you have been told, think of the message of the Scriptures and know that it is the work of the Apostles that we continue."

Évêque Amalrie took another turn about the chapter house. "It may be that you have the right of it, but . . . Hear me out, Padre Bartolimieu. I have been myself afflicted, and I know it was for one unguarded moment that my soul was tainted. God permitted it to happen, the Church does not mind that it happened, and all that I have learned from it is how a good man is the servant of his flesh." He regarded Padre Bartolimieu unhappily. "But the sin is still *there*, and I am never free of it, and nothing I do is unaffected by it."

He was confused again, but Padre Bartolimieu decided to humor the bishop in the hope that he would gain the other man's support for his efforts. "Then let the sin be purged; do the work that God commands us to do."

"And what work is that?" Évêque Amalrie asked softly.

"To cleanse our flocks, to bring them away from error into virtue. We must strive to end the evil that has brought such misfortune to us."

He crossed himself. "I have no more surety, mon Padre. My sin has taken that from me."

"But the demons!" Padre Bartolimieu blurted out. "Think of what they are doing to the nuns!"

"And the nuns to the demons, perhaps," Évêque Amalrie said, his eyes fixing vaguely on the bas relief frieze of the story of Samson.

"But you have shown that the demons are there! If you turn away, you will let the demons triumph!" He wanted to take the man and shake him, to convince him that his course was wrong.

"If they triumph, then it is God's Will; what we do is as nothing. We are vain, puny men, caught in toils we know nothing of." He knelt abruptly and began to pray.

Padre Bartolimieu came over to him. "You are praying. You are seeking guidance. You know what your duty is." He cleared his throat and commenced his expostulation. "I have had a similar trial, and I failed it. I let my people suffer and die because I was a coward, but no more. You will come to this in time, mon Évêque, but for the benefit of the Sisters, who are wretched, troubled women, you must not tarry. You must rise up." The stones reverberated his oratory. "You must recall your faith and your devotion, and you must drive out the demons that have tortured those nuns and show the Devil and the Church that you are staunch in your calling!"

Évêque Amalrie looked up over his clasped hands. "Padre Bartolimieu? Leave me alone."

Taken aback, Padre Bartolimieu faltered in his speech. "You . . . you are not thinking clearly, mon Évêque. You do not recall how the nuns wept when they were lashed and the demons were driven out of them."

"They may have wept for pain. We do not know." He lowered his head again, and for the next hour, no matter what Padre Bartolimieu said, no matter how he accused or exorted, Évêque Amalrie remained on his knees, his head bent over his folded hands.

It was the last day that Père Guibert would be at la Tres Saunte Annunciacion for almost a month, and he was hearing confession before he left; after two hours of listening to the sins of the nuns, his mind was reeling. Most of it was, he knew from long experience, fanciful conjecture, tidbits gleaned from the torments of the sisters truly possessed. The demonic presence was still at work at the convent, and he could not put his thoughts at ease for the welfare of the Sisters. He crossed himself and tried to compose his mind for the next Sister. "Who is ready?" he called out through the chapel door.

Seur Adalin, who had been serving as his page, answered. "It was to have been Seur Tiennette, but a barrel of salt pork has gone off, and she must dispose of it quickly."

"Assure her for me that I will come to her before I leave, so that she need not cease her efforts." There was little enough meat in those barrels as it was, and to lose one augured badly for the convent. "I will give her my blessing, as well, for the kitchen."

"I thank you for her, mon Père," Seur Adalin responded with proper deference.

"Then who will take her place? Is one of the Sisters ready to confess now?" He had hoped it was not Seur Aungelique; that young woman had turned increasingly sullen with her advancing pregnancy.

"Seur Catant would like to speak to you," Seur Adalin informed him.

"Speak to me?—This is time for confession, and it is well that she rid herself of her sins." He was aware that Seur Catant would be willing to repeat all the slights, real and imagined, she had endured over the last few weeks and praise her own forbearance in dealing with her catty Sisters. With a deep breath that just missed being a sigh, he motioned her to come forward. "Enter, ma Fille. I will hear your confession in the name of the Trinity."

She came up to him but did not kneel. Her voice was higher than usual that day, the rasping edge of it more pronounced. "The demon is here; it has been here from the first. Nothing that you or Padre Bartolimieu or Évêque Amalrie has done has changed it. I know that the demon is here and that he possesses the nuns who live and serve here as his own concubines, and they protect him and guard him as they once guarded their chastity. Now they are caught up in the toils of the flesh, and if I love them as my sisters, I must speak. Mustn't I?" At last, she sank to her knees and waited for him to speak.

Reluctantly, Père Guibert blessed her. "What is it that troubles you, ma Fille?"

"It has happened for several nights, and each time I have resolved to tell you, and each time I have relented."

"Yes, yes," he assured her. "What have you seen that causes you this distress? Is it something that you have heard the other nuns discuss, or have you more . . . certainty than that?"

Seur Catant hesitated once more, her breath coming more quickly. "It is always late when this happens. I sleep poorly because of the pains in my shoulders, and because my cell is across the corridor, I have heard what has transpired."

"Across the corridor?" Père Guibert inquired, expecting to hear names other than Seur Ranegonde's.

"Yes, my Sister who suffers terribly with fever. I pity her so for her failing health, and now this, that a demon should rob her of her tranquillity in these days . . ." She paused to shake her head to show how great her sympathy was for Seur Ranegonde. "This demon has taken her and used her."

Père Guibert could not keep from wondering how long Seur Catant had thought about her revelation and how carefully she might have planned this talk, so eloquent were her words. "But you say that this continues late at night?"

"Yes, it continues." She almost smiled but was able to contain herself sufficiently to appear cast down.

"Then you have seen this . . . demon?" He watched her closely. "You have actually seen the demon enter her cell? How could you be sure that it was not a lover?" He would not fault Seur Ranegonde for finding a little pleasure with death hovering so near her in the fever that continued to weaken her.

"If he is a lover, he is most strange, for there is no one in Saunt-Vitre or in Mou Courbet who resembles him." This was announced with satisfaction. "I am not one to be deceived by village youths looking for an idle hour's entertainment. I have taken it upon myself," she went on with real pride, "to follow this demon when he has left, to see which door he used. He has never left the convent. Yet no one has found him."

"Perhaps he has hidden in the hospice?" Père Guibert suggested. "There are many room there that remain empty, and it would be an easy thing for an enterprising lad to find a way in and not take the risk of leaving."

"But what of food and water? What does that creature live upon?" She flung back her head, her coif slipping precariously. "Unless there are other nuns here who are taking what little food we have and giving it to him?"

"I doubt very much that there is anyone in the hospice, but I will order the whole building searched to end such suspicions at last." He would have been glad to be able to do that at once, but Seur Catant was not finished with him. "I have heard such things from their trysts that I am shamed to hear or to admit I have heard." She crossed herself, licking her thin lips as she did. "I am shamed now to tell you of it."

"You need not speak, ma Fille," Père Guibert ventured, trusting that she would not persist but knowing he would be disappointed.

"It is disgusting what they say and do, to hear her cry aloud for his touch and his organ, saying she has no will to keep him away." She rocked back and forth on her knees; her coif bounced on her head, flapping as if a wounded bird had settled there.

"Seur Catant . . . ma Fille—" He was cut off before he could find the suitable phrases to calm her.

"She takes him, and he possesses her!" With a strange gurgling shout, she hurled herself on her side, kicking out so that her habit bunched around her waist. "It is me he wants, me, *me, Me*! It is my faith that has saved me, no matter how he longs for me."

Père Guibert rose, very much alarmed. "Seur Catant! You must not behave in this way! Do not succumb to this possession. You may entreat la Virge to give you her aid, and you will be yourself again." He was already backing away from her, too perplexed to do more than talk. He blessed her and said a hurried prayer in an undervoice.

"What is this?" Seur Adalin cried out as she came through the door. At the sight of Seur Catant, she halted. "Again? What has come over this woman?"

Père Guibert looked down at her. "Évêque Amalrie would say it was a demon entering her and turning her from God."

"What should I do, mon Père?" Seur Adalin asked as she stared down at Seur Catant, who twitched and writhed on the floor. A thin line of foam had come to her lips, and her tongue protruded.

"You had best send for Seur Morgance. She knows the falling sickness; her father and brother suffer from it." He sighed, thinking that the burden was growing too great. "I will stay with her until Seur Morgance arrives. The falling sickness is very ancient, Seur Adalin. In time, she will be herself again."

"If you say it is so, mon Père . . ." She started away, then said to him over her shoulder, "While Seur Catant is being attended to, would you wish to hear Seur Tiennette's confession in the refectory?"

Grateful for this opportunity to get away, he agreed at once, adding, "And I must speak to Mère Léonie. Seur Catant must be placed in another cell for a time." He moved a bit nearer to Seur Catant, noticing that the froth on her mouth was tinged pink from where she had bitten her tongue. Her thrashings increased, and her eyes had rolled up in her head. Gingerly, he knelt beside her and made the sign of the cross. "God and la Virge protect this unfortunate, who languishes in the throes of the falling sickness and has seen visions sent to her by the Devil to torment her to fits." As he continued, he hoped ardently that Seur Morgance would come quickly.

The old sow had littered in the night; before Seur Philomine found her shortly after morning prayers, she had eaten most of three of her piglets, and the two that remained were not sucking as they should. Seur Philomine gazed at the pigs in mounting dismay: the convent was counting on having enough pork to see them through the early winter. After putting other food in for the sow and removing the pitiful bodies of the piglets, she hurried away to find Mère Léonie.

The superior was just coming from the storerooms under the refectory. "I know," she was saying to Seur Victoire, "that new habits are in short supply and there are not enough to issue one to all the Sisters on the Feast of Saunt Bavon. There is not enough new wool to make sufficient habits for all of us by then, but we must try, ma Seur." She gave such a determined smile that Seur Victoire did her best to return it.

"I will speak to the others at once," she assured her superior, then added, "Seur Marguerite is adept with the needle, but during the day she will not leave her bees."

Mère Léonie shook her head slightly. "Poor Seur Marguerite; her whole world is the hive now. Well, she harms no one, and we need the honey. I think Our Lord would permit me to stretch a point and consider her hours at the hive her vigil, for she keeps it with a devotion I could wish the others demonstrated." She had motioned Seur Philomine to wait when the tertiary Sister approached, but now she gave her a nod. "What is it, Seur Philomine? You may be about your tasks, Seur Victoire."

Seur Victoire gave Seur Philomine a terse greeting as she passed. Her habit brushed the floor, disturbing the dust and causing Seur Philomine to sneeze as she began to speak.

"May Our Lord guard you," Mère Léonie said automatically. "You appear concerned, ma Seur."

"It is about the sow," Seur Philomine answered.

"You may discuss it wherever it suits you."

"Then you will accompany me. I must go to Seur Catant. It is a pity about her tongue, but Seur Morgance could not stop her from biting it off, no matter how she tried." She walked more swiftly, her long-legged, clean stride making Seur Philomine trot beside her to keep up.

"I suppose that Évêque Amalrie would say that it was fit punishment for a woman who spread slanders and gossip, but . . ." She did not finish her thoughts.

Seur Philomine could think of nothing to say. "The piglets . . . there are two left, and they are weaklings. I would like to speak with the swineherd in Mou Courbet about getting two or three piglets so that we will have pork in the autumn."

Mère Léonie turned her head and regarded Seur Philomine curiously. "What have we to give the swineherd for his piglets?"

"He might give us one or two for a dispensation of some sort. Père Guibert could arrange it, couldn't he?" She was troubled by the attitude of the superior, who appeared to her to be pleased with the situation. "Do you want us all to starve come Christmas, ma Mère?"

"What a question!" Mère Léonie said with an angry titter. "No, I do not wish to see you or anyone starve." She had reached the narrow stairs that led to the second level where Seur Catant was now kept. "Do you come with me, or do you go to pray?"

"I will see Seur Catant later, when I have had time to compose myself," Seur Philomine answered in her most demure attitude. "I beg your pardon, ma Mère, if you believe that I offended you." She knew that it was the proper thing to say and that if Mère Léonie accepted her apology, she would be unusually fortunate.

"Pray for the afternoon, ma Seur, and we will speak again of this." She started up the stairs, then said to Seur Philomine, "You are not like the rest, you know. They have strong feelings about me, all of them. Except you."

Seur Philomine modified her reply, not wishing to add to her difficulties with her superior. "I am a tertiary Sister, ma Mère, and my vocation is not established. It may be that because of this I am not as much at one with the others and you as the rest of the Sisters."

"Perhaps," Mère Léonie said, resuming her climb.

For the last month, Pierre had slept badly; he had lost flesh, and his face was gray but for the scar, which had become more livid. He paced through his house in

Avignon like a caged animal. *"No!"* he shouted at his visitor. "I have no reason to go there." The sweep of his hand knocked the filled goblet he had offered the other man off the table, and the wine ran red as blood in the rushes.

Père Guibert bowed his head. "I know: every time I leave the convent, I feel I have been released from a dungeon. While I am there, it is an eternity." This confession weighed heavily on him. "That is why I come to you for aid, mon Duc."

"Then arm yourself with more priests!" Pierre growled. "Surely one of the Cardinals would lend you another Évêque for an investigation." He wiped his forehead, trusting it was the sultry weather and not mentioning la Tres Saunte Annunciacion that had caused him to sweat.

"Both Cardinal Belroche and Cardinal Seulfleuve have refused to do anything more." He went on in a different voice. "They are afraid that the Romans will take advantage of the Process and use it to make it seem that the Devil is confounding the Church. They are more worried about Romans than the Devil himself." He started to make the sign of the cross; then his hand dropped. "If these Sisters are lost, then I am lost with them."

Pierre had listened with a scowl deepening on his face. "My cousin is pregnant and says she wants nothing more of me. Her father will discard her rather than bring the child of an unknown man into his House." Then he considered. "She claims that the demon gave it to her, or perhaps that fop Thibault Col." Bitterness made his voice ragged; he signaled the nearest servant to bring more wine. "That Mère Léonie, though," he went on when the servant left the room. "That one would make Saunt Paul lust for her."

Père Guibert blinked at that, startled. "She is a most . . . admirable woman."

"Admirable?" he barked, not daring to laugh. "That woman fires you and eats at you until there is nothing in your heart and mind than her slender body and the degradation she brings with it." He knew that he must not

continue, but the words had been dammed within him
too long, and now that he had given them release, he
could not stop them. "Do you know that she came to my
tent while we were there?" He saw the servant enter the
room, and he hurried to take the two goblets from him.
"Leave us alone," he ordered, then came across the
room to hand one of the goblets to Père Guibert. "She
was with me early in the night, and for the rest of the
night, I could not sleep. My mind was—"

"Possessed?" Père Guibert interjected.

This time he was able to laugh, but the sound of it
was wrong, verging on an angry sob. "Yes! No Devil
could have done more."

"Perhaps . . . it may have been the demon. They
assume such shapes as will draw us all into sin. If
you . . . if you were filled with desire for Mère Léonie,
the demon would . . . take the shape that—that most
. . . pleased you." He stared down into the wine, then
quickly took a draft of it. "I have had dreams there, such
dreams as should make me unfit to hear confession,
but . . . who is there to take my place?"

Now Pierre's laughter was a roar, not genial but not
ferocious. "And what does that make your absolution? By
Saunt Gabriel's horn, we are all in the Pit, mon Père."
He dropped into one of the three chairs in the room and
hooked his knee over the arm of it. He drank off almost
all the wine at once.

"I have listened in humility and the knowledge that
God pardons those who are truly contrite." It sounded as
thin to him as it did to Pierre. "I asked Padre Bartolimieu
to hear them, but he would not, and once he was gone,
what could I do?"

"You might have told the Cardinal that you were unfit. But you want to have the nuns around you, no matter
what you say, and the convent is as much a lure as a
prison to you." He shouted suddenly. "More wine! Bring
the jug!" He winked at Père Guibert and said more
quietly, "They want to listen, you know, but they are
beaten if they are caught at it, and so they stay just out of
earshot, hoping to catch a word or two."

Père Guibert found all this hard to follow, but he

nodded in an obedient manner. "Padre Bartolimieu asked that there be measures taken. He offered to be the one to conduct the investigation."

"I have seen what it is they are doing in Avignon, and you may be certain that no one will make a decision until Clement decides that he wishes action be taken. They are all watching him closely." He gestured to the servant who appeared in the door. "Mine first; then leave the jug on the table. When we are through, you can take it away again."

The servant, a young man with expressionless eyes, did as he had been ordered, putting the jug down with a bit more force than necessary before leaving the chamber.

"Now we may speak more freely," Pierre said, drinking impulsively. "So Padre Bartolimieu wishes to advance in the Church and plans to climb up on the rubble of the convent, does he?"

Père Guibert nodded before drinking. "Padre Bartolimieu *is* ambitious, but he is a good priest."

"If you say so," Pierre responded. "He looks craven to me, and they are always the most ambitious; it makes them forget their cowardice." He emptied his goblet and got unsteadily to his feet to refill it. "What about Évêque Amalrie?"

"Évêque Amalrie has petitioned Cardinal Belroche to permit him to undertake a pilgrimage to the Holy Land," Père Guibert said slowly. "He has refused to be drawn into the investigation in any way."

"Why? I would have thought his pride would carry him through anything," Pierre said, making no effort to guard his slurring tongue.

Père Guibert looked at the wine jug, a lugubrious expression on his worn features. "He confessed to the Cardinal, and the Cardinal . . . would not give him absolution."

"What kind of a Cardinal is that?" The indignation he felt was short-lived. "Well, which of the nuns did he futter, do you know?"

It took more concentration than earlier for Père Guibert to gather his wits. "No," he said, enunciating carefully. "No, it was not one of the nuns. He told the cardinal that a demon in the form of a woman had driven him to madness and to debauchery." He looked up blearily as he heard Pierre howl with mirth and slap his thigh. "What is amusing in a man's degradation?"

"Degradation be damned! That was no demon!" His laughter turned to giggles. "She'll be delighted to hear this."

"What?" Père Guibert poured himself a little more wine, muzzily hoping that it would make him more sober. "On a warm day," he announced to the room at large, "a man must take something for his thirst."

"Orienne will be pleased! She'll be overjoyed. No one has ever thought her a demon before. Occasionally, they call her an angel." He swilled down a fourth goblet of wine, then reeled to his feet. "Poor sod doesn't know what he had. That woman knows more about love than all the saints in the calendar."

"What are you talking about?" The wine had failed to revive him, but it had given him the curious detachment that sometimes came upon him when he was drinking.

"I took him there!" He shook all over with the force of his guffaw. "I wanted to bring him down a peg. We had to break the journey for the night in any case, so I decided we would stop at Une Noveautie. You *do* know the place, don't you, mon Père?" He chuckled at the dawning shock in Père Guibert's eyes. "I asked Orienne if she would amuse our Évêque in the manner she knew best. She told me afterward that he was worse than a twelve-year-old peasant."

"Comtesse Orienne slept with him?" Père Guibert asked, needing to be sure he understood what he was being told.

"Hardly slept. She came to me afterward, and we frolicked most of the night so that she would not be forced to think of Évêque Amalrie anymore." He settled back in his chair.

"This is most unfortunate," Père Guibert said, misery coming over him like a damp cloth.

"Why? The Cardinal knows all about it. No one is

upset but Évêque Amalrie, who need merely spend half an hour in confession to be free of the sin. Still, a walk to Jerusalem would show him a bit of humility."

"Where does that leave the Sisters, then? They will suffer because no one will defend them." Père Guibert could feel tears form in his eyes and spill down his face. "I do not want to go back there because of the dreams. You do not want to go back there because of your lust. What shall happen to the Sisters if everyone turns away from them?"

"They will manage; they have thus far." Pierre shifted restlessly in his chair. "What do we say to explain it if the Church asks? That you and Padre Bartolimieu were mistaken? Or do you put the blame on Évêque Amalrie, off in the Holy Land?" He had another tot, thinking he was being judicious about it. "If we are held to be lacking in this, it might go badly for us and for the Church. Rome could say that we did not take care of our own."

Père Guibert was startled to hear le duc defend the Church's position. "I did not realize you were aware of what is at stake here."

"Oh, there is a vidamie that I have been offered; I have been listening to more churchmen than I have heard before in my life. They want to go to war, but no one has enough men. They want to challenge Rome, but there is no legitimate way to do it without leaving many of the flock exposed to needless danger." He emptied the last of the jug into his goblet. "I do not want to go back to la Tres Saunte Annunciacion; but if you can bring me good reason for such action, I will find my men and we will return."

"How will you justify this to your Cardinal? He will wish to know why you are resuming your guardianship there."

Pierre stared hard at Père Guibert, his bleary eyes narrowing. "I have a cousin there, and no matter what her father does, we are of the same House, and I cannot have a question of diabolism hanging over my becoming vidame." He nodded several times. "Might as well clear it up once and for all."

Slowly, Père Guibert go to his feet. He swayed, but only a little. He had not become completely drunk. "I . . . I will inform the Cardinal. And I will speak to Padre Bartolimieu."

"Oh? Is that pious old swine here?" He rubbed his face briskly. "Your pardon, mon Père."

With great dignity, Père Guibert informed Pierre, "He has been trying to get another investigation under way, as I have. He thought that Évêque Amalrie would aid him, but I have told you what has transpired there."

"The Holy Land? Yes, that was it." He lurched erect. "You leave Padre Bartolimieu out of this if you want my help, is all I can say."

"Very well, but I should let him know that something is being done. He will then turn his attention elsewhere." Père Guibert heard himself and was astonished at how grand he sounded. Delighted by this, he continued with enthusiasm. "You must see, mon Duc, that there can be no deception now."

"Since you are certain it is the demon's work, well and good." He cast his goblet against the wall, the silver clanging as it dented. "We will go back there, and the Devil be damned for a dog's turd."

A coldness washed through Père Guibert, and the lightheartedness of the wine faded like dew in sunlight. "Yes. Yes, mon Duc. We will go back to la Tres Saunte Annunciacion."

Seur Tiennette looked with dismay on the barrels in the pantry. She had opened three of the eight, and so far all had been infested with strange insects like water striders, making their way through the flour and the dried peas. She was sufficiently shocked that she could feel her heart race within her. Her eyes stung, and she dashed her tears away with the back of her wrists. "There is no time for such nonsense," she said aloud.

At final count, she had four of the barrels infested. She knew it meant that she would have to remove the barrels themselves if the insects were to be contained in those barrels they had already reached. "Someone must be prepared to help me. Saunte Virge, how am I to tell them?" At that thought, her dread increased, for she knew that with the convent already in the grip of fear, there was little she could do that would not increase the terror around her.

She left the pantry and made her way back toward the refectory. If only Père Guibert were here, she thought, she might be able to confide in him and be guided by what he said to her. Properly she must inform Mère Léonie, but that was a step she wished to avoid. She felt her cheek and realized that it was quite flushed. As she thought, she reached for the end of her tattered apron and flapped it, trying to fan herself. It was slightly cooler than it had been two weeks before, but the room was still uncomfortably warm, which annoyed her. Her mouth was parched, her throat dry, which she knew was as much from her distress as any actual thirst, yet admitting this only made it worse. She doubted she would be able to move the barrels without something to drink; no amount of prayers would make up for her thirst.

It took her a little while to mark the barrels that needed to go out and another short time to determine the best order in which to move them.

Finally, when she had placed the four barrels in order, she blundered out of the pantry and made her way to the garden, where the well waited, the bucket dangling just out of reach. She grabbed the handle and released the rope. She wound the handle, panting with her need and effort; as soon as she could reach it, she swung it toward her and drank deeply, shutting out the guilt that nagged at her for taking such an action.

When she was satisfied, she went back into the refectory. Her head ached fiercely, and her eyes were almost blinded by the difference between the glare in the garden where the sun struck the whitewashed walls and the shadowed interior. Her steps were unsteady. "This is foolish," she said, not noticing how oddly the words came out. "I know this place."

A corner of the room lifted, and she reached out, puzzled by what she sensed around her. Her knees bent, buckled. There was no pain other than the headache that gripped her with increasing severity. Her lips drew back in a terrible grimace, and she attempted to get back onto her feet—she was able to flap her left hand, but nothing else responded no matter how urgently she commanded her limbs to move. Now even breathing was difficult, and it was almost impossible to fill her lungs enough so that she would not feel she was drowning.

She tried to form the words of a prayer; there was not air enough for her to speak them, had she thought of them. The pain boiled and burned in her skull, and she could do nothing, think of nothing to stop it. As it overwhelmed her, she gave a feeble sigh, knowing that she was damned, her sins unadmitted and unforgiven.

Seur Odile found her shortly before sunset, as she came in out of the garden with an old basket over her arm. "Oh, Seur Tiennette," she called out, "I have found berries growing wild on that fallow rye field. I have picked the ones that are ripe, and we may have them—" Her basket fell on the floor, and the berries scattered across it. Slowly, numbly, Seur Odile crossed herself. "Oh, dear Mère Marie, what . . . ?"

Most of Seur Tiennette's face was engorged with blood, making it appear a ghastly mask that a malicious child might wear at carnival. Seur Tiennette's habit was in disarray from her dying attempts to rise, and her vast white thighs were splayed against the gray of her habit. Flies had begun to settle on the corpse.

"Mère Léonie! *Mère Léonie!*" Seur Odile shrieked as she bolted from the refectory. "Mère Léonie, you must come! You must!" In her headlong flight, she nearly ran into Seur Adalin, who had just come in from the courtyard. "*LET ME GO!*"

Seur Adalin stumbled out of the way, irritated and troubled that Seur Odile should act in such a way. "What is wrong?" she called after the running nun.

"Terrible!" Seur Odile shouted back, uncaring that she was attracting the attention of the entire convent and that the whispers were starting already.

Chapter 15

That night there was little revelry at Une Noveautie. As a result, Comtesse Orienne was bored. She had been listening to her musicians for the better part of the morning, and in the afternoon she had gone out with her falcons, but now that evening was approaching, she could think of nothing that would amuse her but taking one of the servants to her bed.

Jaques appeared in the door of the solar where she sat on the soft cushions looking out into the lavender sky. "There is someone to see you?"

Her brows went up, and her cat's face showed good humor for the first time that day. "Oh? Who?"

"A priest, mistress. I do not know him." Jaques hesitated. "He does not mean to do well by you. It is in his eyes."

Comtesse Orienne shrugged petulantly. "You mean that he will lecture me and then try to convince me to repent? They are predictable, but they are occasionally entertaining," she said, then looked more closely at her servant. "Well? You look troubled."

Jaques hesitated once more. "Mistress, do not go to him. Do you recall that chevalier, the Gascon, who beat you for giving him too much pleasure?"

"How could I *not* recall? He left me with one eye swollen shut for three days and a bruise on my thigh that took more than two weeks to fade." She lifted one hand in an invitation for him to continue.

"They have the same look about them." He knew he had said as much as she would permit, and he lowered his head. "If you must see him, let it not be alone."

This was too much for Comtesse Orienne, who

laughed easily. "Time lies as heavily on your hands as mine, does it, Jaques?"

"It is more than that," he insisted in a mumble.

She rose and came toward him, caressing his cheek. "Your devotion pleases me, Jaques. For that I thank you and will see you suitably rewarded."

He brought his eyes up to meet hers. "I do not warn you for the chance of a reward, mistress."

"You shall have one just the same," she said, her tone low and promising. "Now show me where you have put this priest, and I will try to endure his rantings for an hour or so." She permitted him to lead her down the corridor, using the time to adjust her old-fashioned but provocative gates-of-hell to its best advantage.

"In the smaller salon, mistress," Jaques said, standing aside at the top of the stairs so that she could descend alone. "Have care."

Comtesse Orienne smiled blindly back at him. "You are good to me." She was still smiling when she entered the smaller salon and found Padre Bartolimieu waiting for her, his face thunderous and his fury so apparent that he might have been quilled and clawed. "You are the priest who wishes to see me?"

Padre Bartolimieu ran his eyes over her. "I am the priest. You are the enemy."

Inwardly, Comtesse Orienne faltered, but her smile did not change. "I am no one's enemy, mon Père." She chose a seat some distance from him. "Pray do not stand."

He sat down, reluctantly, on one of the padded benches.

"You are displeased with me?" Comtesse Orienne ventured. "You speak as if I have compelled someone to come here against his will. Or her will."

"You say that, secure in your lies and your wiles." He leaned forward, his jaw thrusting. "You have brought many souls to your master, have you not?"

Comtesse Orienne shook her head impatiently. "I am without a master: it is one of the few joys of being noble and a widow, mon Père. If you are speaking of another master, then I admit I am the dutiful subject of le roi and I am loyal to the Church in Avignon." The entertainment she had hoped this priest would give her was disappointing.

"You have learned your work well, demon. Everything about you is calculated to cause a prudent man to forget his natural caution and to assume that you offer him no greater danger than Venus' pox." He sounded calmer now, though his chin jutted more emphatically.

Now Comtesse Orienne could sense what it was that Jaques had warned her about, and she decided to be more circumspect with her annoying visitor. "Mon Père, perhaps one of your flock has told you that he was brought here against his will or that I compelled him to do acts that he did not desire. And it may be that after leaving here, he may have felt some shame—I do not say that many do, but there must be a few who have decided that they cannot live as I do—and therefore confessed to you. If a man does not choose to be here, I do not want him to remain. I am not a woman who enjoys reluctant lovers, and if that turns a man from me, then well and good; we are neither at loss in that instance." She wished now that she had worn one of her more modest gowns, but with the weather so warm, she had selected the coolest garment she owned. The armseyes on this cotehardie were so deep that a man standing beside her could see most of her body. She moved in the chair so that the gates-of-hell were not quite as open as they had been.

"So you say, while you are given to every voluptuous practice and every seduction. What man would not think himself willing while you are there to work your sorcery upon him and bring him to his ruin?" Padre Bartolimieu glared at her. "You are a vicious snare, made beautiful to the unwary so that you may the more completely devour those who are your victims."

When Comtesse Orienne laughed, there was a quiver in the sound, an echo of the nervousness she felt. "You come here, mon Père, full of purpose and the need to redress a great wrong. I wish no man ill, and if there has been wrong done in my name, I would wish to see it remedied."

"How dare you assume the mask of innocence? You, who are more dangerous than half the hosts of Rome!" He got to his feet. "You have brought a good and holy priest, one who was fired with truth and zeal, to such degradation that he is without strength anymore!" He began to pace, not looking at her as he nursed his rage.

More quietly than before, Comtesse Orienne said, "I know no such priest, mon Père. Those churchmen who come here do so willingly and with glad hearts. When it is over, they do not curse me but pray that I will not repent them too soon." She hoped that her servants were not far away, for she could see that the priest would not easily be persuaded to leave.

Padre Bartolimieu halted by the window and looked out into the vast, overgrown orchard; the scent of apricots was strong, though now it was faintly tinged with the sharp sweetness of rot. "You speak of pleasures, and you will not see them as the odium they are." He began to weep with wrath. "You, who claim to be only as God made you, you, *you* have taken the soul of a good priest, and you have destroyed it. There were tasks that lay before us for the glory of God, and you have deprived us and Our Lord of the victory, so that the forces of hell advance in this land!"

"Mon Pere!" Comtesse Orienne protested.

"You are the spawn of Lilith herself, and you reek of debauchery! You are the portal to damnation, and it lies not in the sides of your garments but between your thighs, where you bring your lovers and cause them more travail than any other woes that the world has to offer. The Kingdom of God is far off as long as such as you walk the earth. You are what has brought the Plague upon us! You are what destroys us all!" His voice had become a howl, almost incoherent with the power of his increasing ire. "Mon Évêque came here, and it was *not* of his own will, you serpent! He was brought here through guile by one who is already your slave."

Comtesse Orienne blinked. "Your *Évêque*? That puny little worm?" She had been hoping to discover the source of his grievance, but she had never suspected that it might be something so minor as that terrified little man with the pouting rosebud mouth that Pierre had requested she bed. "He was here but once, and if he has told you that he did not enjoy himself, then he lies to you. He was like a peasant tasting butter!"

"No!" Padre Bartolimieu rounded on her. "More deceptions, more vilifications! You insinuated yourself into his graces so that he . . . he . . . succumbed to you!"

"That last I will not argue," she said, a degree of amusement bursting through the alarm that ran through her. "He did succumb and would have succumbed more if I had been willing." She leaned back in her chair. "I have not seen him since that day, and it is nothing to me if he never comes here again."

"Now that you have degraded him, you cast him aside so that you may seek new prey!" Padre Bartolimieu accused her. "You will never stop until you have brought down His Holiness! You are the center of corruption in France, and—"

This time she laughed openly, but there was anger in the sound. "I have listened to enough. You have heaped your vituperations on me, and that is sufficient. You will go now, mon Père." She rose with the intention of leaving the salon.

"Wait!" Padre Bartolimieu ordered, taking three quick steps toward her as he fumbled in his sleeve.

"No. You have exhausted your welcome. My servants will escort you to—" Her dismissal ended in a sharp cry as the barbs on his scourge hissed past her face. "You dis*gusting* hypocri—"

This time the lashes caught, the iron hooks at the tips digging into her forehead and cheek, raking and tearing down the side of her face. "Thus do we abjure your work, Satan!" Padre Bartolimieu shrieked in terrible rapture as he swung the scourge again.

Comtesse Orienne screamed, the sound high and shuddering as the pain went through her. "To me! Jaques! *To me!*" The third time the scourge struck her, the agony of it was worse than anything she had felt before. She fell away from the scourge and tried to crawl behind her chair for protection. The smell of her blood was strong in her throat. She coughed and tasted the warm, metallic fluid.

"You destroyed Évêque Amalrie!" Padre Bartolimieu bellowed, and launched himself into the attack once again, the light of battle bright in his face. "You will pay for it now and in hell!"

His scourge struck her shoulder and ripped the linen. He had drawn his arm back and was moving closer to her when strong hands fell on him, restraining him and pulling him away from the whimpering woman on the floor. Knees, fingers, and fists gouged and pummeled him while he tried to break free, but it was to no avail. Two pages, a house steward, and a footman wrestled Padre Bartolimieu to the floor and with pleased efficiency beat him into unconsciousness.

Jaques was the first to approach Comtesse Orienne, who had dragged herself into a corner of the room where she lay in half stupor, her screams now reduced to strange, childlike mewlings. Jaques shook his head as he saw the extent of the damage the metal-tipped lashes had done. Long furrows scored her face and forehead, her nose was torn, and there was so much blood that he could not tell what had become of her right eye. He turned to the others. "Take that man to le duc de Parcignonne. Truss him up like a boar if you must."

"But this is a priest," the footman protested, not wishing to offend the church.

"It would not matter if it were the Pope. Le Duc is her champion, and she has suffered"—he swallowed against a sudden obstruction—"very much at his hands, and it is for le duc to redress her wrongs." He was already trying to think of who he ought to call to tend her, for the injuries Comtesse Orienne had sustained were far beyond what he could treat. "Well, hurry. Get that madman away from here at once!"

The other three exchanged looks but hastened to obey. As they got him to his feet, Padre Bartolimieu began to shout imprecations at the men who restrained him. "You will be hurled into the pit! Demons will consume your entrails!" he raved, but to no avail.

When they had gone, Jaques knelt down and lifted his mistress into his arms, holding her gently, speaking to her quietly as he bore her to her bedchamber with dread in his heart.

In the later part of the night, it was the task of Seur Theodosie to watch over Seur Catant, to see that she did not harm herself. She often sung hymns and Psalms to herself to help the night go by, but this evening, with the first of the autumn storms brewing, heaven seemed to be an unfriendly place as the clouds gathered overhead, blotting out the stars.

"Troubled?" asked a light voice from the end of the corridor.

Seur Theodosie turned to see an intruder. "It is not right for you to be here." She had a brittle tone, one that became more noticeable when she was upset.

"But how uncharitable," Thibault said. "Would you refuse me the chance to comfort the sick? It is a virtue, isn't it?" He had strolled up to her and gave her a wide smile.

"You cannot cozen me, stranger. My good angel warns me that you will do harm if you can." She took up her station with more firmness than before.

Thibault chuckled. "How fierce! And to think I might have tried my wiles on so devoted a Sister. Why, I should cry shame on myself."

"You have no shame," Seur Theodosie said without any fear at all. "You have only the harm you can do." It was invigorating to say these things, express sentiments she had never voiced aloud before in her life. "God will aid me."

Thibault shook his head. "What am I supposed to do? Meet for a contest of strength?"

"We are having that contest now," Seur Theodosie said with conviction. "And as my strength is in God, you will not prevail." She looked at him steadily. "You are one of those who do the work of the Devil." Her confidence was increasing with every word she spoke. "Go away, demon, and take whatever form you must to leave us in peace."

"Do you realize that I can kill you?" Thibault asked in his most charming way.

"Kill me if it must be that. I will go to God, and you will still be what you are." She resumed her hymn, satisfied that she at last understood what her vocation meant to her.

He bent and drew a knife from his boot. "I might cut off your lips so that you cannot sing."

"God hears my soul, not my words," she answered, then stared at him again. "You are very like Mère Léonie, demon."

"Very like," he agreed most soberly. "It is . . . convenient." His face remained composed, but something in his voice smiled its mockery.

In the cell behind her, Seur Catant had awakened again and was shrieking, making garbled, steady cries with the determination of a hungry infant.

"She knows I have come for her, ma Seur." Thibault took another step nearer, the knife held firmly in his hand. "She calls to me, and I answer when I am called."

"If you kill me, know that my death does not alter my beliefs but confirms my faith, demon." She folded her hands and began to sing, the melody of her hymn a strange descant to Seur Catant.

There was a rush of feet at the end of the hall, and Seur Elvire came running, responding to the insistent screams.

"You are not favored this night, ma Seur," Thibault murmured to Seur Theodosie, and closed the space between them, pressing his knife home, through her habit, under her breastbone and up. He moved the blade from side to side, feeling the resistance and slice of tissue in the wrapped steel of the hilt. He held her with his free arm so that she could not slip away from him.

Seur Theodosie trembled and jerked, then blood welled from her mouth and nose; she slumped down the door as Thibault, satisfied, released her.

"What are you doing!" Seur Elvire cried out, gasping. She stood quite still in the corridor, not caring to intrude but fearing more what she could not understand.

Seur Catant's screams drove her almost to distraction, yet she could not bring herself to move.

Then lightning tore through the clouds, and its sudden, deathly glare penetrated the corridor through the windows of the cells. Seur Elvire saw the blood, turned almost indigo by the blanching brightness.

As Thibault disappeared around the corner, Seur Elvire's screams were added to those of Seur Catant, and both were lost in the shattering thunder.

By midafternoon the sky had cleared, but ominous clouds marshaled like hostile cavalry at the horizon, promising another storm by morning. Pierre stood in the bow of his study window, looking out over the magnificence and squalor of Avignon. His interview earlier in the day, during the pelting squall that had been blown up the river from the sea, had left him apprehensive, and reflection on what Cardinal Seulfleuve had told him served only to disturb him more.

"A woman has arrived," his chamberlain said from the door. "She insists on speaking with you."

"Ah." He had been waiting for this since Comtesse Orienne's servants had come to him with Padre Bartolimieu trussed and gagged like a boar after the hunt. "I must see her then, mustn't I?" He had meant this to be a quip, but it sounded like the reading of a verdict. "Where I have given my word, I must uphold it in the face of God, if it comes to that."

"You will see her, then?" the chamberlain asked, surprised that his master should acquiesce so miserably and so readily.

"I am her champion." He came back to his writing table. "Give me a moment, and then I will speak with her in my reception room downstairs."

The chamberlain knew better than to question le duc further when he was in such a humor. He bowed and withdrew to do as he had been ordered, but his thoughts were grim.

Pierre sat and drew one of the rolls of parchment toward him. As he smoothed it open in front of him, he saw that it had not been entirely scraped clean, so that the words of his will crossed lines of almost vanished love lyrics written three centuries before. Putting words on paper had always been a laborious task for le duc de Parcignonne, and never more than now, when he contemplated the disposition of his personal fortune.

> *Given that the hours of man are short and that we may be struck down at any time it pleases God to take us from this life, I, Pierre Fornault, for the sake of my conscience and my House, make the following will in regard to my lands and possessions. To my uncle, Michau d'Ybert, I leave my horses and armor, with the wish that he bestow them on a man-at-arms of sufficient rank and honor to deserve them.*

He sat reading over the paragraph he had written, wondering what else he ought to say. Finaly, he made his decision.

> *The rest of my belongings that are not part of my rank and House, I leave to Holy Church, to buy Masses for the salvation of my soul, which is fallen and tainted by the constraints of honor.*

He prepared wax and fixed his signet to the end of the parchment, then held it flat while the ink dried and wax cooled. He rose, thinking that he would have preferred another means to keep his good name, but no idea came to mind.

When he reached the reception room, servants had brought hot pastries and honied wine to le duc's veiled visitor. He inclined his head. "God give you good day."

Comtesse Orienne looked up through the silk of her veil. "May He protect you and defend the right," she answered, and though her voice was still low, it no longer purred and promised as it had done before.

"You have come to me to champion you," Pierre said without inflection. "You wish me to uphold your name."

"Yes." She watched him, her eye burning behind the soft, sheer fabric. "You gave me your word that you will be my champion." Her tone was flat, as if she discussed the cleaning of fish, but she sat straight on the bench, and the tension in her body shook her. "You did not expect that you would have to do more than see I have a new falcon each spring, and I wanted nothing more than a reward for enduring so uninteresting a lover. But that is changed now." She lifted the end of the veil to carry the goblet of honied wine to her lips. She took great care not to reveal her face.

"I am saddened, Orienne, that you should have suffered." He could think of nothing else to say. "I am troubled that it was a priest who brought you to this. God made them to worship Him and has trusted the rest of us to look after them."

Her laughter was as brief as it was harsh. "And when we look after them, we are punished for our pains. I was punished, Sieur le Duc, and now I want that priest to know a little of what he gave to me." She drank her wine far too quickly and poured herself more at once.

"Honorable combat? Will you accept that?" Pierre asked, wishing to disgrace himself no more than was necessary.

"He is not noble, and you need not concern yourself with his House, for they know nothing of him and do not stand high enough to question anything you do." She did not drink quite so quickly this time, but still she was indulging herself as she had never done in the past.

He thought that perhaps he was trapped in a dream, that no matter what he said or did, it would fade from his thoughts when the morning came. He should have obtained the dispensation and taken Aungelique from the convent in spite of her father's objections. Had he done that, he would never have been trapped in this question of honor. "He is a man of God, and for that I must treat him as a nobleman, ma Comtesse." For a moment, he had forgotten to speak to her, and now he tried to compensate for his lack of courtesy. "The Church will not approve no matter what I do, but they will be more reasonable if I do not offend their priest with a peasant's death."

"But you will kill him?" Comtesse Orienne demanded in a soft, furious tone.

"Unless God guides his hand against me, I will kill him. We will fight with axes so that it will be quick." He had decided that earlier in the day.

"I am unforgiving." With some of her old languor, she turned toward him. "Look for yourself, mon Duc." Slowly, she lifted her veil and faced him, gazing at him steadily with the one eye Padre Bartolimieu had left her. Beneath the gaping socket, there were deep furrows across her cheek, turning from raspberry to puckered white. Her nose, which had been perfect, was cut away on the right side, and what little flesh was left had healed badly, pulling the skin up and back, giving her some of the aspect of a pig's snout. Above her mouth ran another scar, and one corner drooped beneath the white cicatrix of the scourge.

Pierre had seen men maimed and disfigured in battle, but the sight of them did not sicken him as this devastation did, for the men had gone to battle as soldiers with the prospect of injury before them. This was entirely different. He took a deep, unsteady breath. "I will do what I may to avenge you, and the world will judge as it must."

It was no longer possible for Orienne to smile, and the grimace that she was able to produce only served to make her face more hideous. "Thank you, Sieur le Duc, my champion. I am grateful to you."

He acknowledged this by pouring a second goblet full of honied wine and drinking it quickly, but for once in his life, he could not taste the drink or respond to its warmth.

Seur Ranegonde sat opposite Seur Aungelique in the small weaving room on the second floor of the convent. Sunlight angled in the windows, ripe as grain, warm where it touched. The rest of the room was cool, and the wind promised that the year would turn toward the dark again soon.

"What will you do when your infant is born?" Seur Ranegonde asked as she set stitches in a little robe of cast-off linen.

"I will be free of the Church." She tossed her head

as if she were not wearing coif and gorget and wimple. "I
have a place where I will be welcome. The woman who
lives there is a great beauty, and she has let me stay with
her in the past." She went on with her sewing and then
added, "I did not think it would take so long for my
cousin to make proper arrangements for me, but you
know what men are. Well, of course you must; look at
you."

These occasional jibes did not sit well with Seur
Ranegonde, who colored deeply. "No man did this to
me. It was a demon."

"And a demon did this to me, but it was because he
wanted me." Her face grew serious briefly.

Seur Ranegonde protested, "You do not know what
it is to long to confess and to feel the fruits of sin rob you
of your will to admit how greatly you have erred." She
went on sewing.

"Yes." Her eyes flashed with anger and pride. "I was
sent here to be made tractable, and I have not surren-
dered. My great grandmother was chatelaine and defended our lands from rival lords. She upheld the honor
of our House, and she showed herself to be tireless in
battle. She would not have been content in the Church,
and I am not." She threw down the cloth she held.
"When I am free of this place and this thing that turns in
my belly, I will be as she was, and all of France will speak
of me with respect." She got up, striding down the room.
"I do not want your pity, though you are about to give it
to me, aren't you?"

"I . . . you have need of solace, for being so far from
grace, and . . ." Seur Ranegonde was not able to go on.

"But you have fallen from grace as well, haven't you?
Your father will not take your babe, will he? You may be
certain that Père Guibert will not allow it to remain here.
He will send it to Saunt-Elizair to the monastery where
they care for the orphans and foundlings. Doubtless he
will not say that a nun gave birth to it because of a demon
but will lie and tell them that a peasant family died of
Plague. Or it may be he will tell them that it was abandoned by travelers. And it will be in the care of the
monks, who will feed it and put rags on it and will tell it

all its life that it is vile and therefore must be grateful for what little the monks do for it." She laughed, clapping her hands with satisfaction. "That is the life of your baby, ma Seur."

Seur Ranegonde's face had darkened, and now she looked as near to anger as ever she had in her life. "You have no *right* to say this to me, ma Seur. You are the one who was first touched by demons, and you are the one who brought them to us here." She got up from the bench, swaying a little as she balanced herself against the burden of her pregnancy. Her back ached and her face was damp. "I know that I must find it in my heart to pardon you before I die or suffer in hell."

"You are not to speak to me this way!" Seur Aungelique was offended beyond all reason. "You are not of the nobility, and you have no right to speak to the daughter of Michau d'Ybert in this manner!"

"I speak to you as a child of God, for you are that, too!" She glared at the other nun. "You are not deserving of the rank to which you were born, and you have been trying to throw it away since you came here."

"You dare not say this! You are nothing more than—" Seur Aungelique began, preparing for a tantrum.

"Both of you will beg pardon of the other, and to-night, when we have our meal, you will serve your sisters on your knees and beseech each of them to forgive you for this outburst!" Mère Léonie's pale eyes blazed at the two nuns. "I have had enough of your bickering and discontent."

"Ma Mère . . ." Seur Ranegonde was the first who turned away, shamefaced. "I apologize to you and pray that you will find it in your heart to pardon my impropriety."

"And you, Seur Aungelique? Have you anything to say to me?" Mère Léonie stood very tall and regarded the rebellious nun with quiet disdain.

Seur Aungelique's chin lifted high. "My lover would not hesitate to oppose you!"

"Do you think so?" Mère Léonie asked. There was a strange glitter at the back of her eyes. "Each of you may keep vigil in turn, prostrate before the altar."

"Prostrate?" Seur Aungelique repeated, her face turning ugly with indignation. "You wish us to crush our babes?"

"Our Lord will protect them, ma Seur. Go to your cell at once, Seur Aungelique, and think on the sin of pride and how it has brought you to this pass." She made no move, but Seur Aungelique fell back before her. "At once, ma Mère."

"I will be away from here soon, and then I need never speak to you again!" She hurried out of the room, her features set and her head high.

"You as well, ma Seur," Mère Léonie said, less forcefully, to Seur Ranegonde. "From your face, I would think that you have been suffering of late."

"It is the babe. I remember that my mother was similarly afflicted. Her ankles would swell and her hands. When she died in childbed, she said that her flesh and not the babe was to blame." She lowered her head.

"You think of your mother, is that it?" Mère Léonie asked. "You fear that you will die as your mother died and that nothing will save you from that fate."

Seur Ranegonde made a gesture as if to wipe away what she heard. "It is part of my fear, yes. And it . . . I cannot bear thinking of it. I see my mother, and it is myself." She started to cry, her hands covering her face. "I deserve the death, for I let a demon possess me. But I dread it, and when I think of my child, I am in despair."

Mère Léonie made no effort to comfort her. "Père Guibert will do all that he must to see that you are protected and saved, if that is the will of God."

"And if it is not? I will be in the earth, waiting for the Last Judgment, and my babe will be turned out among strangers with no one to care for him."

"Our Lord will care for him," Mère Léonie assured her. "Our Lord cares for all those who are abandoned."

Seur Ranegonde's cry became a thin wail, as if she were the infant she was made wretched for. "I must have more than that." She sank to her knees and clasped Mère Léonie's long, narrow hand. "Ma Mère, I have no right, but I beg you, for the goodness and mercy of this order, promise me you will look after the child and care for it."

The fever spots in her cheeks burned brightly, and tears glazed her eyes.

Mère Léonie did not attempt to withdraw her hand. "Why do you want this, ma Seur?"

"So that my babe will not be lost and left alone. I know what happens to such children, for there were many after the Plague came. They were lean and skittish as cats, and they died under bridges and in deserted buildings."

"In the name of Our Lord, I will take your babe if you do not live to do it. Will that suffice, ma Seur?" Mère Léonie said, disengaging herself from Seur Ranegonde's grasp. "You may deliver as easily as a young mare and be back at prayers before the oil is dry on his forehead."

Seur Ranegonde closed her eyes. "Thank you, thank you, ma Mère. You have saved me if you promise this."

"I would not have thought," Mère Léonie said with a hint of severity, "that it was so simple a thing to save one who has been used by demons."

With a shriek of despair, Seur Ranegonde rushed from the room, leaving Mère Léonie to pick up the two half-finished infants' garments that had been left behind.

When Pierre returned to the monastery, papal soldiers were waiting for him. He stood, framed in the light of the door, and made no move to resist them.

"Pierre Fornault, duc de Parcignonne," said the captain, bringing his halberd forward so that the batwing blade was not far from Pierre's face. "We are here on orders of His Holiness, Clement VII, by grace of God His vicar on earth, Pope of the One True Catholic Church."

Pierre sighed heavily. "My men are outside. They have the body of the priest."

"For the offense of attacking one of the dedicated servants of God and Holy Church, you are to be detained and tried for blasphemy and heresy. Your lands are to be seized by the Church, and your name is to be striken from the roll of honor kept by the seneschal of le roi."

"What I did I did for honor. If that removes my name from the roll, then honor is dead in France." He was fatigued beyond any exhaustion he had known before. He looked at the captain, making no move to oppose him. "Will there be torture, do you think?"

"I do not know" was the answer, but said so quickly that Pierre knew the answer.

"There *will* be torture, then." He lowered his head. "That priest attacked a woman whom I had promised to champion."

"That is not in question here, Fornault. Your acts were against the Church." The captain hesitated. "How many men-at-arms are with you?"

"Two. Ivo and Tristan. They came to see that honor was not compromised." He stared at them. "What was I to do? Let my honor lie in the dust because my word was held for nothing?"

"It is not a question we can answer, Fornault," the captain said implacably. "We are sworn to uphold the honor of the Pope, and you have killed one of his servants."

"And if it had been the honor of the Pope that compelled you to fight, would you have gone against the champion of le roi?" Pierre asked, but without rancor. "You are good soldiers, all of you, and your fame is deserved. God made me noble, good captain, to defend His people on this earth. What would you have me do? Forget that obligation?"

"No," said the captain with more understanding than he had betrayed at first. "You have done as you must, and we will do as we must."

"Then you have nothing more to say to me." He paused, then went on. "My men did not consent in what I did but came only to uphold my honor and the honor of France." He looked around the hall at the armed men, who stood impassively. "Let me speak before you take me. After the monks have had their way with me, I may not wish to vindicate myself."

The captain glanced at his men, knowing that what Pierre requested was improper but reluctant to deny a seigneur de France his right to be heard. "Tell your men they are to remain silent."

Pierre gave a signal; Ivo and Tristan, carrying a laden

stretcher between them, came into the cavernous doorway to the hall of the monastery and stood there in stillness while Pierre spoke.

"It was my cousin who brought me to this, for she had been sent to la Tres Saunte Annunciacion for preferring me to the husband her father chose for her." He cleared his throat. "Padre Bartolimieu came to the convent when it was thought that demons might be there. It was my cousin who first was attacked by them, and the Church wished to determine if it was lust or the instigation of hellish creatures that brought her to her rebellion and her distress." He could hear the monks, standing in the shadows, whisper at this revelation. "My cousin weakened me, and through that the demon came to me, in the form of the nun that I desired, and through this minion of hell, I became a plaything of evil, a degraded and debauched man with little to maintain honor but the worth of my word."

Tristan shifted, wanting to object to this, for he could sense the avidity of the monks as they seized upon his confession and enlarged upon his admission in their minds. The air was as potent as raw wine.

"It was the habit of my cousin to take refuge with Comtesse Orienne when she wearied of convent life, and for that reason, I renewed my acquaintance with la comtesse at her villa Une Noveautie. She gave protection of a kind to Seur Aungelique, but what my cousin learned there was not good for her soul. My guardianship failed, but my obsession did not, and I would not remove myself from its spell. For that, I have lost my honor and my House, and it may be that I have lost my soul."

"You need not say more," the captain interjected, anxious to quiet Pierre before he accused himself of crimes worse than surrender to a demon.

"But I wish to, mon captain. It is necessary that I do." Pierre laid his hand on the hilt of his sword. "Because of the demon, I exposed a good churchman to the sin of lust, and for that he has taken the palm." He spoke more slowly, as if he were falling asleep. "When Padre Bartolimieu could not continue his godly work, he blamed not me, who had provoked the ill that befell him, but the woman who was the instrument of Évêque Amalrie's downfall. For that he went to her and beat her, which was his right as a churchman but not as a priest to a comtesse. For that she demanded vengeance, and I, as her champion, have killed the man, who was also a priest, for the disgrace he brought to her House. For which act, may God pardon me." He drew his sword with his left hand, holding it awkwardly by the pommel, then let it drop, clanging and striking sparks, to the stone floor. He looked at Ivo and Tristan. "You have done well. I dismiss you now and declare that you are innocent of any wrong I have done. Put down that stretcher and leave."

The two men-at-arms hesitated, then lowered their burden to the floor. Ivo looked at the captain. "It was fought well. Sieur le duc killed him cleanly, without cruelty, and with honor." Saying this, he turned on his heel and strode away from the monastery, toward the place where his horse was waiting.

Tristan came to stand beside Pierre. "The death was with one blow, and the priest took it valiantly." He heard one of the monks hiss in disapproval. "We do not know what is right and what is wrong; we do as God inclines us and our Church instructs us."

"Go," Pierre said gently. "The church will deal with la Tres Saunte Annunciacion, as it will deal with me." He motioned Tristan away from him, then faced the captain. "That is all I have to say."

Chapter 16

It was a foul night; cold, blustery rain flung itself across France, bringing the first new snow to the mountains and ruining the late crops still waiting for harvest. In Mou Courbet, the last of the hayricks were soaked and useless; in Saunt-Vitre-lo-Sur, rye and oats were lost.

At la Tres Saunte Annunciacion, only a few grapes were the victims of the storm—most of the plantings had failed already.

"It is too early for the babe," Seur Odile said to Seur Adalin as they heard Seur Ranegonde scream.

"God protect her, it has come early," Seur Adalin said. "One of us must wake Père Guibert."

"May God be thanked that he is here, for who is to hear her confession if not him?" She crossed herself, shivering more from the shuddering cries that Seur Ranegonde gave than from the chill of the corridor.

Seur Adalin asked nervously, "Who keeps vigil in the chapel just now?"

"Seur Marguerite. She is mourning for her bees." Seur Odile gave an exasperated gesture. "What can anyone do when she is as mad as that?"

"We will have to find a way to return her to her cell so that the rest may gather to pray for Seur Ranegonde," Seur Adalin said, looking annoyed.

Two quick panting shrieks cut through the air; both nuns started guiltily at the sound.

"I will wake Père Guibert. You go to Mère Léonie," Seur Adalin said, and without waiting for Seur Odile's response, she hastened away toward the room where Père Guibert slept.

It took some little time for Père Guibert to put on the proper vestments for attending a woman who was delivering so tragically early. He said his prayers as quickly as he could, but when he reached Seur Ranegonde's cell, he could see that he had already taken too long and that she was slipping away from him quickly.

Her eyes had a febrile shine; her short dark hair was matted on her face. She had drawn her chemise down as far as her lifted knees out of modesty, but there was little she could do to cover herself until the infant was out of her and the afterbirth examined. "It hurts," she said breathlessly as Père Guibert made the sign of the cross over her.

"That is the legacy of Eve, ma Fille." He found room to half sit on the side of her raised pallet as he prepared the oil to anoint her forehead. "Give me your confession, ma Fille, so that you may be spared the pains of hell if it is the wish of God that you leave this life."

Seur Philomine, who attended to Seur Ranegonde, signaled Père Guibert. "It will not be long, mon Père, and she is very weak."

Père Guibert nodded, feeling his throat tighten as she spoke. "You must confess, ma Fille!"

With a little sob, Seur Ranegonde looked at him. "It is coming, mon Père, isn't it? It will take my life to have life itself. Won't it?" She took the edge of his sleeve, but her hold was so weak that when he moved his hand, she could not retain it.

"God judges us, ma Fille. It is not for us to decide." He blessed her and began the ritual of Extreme Unction, hardly able to speak the words loudly enough for her to hear them. "Tell me of your sins, ma Fille. Tell me of the lover that gave you this child that shames your habit and the honor of this Order." He had not intended to be so severe, but his nerve was fading rapidly.

"I . . . I have sinned," she said after a moment, and then stiffened with pain, thrashing on the bed with the force of it.

"No. No, ma Seur," Seur Philomine said, reaching to hold Seur Ranegonde still. "It is for your babe to work, not for you."

"It must be *soon!*" Seur Ranegonde cried.

"It will be as God wills, ma Fille," Père Guibert said. He had the fleeting impression that she was not giving birth but drowning. "Confess your wrongs, and God will welcome you to His glory."

"You must hurry, ma Père," Seur Philomine said urgently. "It will not be long before the babe is here, and then . . . she will not be able to hear you."

"Yes, yes," Père Guibert said with ill-concealed aggravation. "Ma Fille, tell me how it is that you carry this babe and who fathered it."

"Let it end, mon Père," she begged as her body shook with her labor.

"Tell me of your lover and how he gained access to you. For the sake of your soul and your babe, ma Fille."

"He came to me. He said I would have a child

by . . . another man because . . . Oh, Saunte Virge
Marie, Sacrée Mère!" She drew her legs up suddenly,
howling once.

"You had more than one lover?" This surprised Père
Guibert, for he found it difficult to believe that she had
had one.

"No . . . no. . . . He visited a man and had seed of
him." She drew in several short, sharp breaths, then
shivered. "It is tearing me apart, mon Père."

"It must be endured, ma Fille," Père Guibert reminded her, though he knew he had gone pale. "You
must tell me. What man?"

" . . . He did not say . . . He never said. Seur
Philomine . . . !"

"It will not be much longer, ma Seur," she said in
a low, even tone. "Do not be frightened, Seur
Ranegonde."

"God will give you grace to . . ." She convulsed
suddenly, then went limp, and it was a moment before
her eyes focused on Père Guibert's face again. "He came,
saying that he would give me a child."

Père Guibert leaned forward. "They say that demons are black and hideous, that they are endowed like
stallions, and that their members are cold as ice."

But Seur Ranegonde was shaking her head, her
feeble protests barely audible. "No. He is tall and
slender, with hair like an angel and eyes . . . lighter than
Mère Léonie's." Her body jerked as if gaffed.

"You must be mistaken," Père Guibert said, horrified. "There is an error."

"Mon Père," Seur Philomine warned him, "hear
her out and grant absolution, I pray you."

Père Guibert rose from Seur Ranegonde's side.
"There must be . . . a mistake!"

In confusion, Seur Ranegonde reached up to detain
Père Guibert. "Help me, mon Père!"

Père Guibert tugged his stole from her fragile grasp.
"*No!* The demon is black, and his member is made of ice.
You cannot save yourself with lies about a youth like . . .
like an angel!" His voice had risen, and he slipped out of

reach of Seur Ranegonde's hands. "That youth was a dream. No demon is as fair as the morning, with such eyes and . . ." He looked wildly about the cell. "You cannot say such things, ma Fille, and go unpunished."

"I am punished," Seur Ranegonde whispered. "I have this child, and it is killing me."

"The child is almost here," Seur Philomine said, distressed to see Père Guibert moving away from Seur Ranegonde. "She must be absolved."

Hastily, Père Guibert sketched a blessing in the air. "I grant you provisional absolution; be contrite, ma Fille, and God will forgive you." He could not help but recall the degrading, captivating dreams he had had earlier in the year, dreams that had cost him many hours of prayer and guilt but that he had desired as ardently as he desired salvation. "Confess your errors to God, ma Fille. There was no pale-haired young man!"

Seur Philomine, who had placed one hand on Seur Ranegonde's swollen abdomen, looked at the priest in disbelief. "Mon Père, you cannot leave . . . you cannot!"

"I must!" He threw open the door. "The nuns are in the chapel. I will tell them to . . . to pray." With that he bolted, leaving Seur Ranegonde to keen her despair as Seur Philomine strove to save her and the wizened, malformed little son that struggled out of his mother's body on a tide of blood long before the dawn broke through the thinning clouds.

By midday, Seur Ranegonde's body had been washed and laid out in the chapel in preparation for burial. Two nuns kept vigil over her corpse and the pitiful infant that lay folded in her arms. Only Seur Marguerite sang for her, and since she was mad, no one thought God would be offended by her prayers.

Père Guibert kept to his room, his head sunk in his hands, his mind in torment. He heard the nuns gather in the chapel, and he heard, distantly and incompletely, the words Mère Léonie spoke over the dead woman. All through it, he could not banish from his mind the memories of dreams that had wrung his body and soul.

"It was a dream. The youth was a dream." The dream would not fade; as he tried to divert his thoughts, his body responded, his flesh jutting out, making a mockery of his misery. With a sudden cry, he thrust his hands into his lap, forcing his offending erection back against his leg, denying it with such vehemence that his skin burned with his disgust. Still he could not banish the dream from his thoughts. The instant he permitted himself to fall silent, he imagined he saw the long, serious, taunting face that had bent over him in his dream and had whispered such promises, rewarded him with such damnable ecstasy.

"No! *No!*" He cried out, appalled at what he felt. He could not endure this humiliation. He thought of the unspeakable things the dream had done to him, of how the youth's firm lips had pressed his mouth and his breast and his manhood. "My God, my God, why do You permit this? Am I not Your sworn servant?" There was no answer to this desperate question. "It was a dream, O God! I would never offend You with such depravity."

It was quite late when Père Guibert at last stole out of his room, down the stairs to the refectory, where he found a kitchen knife to rid himself of that part of himself that gave him such infamy and shame.

The agony that drove through him was worse than anything he had ever known. He had just enough time to see the blood erupt between his legs before he lost consciousness, to lie alone and unattended as his life flowed away.

Tristan arrived at the convent toward the end of the day, less than two hours ahead of the papal troops. He dismounted in the barren orchard, tethering his horse to the empty hive before running to the stable on the side of the building. He heard the slow, unmusical toll of the mourning bell as he entered the stable, and he wondered which of the nuns had died.

The mule nipped at his shoulder as he sought out a resting place in the straw. He wished now he knew where Philomine had her cell; his good sense told him that she would have to come to feed the animals before nightfall, and he trusted that she still performed this task. He did not have long to wait. In a short while, the courtyard door opened and Seur Philomine came into the stable. She held an oil lamp in her hand, which she carried as high as possible.

"Did you fear you had been forgotten?" she asked, reaching down to pat one of the few sheep left in the pen. "You're restless, and I cannot blame you. We are all restless." As she spoke, she gathered up the wooden buckets to refill them with water. "It will not be long, little ones, and you'll be fed." She reached over, taking the pitchfork from its hook on the wall, and began to spear quantities of hay from the loft above. Once she tried to hum, but it brought her perilously near weeping, so she stopped. She had attended to the sheep and the last sow when she heard movement behind her; with her pitchfork raised and ready to strike, she turned toward the sound.

"Philomine," Tristan said, rising from his hiding place. "My love."

Philomine did not lower the pitchfork. "Tristan? You?"

"Yes." He frowned. "What . . . , why?"

She sagged, only to be caught in his arms. "Oh, God, I was afraid . . ." She kissed him as if his lips could blot out that admission.

He kept her close in his embrace. When he was able to speak, he asked. "What has happened here? I have heard such things . . . And you welcome me with a pitchfork."

She pressed her head to his shoulder, feeling the strength of his body through the metal-studded leather tunic he wore. "It has been . . . dreadful. Seur Catant bit off her tongue, and now she howls in her cell, and we must guard her." As his fingers traced down her face to her lips, she kissed them. "Seur Ranegonde died giving birth. Seur Theodosie was murdered. Père Guibert . . ." It was too difficult for her to say it. "Père Guibert is dead."

Tristan was aghast by what she told him, but he mastered himself sufficiently to comfort her before he added to her dismay. "It will be over soon, Philomine. You will not have to live here much longer."

"I wish it were so," she murmured, putting her arms around him at last.

"It must be." He kissed her brow, then her eyelids. "You must come away with me. Now, love."

She wondered why he was suddenly so insistent. "I would want to, if it were possible."

"It *must* be possible," Tristan said, this time with more force and less affection. "You must come with me at once. *Now.*"

"But"—she moved back from him, but not out of the circle of his arms—"I cannot leave. We have not yet buried Père Guibert . . . and it must be tonight it is done."

"Tonight?" Tristan repeated, baffled. "Why at night? Why would . . . How did Père Guibert die that he is to be buried at night?" He looked into her face, trying to read her unhappy expression.

"He . . . he took his own life," she said, her voice sinking to a whisper. "He will have to be buried at the crossroad after moonrise." She trembled. "When it is done, then come for me and I will go anywhere you wish."

The joy that seized him at her compliance was marred by distress. "Now, Philomine. You will not be . . . able to later." He clung to her as he spoke, protecting her with his nearness. "Papal troops are coming."

"What?" She turned her head to stare at him in disbelief. "Papal troops? What nonsense is this?"

"Not nonsense." His chest tightened as he went on. "They took Pierre Fornault for killing that Swiss priest. He . . . he was racked for that, and . . . I have heard that . . . he accused the nuns of diabolism before they were through. Frère Renaut saw it all, and he told me that . . . that the nuns are to be taken . . . as sorceresses, to suffer the fate of sorceresses." He coughed to keep from crying. "Pierre tried to tell me. I thought he meant that he did not want me to fight the men-at-arms when . . . He was trying to—" It was difficult for him to go on. "Then Frère Renaut told me that troops had been ordered. I came away then, as quickly as I could."

"And le duc?" Seur Philomine asked weakly.

"Frère Renaut prayed he was dead." They both were silent, knowing what the monk intended to convey.

"But sorceresses? We are not that. It's . . . absurd!" She grasped his woolen sleeves so tightly that her knuckles showed white. "We are the ones who have suffered, who have resisted the demons in spite of abuse and neglect, and this is what they believed of us, that we are sorceresses?"

"There is not enough time!" He did not release her. "The troops are no more than two hours behind me." He was holding her with all his strength. "Philomine; you must come with me, now, at once, alone!"

"How can I desert them?" Without warning, she gave a wrenching sob. "You must be wrong. They will not betray us so utterly."

"No Philomine, I am not wrong." They clung together in shuddering despair. "One woman, with a man, might get away unnoticed. But there are more than a dozen Sisters here, and they would be noticed if they left at once, especially at night. Come with me, Philomine, before none of us can leave."

She struggled with her wretchedness, attempting to control the grief that threatened to overcome her. "Let me"—she wiped her eyes with the cuff of her sleeve—"let me at least tell Mère Léonie. Someone must know, or I will be one with Judas."

"Can you find her quickly?" He could not argue with her for this, since it was what he would have done himself in her position.

"I will try. If I cannot find her, I will speak to one of the other Sisters so that they will be warned." She touched his face. "I pray that there will be no more burdens for you to carry for my sake."

He kissed her fingers. "Quickly, then, my love." He let go of her reluctantly, not wanting her away from him now that he had her near.

"Yes. Yes, love." She went back into the courtyard,

half running, the skirt of her habit hitched up into her hempen belt so that she could move more freely. She entered the corridor at a trot and went directly to Mère Léonie's study and was shocked to find it empty. She rushed on and in the chapel found Seur Aungelique and Seur Marguerite keeping vigil over the body of Père Guibert, which lay facedown before the altar.

"Our vigil is not finished yet, Seur Philomine," Seur Aungelique said with such boredom that Seur Philomine wished she had the authority to rebuke her.

"Have you seen Mère Léonie? It is most urgent that I speak with her." This lack of conduct on her part earned Seur Philomine a withering sneer.

"So important that you do not recall how to behave. No, to answer your impertinent question, I do not know where Mère Léonie is."

It worried Seur Philomine to entrust Seur Aungelique with her warning, but she had given her word to Tristan that she would not linger. "You must find her at once, ma Seur, in the name of Christ and la Virge Marie."

"By God's nails, ma Seur, you sound distraught." She raised her hand languidly. "Very well, tell me your message. I would just as soon be out of here. The good Père is beginning to stink. Three days is too long to keep a corpse out of the ground." She got up from her post by the altar, her body ungainly with the weight of her pregnancy. "Tell me what has you so distressed, ma Seur."

"It is . . ." She stopped, not wanting to have the words tumble out of her. "There are papal soldiers coming to take all the Sisters to try them as sorceresses."

Seur Aungelique laughed outright. "Where did you hear this tale? They have always said that you are sensible, and this is . . . a tale for little boys."

"It is true. The Church has taken Pierre, and he has confessed that—" Too late, she stopped herself; the stricken, outraged face of Seur Aungelique filled her vision as the young nun rushed at her.

"What lies are these!" Her fingers were curved into claws that reached for her eyes.

"No, no, ma Seur!" Seur Philomine shouted, stumbling back from this attack. "I promise you, I do not lie!"

"You *do*!" She lunged, striking Seur Philomine in the shoulder as she tried to rake her face. "Lies! Lies!".

Seur Marguerite watched the assault in mild puzzlement. "Sisters do not lie to one another, Seur Aungelique," she said as Seur Philomine bolted for the door.

"She said that Pierre said we are sorceresses. He is a man of honor, a duc, by the grace of God and le roi!" She was not able to run after the fleeing Seur Philomine, so she screamed with all the wrath in her, "Seur Philomine has invited the Devil to come for Père Guibert!"

"That is not true," Seur Marguerite protested gently, bending to touch the waxen, clay-colored head of the dead priest. "She said that we are accused of sorcery. She said that there are troops coming to take us all."

Seur Aungelique turned on her, slapping her as she yelled, "It is not true what she told us!"

"Oh." Seur Marguerite stared down at her hands. "But you said you would tell Mère Léonie."

"I will tell her when the vigil is finished. Mère Léonie will decide what is to be done." Her features were distorted still with her anger. "And if any other Sister contradicts me, I will say that she has been suborned by Seur Philomine and the demon who has been sent to torment us. Do you know it would mean pincers and the boot?" She got back on her knees. "When the vigil is over, I will speak to la Mère. I gave my word, and I will honor it." She crossed herself.

Seur Marguerite looked at the other nun with a strange sympathy in her worn features. "We stand in the greatest peril if you are in error."

"You are mad to think that," Seur Aungelique said, her mouth drooping petulantly. "I will see that Seur Philomine pays for her folly." With that promise, she bowed her head and continued the recitation of prayers for the dead.

They had almost made it to Tristan's horse when the first of the soldiers rode into view.

"Run!" Tristan shouted, all but dragging Seur Philomine through the orchard. "They must not see us!"

Seur Philomine had discarded her habit and now
wore a shepherd's cloak over her chemise. In the advancing night, she was chilled so that her teeth chattered
when she tried to answer. Wooden sabots made her
clumsy, and she could not run as swiftly as Tristan did.

On the road, the troops divided into three groups,
one riding toward the empty hospice, one to the tall
doors to the courtyard, and one toward the stable and
the orchard beyond.

"Yes," she panted, "Are they . . . close?"

He did not answer with words; he tugged more
firmly on her arm. The speed of his approach startled his
horse, and the big mare shied, whinnying her alarm.

Not far behind, one of the papal men-at-arms caught
sight of them and set up a shout. "There! Stop them!"

"Oh, God!" Tristan moaned, stretching to grab the
reins as Seur Philomine staggered after him. The mare
reared and broke the leather that held her. In the next
moment, she had bolted.

"Get them!" shouted one of the soldiers, and their
horses raced nearer.

Tristan turned and gave Seur Philomine a swift, desperate embrace. "Hide! In the clearing behind the berry
vines. I will join you!" His kiss was harsh, fast and aching
with love for her. "Do as I say. As you love me!" Before
she could object again, he had turned away to face the
charging horsemen, drawing his sword as he did.

The first quarrel hit him in the shoulder, ripping
flesh and splintering bone. He flailed his arms to keep
erect, and the agony of the wound fogged his mind.
"Philomine!" he shouted. "Go!"

At the sound of his voice, she had faltered, but the
desolation in his cry made her go on, so that she did not
see when the second quarrel struck, catching him on the
side of the neck, lifting him and sending him sprawling,
his head half cut off from his neck where his life's blood
gouted.

"What about the other?" the nearest crossbowman
shouted to his officer.

"A boy? Let him go."

The man-at-arms who had killed Tristan gave him

one last look. "Poor swine, to play with demons that way."

"Don't waste your pity. He and his kind are a danger to all Christians." The officer dismounted. "Tether your horses away from the convent. We don't want any of those women taking them to get away." As he spoke, he was already drawing a mace and a short sword. "Do not kill them unless they fight. The Cardinal wishes to question them before they are sent to their deaths."

"Can we do anything else?" one of the others asked as he swung out of the saddle.

"They're the consorts of demons," his officer reminded him. "Better to bed with a Turkish whore with the pox and a knife than to touch one of these."

The other men strode away toward the stables.

Seur Philomine crouched behind the berry vines and wept as if it were her body that had been transfixed with quarrels.

The convent was empty and still when dawn came. The men-at-arms had refused to remain there once the nuns had been gathered up and loaded into two wagons where they were fettered to benches for the long journey to Avignon. When the wagons had departed, the eerie wail of Seur Catant could be heard long after the jingle, groan, and clop of wagons and hoofs had faded.

When she was certain that no one else would aproach, Seur Philomine came out of hiding. She was full of bitterness, of anger and deep-fanged grief that gave her no respite. With profound misery, she located the body of her dead lover and took a terrible satisfaction in dragging him to where the Sisters were buried, where she scraped out a shallow grave, digging until her fingers were torn and bleeding.

"So you did get away," said someone behind her. "I thought you might."

The sun was in Seur Philomine's eyes as she turned, and she was briefly dazzled by the tall, slender figure that stood behind her. "What? Who . . . ?" She realized that she ought to be afraid, but she could not summon up fear.

"But surely you know me?" Thibault said in Mère Léonie's voice. "You, of all of them, should know me."

Philomine quivered. "Which are you? What are you?"

"I am . . . whatever you wish. Superior, courtier, does it matter?" He went down on one knee and lifted a handful of earth. "Most enterprising."

She shaded her eyes, staring hard at him. "You are the demon, then." It did not alarm her to say this.

"Of course." He cast the earth onto Tristan's livid, ruined face. "Your lover, wasn't he?"

She swallowed hard. "Yes."

Thibault studied the wounds, his head tilted to the side. "He would not have lived, ma Seur."

"Don't call me that!" Philomine ordered him.

"Abjuring your calling? But you are a tertiary Sister, aren't you? You have less to repudiate than the others." He settled back on his heel, bracing his elbow on his other knee. "All the others were tractable in their ways, but not you. Or poor Seur Marguerite."

Philomine began the slow task of pulling dirt over Tristan's body. "And Seur Aungelique?"

Thibault chuckled, a sound like small things breaking. "She was the most tractable of all if one addressed her properly." He watched her. "Do you want assistance?"

"No."

"As you wish." He dusted his hands off, then got to his feet. "Do not be long at that; we have far to go today."

Irate tears stung her eyes, the first she had shed since she had found Tristan's body. "I will go nowhere—*nowhere!*—with you."

He looked down at her. "They will send more men-at-arms soon, and if you are here, they will find you and arrest you. Your legs will be turned to jelly in the boot, or your guts will be pulled out of your mouth with the wet knotted cord, and you will be consigned to the flames. What would be the point of it, Philomine?"

"I will seek refuge . . ." She broke off, looking away from him. "There must be a place I can go."

"And where the men-at-arms will find you. And

those who sheltered you will suffer the same fate you will." He squinted as he looked over the fields. "I have no control over you; you may believe that or not, but for once it is the truth."

Philomine stopped her work and regarded him with the first stirrings of curiosity. "Why do you say that?"

He shrugged. "What point is there in lying? You know too well how to see my deceptions."

In spite of herself, she asked, "Why is that?"

He chuckled again. "Because, my little bird, you want nothing of me. You have had what you wanted and accepted it as it was. We have no hold on that, not I or any of those like me who serve Our Lord on the earth."

She blinked. "You are not a demon?"

There was no trace of laughter in him now. "Do you doubt it?"

She shook her head. "No," she told him quietly, and resumed the burial.

"You will need to be away from here soon," Thibault said a little while later.

The grave was half filled now, and she was sweating with the effort of the work. "And it would be better to be with you?"

"Little though you may believe it, yes, it would." He turned toward the orchard. "Poor Seur Marguerite; she wanted to take her hives with her, though they are empty." He snapped his fingers twice.

Philomine wanted to shriek at Thibault; instead, she fixed him with a contemptuous stare.

"Our Lord will protect her." And then he laughed with such enormous malice that Philomine trembled to hear it. "Our Lord protects you all."

"That is heresy," she said without thinking.

"And blasphemy and all the rest of it." He walked around the grave. "You will need another hour to finish, Philomine. Then you must decide."

"I would be a fool to take anything that comes from you." She knew beyond question that it was true, but Thibault caused her such devastation of spirit that she found it prostrating to think of it.

"Possibly," he allowed, still speaking in Mère

Léonie's voice. When he continued, he sounded distant, speculative. "I would take you to a woman who has more need of you than of me—for the moment. She languishes and suffers and will take solace of no one. For that she must be pitied, which I would do if I were capable of it. I would pity you all."

Philomine cut her hand on a sharp stone and stopped her work to suck it. She kept her eyes on Thibault, watching him attentively as he explained.

"She will destroy herself shortly if she does not have someone with her, someone who did not know her before. You have no one to take you in, and you are not easily dismayed." He favored her with his mercurial smile. "She was beautiful once, but now she is quite hideous. With you to be with her, she may once again wish to live, and when that happens—" He stopped.

"When that happens, what?" she asked, irritated at herself for indulging him.

"Then she will yearn for . . . things. And she will not be able to have them, not as she did before." He looked down at her, holding out his long, slender hand. "Here. Wrap those cuts before you go on."

"Why should I?" She felt anger growing in her, blotting out the sorrow that possessed her.

"Because it would not suit my purposes to have you lost to infection," he answered coldly.

She recognized that he was telling her the truth, which infuriated her. "Why should I live to aid you when it was you who brought down the convent and destroyed my Sisters?"

"You are sure of that, are you? But I did nothing that might not have happened without me." He dropped his hand when she did not take it.

"Seur Ranegonde would have died in childbirth? Seur Aungelique would have been wanton? Père Guibert would have . . ." She was not able to say what he had done.

"Seur Ranegonde wanted to be overpowered—that was her desire; I did not force it on her. Seur Aungelique was made wanton by God. I did not make her so. Père Guibert had his appetites, and I did nothing more than indulge them. Le duc de Parcignonne had his desires, as well, and when he longed for them, I complied. That is all I may ever do." He offered his hand again, and this time she took it, permitting him to lift her out of the grave.

"Do you have a linen strip?" When he did not answer, she bent and tore away part of the hem of her chemise, which she wrapped three times around her hand.

"You manage well." The compliment was sarcastic, and she was about to give him the most cutting retort she could think of when he took her chin between his thumb and forefinger and tilted her head up toward him. "Oh, yes, you are burning with grief now. You believe that what love you had for that . . . carrion in the grave will suffice a lifetime." She tried to break free of him, but he pinched harder, so that she winced and was still. "But there may come a time, little bird, when you have desires that torment you, though the bitterness in your heart will rob you of courage and your strength to love. Then you will long for me, for the pleasures I bring. My illusion can be more delightful than what is real, little bird. Remember that."

She pushed on his arm, and he dropped his hand at once. "You are repugnant to me!"

He bowed slightly. "That is a start. There was a time when you were only indifferent. In a year, who knows what you may want."

Philomine gave him no response; she sank to her knees and went back to filling in Tristan's grave.

Thibault reached out and touched her short brown hair, tweaking one of the curls. His hand dropped to her shoulder, long fingers pressing hard. "See how strong your anger is?" Abruptly, he turned and walked away from her.

As she listened to his footsteps fade, Philomine pounded her closed fists on the ground, once, twice, three times. Rage and loneliness swept through her soul like a winter wind, and she wished that it had been she, not Tristan, in the grave. Slowly, carefully, she shoved the earth into the hole until instead of a declivity, there was a long, raw mound, like a fresh, raised scar. She remained on her knees, her hands pressed together as she tried to recall the prayers that would aid him when he came to God. The words eluded her. He was gone, and the loss of him engulfed her. He lay only a few feet from her, but he was as far away from her as if he had sunk to the deepest point in the most distant sea. In time, she would forget the weight of his hand, the salt of his body. She had told Seur Aungelique that she would live to affirm her love of him, but without Tristan the love was hollow and he another ghost in this world of ghosts. The more she searched her mind, the less consolation she found there.

Some little time later, she got to her feet and started away from the grave. It was then that she saw Thibault standing in the shadow of the convent walls, waiting for her.